Under the Radar

Under the Radar

A Novel

JAMES HAMILTON-PATERSON

faber and faber

First published in 2013
by Faber and Faber Limited
Bloomsbury House,
74–77 Great Russell Street,
London WC1B 3DA

Typeset by Faber and Faber Ltd
Printed by CPI (UK) Ltd, Croydon, CRO 4YY

A CIP record for this book
is available from the British Library

ISBN 978–0–571–27398–0

FSC
www.fsc.org
MIX
Paper from
responsible sources
FSC® C101712

2 4 6 8 10 9 7 5 3 1

For Len Deighton

Acknowledgements

Grateful thanks to: Nigel Baldwin, Neil Belton, Richard Bentham, Tony Blackman, John Farley, Jeremy Greaves, John Grindrod, Andrew Hewson, Ray Humphrey, Jeff Jefford, Mike Pearson, Robert Pleming, Brian Rivas, Robby Robinson, Chris Royle, Clive Rustin, Patrick Scrivenor, Michael Somers, The National Archives, Edward Wilson.

Restraint? Why are you so concerned with saving their lives? The whole idea is to kill the bastards. At the end of the war if there are two Americans and one Russian left alive, we win.

General Thomas Power, Commander-in-Chief Strategic Air Command, 1957–64, in reply to a suggestion that SAC might hold back from bombing Soviet cities in the early stages of a war

1961

1

'You have control,' said the voice in his headphones.

'I have control,' Amos acknowledged.

'And if you screw up your landing at Kindley I shall be really quite vexed. Not that you will, of course. Still, must put on a good show for the Yanks.'

Amos smiled into his oxygen mask as he let the Vulcan climb out of Goose Bay, Labrador towards their planned ceiling of fifty thousand feet. Typical Muffin, he thought, glancing almost affectionately at the man beside him in the left-hand seat who was so close their shoulders were touching. Wing Commander 'Muffin' Mewell DFC and bar was thirty-eight, which to Amos made him old enough to have seen the ice sheets retreat from Guildford and mammoths wander the South Downs. In fact, in RAF terms he was even more venerable. Mewell had actually flown with 617 Squadron on the Dams raid in 1943 as a twenty-year-old navigator and soon afterwards had applied to be retrained as a pilot. He had eventually been shot down and remained a PoW until the war's end. Now, sixteen years later, the Vulcan's captain was leaning back in his seat with his eyes closed.

Sitting shoulder-to-shoulder in the cramped compartment immediately behind the cockpit were the three crewmen. For this trip a fourth man had been added: the aircraft's crew chief. Strapped uncomfortably into his ad hoc seat on the floor, he would be responsible for supervising refuelling and any maintenance on the trip but would not be allowed on the actual exercise. Now Viv, the nav plotter, came on the intercom with a course correction that would take them slightly east of Halifax with a clear run over yet more empty ocean almost due south to Bermuda: some twelve hundred nautical miles. He added that the other three Vulcans in their flight were airborne and following. Amos confirmed the correction and tilted the great white delta a few points to port as it climbed. Once they had levelled off well above any transatlantic commercial aircraft he could go to autopilot, although he was too keyed up to relax much. He had snatched an hour's sleep on the five-hour first leg out from Scampton to Labrador while 'Muffin' was flying and now here he was, a mere stripling of twenty-four, in charge of one of Britain's most potent and charismatic nuclear bombers for as long as the captain slept. This was not a time to make an ass of himself.

Amos could still hardly believe his luck in having been swept up in a chain of events that had begun several months ago, and about which he had known nothing until almost the last moment. Like so much else currently affecting Bomber Command the chain had begun with a NATO panic. Half a dozen years ago, with the Cold War getting colder by the week, Canada and the United States had suddenly realised how vulnerable they would be to attack by nuclear-armed Soviet bombers flying directly in over the Arctic. The decision was taken to build lines of radar installations stretching across the North American continent to provide advance warning. Together these electronic barriers constituted North American Air Defense Command, or NORAD. In theory, the system would have afforded some three hours' warning of an attack. In practice, it had to be tested. Hence this exercise, Operation Skyshield, the second of its kind, and this time the RAF had been invited. The RAF decided it could spare eight Vulcans. Skyshield II had been planned for mid-October 1961 and by September all eight aircraft had begun intensive training in the area around the Orkneys. They flew up almost daily from Lincolnshire to practise co-ordinating their electronic countermeasures and determining the exact extent to which their radar defences interfered with each other and at what heights and ranges.

Then within days a flu epidemic struck, affecting RAF personnel all over eastern Britain, including the crews practising for Skyshield II. Replacements were quickly drafted in from other squadrons. As a qualified Vulcan co-pilot Flight Lieutenant Amos McKenna had suddenly found himself ordered to report to RAF Scampton on temporary secondment. And so it was that a bare month later he was sitting in the right-hand seat of XJ786 heading for Kindley Air Force Base in Bermuda from where, in a couple of days' time, he would be taking part in a mock attack against New York.

The plan was for four of the Vulcans to approach North American airspace from the south and the other four to do so from the north, in rough mimicry of what Soviet bombers might do from Cuba as well as from their Arctic bases in the Kola Peninsula near Murmansk. His own flight had left Scampton in advance, having that much further to go. The other four aircraft, having first deployed to Lossiemouth, were due out next day. They, too, would fly to Goose Bay, from where they would launch their own attack the day after that. Amos had never been to Bermuda but 'Yourshout' Maybury had told him to pack a pair of swimming trunks in case he got the chance of a quick dip: one of the perks of having struck lucky. None of his mates destined for Labrador in mid-October was thinking of swimming.

This leg was a mere three hours of monotonous flying and he had to make an effort not to emulate his senior officer slumped and dozing in the seat next to him. Amos had long discovered that he was susceptible to crossing time zones. On the morning's flight across the Atlantic from Scampton to Goose they had gained four hours: taking off at 10:30, the four Vulcans in his group had landed at noon in time for lunch and a rest while the aircraft were refuelled. He had made sure to limit his liquid intake, first-rate bladder control being a prerequisite for V-bomber pilots; but the food had been generous and he felt a certain drowsiness descending. The time was now 15:20 local, getting on for half-past seven in the evening according to his body clock. He scanned the instruments in front of him, an automatic check as unconscious as a tic. They were now at their planned altitude, as Viv suddenly confirmed over the intercom. He reached down by his left thigh to the autopilot control panel between the seats and found it hidden beneath the sleeve of Muffin's flying suit. Once, on an exercise to an air base in Nebraska, he had flown in one of Strategic Air Command's huge B-52 bombers whose cockpit (Amos recalled wistfully) was the size of a tennis court compared with that of the Vulcan. He brushed his superior's sleeve aside and set the autopilot, trimming for level flight at a cruising speed of Mach .85.

Somehow the hours passed. The trouble with flying so high was that there was nothing to see, a lack of visual interest that was anyway not helped by the cockpit's restricted vision. After an interminable period the headphones in his cloth helmet at last clicked and 'Bunny' Carmichael, the air electronics officer (or AEO) sitting a few feet behind him, announced that he had made radio contact with Kindley. Immediately afterwards Viv gave Amos a slight course correction and told him to begin his descent. As they lost height the sun, seen through an increasing thickness of atmosphere, became a deeper orange and seemed to sink. It was getting on for 18:00 hours local on 12 October: even in Bermuda the nights were beginning to draw in. He found himself looking forward to dinner. Kindley AFB was, of course, an American base on a British island and the Yanks usually did themselves remarkably well when it came to eating; indeed, both the food and the quarters were generally a good deal cushier than their equivalents back home.

As he altered course to bring them in from the east he suddenly glimpsed the islands out of the porthole window beside his head: a little green archipelago set in an otherwise unbroken expanse of wrinkled gold.

'I presume that means there's an evening breeze blowing down there,' said Muffin unexpectedly at his side. Had the canny old bugger actually dozed off at all? Amos wondered. 'I've flown into Kindley five or six times now, and on a couple of occasions they brought us in from the west. It doesn't much matter to us because we've got nearly ten thousand feet of runway to play with. Did I ever tell you I once landed and stopped a Vulcan in two thousand feet?'

'Is that a challenge?'

'Certainly not. You do your landing how you like. There's plenty of space and a bit of a headwind. No point in wasting a chute. That's the great thing about American runways: they're so long one can practically run out of fuel just taxiing from one end to the other. Take your time. We're the lead aircraft. The others will follow. You realise 'Bing' Cross will be lurking?'

'What?'

'Yes, God knows what he's doing here. Apparently this exercise on Saturday is going to be a very brassy occasion. Just about everybody you can think of with scrambled eggs on his cap will be lurking. But you can bet Bing will be watching us arrive. So squadron's honour at stake, and all that. Now, do you want me to call out some heights and speeds for you?'

'Roger that.' Amos put the presence of Bomber Command's C-in-C to the back of his mind and concentrated on his circuit over the sea. Behind him, he knew, the other three Vulcans would be strung out with a three-quarter mile safety margin between each, setting up for their approach directly into the setting sun. With a little turbulence over the ocean and with gear down and air brakes out he was at 132 knots, just above the stipulated safe minimum speed, as the end of the runway slid beneath the aircraft. He held his breath as a hundred tons touched down like a marshmallow settling into custard. Jammy sod – he thought to himself – pulling off a greaser just when needed. Keeping half an eye on the edge of the speeding runway through the circular side window, Amos held XJ786 straight down its centre, nose high, using the huge delta wing to act as an air brake. In this attitude both pilots had no forward vision at all other than of the sky, but their attention was anyway fixed on the instruments. As the speed bled off Amos gently lowered the nose until the nose wheels touched and they rolled out towards the designated turn-off.

'Well, I don't know. Anyone might think you were getting the hang of it,' Mewell observed as though he was an instructor in a Chipmunk and Amos a student doing his first circuits-and-bumps. Amos smiled into his mask, recognising this as praise.

Soon, drawn up neatly on the flight line, the all-white Vulcans stood out among the American aircraft parked nearby. They looked particularly futuristic against a squadron of propeller-driven B-50 Superfortresses: basically Second World War-vintage aircraft now relegated to weather reconnaissance. As always, the British bombers excited attention. It was not only a matter of their looks: rumours of their fighter-like agility had preceded them. As the newly arrived airmen disembarked, crew buses were ready to meet them and take them off to their quarters.

Ninety minutes later, having showered and changed into the mess kit they had been ordered to bring with them, the Vulcans' crews assembled in the officers' mess. The base commandant and the redoubtable Bing Cross were already standing by the bar, drinks to hand. Air Marshal Sir Kenneth Cross had taken over from Sir Harry Broadhurst as head of Bomber Command a couple of years earlier, and like his predecessor had a brilliant war record as a pilot. With his greying moustache he looked every inch the popular image of an RAF veteran, but there was nothing old-fashioned about the Soviet threat he was facing. He had resolved to meet it by instilling an unprecedented degree of alertness in his men that was much appreciated by his American counterpart in SAC. The tension generated by his stern insistence on discipline and constant exercises had percolated to even the least willing corners of Bomber Command.

Now, making his excuses to his American host, he marshalled the twenty RAF men into a quiet corner of the mess for a brief word before dinner.

'You may be surprised to see me here,' he said. 'The astuter among you will deduce it's a measure of how seriously we and our American and Canadian colleagues are taking this Skyshield exercise on Saturday. It's obviously of vital importance for us to discover just how good NORAD's radar defences really are. A sneak attack by the Soviets would be devastating. It could even be decisive. As you know, next year we will have that advance-warning radar system of our own at Fylingdales, which will join Thule and Cape Cod to give us longer warning. Even so, they will only buy us minutes. So what I want to say, chaps, is *"Vigilamus"* – which I gather is to be the motto of the Fylingdales station. For those of you who've forgotten their Latin, that means "We are watching". And you can be damned sure we shall be on Saturday.

'A word of warning. You are *not* to speak of this exercise off-base. From the Bermudans' point of view your visit is just a routine mission, nothing special, all right? And as for my own presence here, it is, quite simply, denied. I am not here, gentlemen – is that clear?' There were murmurs of assent. 'Oh – and one final point. If it doesn't seem an odd thing to say in the circumstances –' the Air Marshal cast a glance over his shoulder and lowered his voice '– good luck on Saturday. May Bomber Command show our allies who's boss when it comes to acting the part of the Soviet air force. OK then, enough of this. We should get back to our hosts.'

*

Saturday morning found the four Vulcans airborne once more, on a north-westerly heading for New York City. XJ786 was the designated lead aircraft, for no better reason than that Wing Commander Mewell was the ranking senior officer. Today he was flying and Amos sat attentively waiting for Bunny Carmichael to announce the first radar contact and possible hostile engagement. Although too seasoned in exercises of all kinds to feel particularly excited at the prospect, the Vulcan's entire five-man complement was nevertheless tensely aware that both squadron and national honour demanded an exceptionally professional performance.

The previous afternoon Amos and most of the other crewmen had managed to get their swim at Clearwater Beach. ('See?' said Yourshout. 'Don't tell me it wasn't worth bringing your trunks. You owe me a pint.') The rest of the day had been spent in getting the Operation Order off by heart, planning tactics and routes, and all with an eye to the forecast weather. The whole exercise might well have been top secret as far as the Bermudans were concerned, but on-base at Kindley even the mess cat would have sensed there was something major brewing. Apart from anything else all non-military aircraft along the American north-eastern seaboard would be grounded for twelve hours as from Saturday at 06:00. This included everything that could fly, from private planes to airliners. Such a drastic restriction was enough to make it internationally evident that a military exercise of unprecedented size and importance was taking place. Amos and his comrades were betting that the Soviets would be tipping off every agent and sleeper they had on the ground to go out and observe today.

What this ban on civil flying meant was that any other aircraft the Vulcans might encounter would belong to either the American or the Canadian air force, which simplified things. However, the Vulcans were not alone in masquerading as Soviet bombers. Large numbers of Strategic Air Command's B-47s and B-52s would be doing the same, though at lower altitudes. Altogether there would be hundreds of military aircraft in the air at every level, with the constant danger of collision. For that reason scrupulous altitude separation was vital. But that was not the sole reason why all civil aircraft had been grounded. The incoming bombers would be using their full range of ECMs or electronic countermeasures equipment to try to block NORAD's radars as well as that of the fighters sent up to intercept them. This would not only include powerful jamming signals but also 'chaff': strips of foil dropped from the bombers to confuse radar. For much of today, thousands of square miles of American and Canadian airspace would be crackling with electronic interference that risked swamping any civil airliner's navigation and communications systems and sending it wildly off-course.

Fourteen hundred miles to the north the other four Vulcans from 83 Squadron would be taking off from Goose Bay and flying for an hour eastwards out over the Labrador Sea. There they would rendezvous with SAC's assembling armada of bombers before the whole lot turned westwards again as though they were Soviet intruders that had just crossed Greenland and were approaching Canadian airspace. The Vulcans were expected to continue southwestward at high level as though launching an attack on Montreal and Ottawa, then turn back to land at Loring in the very northeastern corner of Maine, right on the Canadian border.

For the Vulcans flying up from Bermuda, the course of XJ786 and its three companions was plotted to cross New York City, then to head north-eastwards over Connecticut, Massachusetts and Maine, approaching Loring via Portland and Bangor. They were long sorties: both flights of Vulcans would be covering about two thousand five hundred miles each, more than five hours' combat flying with all crews maintaining maximum alertness.

The strange thing was, Amos thought, that although dropping nuclear bombs on people was the ultimate physical assault, the process involved was almost entirely electronic. They were about to run the gauntlet of every airborne defence the Americans and Canadians could muster, with real fighters trying to achieve radar lock-on to real bombers and ground-to-air missile batteries doing likewise. Thousands of tons of steel and alloy would be hurtling about the sky, all trying to intercept or avoid each other at supersonic closing speeds; yet nobody in the Vulcans was likely to see or hear a thing. They were up at fifty thousand feet or higher with lousy visibility from the cockpit and none whatever in the compartment behind, which was kept in darkness so the three backward-facing technicians could read their various cathode ray tubes and dials.

'AEO to Captain,' Bunny Carmichael's voice suddenly broke into Amos's reflections. 'We're two hundred nautical miles off New

York City. We'll have been under surveillance from their early warning radars for some time now. I've gone to Red Shrimp and Blue Diver. Both on line and normal.'

'Thanks, Bunny,' said Muffin.

Red Shrimp was a powerful noise jammer that would hopefully confuse the ground radars, while Blue Diver was designed to do the same to missile-guidance systems. Although no-one was going to launch missiles today, the radar technicians at the sites would nevertheless be doing their best to achieve lock-on and additional ECM noise would reduce their chances.

'We're about to trigger the Texas Towers L-band early warning, Skip,' said Carmichael. 'And we're just joining the bomber pack.'

'Roger.'

The Texas Towers stood in treacherous waters far offshore, one on the Georges Shoal, east of Cape Cod, the other on the Nantucket shoals, south-east of Rhode Island. Both radar stations were directly linked to USAF bases, so quite shortly the incoming bombers could expect attention from jet fighters out of bases like Montauk on Long Island.

'What aircraft do we have below us now?' asked Muffin.

'Four layers. B-52s at flight level three hundred, B-47s at two hundred and one hundred, and more B-52s down at about twenty. My guess is those big guys at the bottom of the heap will go down still further and try to sneak in on the carpet. Yes – they're losing height. Down to fifteen hundred feet now.'

'Roger that.'

'Christ, these scopes are a mass of contacts. It looks like Piccadilly Circus on Cup Final night,' Carmichael said. 'Deploying chaff *now*.'

Amos knew that the AEO would be releasing packets from the launcher beneath the port wing together with reels of 'rope', lengths of metal foil that unwound and floated upright in the air, held vertically by a little square of paper that acted as a miniature parachute. Beside him the wing commander triggered his intercom switch.

'Captain here. Good luck everybody. You heard what Air Marshal Cross said the other night. Today we're the bad guys, so let's give the Yanks something to think about while 83 Squadron take care of the Canucks up north. Bunny, keep us informed as we go.'

The briefing had warned the crews out of Bermuda to expect radar contacts by defending American interceptors once they had crossed longitude 65° W. Yet that was a good four hundred and fifty miles out into the Atlantic from New York City, a return trip to base of at least a thousand miles: a great distance for a single-seat fighter even without having to climb to meet the Vulcans at their level. Amos didn't imagine that the layers of SAC bombers beneath them were any more worried yet than he was. When they did come, the first fighters would be those with the longest range: F-101 Voodoos from bases like Dover in Delaware, Suffolk on Long Island and Otis on Cape Cod. As the bombers neared the coast the Voodoos would be reinforced by F-102 Delta Daggers (known as 'Deuces') and F-106 Delta Darts ('Sixes') from Westover in Massachusetts and McGuire in New Jersey.

From the AEO's regular updates the layers of bombers beneath the Vulcans were increasingly engaged as they neared the coast. It was not easy to guess what was going on with any precision since the mass jamming of the radar and radio frequencies was so intense. Bomber pilots counted themselves as 'downed' if the radars of either an interceptor or a ground missile battery achieved 'lock-on' for more than ten seconds. It was not until they were less than thirty miles from New York City that Bunny reported radar contact by a fighter coming up very fast behind the Vulcan but still some eight thousand feet below. He switched on the radar in the aircraft's tail that warned of anyone closing in from behind while putting out a fresh barrage of chaff. Almost immediately contact was lost.

'He'll have us on visual, though,' Muffin said to Amos. 'But he'll be closing quite slowly now. Less atmosphere up here and he'll be aware of all the fuel he's already burned from a scramble start.'

'We're currently at flight level five-sixty,' said Amos. 'Voodoos, Deuces and Sixes can all get above fifty thousand feet.'

'Worried?' asked Mewell with a sidelong smile.

'He's quite close,' broke in Bunny. 'He's about half a mile to port, a couple of thousand feet below. He'll be able to see us.'

'Mark 1 eyeball,' was the captain's rejoinder. 'Best of all systems. In real combat he could try to shoot us down with his cannon. Let's depress him a little.'

With that Mewell put the Vulcan into a tight turn to starboard and began jinking this way and that. The vast delta wing got enough purchase on the thin atmosphere for everyone aboard to feel the Gs building up. Almost at once there came a triumphant cry from the AEO.

'You've lost him, Chief. We've out-turned him easily. OK, confirmed, he's now seven miles away and descending fast. Just falling out of the sky.'

'Bingo'd, I'll bet. He'll be watching the fuel gauges every mile of the way,' said Muffin with satisfaction. 'Viv, give me a course to take us back round and directly over the city and then pick up our route to Boston. Rusty, I want to bomb New York.'

'OK, Chief.' This was Maurice Irons, the nav radar, the third man in the back whose job was essentially that of the old-fashioned bomb aimer, aided by some highly sophisticated radar targeting equipment. 'There's too much jamming going on to get a good fix.'

'Can you do a visual with your T.4 sight?'

'Roger. Good vis today. Long Island to the right. Manhattan coming up . . . Yup. Right on target. I've got a picture of that.'

'Captain, stand by for new course.'

As the Vulcan swung away to starboard to follow the coast Muffin said, 'Bloody good, Rusty. That'll give the Yanks something to worry about. We've just dropped a hydrogen bomb plumb spang on Central Park. Think of us as radical landscapers. The twentieth century's answer to Capability Brown.'

'*Who?*' said a voice.

'Three contacts closing fast from behind,' broke in Bunny. 'Two a couple of thousand feet below, one on our level. No lock-ons.'

'Can I break right?'

'Go-go-go.'

Once again the wing commander threw the aircraft into a steep bank.

'He's overshot. He'll never get back. Mach 1.4. His turning circle up here will be forty miles if he's lucky.'

There was unmistakable boyish elation in the young man's voice to which Amos felt himself respond. Bloody hell, it wasn't every day that you won a dogfight high over New York with the best fighters the USAF could deploy. Over the *ruins* of New York, too, since your aircraft had just blotted the city from the map . . . It was definitely not the moment to worry that big Soviet bombers like the Tu-16 'Badger' and the Tu-95 'Bear' might in theory also do what they had done, even though neither aircraft could climb as high as the Vulcan and nor were they anything like as manoeuvrable. The chances were they would be shot down. But then, in the general confusion it only needed one to get through.

'AEO, any sight of our own lads?'

'Hard to tell, they're putting out so much rope and chaff. Two were behind us, eleven and fifteen miles, I've lost the other. It could be this blip I'm getting way up at sixty thousand. Must be. Nobody else can get up there except for one of their Canberras or B-57s or whatever they're calling them, and this is a bigger return. Has to be a Vulcan but it could be a rope image and they're some way off now. They're all jamming like mad. Probably helped our own approach.'

'Thirty miles to Boston, Skip,' called Viv.

'Right, we'll bomb that, too. Get that, Rusty?'

'Roger.'

'AEO to Captain,' Bunny broke in. 'I'm in contact with Loring. We've got a divert, we've got a divert. Loring's no go, socked in, mist and rain. Vis twenty per cent and falling. We're diverted to Plattsburgh. Course correction coming up.'

'Roger that. But we'll just wipe out Boston first.'

'Where's Plattsburgh?' Amos asked Muffin.

'Northern New York State on Lake Champlain, up near the Canadian border. About eighty miles south of Montreal, as far as I remember. I'd guess a couple of hundred miles north-west of here. SAC station, if it's the one I'm thinking of. Just bombers. Dropped in there once a few years ago on some exercise or other. So many bloody exercises you can't remember where the hell you *have* been.'

'Or why.'

The wing commander shot Amos a glance, his eyes above the oxygen mask unreadable. 'There is no *why*, Pins. You just *do* it.'

Uncertain as to whether he had just been upbraided, and mildly unnerved by his superior's sudden use of the nickname that had followed him from his student days at Cranwell after an embarrassing episode involving an ejector seat, Amos was relieved when Viv broke in at this point with the course correction and warned Plattsburgh of their approach. The air traffic controller there would give them altitude instructions a hundred miles out. This was the distance from their original destination where the exercise would have been deemed to finish for the Vulcans.

'All ECM suspended, Skip,' said Bunny. 'No hostiles near us. I think they've called it off.'

Twenty minutes later XJ786 touched down beside the lake on runway three-five at Plattsburgh AFB. The other three Vulcans followed in the next fifteen minutes, their white triangles emerging from the clouds as traffic control slotted them between returning B-47 bombers and Boeing KC-97 tankers. There were even some fighters screaming down to land with puffs of tyre smoke.

'Strewth, what a caper,' said Muffin as he let Amos taxi in and park. The men swiftly completed their post-flight checklists. 'I'm knackered. Getting old.' Yawning, the wing commander removed his cloth helmet and ran his hands through hair that was already showing silvery strands. 'Well done, lads. Good stuff. One day you can tell your kids you wiped out New York City and Boston – but not before the Official Secrets Act expires or you'll be sent to the Tower. Right, we're unexpected guests here, so best behaviour and all that jazz. And don't rub their noses in it – we're all on the same side, don't forget. Plus we've still got a lot more flying to do in this country in the next few days.'

In the excitement of Skyshield Amos had almost forgotten that before they could return to England they would be flying sorties in an exercise called Big Photo. They hadn't been briefed on this yet but had gathered they would be pitting the Vulcans' ECM equipment against ground radars that the Americans had set up to mimic Soviet SAM missile sites. Well, tomorrow was another day. As they disembarked they could see that Plattsburgh was unmistakably a bomber base. The B-47s were coming home like weary crows at the end of a long day. They learned later that some of the crews had flown in for Skyshield from Europe as well as from bases all over the US, and thanks to air-to-air refuelling many had been airborne for the best part of twelve hours. They, too, were disembarking unsteadily and filing into buses. Beneath the grey sky a cool breeze blew the scent of burned kerosene and carried with it the sundry moans and blasts of aero engines. It was a scene familiar to airmen everywhere. XJ786's crew handed each other's flight bags down before themselves climbing stiffly down the yellow ladder to the stained concrete.

'The thing about life in the RAF which the adverts don't mention,' observed Bunny, 'is that you never know where the fuck you're going to be sleeping from one day to the next. Life's just one long camping trip.'

'Never mind the sleeping – oh wow!' said Rusty Irons with a sigh of pleasure as he pissed against a still-hot tyre. A small cloud of vapour drifted up. 'Bloody desperate, I was. You can't beat a Jimmy Riddle after a sortie.'

Just then, to everyone else's relief, a crew bus drew up and they climbed aboard.

*

Once they had showered and changed out of their flying gear, the crews of all four Vulcans met up to compare notes. The results surprised even them. Each of their aircraft had registered radar hits but none for a lock-on long enough for them to be 'downed'. All had successfully evaded their attackers by effective use of ECM. They had just heard that the four Vulcans from 83 Squadron had also been diverted from Loring, in their case to Ernest Harmon AFB in Stephenville, Newfoundland. There was no news yet of how they had got on in the exercise, but the results of the flights up from Bermuda were both triumphant and sobering. The four bombers had managed to 'invade' the seaboard of north-eastern America and, in a real war, could have obliterated several of its major cities.

'Shit-a-brick, it's back to the drawing-board for someone,' Mewell observed. 'Not for us, though, and definitely not tonight. Time to sample SAC's hospitality, don't you think?'

The next day RAF and USAF crews alike were amused by the reports on the mess TV of what Skyshield Saturday had looked like from the ground. It had evidently been plane-spotter's heaven as the waves of bombers at varying heights were met by the milling gnats of fighters. The sky had echoed to the constant thunder of jet engines and sonic bangs. More than one panicky radio station had reported a Soviet invasion. Citizens old enough to remember Orson Welles's 1938 radio play *The War of the Worlds* swore they had seen squads of short, squat creatures in metallic uniforms massing in the fields of Connecticut. When Sunday morning dawned it looked as though Christmas had arrived early. The countryside and hedgerows of the eastern United States glittered and sparkled beneath many tons of the tinsel-like filaments of chaff and strands of 'rope' that the hundreds of aircraft had deployed.

On Monday the 16th came news that the weather at Loring had cleared, and Amos and his crewmates regretfully left Plattsburgh for the next exercise. They made sure the four Vulcans put on a bit of a show for their poor benighted SAC friends by doing what B-47s couldn't do, which was to take off in pairs, fighter style, leap into the air and climb steeply out at an angle that would not have disgraced a single-seat interceptor. They turned to starboard over Lake Champlain for the short hop to Loring leaving trails of dark smoke that disappeared into the grey overcast.

At Loring they met up with their colleagues from 83 Squadron, who had themselves just flown in from Newfoundland to take part in the next exercise. It emerged that one of their Vulcans had been 'downed' by an F-101 Voodoo over Canada on Saturday; the other three had got through. In all, seven of Bomber Command's aircraft had successfully penetrated North American airspace. Washington, Baltimore, Philadelphia, New York, Boston, Montreal and Ottawa: *gone*. The men looked at each other.

'I blame the Founding Fathers,' said Bunny Carmichael. 'America was colonised from the east, so most of their principal cities are strung out along this side of the continent, aren't they? Big mistake. As my old nan used to say, 'Never put all your eggs on one seaboard.'

'What was she, then, chorus girl at the Pentagon?'

'Nah, she couldn't kick high enough because of the arthritis.'

The jocularity concealed a slight feeling of anti-climax among the men from Scampton. It was further intensified by the complete absence of any kind of official debriefing. This was most unusual in the wake of an exercise. Apart from their own success, how had all the others done? The hundreds of B-52s and B-47s and B-57s, any of which was capable of delivering nuclear weapons? Silence. Like Plattsburgh, Loring was also an SAC station, and the only information the Britons could glean came from chatting with their opposite numbers from the American bomber crews. Not surprisingly, a lot of the bombers at lower altitudes had been intercepted and 'killed', but many hadn't, in particular some of the B-52s that had gone in lowest of all.

'I'm not surprised you guys got through if you were up at fifty-six thousand, for Pete's sake,' said one B-52 captain. 'That's gotta be cheating.'

'That's the height we were told to fly at,' Wing Commander Mewell said pacifically.

'Yeah, sure, I didn't mean you were out of order, just that it was unrealistic. Those Vulcans of yours can fly far higher than anything the Russkies have. We're told no Bear or Badger can make more than about forty-five thousand.'

'Maybe the Soviets have something in the pipeline we don't know about.'

'Well, I sure hope to Christ you Brits aren't going to sell them Vulcans like you sold them jet engines after the war.'

'Ouch.'

One of 83 Squadron's pilots reported that he'd been chatting to an F-102 pilot in a bar at Ernest Harmon. The Vulcan man, in common with all his fellows, had made no visual sightings himself but the pilot of the Deuce had spotted a Vulcan from below. 'He was tracking a B-52 and saw us about twenty thousand feet above him. His reaction was "What the eff is that effing thing up there?" and tried a snap-up attack but said he just about fell out of the sky in the attempt.'

'Theoretically we could have gone higher, you know,' said Mewell mildly. 'One of our guys tells me he managed to slide up to around fifty-eight before getting within early warning cover.'

The USAF man merely shook his head before brightening. 'Sure, but if that had been a real attack we'd have gone to missiles. This base, Loring? We're the biggest in SAC. We store nukes here and we're ringed with Nike Ajax sites. You stick a nuclear warhead on one of those mothers and it doesn't matter if it misses you by a few hundred feet. It's still going to make your eyes water, right? Anyway, we all showed up on their screens from the moment we were airborne on Saturday.'

'Of course we did,' Amos broke in. 'But as I understand it the point of the exercise was to test NORAD, which isn't blips on radar so much as what you do about them. Surely North American

Air Defense means, well, defending against an incoming enemy. Speaking for my own lot on Saturday, none of the defenders could reach us, not even your Sixes, and we were briefed that they'll hit Mach 2 at forty thousand feet and are good to reach well over fifty thousand.' Amos was embarrassed to intercept a warning glance from his senior officer and subsided.

'Yeah, well, like I said, if it had been for real you guys would've been taken out by missiles, ECM or no ECM.'

'You hope. You don't know our ECM.'

The next night a cocktail party and supper was held at the Officers' Club to welcome the RAF detachment. The day after that, using Loring as their base, the eight Vulcans flew various sorties in which they tested their equipment against simulated surface-to-air missile sites as well as making radar bomb scoring attacks on American targets at which hits and misses were very accurately measured electronically. A 'highly classified' aura surrounded the whole venture. From the airmen's point of view, it was just another exercise and the results were none of their concern.

From then on the RAF crews gave themselves up to fraternising with their USAF colleagues. The final social event of the British visit to Loring was a return party they threw for their American hosts: a binge involving the usual ritual exchange of shields and plaques, squadron ties and badges. On 20 October, somewhat reluctantly, the Vulcans flew back to Scampton. All crews agreed it had been an ace exercise, but once back home they were very surprised not to be debriefed on the mission in the usual fashion. It was obvious to them that certain sectors of NORAD had been found wanting, which seemed worthy of mention. At the very least they expected Bomber Command's research branch would be eager to know a good few particulars of the Vulcans' performance. However, it appeared the USAF were sitting on all the results and from then on official silence blanketed the biggest joint exercise in which the RAF had ever taken part.[†]

Within twenty-four hours Amos was returned to his old squadron and memories of Skyshield II were swiftly buried by fresh exercises. After another year's co-piloting he was sent off to No. 230 Operational Conversion Unit at Waddington to be turned into a full-blown Vulcan captain. Somewhere around that time he heard on the grapevine that 'Muffin' Mewell had been promoted group captain and had been given command of Wearsby station in Lincolnshire. The next few years passed in a haze of kerosene smoke and the endless daily rehearsals for heading off a third world war, and Skyshield II became just another fading memory.

---

† See Appendix 1, p. 287.

1964-5

2

As he pedalled along, Amos was once again struck by how beautiful an airfield could be. In the clear light of an early Lincolnshire morning the gently rolling fields in the distance were darkly marked with lines of elms emerging from a stealthy ground mist: familiar shapes without which no English landscape would ever be truly complete. This hardening panorama, he now decided, performed the same function as the background of a Renaissance painting. There, behind the rallying men and horses, gorgeous with flags and harness, a far-off river might wind placidly past unheeding villages and olive groves. Here, the pale tower of the medieval church in Market Tewsbury five miles away seemed equally unwitting of the engines of war marshalled in the foreground. And just as an art-lover could read a painting's iconography and marvel at details of sword and armour, so could an airman's heart lift at the sight of the great ghost-white bombers on their dispersals like pale cattle caught sleeping at dawn. Yet human ingenuity had designed them to spring into the air within minutes and fly faster than the footprint of the sun.

Lately, Amos had taken to starting the day with a visit to one of the airfield's remoter corners. There was seldom anyone about although, as on any active station, there were always sounds of industry from some quarter. This morning it was from the crews working overnight in one of the vast hangars to bring a Vulcan back to serviceability. On the cool, still air as he passed came the distant chugging of a mobile generator and the faint screech of a power tool. His cycle tyres whined softly over the perimeter track's ribbed concrete. Out here, where less than twenty years earlier bombed-up Lancasters had waddled from dispersal, the expansion joints between the sections of pavement were still filled with bitumen. Nowadays, spilt kerosene and the searing heat of jet engines too easily dissolved or burned such tar fillings so out on the pan all the old joints had been reamed out and replaced with concrete. This perimeter road, however, remained a fossil from the Second World War, still functional in these chill and perilous times.

This and associated trivia freewheeled through Amos's mind as he cranked his bicycle along in the growing light. Off to his right stood an immense black water tank on tall iron legs with cross-bracing, another relic from the previous war. It still functioned as an emergency supply and had always been a useful point of reference for pilots on final approach. Ahead of him there now appeared the figures of a military policeman and his Alsatian dog returning from a night's patrolling of the inner perimeter fence. He braked to a halt as the man raised his hand in slightly more than greeting.

'Morning, Corporal. Quiet night?' He handed over his F.1250. There had been a security scare recently.

'Morning, sir. Thought I recognised you. Quiet enough, it's been.' The immaculately blancoed white webbing of the man's belt, holster and shoulder strap gleamed in the early light. As the policeman bent his head to read the ID Amos could see beads of dew on his service cap's white top.

'And how's Air Dog Bonzo this morning?' Amos addressed the question facetiously to the Alsatian. 'No Russky spies to get your teeth into?' The animal merely fixed him with a blank, killer's gaze. There was a dusting of dew on its back and mud had oozed up between its toes.

'Thank you, sir.' The MP handed back the folder. 'Long way from married quarters, sir.'

'You married, Corporal?'

'Not quite, sir.'

'Just you wait. You'll soon find a bit of distance essential now and then.'

When the guard and his dog were dots on the track behind him Amos turned in at the edge of the woods that screened the fire dump equally from the personnel on base and from the occasional British taxpayer travelling the B road a couple of hundred yards away beyond the airfield's high outer fence. A favourite destination of his, the place drew him as the archaeological site it was. Less than two years previously RAF Wearsby had been a Fighter Command station. Then, after welling anxiety in Whitehall and Washington about the Soviets' ability to deliver a nuclear strike, Bomber Command had taken up residence instead. The Airfield Construction Branch had worked night and day to lengthen the main runway and build a series of individual operational readiness platforms leading off it so that each bomber had immediate access to it for scramble take-offs. The crews had been busy right up to a month ago building blast pens, hardened aircraft shelters and the reinforced bunkers where Blue Steel nuclear bombs were stored. The two previous squadrons had flown off in their Hunters to Jever and Gütersloh in Germany and the great delta-winged V-bombers had moved in, three of them brand new from the Avro works, their anti-flash white finish smelling of fresh cellulose. Since the strategic catchword these days was 'deterrent', they were facetiously deemed to constitute part of Britain's Great White Deterrent, a phrase which the service had reliably downgraded to Great White Detergent in honour of the novelty value of washing powders like Omo and Tide. The very word detergent brought with it an air of modernity, a suggestion of effortless efficiency.

In all the recent hectic activity at Wearsby the station's fire dump seemed to have been overlooked. Tucked away in its distant corner, it remained an oasis immune from the new Ministry of Aviation's world of strategic urgency. It simply went on giving a last home to the victims of mechanical failure, pilot error and sheer bad luck. Lincolnshire – like much of East Anglia – was dotted with airfields of all kinds and despite Wearsby's nuclear status it was also a Master Diversion Airfield, guaranteed open all year round (weather permitting) for emergency landings, civil or military. It was surprising how often it played host to pilots declaring an emergency. It might be some fighter jock far from home whose engine had surged, flamed out and refused to relight who thought he still had the altitude and was bullish enough to try to 'dead-stick' it onto Wearsby's long runway instead of ejecting and letting the aircraft fall where it might. Another could be down to his last hundred pounds of fuel while searching fruitlessly in a thick sea mist for his home base. Or else a fledgling pilot from Cranwell became lost on a night flying exercise and put down at Wearsby, typically so overjoyed to find terra firma again that he would forget to lower his landing gear first. The physical remains of such episodes, once they had been designated Category 5 – written off as beyond repair – were struck off charge, lifted onto a battered Queen Mary low-loader and hauled off to the fire dump. And it was here that Amos sometimes came for a reflective visit before the day's routines summoned him elsewhere. It was something he tried to keep from his crew, none of whom was married. They would have seen it as disquietingly morbid, their own spare time being reserved for more extroverted pursuits. As his crew chief 'Baldy' Hodge would remark with the sour wisdom of a married man in his mid-thirties, 'Growing old is compulsory; growing up is not.'

On entering the dump a visitor was confronted by four main rows of scrap, in places piled twenty or more feet high, separated by broad concrete lanes stretching some fifty yards to a pair of Nissen huts at the back that still wore the fading blotches of wartime camouflage paint. The wrecked aircraft were pretty much stratified by era, the majority dating from Fighter Command's recent occupancy. The oldest types that formed the bottom layers had been propeller-driven. Off to one side were several stacks of Meteor fuselages that had been whimsically propped on their noses, wigwam-like, with tail fins interlocked. From their plain metal finish and the yellow bands painted around wings and fuselage it was clear that many had been training aircraft: a mere handful of the nearly nine hundred Meteors the RAF had lost in service. Everywhere the early sunlight glistened on the dew-beaded remains of cockpit canopies, the crazed perspex of the older models already acquiring a brownish tinge from exposure to the elements. One of the rows of scrap was composed entirely of wings and other flying surfaces, at the bottom of which some were recognisable among the tangle of oxidising alloy as having belonged to old monoplanes such as Harvards or Typhoons. Immediately above this layer were more relics of the RAF's earliest jet fighters: Meteors, Vampires and Venoms. Wherever water could pool, moss and even small seedlings had sprung up, especially in the tiers devoted to fuselages, where brilliant green algae favoured the rails in which cockpit canopies had once slid. In one pilot's seat a crop of groundsel had colonised its sodden and decaying foam stuffing.

From a neighbouring lane the towering jib of a Coles Mk 5 crane was outlined against the paling sky, its steel hawsers dangling slack above the tailless fuselage of a Canberra that had landed short some weeks earlier, caught its wheels in an unseen drainage ditch and cartwheeled onto the airfield. Two dead on the spot and the third within minutes of the crash crews' arrival. All its high-altitude photos of East Germany were lost in the ensuing fire. The crane rested its heavy grab impassively on the Canberra's blistered hide as if holding it down against some atavistic struggle the fuselage was making to heave itself back into the air. Wire pulleys, thought Amos. Typical of the RAF to make do with a museum piece. But then, why waste a modern crane on a junkyard?

Unlike most airmen, Amos found the fire dump perversely comforting. Aircrew generally avoided confronting the evidence of the death or disaster that was anyway seldom far from their daily lives. Of necessity they inhabited a blessed present squeezed between the dangers of yesterday and the probable nuclear holocaust of tomorrow. Everybody knew of someone who had died. Some had gone instantaneously, some nastily, some even absurdly – like the ground crewman in Aden who had been replacing a faulty relay in the bomb bay of a Valiant. The aircraft was to be flown back on a UK ranger, to the delight of its crew, for a complete overhaul of the bomb-bay heating system which constantly failed. By some freakish screw-up the technician had been shut into the bay by an inattentive crew chief. The aircraft had taken off from Khormaksar, flown back to the UK at fifty thousand feet with a refuelling stop in Akrotiri, and at the last minute had been diverted to Wearsby because of an accident on its home base. Before landing the Valiant had done a low, slow run over the airfield with its bomb doors open to test them, watched by binoculars from the control tower. The deep-frozen ground crewman in his frost-covered khaki shorts fell three hundred feet onto the main runway and shattered like marble, white and crimson chunks bounding away across the grass on either side. Still other deaths remained pure enigmas. Handsome Peter Torrance had gone off in a leftover

Hunter F.6 to test its Aden cannon by shooting a few holes in Knock Deep, off Felixstowe, a fifty-minute sortie at most, and had simply vanished. No radio message, no thin slick of kerosene, let alone wreckage. He had promised to be back in time for *Yogi Bear* on the mess TV at 17:00 and broke his word by flying off into everlasting silence.

But that wasn't the salutary part of all this: there was nothing new to be learned from sudden death. For Amos the real point was the temporary nature of the whole strategic enterprise, from summit-level politics to outdated hardware. He found it ironic, even reassuring, that the top secrets of fifteen years ago were now junk buried beneath later layers of other top secrets, with the most recent and secret of all open to the skies and held down by the rusted grab of an obsolete crane. They were casualties of the hectic technological advances which the Cold War mandated. Everyone on the station knew that some of Britain's most ground-breaking experimental aircraft were scrapped by government decree before they had ever flown, winding up as targets on the artillery ranges at Shoeburyness. Millions of pounds' worth of ingenuity, labour and materials blown up by a bunch of pongos.

Yet it wasn't really a simple issue of outrageous waste, as the newspapers claimed. If you flew a V-bomber you knew only too well the difficulty of designing new weapons on the edge of what was technically feasible. Unavoidably such weapons had long lead times, and an unexpected breakthrough on your opponent's part might change the whole strategic plan overnight, rendering the latest interceptor or radar set obsolete before it was even rolled out. No NATO airman was ever likely to forget that day in 1960 when the American Gary Powers had been shot down deep over Russia in his U-2 reconnaissance aircraft by a Soviet surface-to-air missile. Nor had the Yanks been alone in thinking themselves safe at an altitude of over eighty thousand feet; *everyone* in the West had been counting on sheer height for protection. That one SAM had demonstrated they were safe no longer. It was an immense technological and political coup for the Russians; and in Powers's later public trial Khrushchev had rubbed it in. The real worry was that the USSR had revealed itself as a good two or three years more advanced in missile-guidance systems than the West's intelligence services had believed. In how many other fields might it already be equal – or even superior – to the best NATO could offer?

So here in a relatively forgotten corner of RAF Wearsby the strengthening light revealed the sedimentary layers of the best the RAF could once offer: a geology of ex-secrets. Amos wandered to the end of a row and opened the door of the right-hand Nissen hut. The air inside was cold and smelt of kerosene. A few more or less intact engines rested neatly on steel trestles with drip trays beneath them. Periodically, he knew, a heavy lorry would call for them, presumably to take them back to Bristols or Rolls-Royce for rebuilding. Other lorries collected the more battered engines piled to one side so their valuable alloys could be reclaimed. The second hut was locked and mainly contained salvaged instruments and avionics other than radar. Anything to do with radar and electronic countermeasures was far too sensitive to be left in a shed, no matter how well locked and patrolled by RAF police with Alsatians. Some way off was an open area of blackened soil. This was where combustible stuff was periodically burned to give the fire crews some practice. On a still day the viscid column of smoke from shredded aero tyres and engine oil provided a marker that could be seen for miles around. Evidently the last things to go had been some seats, presumably from a crashed transport. Their skeletons, orange with heat or rust, were still tangled at the centre of the bonfire site whose edges were marked by odd lengths of half-charred hydraulic tubing like stubs of liquorice.

Between the huts rested the flattened remains of a Sycamore helicopter. For Amos this wreckage had become the dump's focal point, almost a private shrine. By sheer chance he had happened to witness the accident, which took place in Wearsby's airspace. He had been replacing a windscreen wiper on his tatty Hillman one unusually slack day towards noon when, as habitually as any airman, he had glanced up at the sound of aero engines. A huge Beverley transport was lumbering over a corner of the field at about fifteen hundred feet, not with any obvious intention of landing but at what looked like close to stalling speed. Buzzing beneath it and far too close, like a cleg trying to settle on a cow, was a small helicopter. At that moment Amos had a powerful premonition of disaster that leaped through him like voltage. Possibly the helicopter's pilot misjudged the distance or else his Sycamore was caught in the vortex that the massive transport was generating, which amounted to the same thing. Its main rotor touched one of the transport's fixed undercarriage legs, instantly shattering its blades which were hurled aside like twigs. The suddenly relieved engine raced itself to destruction within seconds and the helicopter twirled from the sky, falling towards the distant outskirts of Market Tewsbury. It disappeared from view behind the station's chapel while the Beverley droned on, seemingly unaware of anything amiss, not deviating from its course until it, too, vanished.

Bloody fool, Amos thought almost viciously, turning back to finish with the wiper. Only an idiot would fly a helicopter that close. What did he think would happen? It was the familiar reaction with which airmen so often masked distress and fear. Immortality was naturally granted to those who were not that stupid . . . Amos had witnessed several fatal accidents in his flying career and thought little more about this one until he overheard some

35

gossip and caught the unfortunate pilot's name: O'Shea. Simultaneously the small shock raced through him again. Surely not *Marty* O'Shea? But inevitably it was. Apparently the pilot of the Beverley had reported foreign object damage to his starboard wheels on take-off, and as the nearest aircraft Marty's Sycamore had been diverted to make a visual inspection. It had simply flown too close. Although Marty and his no. 2 were wearing parachutes, neither had managed even to release his seat harness: centrifugal force must have pinned them where they sat. Wrenched violently in all directions, they might dimly have perceived for a few seconds that they were doomed. The Sycamore had slammed into the ground upside down, digging itself a grave several feet deep. The removal of the two men had taken place piecemeal; and although fire hoses had later flushed out the wreckage it still smelt and attracted flies whenever the sun was on it in Wearsby's dump. Pilot error, the Accidents Investigation Branch inspectors had reluctantly concluded.

It had hit Amos hard. Marty and he had been at Cranwell together and had shared many a daft escapade. They had been at the same drunken dance in Grantham the night they met Avril and Jo. In what Amos now ruefully considered the daftest escapade of all, Marty had married Avril and he had married Jo. It had been all the dafter because at the time the RAF reinforced its disapproval of officers marrying before they were twenty-five by not assigning them married quarters even when they were available, which was seldom, and frequently obliging young couples to buy their own caravans to live in and to move them at their own expense when they were posted. The promise of a life of Calor gas lighting, Elsan toilets and a likely bus ride for the wife to reach the NAAFI shop surely argued true love.

That had been in 1957. Or was it 1958? On graduation Marty had opted for a rotary-wing course and had stuck with helicopters, winding up flying rescue missions with Coastal Command. For some years he and Amos had seen little of each other until Marty was posted not far from Wearsby, somewhere out by the Wash. Jo and Avril, who had remained in touch by occasional letter, still met quite often. These days Jo contrived to spend ever more time with her widowed friend and two small fatherless children and had ever less to say when she fetched up back at Wearsby. 'This whole world of yours,' she would gaze stonily out of their married quarters' metal-framed windows at the identical brick blocks of flats on either side. 'It stinks of death, Amos. You do realise that?'

I'm every bit as upset about Marty as you are, he would think to himself, reflecting that he'd known his friend rather longer than he'd known his wife but managing to stop himself from saying so. One had to make allowances for the womenfolk, everyone recognised that. Most of the time they were as keenly wedded to the ethic of the service as their men; but every so often an emotional side could surface when they seemed to forget the overriding demands of this attritional war against communism in which they were all, willy-nilly, combatants. Amos preferred not to risk one of Jo's disparaging retorts about 'male bonding', whatever that was. No doubt some phrase she had picked up from the *Reader's Digest* to which she subscribed at a Forces discount. It paid to increase your word power, Amos thought bleakly. 'You married into the services, Jo,' he protested as quietly as he could, nettled more by the idea of embarking yet again on a tedious circle of repartee than he was by her implied accusations.

'*Into*, yes. But I didn't marry the Royal bloody Air Force. "I Give My All". What kind of a daft squadron motto is that? Not to me, you don't, and I'm your wife.'

'I think I'm supposed to give it to my monarch,' he told her mildly. 'Private life gets whatever's left over.'

'Slim pickings.'

'Maybe. But at Cranwell I took an oath of allegiance to "Queen Elizabeth, her heirs and successors".'

'And may I remind you that you also took an oath of allegiance to me. Your marriage vows – affirmed before God, in case you've forgotten.'

'We knew all that beforehand, Jo, remember? Frankly, I don't mind giving my all if it prevents the world being obliterated with nuclear weapons. I've never made a secret of it. I *like* being a cold warrior. I regret but believe in its absolute necessity. It's what I've been trained for.'

He supposed it was the shock of her friend's widowhood causing this bitterness. That and the new regime of QRAs – quick reaction alerts – to say nothing of his frequent absences on exercises and sorties to far-flung places around the globe. 'It's the job, Jo. We can't ease up. Do you want Britain turned into a wasteland of fused glass just because we've been caught napping by a pre-emptive Soviet attack? You can't trust the Communists an inch, you know that.' But it remained acknowledged and unspoken that the constant state of alert could break normal life, collapse marriages. It was the poisonous fallout of a confrontation structured to ensure no nuclear bomb would ever be dropped in anger. Security was such that wives quickly sensed what questions not to ask about their husbands' work, the operations they flew, and least of all about the weapons and equipment they deployed. And there were even a few women who outranked their husbands, or whose jobs made them privy to information they couldn't share in bed.

'Shit-a-brick, that's the *deal*,' Amos told the stratified heaps of sheet metal in the fire dump as he stood in the morning light full of righteous exasperation. Unexpected absences, certain no-go areas – they were surely the trade-off for cheap living, for allowances and pensions, the best medical attention, paid holidays, even the occasional free flight care of Transport Command to sunny places like Singapore or Aden or Nairobi. Not for the first time – by no means for the first time – he was aggrieved enough by his own rhetoric to add aloud, 'Bloody women.' What a ridiculous mistake to have made: starting out his adult life by swearing solemn oaths to not one but two of them. At least the Queen didn't moan at him over breakfast. One of these days, he thought with a tiny lift of satisfaction, I shan't be able to stop myself telling Jo that I love flying more than I love her. Never mind the initial drilling and bull back at Cranwell, learning to fly had been wonderful. And now years of disciplined study and practice as well as the Operational Conversion Unit course have finally put me in the left-hand seat of a nuclear bomber. The responsibility would probably scare me shitless if I ever allowed myself to think like that instead of treating it as the best thing in my life... For a moment Amos thought fondly of his crew: professionals all who loved what they were doing and believed in it. By comparison the domestic and emotional world was strangely aimless, its civilian inhabitants amateurish and clumsy. From where he stood he could glimpse between two elms one of his squadron's Vulcans nearly a mile away. For a long moment its dew-beaded tail fin blushed beneath a pinkish ray of the rising sun and again he felt his heart lift as once a cavalryman's might at the magnificence of a charger in peak condition. It was more than the mere tool of his trade, a piece of service-issue equipment. Wives sometimes referred sourly to their husband's aircraft as 'the other woman'. That's the *deal*, he thought again.

In the strengthening light Amos glanced around before laying an affectionate hand on the Sycamore's shattered carcase.

'Bless you, Marty,' he murmured a little self-consciously. '*You* knew what it was about. Good hunting to you, old boy, wherever

39

you may be.' The words said themselves without the least belief in anything beyond the point of impact; but the sentiment filled his eyes with momentary tears.

After a few more minutes in this junkyard-turned-shrine he glanced at his watch and pedalled away. The day had begun. Within a matter of hours the weather had turned and he was suited up and sitting patiently in the captain's seat of XM580 on yet another QRA.

3

Ever since the Cuban missile crisis in 1962 a proportion of the V-force – one aircraft in each squadron – was always held at readiness state one-five. That is, the bombers could be in the air with their Blue Steel nuclear weapon at fifteen minutes' notice, hence the 'quick reaction alert' designation. Tannoys screwed to buildings on every part of the airfield could exert their raucous klaxon tyranny at any time, day or night. This might be followed by the stentorian announcement: 'Exercise Edom! Exercise Edom! Readiness state zero-five!' The booming voice relayed from Bomber Command's HQ at High Wycombe would go rolling away into the Lincolnshire countryside, often clearly audible in nearby towns and villages. The nominated crews who had been waiting, suited up, for anything up to twenty-four hours would make a dash for their aircraft which were already in a state of cockpit readiness with the pre-take-off checks complete, there to await the next instruction.

The theory was that since most bomber airfields held two or three, sometimes even four squadrons, Britain could generate some ninety or more nuclear-armed bombers within the four minutes' notice of incoming Soviet missiles the Fylingdales radars would theoretically give. In practice it was assumed that escalating international tension would buy several days' additional warning time for the V-force, allowing it to be deployed to thirty-six secondary airfields scattered throughout the British Isles. Whitehall was banking on the Soviets never being mad enough to launch a pre-emptive 'bolt from the blue' attack on the Lincolnshire and East Anglian main bases because the Americans, forewarned, could then annihilate the USSR with retaliatory attacks more or less at their leisure. But with the RAF's Vulcans and Victors and Valiants at full cockpit readiness anywhere between the Lizard and the Orkneys it was reckoned that a good few would be able to get off the ground in time and, even allowing for some of them being intercepted by missiles or fighters en route for Moscow, Stanley Baldwin's pre-Second World War adage that 'the bomber will always get through' was still widely enough believed by all sides for its deterrent threat to be effective.

Now Squadron Leader Amos McKenna and his crew were sitting in their Vulcan on its dedicated dispersal pan at the far end of Wearsby airfield. They had been there for an hour and a half already on zero-five alert, strapped in while wearing a flying suit, an air-ventilated suit, G-trousers and G-waistcoat. They had already missed lunch and were beginning to be both hungry and thirsty. From long experience they had known not to drink too much liquid that morning. There was provision for 'easement' aboard the bomber in the shape of chrome-stoppered rubber tubes ending in piss bags, known to all as 'rubber kippers'. However, the sundry straps and tightly laced garments offered too daunting a prospect for any but the most desperate. Somehow the exigencies of a national emergency always managed to take precedence over mere bodily functions and subdue them except – as at least two crew members could remember – in the case of a co-pilot they'd once been assigned who had eaten an unwary chicken curry in Market Tewsbury's Moti Mahal a few hours before a high-altitude sortie. The curry had had real authority and there was no provision aboard a V-bomber for that sort of emergency, least of all at fifty thousand feet, and the luckless man was unwise enough to confide his acute sufferings over the intercom. Helpful advice was immediately forthcoming from the rear compartment. 'Bomb doors to open.' 'Better out than in.' 'Go on – you know you want to.' And eventually, strapped firmly into his ejector seat as he was, there had been no alternative. For the rest of the flight an apprehensive silence settled over the crew. The man even carried out the landing in order to keep up his currency, a perfect greaser despite a gusty crosswind. ('If that's flying by the seat of one's pants I wish more pilots shat themselves,' the AEO remarked to his neighbour as they were taxiing back.) The pilot was known for a while as 'Skidmarks' but by the time he was posted to train for a captain's seat he was universally known as 'Vindaloo', a name probably destined to follow him for the rest of his RAF career, and one he would never explain to his family.

From his seat twenty feet above the concrete pan Amos smiled to himself at the recollection before dragging his attention back to the present. As always, the insistent 'beep' of the Telebrief in his earphones was inducing its own kind of nervous tension in him. For as long as the aircraft was held on readiness, its intercom system was linked directly by umbilical cable to the Bomber Controller at High Wycombe, who would issue the next orders. The beep, repeated every ten or fifteen seconds, was fed into the line to show that it remained open and live. The same sound was being listened to aboard crewed-in bombers on the same QRA all over eastern England. It was also audible in the headphones worn by Baldy Hodge, the crew chief, who was huddled below sheltering from the rain beneath the Vulcan's ample wing. After an hour of it Amos found himself waiting for the next beep much as the victims of Chinese water torture must have waited for the next drop. Suddenly an imperious voice came on the line.

'Attention. Attention. This is Bomber Controller. For Wittering, Wearsby and Finningley wings: maintain readiness state zero-five. I repeat: Wittering, Wearsby and Finningley wings: maintain readiness state zero-five. Bomber Controller out.'

'Ahh, buggeration,' came Bob Mutton's voice over the intercom. 'How much frigging longer, eh? We could do with some nosh back here, Skip.'

'So we could up here, Baa,' Amos told his nav plotter as the monotonous beep resumed. 'We've been here before. You know what'll happen the moment we get the soup heated and the sandwiches broken out: they'll call a scramble and we'll be in the shit. Better to hang on.'

'We've tried feeding him grass but it just makes him fart.' This was the nav radar, Vic Ferrit. Amos allowed a couple more exchanges of banter before commanding silence. Although he knew it to be impossible, he could never quite disabuse himself of the idea that these crewed-in conversations might somehow be audible to the brass hats in their High Wycombe nerve centre. Perhaps it would be salutary if they were. It might convince the powers that be that the men they were commanding from their distant bunker were under a constant strain that could be a little relieved by ribaldry. The endless repetitive checks to achieve cockpit readiness took their toll. So did the practically daily sessions of target study in 'the Vault' in Station Ops. Before each QRA the air electronics officer and the nav plotter were given a target in Russia but not the route they needed to reach it: that was something they had to work out for themselves before the klaxon sounded and they dashed for the aircraft. Amos often wondered if the upper echelons of Bomber Command weren't too cut off from the consequences of their demands.

One of the oddities of this new kind of warfare, he reflected, was that the more concerted the bombers' response was required to be, the more each crew ended up in isolation. The view from the Vulcan's cockpit was never good, and the rain falling outside from a gloomy low ceiling of clouds made it still worse. Almost immobilised in their seats by straps and bulky layers of clothing, with news from outside blanked out by the Telebrief's beep in their headphones, it was easy for the two pilots crammed together in the narrow cockpit to feel cut off from the world, suspended in a capsule of slowed-down existence. They had an inkling of how Yuri Gagarin must have felt orbiting the earth in his titanium ball three years earlier. Nor were conditions any better in the crew's compartment behind them. It was at moments like this, simultaneously tedious and nerve-fraying, that Amos saw his aircraft less as a friendly beast and more as the weapon it always was, its human component stuffed into cramped holes up in the nose with the rest of the immense fuselage given over to the capacious bomb bay and the nine heavy dustbin-sized drums of ECM gear in the tail.

And truly isolated they would be if ever it came to the real thing and they took off with a live nuclear weapon they were committed to drop somewhere in western Russia. It would mean that Britain had already been attacked; and as they flew eastwards they would know there would be no coded message telling them to return. They would listen out for it, of course. In default of an official re-call on the usual military wavelengths the Vulcan's radio compass could be tuned to the BBC Home Service, which in the last re-sort would broadcast the recall code – assuming that Broadcasting House itself still existed. But there would be nothing left to return to and nowhere to land: no airfield, no families, friends, wives, children – nothing but glowing rubble. Then they really would be on their own. They had been told they should make for Turkey and land there, but they all knew there would be little fuel left for such a diversion after dropping the bomb. No-one liked to think of these things, of course; and because they all had absolute faith in the V-force as an effective deterrent they none of them believed it would ever come to that. Even committed Communists were only human and not irrational madmen. But still the images of Armageddon lurked disguised in their dreams, now and then given flickering shape by recent films shown at Wearsby's little Astra cinema such as *Dr Strangelove* and *Fail-Safe*. Those cinematic reminders were probably salutary, anyway. The rituals of constant rehearsal could all too easily lead to forgetting what the final picture might look like if things went badly wrong.

The imperious voice once again broke into the thoughts of everyone aboard XM580. 'Attention, Attention. This is Bomber Controller. For Wearsby wing only, revert to readiness state one-five. I repeat, for Wearsby wing only, revert to readiness state one-five. Bomber Controller out.'

'Yippee!' 'About bloody time too, and all.' Headphones were shed and ears massaged to the tinkling of harnesses being thrown off and connectors clanking against metal. Fifteen minutes' readiness was the baseline and meant the crew could disembark. Amos and his men ran their shortened shutdown checks. Someone pulled a lever, the hatch opened and cold Lincolnshire air gusted in. Crew Chief Hodge appeared below to reach up and pull down the extension of the yellow-painted ladder. The men swiftly disembarked, encumbered by their go-bags and the awkward aluminium ration boxes and Thermos flasks.

'Thanks, Chiefie,' said Amos as he reached the ground and viewed the dismal rain-swept expanse of concrete around the aircraft. 'I'm afraid your wait was more miserable than ours.'

'We get used to it, don't we?' came the morose response. 'At least it's not night and snowing. Anything on your 700?'

'No – all up and running as per.' He handed over the form he'd signed and went to board the Bedford coach that drove the crew off in a cloud of spray to the operational readiness huts and their much-delayed picnic lunch.

*

When Amos's own posting to 319 Squadron at Wearsby had come through he treated it phlegmatically, as one always did. Being shunted around the country at a moment's notice was all part of being in the service. The usual disruptions to private life ensued: the digs to be found if no married quarters were available on-station, as they never were; relations with new colleagues to be cautiously negotiated and, with luck, new friends to be made – all these were familiar enough. But on this occasion Amos had felt it was a definite plus that his old boss was the station com-mander. Amos both respected Mewell and liked him. Once at Wearsby he soon discovered that, unlike the commanders of cer-tain other stations, Group Captain 'Muffin' Mewell was popular with the men he commanded. This was partly due to his war re-cord, partly because he was easy-going, and also because he still flew whenever he could get the opportunity, which these days was seldom enough. When administrative affairs became too much for him he was more often seen driving his Allard J2 along Wearsby's runway and perimeter at racetrack speeds, pipe clenched between his teeth. Occasionally he would do this with the station mascot, a Barbary ape from Gibraltar named Ponsonby, strapped in beside him. Ponsonby would wear his miniature blue uniform jacket with the single pilot officer's rings on the sleeves. The animal, who was considerably addicted to gin, would stare fixedly from behind his half-moon windshield as the little green car sped about the land-scape amid the gruff blare of its massive Cadillac engine.

47

Now the group captain took Amos's elbow as he was standing in the bar before going into the mess for dinner.

'Word in your ear, Pins,' said Muffin. The CO steered him away from the group he'd been with and set his beer mug down on a small table in a quiet corner. 'Won't take long. But time's short and we don't want too much formality.' He produced a tobacco pouch from his pocket and busied himself as he spoke. 'I've had a directive. Absolutely hush-hush, of course.' He looked up and Amos gave him a tacit nod. 'High Wycombe want me to form a special flight for what they describe as "under-the-radar missions" – although I don't know if we need take that literally. But apparently there's some unusual stuff they want done from time to time and I thought you might be the chap to help out. You and your crew have been classified Select Star, which as far as I'm concerned says it all. I'd ask you to nominate one other captain and crew and if I like your choice we'll hive you off as a special two-ship flight for whatever it is they need you to do. Thoughts?' Having lit his pipe Mewell stuck his nose into his beer mug but Amos noticed he kept his eyes turned towards him over the rim.

'Well, sir, I . . . Thank you, sir. I *think*.'

'Quite. Pig in a poke, eh? Exactly. And we all know the axiom that all service recruits learn on their first day.'

'Never volunteer.' Amos smiled. 'You put it craftily, sir. I don't know whether I'm volunteering or have already been chosen. Both, I suspect.'

'Your wariness does you credit. Apart from the nature of the pig itself, you're bothered the other crews will think you're considered a cut above them, teacher's pet sort of thing. *I* would be. I'd be worried about the jokes, let alone the hammering on the rugger pitch.'

'That did cross my mind, sir,' Amos admitted. A familiar weariness welled up. It sometimes seemed he had never left school. A

48

headmasterly hierarchy had persisted into his adulthood, and the fight against nuclear war was to be entrusted to hand-picked prefects wearing their house colours. At such moments he glimpsed within himself an urge to blot his copybook definitively, to be caught doing something far more shameful than merely smoking behind the fives courts. His most calming inner vision had always been of the school well alight, every window a rectangle of orange flame as an immense cloud of greasy black smoke rolled away across Sussex.

'Point is,' Mewell was saying, 'we'll do all we can to minimise that. You will be privileged in one obvious sense, which is that if my informants are right you'll be doing a lot fewer QRAs. Enough in itself to make the other crews envious. But to make up for that your life will become even less predictable. You won't be on a roster so you'll seldom know what to expect. You could be hauled out of bed at zero notice. Ditto your crews, of course. Pretty destructive of private life, it could be.'

'We all signed up, sir.'

'Good man. Do I take it that's a yes?'

'Can we all be sure of keeping up our currency, sir? I don't want to get suspended for a month because I haven't done enough night landings.'

'Oh God, chinagraph and perspex!' It was apparent the group captain had strong feelings on the subject. 'How those bloody wall boards rule our lives with their ghastly little boxes of blue ticks and red crosses! Never used to be like that. If you needed to fly, you got in and flew. These days everything has to be done in triplicate. Personally I blame Old Iron Pants LeMay and our SAC cousins over the ditch for all this manic time-and-motion, super-efficiency bollocks. Not that you ever heard me say that. I suppose preventing nuclear war *should* demand super-efficiency . . . Yes, of course it should. Quite right. Still . . .' Mewell once more stuck his nose in his mug, clearly nostalgic for the relaxed practices of his own earlier years in the RAF. 'We'll do our best to keep you all current. That's a promise. So, any thoughts yet about a second crew?'

'Terry Meeres is a good captain, sir.'

'So he is. But . . . wait a bit. Who's his AEO?'

'Ken Pilcher.'

'Thought so. H'm. Pilcher's our best scrum-half. Can't see how we can put Waddo in their place if he's at fifty thousand feet.' Wearsby's rivalry with Waddington was particularly keen on the rugby pitch. 'So it may be a toss-up between the trophy back on its shelf in our mess and *possibly* – only possibly, mind – helping to avoid World War Three. What I believe our Yankee friends would refer to as a tough call. They're a Select crew, aren't they, Meeres's lot? Can't ignore that, I suppose. All right. Consider the bullet bitten. That's that, then. Another pint before we go in?'

The drinkers in impeccable mess kit parted to let their commanding officer through to the bar where he inserted himself next to Wheezing Jesus, the padre. Whatever elation Amos might have felt was held in check by a wary foreboding. Never mind not volunteering: it was never entirely good news in the services to be selected for anything. It could well have unguessable repercussions for one's career. Which yet again led him to slightly dismal speculation about the direction his private life was taking.

4

With wifely insouciance Jo had appropriated Amos's car for one of her visits to her old friend Avril O'Shea. Avril wasn't on the phone and Jo realised she was taking a chance; but it was a beautiful late summer's day and the more miles she put between herself and Wearsby the more her spirits had lifted. Avril now led the way into the garden where her two children were playing in a sandpit. A battered Dansette transistor radio was making tinny noises on an upturned fruit crate. She turned it off. Looking at the cherry tree and the elm in one corner Jo said, 'It's a really nice house and garden. You are lucky, Rilly,' thinking of the lawn in front of the married quarters block at Wearsby, an unloved expanse of grass shaved to the bone whose main function seemed to be to display a prominent fire hydrant.

'Only rented, and I don't know how much longer we can afford to stay here. I told you how wonderful the squadron was after Marty crashed, didn't I? You know the normal treatment of anyone who no longer qualifies for quarters – instant order of the boot. They're all heart, those bastards. Can you believe the barrack warden actually paid me a call the day after the funeral? I realise they've got a waiting list, but even so. Then our friends rallied round and Wingco Admin stalled things in our favour. The Benevolent Fund paid most of the rent and then a really nice bloke helped me find this place and the Fund's still helping, God bless them. But who knows how long it will last? We're living on borrowed time here, and that's the truth of it.'

'I suppose you could still go home?'

'I couldn't face it, Jo. Mum and Dad and Katy. You remember how it is there. Dad at home all day, moaning. *And* Grantham. Too much like going backwards, you know? Besides, there wouldn't be room, not with these two,' she nodded towards the sandpit. 'Spalding's a good compromise. Not too far from my friends in the squadron and close enough to Grantham. Still, I won't pretend money isn't bloody tight.'

Jo knew that Avril's widow's pension would be exactly half what Marty would have got had he left the RAF, which itself wouldn't have been much for a man with only six or so years in. 'And if you ever do remarry, that little pension of yours stops at once.'

'You needn't remind me. Generous buggers, aren't they? As for remarrying . . . Well, I suppose if the Aga Khan or the Shah of Persia made me an offer I'd have at least to *consider*. Even Lord Docker would do. For the children's sake, of course.'

'Of course.' They both laughed. Jo glanced at the book on the grass beside her friend's chair. It was evident her surprise visit had interrupted Avril while reading something called (Jo squinted sideways) *Orang-utans Are not the Only Apes* by Dr Prudence Summertown. Avril followed her friend's inquisitive gaze.

'I wouldn't mind being her,' she said, indicating the book. 'Well, sort of. Do you know about her? She spent years in Borneo just living with orang-utans.'

'What, those great hairy monkeys?'

'They're apes, not monkeys.'

'I didn't know there was a difference. Is it like Gerald Durrell? *My Family and Other Animals* – I loved that.'

'That's exactly what I hoped it'd be like. After all, the Readers' Union adopted it as their book of the month. But really it's more sort of scientific than funny. This Dr Summertown's definitely a scientist. She goes into amazing detail about her apes' habits. Her own, too. It's, well it's actually a bit *shocking* in places.' Avril giggled a little. Both women watched the two children packing old condensed milk tins with sand.

'Go on,' Jo insisted.

'It turns out they're often,' Avril dropped her voice, 'you know, *lesbians*' (this word being mouthed rather than spoken, with much labial exaggeration).

'Heavens, Avril . . . You mean, women scientists?'

'No, silly, these orang-utans. Even when there were males around. In fact, one of the males tried it on with poor Prudence and she had to fight it off. But there's one place where she and her favourite female . . . But perhaps it's just my dirty mind.' Another nervous laugh. 'Obviously she doesn't spell it out. How could she? But she did live very close to the troop, I think it's called. Of course, she's a proper scientist from Cambridge so I suppose it's all part of the job to get intimate with the animals you're studying. Even so . . . *Yeeuchh!* – all that ginger fur. Not this girl's idea of a night out.'

Both friends fell silent as though musing on the quirkiness of other people's professions.

'What do you think she meant by her title?' Jo asked. 'It's not exactly catchy.'

'I suppose that maybe human beings are also apes? Dunno. She hasn't explained that yet.'

'It could be she meant her own behaviour was, well, a bit ape-like.'

'Mm. But she doesn't seem interested in morality. She just watches and notes down what she thinks she sees. Actually, she's not really very much like Gerald Durrell at all. To be honest, she often seems more interested in Prudence Summertown than in her apes. There's a lot of stuff about her childhood in Acton, much drearier than Gerald Durrell's on Corfu. Still, she's quite sympathetic about when she eventually flew home from Singapore. Apparently she spent a lot of the flight in the lav, drenching herself in the free cologne.'

'To get rid of the ape smell? I don't blame her.'

'No, I think it was more because after months and months of jungle living she suddenly found herself desperately longing for all the nice feminine things of civilisation.'

'I can guess what scent it was,' said Jo. 'Bet you anything it was Elizabeth Arden's "Blue Grass". It always is on those long flights. They say BOAC buys it by the gallon.'

'That's exactly what it was,' said her friend with an admiring glance. 'She says so. She has this sort of swooning fit in the lav because it suddenly smells so wonderful and it's all free.'

'I always imagined Elizabeth Arden as a fat Frenchman sitting in a darkened room surrounded by bottles and those strips of filter paper. There was an article in *Reader's Digest* the other month about the people who dream up new perfumes. Apparently they call the top ones "big noses" and they're not allowed to eat strongly flavoured food.'

'I'd have thought that would rule out the French. All that garlic.'

'And those awful cigarettes. They're a niffy lot. Don't forget Amos and I had our honeymoon in France. And as for their *lavatories*! I'm amazed they haven't all evolved very small noses out of national self-defence. But some of them do have huge conks.'

'And you know what they say . . .'

'Now, now, girl: keep it clean.'

'It's not easy,' admitted Avril with a little chirp of a sigh. 'Poor Marty's been gone, God, do you realise it's six *months* last week? And, well, biology makes one restless, doesn't it?'

Far off in a corner of the sky an invisible thunderous banner was being towed up into the heavens by a diminishing white triangle Jo found and followed with her eyes until it was out of sight.

'One of yours?' Avril asked, watching her.

'Could well be. Where are we?' she looked round at the sun. 'Heading south-east. Waddington and Scampton are too far north. Ditto Coningsby. I'd bet Wearsby. Might well be Amos himself. I can't remember what he said he'd be doing today. Not that I really believe it when he tells me things. He's far too security-conscious to give anything away. At least you didn't have that to contend with all the time, Rilly. Nothing very top secret about helicopters.'

The girl in the sandpit burst into loud wails. It appeared that her brother had just stamped on her sandcastle.

'*Boys*,' sighed their mother, getting up. 'They're just naturally de-structive, aren't they? Poor old Fuzzy,' she gathered up her howling daughter. 'That was mean, Petey,' she added aside. Admonished, the little boy glowered and smacked at the sand with his wooden spoon. Once peace had broken out again Avril returned and re-filled her friend's glass with lime squash. 'Little sod. I know Dr Spock says you must never hit a child, but by golly one's tempted at times. I think he's better with other boys, actually. They just seem to spend the time quite happily fighting and falling off things. I told you, didn't I, that from the moment he learned to walk Petey was trying to run up trees? I spent my time in the station clin-ic explaining that no, Marty and I hadn't given him the black eye and the thick lip, he'd done it all by himself. My brilliant son was convinced that the faster he ran at a tree, the higher up it'd get. Marty thinks he'd been watching the cat. *Thought*, I mean.' A laugh. 'Brains of peahens, boys, if you ask me, although I really shouldn't say that about Petey because he's already reading a bit, which isn't bad for his age. Still . . .' A silence, broken only by squeaks from the sandpit.

'I know what you mean about biology,' said Jo.

Her friend studied a midge caught in the surface tension of her drink. 'Things still iffy in that department, then?'

'Iffy *and* whenny. Ever since he got back from OCU and was made a captain Amos has been a perpetual absentee. Even on the rare occasions he's home, if you know what I mean. I told you it was OK at the beginning when we kept trying for a child, but after a while he sort of gave it up as a bad job. Or else he had so much flying to do and stuff to learn he just came home and slept like a log. A waterlogged log when he'd been in the mess with the crews. Especially with that young AEO of his, Gavin Rickards.'

Avril dabbed the midge from her lime juice with a fingertip. 'Rickards. Rickards. Is that the one you said looks like a schoolboy and drives an Austin-Healey Sprite his father gave him?'

'That's him. When you see him you think, God, that kid ought to be in class studying for his bloody A levels. Instead of which he's an air electronics officer aboard a Vulcan bomber, jointly responsible for delivering their basket of sunshine to the Russians. That's what they call it, you know. Amos is only a couple of years older but all the work and responsibility have aged him. He feels older than twenty-seven suddenly.'

'It's obviously official policy to get these crews really close-knit,' said Avril. 'Each relying on each, like the Three Musketeers. Dear old Marty was really fond of Amos, of course, but sometimes he could be a bit satirical about the mystique surrounding your V-bomber crews. He used to call them "finely meshed cogs in an intricate machine", something like that, in a funny voice. He was quoting some publicity he'd read. He'd give one of those great mocking laughs of his and say, "Not as frigging intricate as the machines I fly. Anyone could fly a Vulcan with a bloody great wing like that. Those things can practically land and take off by themselves. I'd like to see those wonder-boys hold a helicopter in a motionless hover six feet off the ground in a gale." Did I tell you he was about to go on a twin-rotors course? He wanted to upgrade to Belvederes. What he was really hoping for was a posting to the Far East. You know, the Confrontation. He had his heart set on a bit of jungle action in Borneo, did Marty – though not Dr Summertown's kind.' A wan smile. 'He told me we're using Belvederes out there to supply the forces on the ground – air drops and evacs in the most inaccessible places. When you think about it, he might just as easily have been killed doing a supply drop in the jungle as ferrying a stupid little Sycamore fifty miles to get some minor part replaced.'

'It's the way it goes.'

'I know, I know. But God, I do miss him.' She buried her face in her glass to hide the sudden tears. 'Two children and no father,' she said at length. 'You don't know what alone is until there's just you and two utterly dependent kids. Petey keeps asking when's Daddy coming home, but not so often now. Well, six months – it's a big fraction of his entire lifetime, isn't it? It already feels like the whole of *my* bloody lifetime. And to think that we put off having children for all those years just so he could get properly promoted and settled. What will we do? Everything's so . . . *shapeless* now.'

'I've been asking myself the same question recently. Between you and me, Rilly, I'm getting pretty fed up with Amos. He's always sort of heavy at home but whenever I see him with his crewmates he's light again, like the Amos I used to know when we first met. What the hell did we think we were doing, you and I, a couple of Grantham girls becoming service wives? I mean, it wasn't as if we didn't know about the accident rate, the sudden postings and absentee husbands, all that. Living in caravans. No say in anything. What I mean is, Rilly, what on earth got into us?'

'Love, probably. You forget practical things when you're under the influence. Or at least I did.'

'Mm.' Jo set her empty glass down. 'I'm . . . I'm . . .' She gave up. 'Yes?'

'I was going to say I'm not sure I ever had that excuse. Oh, I did love Amos, no doubt about that. But at the same time I wasn't blind to the drawbacks of being a service wife. We all just hoped for the best, didn't we? Love conquers all. I now think it may be a blessing we don't have children. Much as I should have loved them.'

'Amos was a terrific catch,' Avril said encouragingly. 'Film star good looks and a hell of a nice guy, too. And you got him. My Marty would never have won a beauty competition, would he? Not that I cared. Once he'd got me into Mavis – you remember that ratty old Humber Super Snipe of his? – I was gone. But I could always see it was more *complicated* with you two.'

'It bloody well was. I could only get to work on Amos once he'd had a few drinks to break the ice. Remember those evenings in the Serpent's Tooth? He was such a shy boy. Still is, though I suppose it's an odd thing to say of a Vulcan captain. You don't really associate dropping nuclear bombs with shyness, do you?'

'Marty once said something about him that I've never forgotten. He said, "Old Amos has a broad streak of chastity in him." I had to laugh.'

Voices were raised in the sandpit.

Avril glanced at the sun. 'It's nearly jam sandwich time,' she said. 'Will you kill me if I ask you something personal, Jo? I mean, you don't have to answer it. It's not really a question, more just wondering aloud. It was Dr Summertown and those apes of hers that got me thinking.'

'Oh?'

'You know – their odd behaviour. Surely you must have wondered yourself now and then? About Amos, I mean. You must admit that, looking back, he always did seem to have much better relations with his men friends than he did with us girls. Even down the dance hall with a few drinks inside him. Well, *especially* then, actually. Don't get me wrong, Jo, I'm not saying he's, well, you know. But maybe just a bit?'

'The one thing I can promise you Amos most certainly is not,' Jo said a little stiffly, 'is a Communist.'

'No, of course I didn't mean that.'

Jo's expression grew puzzled. 'But I always thought men like *that*, the ones you're saying, are mostly Communists as well. Look at all those spy scandals we've been having, the papers have been full of them. What's his name, Vassall? And the one that's just died – Guy Burgess? And don't you remember that bloke who used to work behind the bar in the Serpent – the la-di-da one? They put him away a couple of years ago – Mum sent me the cutting. They said he was corrupting national servicemen and getting information out of them for political purposes.'

'Yeah, *if* you can believe it,' snorted Avril. 'How much useful information are you going to get out of eighteen-year-old conscripts? The latest top-secret British way of peeling potatoes and white-washing coal? No, I remember him. He was the one they used to call Julie. They caught him doing things in the Gents behind the town hall, and that's against the law. Nothing to do with communism. I think he got eighteen months.'

The two sandy children chose this moment to prance up and tell their mother that they were hungry.

'I could do with a pot of tea myself,' said Avril. 'Let's go in and see what we can find. Then we'll have a hose-bath. All right?'

After tea the two children danced naked on the lawn with squeals of pleasure while Jo and Avril took turns to play the hose on them and remove their liberal covering of sand and jam. An image of them shining like little pink seals remained in Jo's mind on her return journey, suffusing her with a faint sense of envy. However much trouble children were, however boring and insistent, they undeniably filled a mother's life and fixed her days' boundaries for years to come. There was a lot to be said for that. Jo had one or two good friends at Wearsby – mostly other wives, it was true, and a couple of them also without children. But the flat tulip fields outside Spalding and the yawning dome of sky above Lincolnshire suddenly seemed appallingly empty. The prospect of returning to her quarters and the view of wartime brick buildings with the back of a hangar off to one side, its fading camouflage in oblique blotches that somehow became mournful in the evening light, hollowed her out with a sudden, almost irritable, sense of futility. It had all been a dreadful mistake. No, it hadn't been. A squadron leader's wife had some standing, after all. But if only the squadron leader himself would sometimes be *there*, the presence she still craved, the return she waited for as she read her magazines and sipped her Nescafé.

As she drove on, what Avril had been saying about him stubbornly refused to be silenced. Might it be true? She really knew nothing about things like that, nothing apart from her friends' occasional jocular references with lowered voice to something they'd read in 'The Screws', as they called *The News of the World*. A line from some long-ago school religious knowledge class suddenly popped up from nowhere and, like Mary, Jo kept all these things and pondered them in her heart.

5

The group captain's choosing him to lead a special flight for unknown operations was weighing more heavily on his mind than
Amos cared to admit. A couple of weeks had passed without any
further mention of the plan, but he knew that meant nothing.
Whatever was afoot would sooner or later materialise. Meanwhile
it gave him ample opportunity to worry about whether he would
be equal to the task, whatever it was. He only hoped it wouldn't in-
volve overflying Soviet Bloc territory on clandestine missions.

In the last few years Amos had thought increasingly about capture and interrogation: about loyalty, in short. In the closeness of
the cockpit, in the hugger-mugger of the bar, in the ops block
briefing room, everybody felt the same confident camaraderie. But
cut off and on his own on the wrong side of the Iron Curtain,
maybe injured and exhausted and certainly frightened, how would
he shape up? Name and number: that was the only information
you were authorised to give. The rest had to be silence, provided
you could hold out until a crucial date had passed, your captors
gave up or perhaps found a better source.

It wasn't really a matter of not betraying one's country, which
God knew was old enough to take care of itself. It was obvious
the country would already be lost if its fortunes could hang on
anything a wretched squadron leader might know. No, it was the
thought of betraying his mates, his crew, that obsessed him. While
he was training a few years earlier it had seemed to Amos that

he was always bumping into officers who had survived capture by North Koreans or Chinese during the Korean War. Some were British military men who had come to give talks but most were Americans, usually airmen whose F-86 Sabres had been downed on the wrong side of the Yalu river and had been lucky enough to reach the ground alive and return. One day, thought Amos, it might be acknowledged or even written about: the extent to which everybody in this Cold War – military and civilian alike – was haunted by the notion of borders, frontiers, blocs. A tiny gap in the Iron Curtain like Checkpoint Charlie in Berlin, with its multiple barriers and armed guards with wheeled mirrors for looking under cars, became a mythic node like the entry to Tartarus. On the other side lay a menacing world of the utterly foreign, of brutal snares and traps; of arrest and interrogation and being for ever cut off from help. Any friendly gesture was a bitter ruse. He had heard the story of a captured RAF pilot from Bermondsey who had been kept in solitary in a bare, whitewashed cell and who had resisted all interrogation. Then one day after being returned half-conscious to his freezing hutch he found in the middle of the floor a small pink rectangle of paper with a hole punched in it and a list in tiny print: Southwark Pk., The Crown, Abbey St., Ldn. Bridge. It was a bus ticket from home, and it broke him.

It scarcely mattered whether the story was genuine; Amos believed absolutely in its truth. He knew that he, too, could be broken by something so familiar, by a token from the warm, lost world on the far side of that fatal frontier. His training had never reduced him to that extent, but it had supplied a recurrent memory of fear and duress that came for a while and replayed itself over and over like a tune that can't be got rid of. He would break off and once more be lost in total blackness. The dark had been appalling. He had blundered slowly through the forest, his gloves held in front of him, exhausted and frozen. His hands were so cold they had no more feeling left in them than the buffers on the front of a steam locomotive. They banged bluntly into tree trunks or, each time he tripped and fell, skidded off rocks beneath the thin layer of snow. He would sprawl there for a while, winded, the snow numbing the flap of hairy scalp that a stub of fir branch had torn loose above his left ear when he walked into it, drenching his face and neck with blood. He knew he might just as easily have lost an eye.

His sole glimmers of light were phosphorescent: the face of his watch and the luminous green triangle that revolved on the tiny compass he wore on its lanyard around his neck. The crash of his own fall seemed to echo around the forest. His pursuers had surely heard it and would even now be stealthily closing in: men who not only knew the forest but who were past masters at wood-craft, able like wolves to move silently. Was he imagining things or had there been the brief flash of a torch somewhere off to the right of where he lay? Homa had a torch: his buddy Homa. Dare he risk calling out? It was sixteen hours now since they had be-come separated while trying to avoid that bloody farm dog. He thought Homa had got away with a chicken as planned, and they had arranged to meet up in the hanging wood that rose behind a dilapidated barn. But when eventually he was plunging breath-lessly uphill through the trees towards the rendezvous point, he heard no sign of Homa's parallel progress. Had he been caught? Amos had waited ten minutes, itching with nerves and impatience, before giving up and moving on. He now reckoned he still had a good six miles to cover to the frontier. Much as his body was pleading for rest he couldn't afford to lie there in the snow getting rapidly colder and weaker. He hadn't eaten for a day and a half, not since the scorched potatoes he and Homa had built a fire over before devouring them half raw, as apprehensive about the loss of time as about the thin smoke giving away their position.

So up on his feet again, the crust of blood and stubble a rigid plate clamped to the left side of his head. If he could get out of this damned forest by dawn he would be in a better position to cover the remaining distance before nightfall the next day. Then under cover of renewed darkness he would face the biggest obstacle of all: the frontier with its guards and trip wires that would send up magnesium flares. Maybe Homa was ahead of him? He surely couldn't be far away unless he'd been caught. They were both aiming for the same spot and it was hard to imagine he could have avoided this forest entirely. So Amos resumed his sleep-walker's progress, leaden arms thrust out in front to ward off the tree trunks, stopping frequently to steady the whirling luminous dots on the compass to check that his course was as near south-south-west as he could manage. For the first time the thought of capture was beginning to seem almost welcome. At least it would mean an end to this living famished in the wilds, hunted like an animal. The worst would have happened and from then on it was a matter of resisting interrogation. But the voice of an instructor came back to him, warning him of the danger of this kind of thinking. Once one began longing for it to be over, capture became ever more likely. So he went blunderingly on, aware that the ground was getting steeper and drawing hope from his memory of the map which showed that the forest stopped halfway up the flank of this particular minor mountain.

And what a brilliant example all this had been of the brain's ability to confuse different types of reality! Half of Amos was desperately trying to escape from East Germany with GDR border guards in hot pursuit; the other half knew he was taking part in a compulsory 'escape and evasion' exercise run by the USAF Survival School in southern Bavaria. Based at a barracks on the eastern outskirts of Bad Tölz, Flint Kaserne had the worst reputation of any of these courses. 'It doesn't get badder than Bad Tölz,' the saying went. The barracks was a huge fortress-like affair that had been built in the 1930s to provide Sandhurst-style training for the Waffen-SS. It had exclusive access to thousands of hectares of wooded hills that stretched to the Austrian border a dozen miles to the south. Nowadays it was home to the 10th Special Forces Airborne Group, who were not known for their easy-going approach to capture by Communists. The RAF hierarchy, eager to show their American allies they were no less serious and motivated, made an E&E course a necessary part of becoming V-bomber aircrew, and it was often at Bad Tölz. By the time Amos came to do it in the late fifties it had acquired enough notoriety to become a source of mild dread, requiring as it did a six-week fitness course in preparation.

Once at Flint Kaserne Amos began five days of classes starting at seven in the morning, many of them given by men who had done it for real in Korea. There were maybe a hundred others on the course with him, mostly Americans from all three services but with a fair sprinkling of fellow-Brits including several Royal Marines. He gathered that each year the course was slightly different, being modified in the light of previous experience. Thus it was hoped that the three deaths from hypothermia in last year's course might be avoided this year by magnanimously allowing 'escapees' to take the remnants of silk parachutes with them to wrap themselves in at night. They also had instruction from an East German border guard who had recently defected by swimming across a canal and who knew a good deal about the latest deployment of the GDR's Grenztruppen. Other instruction included lock-picking, given by an articulate American villain who had recently been released from a jail in Kansas City after completing his third sentence for house-breaking. This was a skill Amos had been happy to acquire and which later was to come in useful for dealing with the Yale lock on his own front door when he lost his key.

But the demonstration that made the most impression on him was that of interrogation. The trainees were seated in a darkened hall in front of which a huge sheet of perspex had been erected, sealing it off from the stage. They were ordered to watch in strict silence: not a cough, not a sneeze, not a movement. Onto the stage was led a man who had been taken 'prisoner' in a previous exercise. Ever since then, according to the instructor, he had been kept incommunicado in a bare concrete cell on a bread-and-water diet. Already exhausted from five days and nights spent living rough in the Bavarian countryside before being captured, he was evidently so bemused and demoralised that he believed in the absolute reality of the play that had been so carefully scripted around him. Handcuffed to a wooden chair in the glare of high-powered lamps, he was repeatedly questioned by his 'Russian' tormentors, who did indeed speak fluent Russian and only heavily accented English.

Not a man in the invisible audience but saw himself in the victim's position, most especially when the chief interrogator gave an order and a box with a dial and a crank was brought in and placed on the table in front of the prisoner, together with two crocodile-clip electrodes connected to the box by yellow insulated cables. Again the man was questioned, now with repeated face-slapping, and once more he would give only his name and number in a weak voice, tears glistening on his cheeks. He sounded like an American. The voltage generator was never used but sat there radiating menace. After forty-five minutes of shouting and brow-beating the prisoner was led off, presumably to be swiftly 'freed', congratulated and fed, while Amos and the rest of the course surreptitiously wiped the sweat from their palms on their trousers. Was that what awaited them if they were caught? Would they, too, lose touch with reality and become tearful in front of an invisible audience?

The next day, dressed in civilian clothes and issued with a small pack containing minimal survival gear such as a downed pilot might carry (compass, map, knife, matches, parachute silk), a group of 'escapers' including Amos and Homa was trucked to a snow-streaked clearing in the forest and given the co-ordinates of a position many miles away where a tent would represent safety on the far side of a ring of defences. They were given up to five days to reach it, after which some very irritated search parties would be sent out. From boxes at the back of the truck various animals were taken and one given to each pair: a rabbit, a chicken, a tiny piglet. Amos and Homa were handed a small mongrel dog trembling with bewilderment. The truck drove away.

'What the hell do we do with these?' Amos asked, as the others stood around awkwardly in the clearing with their unwelcome livestock.

'Whaddaya think?' said Homa. He produced his knife and, taking the dog's muzzle in one hand, deftly cut the artery in the animal's neck before it or anybody else knew what was happening, directing the crimson spurts of blood away from his clothes. 'This could be the only thing we get to eat in days.' The dog began gurgling and jerking and Homa released its muzzle, letting it hang head downwards while its life ebbed swiftly with a few last whimpers into the Bavarian mud.

'That's just not on, you know,' said a tall Royal Navy lieutenant, very white in the face. He was holding a rabbit.

'You want to eat acorns for the next few days, be my fucking guest. This course is about survival, buster, and I intend to survive. I'm a country boy and this here's a skill no Special Forces asshole needs to teach me.'

Homa squatted and adroitly paunched the animal, tipping its guts out into the snow in a steaming heap. Having severed its paws, he began working his hand carefully around between the fur and the underlying membrane, skinning it as one would a hare. He pulled the pelt inside out down both hind legs, its pale blue under-side innocent in the wan sunlight. In a matter of minutes he had dumped the fur and kicked snow over it and the entrails and had jointed the carcase, giving half to Amos to put in his pack. The head Homa kept for himself with its bulging eyes, ear cavities and grinning teeth. 'The brain's pure protein,' he said. 'Stick it in a tin mug over a fire and you've got yourself some real energy. Come on, Amos: we're heading out. See you lot later. Good luck.' And with that he and Amos set off into the woods. Looking back, Amos saw that one or two of the others had begun making clumsy attempts to dispatch their animals but the navy man had evidently decided to release his rabbit, last seen scuttling rapidly towards the nearest undergrowth.

And now it was three or maybe four days later. Homa had van-ished and Amos was on his own at 06:00 in the frozen forest. He was ravenously hungry and decided he would light a fire at first light, come what may, if only to bring some warmth back into his hands. He still had two half-burned potatoes in his pack. The joints of dog had long gone, the small bones smashed with stones for the smears of marrow they contained. On the first day he and Homa had found an abandoned orchard and had picked up a few fallen apples among the autumn leaves beneath the snow that were still not quite rotted. 'Cider apples,' Homa had said knowledge-ably. 'Not great but better than nothing.' The one Amos ate had given him diarrhoea, merely adding to his misery. Snow and half-frozen leaves were not much of a substitute even for the RAF's awful glazed lavatory paper.

Yet dogged perseverance paid off, and eventual daylight brought easier going to the point where he reached his goal at about three in the afternoon. Hidden in the undergrowth, Amos surveyed the bare hillock on top of which was pitched a white tent. Armed men dressed as Russian soldiers in fur hats patrolled the surrounding ground at irregular intervals. Amos could see no sign of either Homa or any of the others in his group. Maybe they had long since won through to the tent or else had been captured. Either way they would even now be back at Flint Kaserne having had hot showers and a square meal, their ordeal safely behind them.

In any case there was nothing for it but to lie up in the woods and wait for darkness. At nightfall it began snowing again and Amos was so stiff with cold he wondered it he would be able to stand, much less make a dash while avoiding guards and trip wires. From his prone position at the edge of the wood he could see the tent, now illuminated from within and not more than a hundred yards away. Suddenly there was a dull bang and the entire area was lit with the scorching white glare of a magnesium flare. It revealed a dark figure who had evidently forgotten the instruction to freeze and keep his head bowed. At a pinch he might have passed for an old tree trunk had it not been for the wild white face he was turning in every direction in order to spot the nearest guard. Seeing none, he broke into a dash for the tent whereupon two burly figures in fur hats rose from the ground and intercepted him just as the flare fell to earth and went out. In the sudden dark he gave a rabbit's scream.

As though his body was out-thinking his mind, Amos felt himself get to his feet and break into a swift trot, striking an oblique angle upwards in the rough direction of the tent so as to elude the guards. By some miracle he managed to avoid setting off another flare and in the confusion of the captured man's loud protests he gained the back of the tent and went in. A lean and crew-cut Special Forces top sergeant shook him by the hand and said 'Congratulations, soldier.' He was given hot coffee and a jelly sandwich, after which he was escorted down the far side of the hill to a waiting Jeep and it was over.

It turned out that he was by no means the last of his group. It also emerged that the man whose capture had provided cover for Amos's 'escape' was the Royal Naval lieutenant who had liberated his rabbit rather than kill it. Apparently he and his buddy had snacked on raw turnips. He was surprisingly cheerful despite having been caught at the last moment, and proud of having survived without bloodshed. As they collected their certificates as having 'successfully completed the course of training given at Bad Tölz, Germany', the lieutenant said, 'Harry icers: that's how I'll remember this whole caper. That and not becoming a carnivore, unlike certain crabs I can think of.'

'I was taught to eat what was put before me, and be thankful,' retorted Amos. 'I suppose a diet of root crops does explain why you fish heads so often lack the energy to leave port.'

Inter-service rivalry having been satisfied, they parted on good terms. But before Amos caught the train for the long haul to the Hook of Holland he made a discovery that told him he'd always been far more on his own than he'd believed. Back in the stone corridors of Flint Kaserne, with half his hair shaved off and a row of black stitches beneath a band of white surgical plaster, he'd bumped into Homa, now wearing Special Forces uniform.

After a moment's surprise Amos shook his head sadly and said with sudden enlightenment: 'You were never my buddy, were you?'

'Correct. Sorry about that. My job was to show you guys it was for real, how to kill your own food, how to survive, and then fade.'

'Well, fuck you,' said Amos.

'Yeah,' said Homa, nodding. 'No hard feelings.'

'Oh, terrific. I froze my balls off waiting for you in that wood behind the barn and then did the whole thing on my tod and I'm supposed to be *grateful*?'

'It's a thought. All you'll get from me is that I was under orders, OK? Somebody must have wanted you to complete the course alone, which you did, and made a pretty good fist of it for a jet-jockey. One day you might have to hit the silk over enemy territory and you'll be on your own, right? No buddies in Ivanland. You shaped up pretty good.'

On the way home Amos thought this was probably as close to praise as he was ever going to get for his stint at Bad Tölz. Still, he'd got his certificate and could now add it to that from the ditching course, which had involved parachuting into the sea off Weymouth in full flying kit in January. He was well on his way to combat status. Good. But it did throw up that question of loyalty: how far to trust a buddy and how much to go it alone. It would have to remain unsettled.

6

The special flight that Group Captain Mewell had been instructed to form was now officially in existence, as evidenced by the squadron notice boards. On these it appeared as 'P' Flight, whimsically named after Ponsonby, the station's mascot. As arranged, it consisted of two crews: Amos McKenna's and Terry Meeres's, with hints that a further two might be assigned 'in case of future need'. If anybody knew what even the present need was they weren't telling. This was in the time-honoured RAF tradition of keeping people in the dark until the last possible moment. Consequently there was a good deal of nervous speculation among the crews as to what their job might entail. Some discussion took place quietly over lunch at a corner table in the mess.

'If it hadn't been for that test ban treaty last year I'd have said we were going to sniff-and-bottle somewhere,' said Stephen Sanders, Meeres's nav plotter. 'One of those Chinese tests, for instance. They'd have sent us out to Midway or Singapore and the Met people would give us the winds at various altitudes and we'd have to plot courses to intercept the fallout.'

'It's still not impossible,' Amos said. 'It's only a ban on atmospheric tests and the underground ones sometimes leak, apparently.'

'I did a sniff-and-bottle once in a PR.9 Canberra,' said Meeres's co-pilot, Ludo Franek, reminiscently. 'They tacked on a couple of underwing pods and sent us up from Spitsbergen, way out over the Barents Sea and Franz Josef Land. The Russkies had just exploded some gigantic bomb in Novaya Zemlya and the boffins wanted samples of the fallout to analyse the isotopes or whatever it is.'

'You must have been worried about being meaconned and lured into Soviet airspace,' said Ken Pilcher.

'Straying? Christ, we were well inside. We'd been told to go as high as possible and with luck, if a Guideline found us, we'd crash into the sea and vanish. I told Group Captain Ops this was a new definition of the word "luck". "Don't you worry, old boy," he said. "There aren't any missile sites within a hundred nautical miles of where you'll be, and their fighters will be out of fuel before they can get within twenty thousand feet of you."'

'So you went high.'

'Never been higher. Up to sixty-two thousand. Talk about paralysed. You know Canberras: you either bake or freeze. We froze. We were so cold after nearly five hours in the air they practically had to use steam hoses to get us out of the aircraft when we got back. And that was another thing. They made us taxi to a quarantine area on the far side of the field where we were met by a bunch of moonmen in radiation suits. Masks, breathing apparatus, gauntlets, lead-lined jock straps, Geiger counters – the whole caboodle. They unhitched our pods and put them into specially lined boxes and drove them away on a trailer. Then some others ran Geiger counters over the aircraft and decided it should be decontaminated. And there *we* were, my navigator and I, having flown through the fallout and sampled it and carried it all the way back, still in our ordinary flying suits, frozen like ice lollies, and nobody paying us the slightest attention. We had to hitch a lift back to get a hot shower and a bowl of soup. No-one ever tested *us* for radiation. Never even saw the MO for a check-up. After a week of hanging around we were rotated back to Scotland. That was a few years ago, though. Today we might at least be given iodine pills.'

'I thought I'd noticed a strange glow from you in the cockpit at night,' said Terry Meeres. 'I put it down to your halo.' His co-pilot was a devout Catholic who never flew without his rosary.

'Oh, do look, Mark,' a voice broke in from over their shoulders. 'The Dam Busters are having a top-secret lunch.' Two airmen paused on their way past the table.

'I say, wizard prang, Fishy. Can I have your egg if you don't come back?'

'Bugger off, you two,' said Ken Pilcher wearily, 'or we'll be wondering whose Vulcan we noticed sitting on its tail this morning out there on the pan. Oh whoops. Tow it away and knock out the dents.'

The jibe evidently struck home since the other's tone became defensive. 'Sod off, Pilcher – that was hardly our fault. The auto refuelling system was on the blink and the rear tanks filled first.'

'Maybe your crew chief should have been in the cockpit selecting the tanks manually rather than trusting to the wonders of automation. But that's probably a little advanced for you lot. Still, we were all impressed that you've trained a Vulcan to sit up and beg. It can't be easy and I'm sure it's expensive.'

'I don't think we want to have lunch with these snooty people, Mark,' said the first speaker. 'They've grown a bit too grand for their former mates.'

'Oh, it's only your table manners,' Pilcher called after them reassuringly. 'We still love your honest, boyish selves.'

Just as Amos had feared, the superficially good-natured badinage revealed that the other crews weren't taking too kindly to 'P' Flight's special status, but he couldn't think of anything to do about it for the moment.

'Sniffing missions had crossed my mind, too,' he resumed quietly. 'I gather BOAC have installed discreet sniffers on some of their airliners but that can't be as good as getting close to the test site.'

His nav plotter said, 'Maybe they're working on some spiffy new navigation system and we'll all be going to Gan for extensive testing between there and South Africa. Get our knees brown. Sun, sand, surf and dollies in grass skirts offering us their lovely firm coconuts.'

'Baa Mutton, goodwill ambassador and NSU vector to the Indian Ocean.'

'Widely known for his unbreakable penicillin habit.'

But that same afternoon the two crews read a notice summoning them for a briefing next morning. This took place in a room in the ops block whose door was guarded by two armed policemen. Inside, the floor gleamed with Ronuk polish, orange traces of wax visible here and there between the boards. The ten crewmen sitting at tables stood up when Group Captain Mewell came in, the overhead lighting glinting on the glassine fronts of the photo ID badges they all wore on their left breast pockets.

'Be seated, gentlemen,' said their CO as the door closed behind him. 'You'll be glad to know they've at last seen fit to tell me what missions you're to prepare for. You will be given detailed briefings later but to prevent speculation and to ease your minds I thought I'd better outline the general scheme so far as I understand it. There are two main tasks at present, one involving a new electronic countermeasure and the other a new weapons system. I'll take the ECM first.

'I've had this explained to me by a bloke from the Royal Radar Establishment in Malvern. Apparently it's his idea and he seemed pretty proud of it. Frankly, I couldn't make head or tail of the technical stuff – it's way over my old-fashioned head. That's the province of you two AEOs,' he nodded at Rickards and Pilcher.

'You're the experts and you'll be properly briefed by a boffin later. What I'm clear about is that it's an ingenious method for fooling the Russians' radar. We all know our present system is powerful and offers good defence at various wavelengths, but it's still basically just jamming and chaff.

'Anyway, this new system is code-named Oilcan and it's absolutely top secret. Note that, please. It's going to put us back on the offensive rather than having to rely passively on our Red Shrimp and Blue Diver noise jammers as at present – useful as those are. Squadron Leader McKenna will vouch for what a good job they did when we flew together in that Skyshield exercise two or three years ago. What Oilcan does, apparently, is not jam the Soviets' radar so much as fool it. It replaces your echo on their screen with one that's so powerful it overloads their system, and to protect itself from burnout it has to reduce its sensitivity drastically. This makes your image appear to be retreating and their radar follows what in effect is a phantom target, still locked on to your jamming. At that moment Oilcan switches off your jammers and *poof!* you disappear from their screens. It involves something called "range gates", I believe; but as I say, I don't really understand it. However, if it works it does sound rather brilliant.'

From an office along the corridor outside there came the perky trumpet lead-in to *Music While You Work* on somebody's radio, instantly stifled behind a closing door. The homely aural intrusion provoked some smiles in the room.

'Right, that's Oilcan. Just remember, it has been decided at the highest level that it must remain a national secret for the present. Not even our American cousins will be told. I have been assured that the team at Malvern who developed it did so out of sight of the American personnel seconded there. And that also goes for their National Security Agency people stationed over at GCHQ in Chel-

76

tenham. So far as we know they too are none the wiser.

'There must be a reason for this, but I don't know what it is and neither do you need to know. No doubt there are political wheels within wheels but all that affects us are our orders. And those, gentlemen, are not to breathe a single, solitary word to anybody, and above all not to any American colleague you may meet either here or on deployment in the US, on pain of a guaranteed court-martial. Is that absolutely clear?'

The room was filled with murmurs of nervous assent as the men stirred uneasily. As security-conscious as they already were, this additional level of secrecy sounded draconian.

'There is priority in getting Oilcan installed in both your aircraft as soon as humanly possible.' He unbuttoned the flap of his breast pocket and found a slip of paper. 'You'll be going out to practise using it when we've found a spot where neither the Russians nor the Americans will overhear, which is none too easy. I'm not just thinking of Fylingdales but of all those wretched Russian "trawlers" stooging about chock-full of SIGINT equipment. Right: any questions so far?'

Ken Pilcher raised a hand. 'I've got one, sir. Why use Vulcans to test this Oilcan thing? What's wrong with Canberras? Or even Shackletons? Mightn't they attract less attention?'

'Probably. But it's V-bombers that are our deterrent force and not Shackletons. We need to use the aircraft we normally fly. From most angles it's the Vulcan that produces the biggest radar return. As we all know, a whacking great delta can send back a whacking great echo.'[†]

Another door opened down the corridor outside and Dusty Springfield swept out, just not knowing what to do with herself,

---

† See Appendix 2, p. 293.

before the closing door cut her off. Amos thought there was something absurd about these abrupt, weird juxtapositions of two worlds: the Top Twenty accompanying things so secret they could hardly be thought about.

'Now,' Mewell was saying, 'the second thing you'll be testing is equally new and experimental. Despite all the bomb comps and target practice we do, everyone knows that pinpoint accuracy isn't absolutely vital when it's a nuclear warhead you're delivering. A couple of hundred yards more or less isn't going to make much difference. However, we *are* Bomber Command and we may still be called on at any time to drop conventional iron bombs on uppity fuzzy-wuzzies threatening Her Majesty's territories overseas. Things are looking pretty dicey in the Yemen at the moment, not to mention points east. In which case accuracy matters very much indeed. We've all recently heard grim stories from Vietnam of the Yanks bombing their own troops by mistake. God knows blue-on-blue is easily done in war: I'm afraid we've done it ourselves. So obviously some method of precision-guiding munitions to their target would be a great advance.

'Up to now we've been concentrating on making ever more accurate bomb sights. But at the same time we, the Americans and the Russians have been experimenting with sticking a TV camera into the nose of the bomb, which as it falls relays a picture to the bomb aimer or nav plotter so he can guide it onto the target with his little joystick. However, the latest idea is to do away with the camera and use something called a laser instead. I gather this is a beam of highly concentrated light even thinner than a pencil. Again, I certainly don't understand the ins and outs of the physics involved, but there'll be a boffin coming down to talk to you nav plotters, too. Questions?'

From somewhere far away in the distance there filtered the familiar sound of four Olympus engines spooling up to full take-off power with the unmistakable honking wail their intakes made as they gulped tons of air every second. Swiftly this neared, melding into the darker noise of the jets themselves which in turn bounced low-frequency sound around the room before the speeding Vulcan passed diagonally away from the ops block along the main runway, its actual lift-off being screened by two hangars. The rumble died.

When he could make himself heard, Amos said: 'Obviously these two systems are going to mean some new equipment installed in our aircraft so presumably they'll be u/s for some time. Do we get any flying in the meantime?'

Mewell smiled. 'Point taken. Yes, I'm afraid your two aircraft will have to go back to Woodford. You will have heard there's a new paint scheme being phased in for all V-bombers to take account of our shift in tactics from high to low level. So your two aircraft will be the first to be repainted and this new equipment will be installed at the same time. They say a fortnight, ten days if we're lucky. Apparently the Oilcan set-up requires a lot of extra power so they need to stuff more cooling gear into the back. As for flying, you've noticed we're hosting Canberras here on rotation from Germany. We'll see if we can't arrange you some hours on those. Failing that, there's always an assortment of passing traffic at Wearsby and I'm sure you'll be able to wangle yourselves a bit of air time in some of it – as you always do in any case.' This provoked some not very abashed smiles from the four pilots in the room. 'Personally, I'd dearly like to import some Tiger Moths from wherever they're still flying them – I don't know, a university squadron perhaps? A few hours of real stick-and-rudder stuff does wonders for airmanship after all those hours tooling along on autopilot in a pressurised metal bullet like the Vulcan. Open-cockpit stuff – that's proper flying,' Mewell added with a touch of wistfulness. 'Happy memories, gentlemen, happy memories.'

Typical Muffin – Amos thought afterwards – managing to inject a little nostalgia into Cold War technology. Still, anyone with his war record was entitled to it. This was a recognition that, on the whole, the officers at Wearsby wouldn't have swapped their station commander for any other brass hat in Bomber Command.

7

Chief Technician Ernest 'Baldy' Hodge sat on the bus and watched the hedgerows pass in an unfocused blur. He was thinking grumpily that one day soon he would no longer be dependent on this uncomfortable and laborious mode of public transport, constantly stopping in the middle of nowhere to pick up elderly shoppers. This was one of his periodic trips to Grantham, a journey that involved changing buses in Market Tewsbury as well as a good deal of patience. He would usually make the trip on his day off; but since his personal Vulcan, XM580, was away being re-equipped and repainted he had some otherwise scarce time on his hands. He was not the sort of man to be reassigned to temporary duties elsewhere. Nothing you could put your finger on, exactly; just something about him that prevented even the engineer wing commander in charge of the maintenance unit from taking advantage of the fact that for a couple of weeks one of his chief technicians was severely underemployed.

A disgruntled, self-righteous man this Hodge, with his translucent red ears: a combative person, much given to sour rejoinders in sergeants' mess and dispersal hut where, even among his peers and despite his gleaming scalp, he was considered the chief 'hairy'. It was widely accepted that you didn't tangle with Hodge. He had countersigned his cynical persona by having a blue sword tattooed inside one meaty forearm with the legend 'Dishonour Before Death' around the sword's tip in Gothic script. Nobody had ever thought for a moment that this inversion of the traditional military motto had been a mistake on the part of the tattooist. Baldy was famous at Wearsby for having thrown an orderly officer into the frozen fishpond outside the sergeants' mess one night for daring to try closing the bar at 23:00 as per standing orders. He was carpeted and fined, which only increased his perennial resentment over money, his pay being the same as that of a junior engineer officer ten years younger: some £1,218 per annum which, as a married man of thirty-four, Baldy Hodge considered wholly inadequate for an experienced aircraft servicing chief responsible for the proper functioning of one of Britain's V-bombers. Money matters were seldom far from his calculations and conversation and, what with one thing and another, had he not been so competent and reliable in his work he would have been altogether intolerable. However, where his work was concerned C/T Hodge did things by the book; and although no-one – probably not even his wife – could honestly say they actively enjoyed his company, Amos and the rest of XM580's crew were glad to have him aboard in a sixth seat on certain trips to foreign airfields where the ground crew's standards might not be up to Baldy's. If anyone could keep their aircraft going, he could.

At last they drew into Grantham bus station. Hodge hung his burly frame menacingly over two stout women with headscarves and creaking wicker baskets easing themselves arthritically down the bus's steps. They both paused to call a thank-you to the driver.

'Take your time, missus, I would,' said Hodge witheringly as, released at last, he set off briskly up the High Street to Swinegate. It was a sunny day and he found his mood pleasantly expectant as he came in sight of the familiar corner shop. P. & S. Finstock was a typical tobacconist and newsagent: utterly unremarkable, in fact, with its worn lino and the smell of newsprint and paraffin.

There was a large tabby cat asleep in the flyblown window beneath a copious display of handwritten cards advertising accommodation, lessons in book-keeping, secondhand cots, a breeding pair of pigeons. A decrepit old man with burst slippers and a walking stick clutching a packet of Woodbines was inching his way out as Hodge entered.

Inside, the shop was empty and silent save for a bluebottle that was probably destined to join the corpses on one or other of the yellowed scrolls of flypaper Sellotaped to the ceiling. The shelves behind the counter were lined with big, screw-topped sweet jars and stacked packets of cigarettes. Bottles of fizzy drinks stood on the floor in one corner. The counter was piled with neatly segregated newspapers. From somewhere in the interior came the whistle of a kettle and before long a man in a sagging cardigan appeared with a mug of tea in one hand and a half-smoked cigarette in the other. On seeing Baldy Hodge he set the mug down and parked the cigarette on the scorch-marked edge of the counter.

'Morning, Mr Parsons,' he said. 'And not a bad one, either. Hope I didn't keep you waiting? She's out shopping so I have to make my own tea. Your post's here. Arrived Thursday, it did. No, tell a lie, it was last Tuesday. Postman had to wait because the coalman was delivering and the cover was off the coal hole outside the door there. Half a ton of nutty slack, and more bloody slack than nuts, I can tell you. Had to stand over the bugger to make sure of a couple of hundredweight of lumps at least. And the price these days! Well, I told him, if that's how you treat your customers I can always go back to Charringtons, can't I? Thought I was doing you a favour, switching. You take your horse and cart and hop it back to the Co-op and tell them to pull their socks up. Who wants a great heap of coal dust in their cellar?' He reached beneath the counter, squinting, before producing a large brown envelope bearing a row of the familiar blue French stamps. 'All the way from gay Paree,' he said, winking odiously. 'Will there be anything else, then? Your usual mint humbugs?'

'No, I'll have a quarter of sherbet lemons today,' said Baldy. 'I feel like a change,' he added with an effort at chattiness to match the shopkeeper's while inwardly fuming with impatience.

'Right you are, then.' The man took down a jar and shook a rattling heap of yellow sweets into the brass scoop of a small pair of scales, then poured them neatly into a paper bag which he twirled expertly by the corners. 'That's two bob for the post and threepence for the sherbets. Half a crown? Ta.' He rang up the till and handed Baldy his threepenny bit change. 'Thanks very much, Mr Parsons. We'll meet again, as Vera Lynn used to say.'

'Yeah,' said Baldy, stepping out into the sunshine of Swinegate with the envelope securely tucked under his arm. He made his way back towards the High Street before ducking into the saloon bar of a pub that hadn't yet begun to fill up with lunchtime customers. Reassured to find he had the gloomy room to himself, he carried his Double Diamond to a distant corner table. He took a large gulp of the beer before setting the mug down and opening the envelope. He noted it was addressed to plain John Parsons. Had the name appeared with an initial he would have known he needed to arrange a new accommodation address. He wondered what the envelope contained this time. It was usually some general interest magazine all in French. Once it had been knitting patterns and the last time it had been about horses, so far as he could judge from the pictures. Baldy Hodge was not a linguist. On the contrary, he prided himself on not knowing a word of Froggish, as he called it. He had no time for all that *parley-voo* and *owf veedersayn* stuff. It didn't seem to have done them much good in two world wars.

He drew out the magazine and immediately pushed it guiltily

down beneath the table's edge. The bastards! This time they'd sent him something typically French, all right, and it required no translation. He shot a glance at the room. There was nobody about. The barman was round the corner, dealing with customers in the public bar from which came voices and an eddy of smoke. He looked down again at his lap. Nudes on every page. And – good God! – not just women, either. This wasn't *Health & Efficiency* by a long chalk: there were people actually, well, *doing* it. You could see everything. Baldy felt himself blush. He was, of course, a man of the world, as he often informed his subordinates at Wearsby; but really, there were limits. The dirty-minded so-and-sos! Still . . . With another furtive glance around he turned to the centre spread. At least the important thing was there. Under cover of the table he drew out a sheaf of dark blue five-pound notes – the new ones, he noted, with the Queen's portrait. To think of sandwiching Her Majesty between pictures of that kind of filth! But what else could you expect from foreigners? He licked his fingers and surreptitiously counted the notes. Twenty, all right. That cheered things up. Another step towards the car of his dreams. He was buggered if he was going to settle for some dull runabout. He'd put that little toy Austin-Healey of young Rickards to shame. He couldn't wait to see people's faces at Wearsby when he burbled up in one of the new 4.2 E-Types. They'd be out in October for £2,100. Leather upholstery and that long, gleaming bonnet. One of those babies would release anybody's inner James Bond and no mistake.

With another glance at the room Hodge swiftly tucked the money into his inside pocket, shoved the magazine back into its envelope and downed the rest of his beer. Just like the adverts claimed, he thought as he returned the empty mug to the counter: a Double Diamond works wonders. He went out into the sunshine with something of a spring in his step. He called in at the Post Office where he deposited eighty pounds in his account. He tucked the remaining fivers into his savings book and strolled back towards the bus station. He never noticed the young man with the blue windcheater and crisp haircut who kept pace with him, but always at a careful distance.

8

One morning a note from the barrack warden informed Amos and Jo they were being moved from the flat into a house of their own. This turned out to be a brick semi-detached with three bedrooms in a close whose rear overlooked the sports field and the station's chapel. The previous occupants were an American family who had just been posted back to the States. The surprise news was disquieting to them both, and for reasons neither was yet quite willing to disclose to the other.

'Oh Amos, at last a house of our own!' Jo said, satirically clasping her hands at her throat like a Hollywood housewife overjoyed with her new cooker. 'And we'll be right next to Ronald and Kay.'

'And their children. And their dog.'

'It will do wonders for my social life but I don't suppose it'll have any effect on yours.'

Ignoring her sarcasm, Amos said, 'I want to know what it means.'

'It seems to mean that at last we get a proper family home of our own.'

'Huh. That's the theory, my dear. In *practice* this is the RAF. Nothing ever comes without strings. There are politics at work here, Jo. Think about it. Married quarters are like hen's teeth. Yet they're suddenly moving a childless couple into a house with three bedrooms. Why? Who authorised that? It makes no sense and it'll undoubtedly get a lot of needier people pissed off because we've jumped the queue.'

'Does that mean we now have to have children whether we like it or not?'

The house was a fifties brick semi in a small estate comprising a cluster of roads named for pioneers of British flight. Tucked behind Cody Road and Rolls Drive, Brabazon Close was the one that gave its residents the most convincing impression that they were not living on an active Bomber Command station so much as on the leafy fringes of civilian suburbia. The rugger posts visible from the back windows might have been those of a school playing field; the trees beyond might have screened off a golf course instead of the grassy mounds of buried fuel tanks with their jutting black ventilation cowls; and between the intermittent roaring of aero engines the twittering of birds could be heard even with the windows closed.

The move was accomplished in a single morning while Amos was on duty. Between them they didn't have much in the way of possessions, and the house was already furnished as though by a boarding-house landlady who didn't trust her tenants not to put their feet on the chairs. The plywood kitchen cupboards were lined with sheets of wrinkled green Fablon marked with the rings of other people's pots and pans. In a battered tin ashtray on the Formica-topped kitchen table was a small gummy bladder that had once contained lighter fuel. There was also a used pipe-cleaner and an American book of matches with the slogan RE-UP NOW! inside the cover. Amos recognised this as urging US troops to re-enlist for the rapid build-up currently under way in Vietnam. The institution-green carpet in the lounge flaunted odd stains and the dents of furniture that had been moved.

Two of the three bedrooms upstairs contained a single bed. In one room there were children's handprints on the pink distempered walls. In the bathroom the medicine cabinet above the washbasin was empty but for a strong smell of nail varnish remover and a crumpled yellow tube of Kolynos toothpaste. Hot water was supplied by a gas water heater on the wall over the bath which, once Amos had lit its pilot jet and opened a tap, ignited with an explosive thump that rattled the window panes and very slowly heated the water with industrial clamour before dying abruptly with a click. In the cupboard under the stairs he found the meter that required a rich diet of shillings. He decided that until the RAF was your landlady you had no idea of the real meaning of the word 'skinflint'.

Jo was gazing in horror at the double bed in what the architect had possibly thought of as the 'master bedroom'. The stained mattress was slightly awry and visible on the inside of the wooden base was a black Ministry of Supply broad arrow. The varnished deal headboard showed twin darker patches where numberless sebaceous scalps had rubbed.

'This is plain sordid, Amos,' she said decisively. 'I'm not sleeping on that. We might as well be in a prison.'

'Oh, it's just institution furniture,' he said.

'No doubt you got used to this sort of thing in that private school of yours, not minding that generations of disgusting adolescents had left their mark on what you slept on. It won't do for me. You can go and get that divan base from the flat. I know it's RAF property but we had it new and the springs are good and however grubby it may be at least it's our own grub.'

Her rebellion was perfectly reasonable, Amos thought as he stared out of the bedroom window. The bed was indeed a disgrace: an object more suited to commercial travellers' lodgings or to a cheap hotel on the Continent. He was suddenly assailed by an image of himself and Jo as a couple on the *Titanic* complaining about the furniture in their cabin, and couldn't help a tight little smile. Outside, flocks of starlings mustered in the late-afternoon light. On the playing field two boys were doggedly trying to get their control-line model aircraft to start, flicking its propeller over and over as darkness raced towards them over the planet's edge. He was suddenly swept with a brief but terrifying conviction that nothing would last.

'There's one thing,' Jo was saying, her tone faintly savage. 'You could hardly be closer for your rugger, could you?'

Maybe it would be an asset for her to have Kay Hendry next door. Kay's wing commander husband Ronald spent a good deal of his time in Germany, being temporarily involved with some arcane aspect of the nuclear weapons stored there for the RAF's Canberra light bombers, while Kay taught in the local village primary school where their two children also went. That meant she was around most afternoons and evenings and might make a pretty good companion for Jo. Girls liked all that hobnobbing over tea and biscuits. But really it was high time Jo got herself a job, Amos thought. Half her trouble is that she doesn't *do* anything. Why couldn't she become, I don't know, a librarian in Market Tewsbury? She's no fool and obviously likes reading. It would surely be a lot more fulfilling than mooning about all day drinking endless cups of instant coffee and reading those brainless magazines of hers.

A mere three days later, to his astonishment and relief, Jo announced she had become a vet's assistant in Mossop. The practice was the only one this side of Grantham and was big, dealing mainly with farm animals and only secondarily with pets. The two vets who ran it needed a new receptionist and on Kay Hendry's recommendation Jo had applied for the post and immediately got it. That evening Amos returned to find an enormous buck rabbit loping around the kitchen in between nibbling at a carrot in one corner.

'Isn't he gorgeous, Amos? Just feel his ears: they're lovely and silky and floppy. He was born in captivity but then just abandoned by some people who thought he could fend for himself in the wild. But he couldn't and was starving to death when someone brought him in. That was a fortnight ago and just look at him now.'

Amos did, and was not reassured.

'Is he house-trained?'

'Perfectly. Look over there.'

In the corner beside the fridge was a naked tray of earth on a sheet of newspaper. It was surrounded by a scattering of pellets like glistening coffee beans.

'Well, fine, why not? I bet we're unique on the station. The only people with a live-in rabbit. It's not called Bugs, I hope?'

'No, I'm calling him Vulcan. Very occasionally some of his bombs get quite close to the target.'

'Very satirical.' The sharp little sally reminded Amos of why he had first found her attractive. She was no empty-headed dolly bird, unlike most of the others who bussed into Market Tewsbury from the surrounding countryside on Saturday evenings to dance in the hall at the back of the pub, their half-frozen white thighs defenceless beneath their mini skirts. But such reflections only depressed him further. This side of his life was increasingly an irritant, a distraction from his real centre of interest. He had joined the air force to fly, not to become mired in domestic encumbrances. Much as he had loved Jo when they were first married, he couldn't conceal from himself that his intensest emotion these days was for his mission, his aircraft and his crew. He could more easily and agreeably imagine spending the rest of his life in the company of, well, Gavin Rickards, than he could doing so with Jo, who seemed to have no further secrets to yield up. And now this new housing, with its implied official enforcement of family status, felt like imprisonment for the crime of marriage he now realised he should never have committed.

As if to make things still worse, within days he and Jo were invited to a Saturday evening welcoming party around the corner in de Havilland Road. Their hosts were Squadron Leader Dominic Purdue and his wife Joy. It was a slightly odd experience walking into the Purdues' house since it was identical to their own, down to the furnishings and décor. It was a bit like coming home and discovering strangers had moved in, except that the Purdues were no strangers. Like his late friend the helicopter pilot Marty O'Shea, Dominic had been in the same Entry as Amos at Cranwell and their careers had run along parallel courses except that Purdue had ended up in 599 Squadron flying Canberras. He had been based at Wearsby for the last two years while the squadron's various flights rotated to Germany, Cyprus and further afield.

'Welcome to Marital Mansions,' he greeted Amos as his wife collared Jo and led her off. 'We thought you'd never make it to these refined parts. Think of this as Wearsby's Hampstead Garden Suburb. We're all assuming you must have bribed somebody. No doubt you've got some compromising photos to hold over the barrack warden's head. Anyway, it's now your duty to get stinko unless you're flying tomorrow.'

'I may not bother to get out of bed tomorrow,' Amos assured him. 'Not even if Wheezing Jesus tries to haul me off to chapel.'

'Least of all, I should think. Nasty cold place full of damn silly pronouncements.' Dominic looked around hastily for possibly offended ladies and, finding none, thrust a tumblerful of scotch at Amos. 'I guess you'll have heard that my 'B' Flight has blotted its copybook?'

'There were some murmurs on the grapevine this morning but

to tell the truth I've been kept so busy I missed the full story. Something about a car crash, was it?'

'I'll say, but luckily no human casualties. They were playing the BABS game after a session in the Tooth. Pissed as farts, of course. They very nearly made it back, too, but at the last moment they pranged the phone box outside the main gate here, ricocheted across the road and wrote off that CND protest sign in the field opposite.'

'Hey, that can't be bad. High time it went,' said Amos enthusiastically. 'Good for them, I say.'

'Absolutely. Everyone agrees. But whatever he may think, our CO can't say so. He's grounded the lot of them *and* is making them pay for a new phone box. They'll probably have to do a refresher on Meteors or something humiliating before being allowed back on Canberras. The boys are having a whip-round for them. Chip in?'

'You bet. Anyone who has managed to Cat 5 that banner gets my vote.'

The banner in question was an enormous affair that supporters of the Campaign for Nuclear Disarmament had erected in a sympathetic farmer's field slap opposite Wearsby's main gate. Its slogan read 'WE WERE ONLY OBEYING ORDERS' WAS NO DEFENCE AT NUREMBERG. Underneath was the CND's motif of an upside-down Y in a circle. It had been there for months. At first the airmen had planned excursions to sabotage it but gradually a general feeling had spread that it was too pathetic a target for professional pranksters like themselves to bother with. It was just another confirmation that most civilians simply didn't understand the real world they were living in. Still, that didn't mean 599's 'B' Flight weren't due a vote of thanks for writing it off, and in such spectacular fashion.

The two friends smiled and shook their heads, both no doubt remembering similar escapades of their own. Nearly everyone had played the BABS game at one time or another. It was named after the old Beam Approach Beacon System on which Canberra crews had trained: a somewhat primitive aid dating from the war for lining up an aircraft correctly for landing. In fact the Canberras' version was even more primitive in that it depended on spoken instructions given by the navigator to the pilot as he made his final approach. The navigator watched a cathode ray tube that showed how much the aircraft was deviating to the left or right of the correct path. If it strayed to the left he called out to the pilot 'Dot'; and if to the right, 'Dash'. The further it strayed, the more he repeated it: 'Dot-dot,' or maybe a more urgently shouted 'Dash-dash-dash!' A rare, correct line straight up the middle of the runway would evoke the call 'Steady!'

The game, best played when returning legless in someone's car after an evening at a pub, involved blindfolding the driver. A back-seat 'navigator' was nominated to guide him by calling out dots and dashes. At chucking-out time in the wilds of Lincolnshire there were few other vehicles on the roads and it was surprising how far BABS players could drive without calamity. On this occasion it seemed they had managed to cover almost the entire four miles back to Wearsby's gate guardian, a decaying Whitley bomber, before writing off the phone box and the CND banner. This cruel luck was now to be punished further, which was doubtless no surprise to the roisterers themselves. Such exploits, together with the more physically hazardous of the traditional mess games, had long been outlawed for crews responsible for delivering the country's nuclear deterrent. Drunken driving in the neighbourhood of RAF stations was hardly a rarity, and the local police usually dismissed it with a caution as boys being boys. But if a bomber crewman broke a leg or a collarbone in a mess game it was counted as a self-inflicted injury and was severely punished. (Breaking them in a rugger match for the honour of the station was a different matter, of course.)

'Still,' said Amos sympathetically, 'I suppose that's what comes of playing silly buggers. I bet they got a dressing-down.'

'A real headmaster's scolding, I gather. Actually, they're lucky not to be on fizzers. A court martial doesn't look too good in the old record. Instead they got the usual homily about such larks being incompatible with the high seriousness of nuclear deterrence, blah blah, squadron honour and responsibility, more blah, and not forgetting to mention that it costs the best part of a hundred thousand quid to train each crew member. Plus of course having their pocket money docked. It's the pilots I pity. They're all good lads but if they're grounded long enough they'll lose their currency, go back to retake the tests, get the hours in, all that jazz. Mind you, we all know that could change overnight if there's an emergency. They'd be back in their cockpits within minutes. Your glass is empty, old boy,' Dominic suddenly pointed out. 'Can't have that. Nobody stays sober long in Marital Mansions.'

The house filled up with familiar faces, the men tending to congregate in the sitting room talking shop while the women migrated to the kitchen, from which emanated periodic bursts of ribald laughter and plates of bridge rolls. Three rapidly thinning crates of Worthington ale stood in the fireplace. Several of the men wanted to know the inside story on the two Vulcans nominated as the Ponsonby flight in 319 Squadron. Predictably, it had become the source of inspired gossip all over the station.

'Secret mission, I heard,' said Jim Ledbetter confidentially. 'They're going to kidnap Khrushchev from his dacha. Then they'll bring him back to Wearsby and quarter him here under lock and key with all his meals brought in from the sergeants' mess.'

'Poor sod. Think of the weight he'll lose.' There was general laughter at this. The appalling quality of the food there was notorious and NCOs' increasingly bitter complaints were reaching ears that were usually too senior to be troubled by such things.

'No, no, that's not it,' said Andy Fyfe. 'It's dead obvious when you think about it. Apart from the crews and the lineys, who's allowed aboard a Vulcan?'

'No-one.'

'Exactly. And you've got an armed MP with a dog and six spare rounds for his revolver guarding each aircraft.'

'I've got it,' said someone. 'Customs and Excise.'

'Go to the top of the class, Bernie. Don't you see? Not even Customs and Excise are allowed aboard. So they detail off these two Vulcans with panniers in their bomb bays and fly them around the world topping them up with contraband goods. No-one can touch them. Pearls, opium, diamonds, booze, blue films . . . It's the perfect racket for generating funds for the RAF. I happen to know the idea comes straight from the Air Ministry. They're not as stupid as some people claim.'

The burst of laughter that greeted this flight of fancy brought Joy Purdue hurrying in to remind them of the children sleeping upstairs. There was a token lull. Amos heard himself say, in the careful, serious tone of the half-drunk, 'Honest – I really don't know what "P" Flight's for. Some weird admin idea of Muffin's. Who knows? We're all a bit baffled.'

'Oh bollocks.' Conviviality broke out again and eventually several of the other wives began persuading their husbands that it might be time to go home.

'Shame, really,' said Jim Ledbetter, whose shirt bore a brown stain of Mackeson's stout. 'I feel in the mood for a prank. How about, how about – no, you chaps, listen – how about we put that clapped-out car of the padre's up on the chapel roof?'

'How? It's a *high* building. Tall, you know.'

'We can get a crane, can't we? Bound to be one somewhere. Drive it over here and Bob's your uncle. Dead snip.'

'No, Jim,' his wife said firmly. 'You're a big boy now and you've had enough. We're going home.'

'Terrible spoilsports, these women,' said Jim. 'No sense of fun. Absolutely won notever.'

'I must say I'd have liked to see Wheezing Jesus's face,' admitted Andy. 'It would have been something. A Morris ascends into heaven.'

At this point Jo thanked her hostess, Dominic being asleep near the fireplace, and led Amos eighty yards back to their house and unsteadily into the hall, where he tripped over the rabbit Vulcan. A little later he and Jo were lying side by side in their bedroom, quite naked but for one sock and a shirt that Amos had overlooked. He dimly knew that with his inhibitions subdued by alcohol this ought to be an erotic moment. Yet for the life of him he couldn't stop completely inappropriate images from spinning through his mind like a series of slideshow pictures. First there was a close-up of a Vulcan's tyre streaked with liquid that had sent Baldy Hodge into a tizzy thinking it was a hydraulic leak until it was identified as a leaking police dog. Then there was the padre's car on the chapel roof, surreal and splendid in the moonlight. After that a brief flash of the BABS game, interspersed with Joy Purdue's amazing breasts which made him think of nothing very much but pink glimpses of people's faces. These ended mysteriously with a close-up of his own crewman, the boyish Gavin Rickards, with whom he now thought he might have been at school. He slept.

9

The flight of fancy about open-cockpit aircraft that Group Captain Mewell had had during his briefing of 'P' Flight suddenly took practical shape. A series of phone calls enabled him to secure the loan of an ideal machine. This was a Bücker Jungmann that had apparently been abandoned in a hangar at Martlesham Heath when the RAF had pulled out the previous year. This was the type the Luftwaffe had adopted as its basic trainer from the mid-1930s and had built by the thousand. Somehow this particular example had found its way to Suffolk. The owner, a reserve officer, was planning to fly it in club aerobatic competitions and had recently rebuilt the engine. He seemed quite content to lend it to a man who had once flown with the Dam Busters.

Mewell was overjoyed. The Jungmann sat on a patch of grass by 'B' hangar, a bright yellow biplane smelling sweetly of fresh Titanine dope. Smaller than a Tiger Moth, it looked like a toy or maybe a large version of the radio-controlled models the Wearsby enthusiasts flew at weekends. Mewell had dug out his old goggles and leather flying helmet but otherwise wore nothing but his uniform. A couple of erks watched with a valiant attempt at solemnity as their commanding officer folded down both access panels in the sides of the front cockpit and squeezed in. He was quite a tall man and, once wedged, found he could barely get his knees far enough up under the fuel tank in order to put his feet on the pedals. Wincingly, he levered himself out again and sat himself in the student's cockpit behind. This was not only more spacious but better instrumented. Well, I am forty-one, he thought as he strapped himself in. Not quite the flexible twenty-year-old I once was. While familiarising himself with the layout he was glad he'd picked up a bit of German in the prison camp during the war and so was able to translate some of the inscriptions on controls and gauges. Finally he began the start-up ritual. He set the brakes and at his wave one of the helpers held a wing tip while the other laid a hand on the propeller.

'Fuel on, switches off, throttle closed,' called the erk.

Mewell checked that the choke was set. 'Fuel on, switches off, throttle closed.'

'Throttle set. Contact.'

'Throttle set. Contact.'

The propeller swung and the engine caught with a ragged tuft of blue smoke that was immediately shredded by the ensuing gale. Mewell settled it back to a tickover whose gassy chatter did more even than the smell of dope to take him pleasurably back to his youth and his own wartime training as a fledgling pilot. Conflict might still have been raging and his comrades decimated but a new life had spread out ahead of him disguised as an expanse of green and springy turf capped by a limitless dome of blue sky. The promise of a great freedom welled within him like adrenaline. Seeing that both erks were standing clear he raised his hand, settled his goggles, gunned the engine and bumped towards the nearest taxiway. No need to use a runway designed for bombers: a couple of hundred yards of grass alongside the taxiway were ample. There was no radio, so he had previously worked out a system with the runway caravan. He lined himself up and set the brakes, eyeing the orange windsock at the end of the airfield to check the wind.

A window in the caravan opened, an arm appeared and a lamp

flashed green. Having first remembered to lock the steerable tail-wheel, Mewell pushed the throttle open and began his run. At twenty-five knots the tail came up and he could see ahead through the grey blur of the propeller. At sixty knots he was off the ground and climbing away, banking slightly to starboard to take him over the fire dump, across the woods and away from Wearsby. He headed eastwards over fenland, climbing to five thousand feet before trying a gentle first roll. Lincolnshire's green patchwork swung up and over the cockpit followed by blue space. It was perfect. His heart sang in the wind that streamed into his face at various angles as he sent the little yellow biplane cavorting about the sky like a foal leaping and kicking its legs in an access of spring fever.

For forty minutes Group Captain Mewell worked the rust out of his aerobatics and he was soon able to judge how much extra power and speed were needed to perform more complex manoeuvres like outside loops. He noted the exact point at which the speed fell off, the normally taut controls grew soggy and one wing fell away in a stall. Nose down and happily recovering in a few hundred feet, Mewell decided that flying is by its very nature a youthful activity. To fly is to be young. To fly oneself, that is, not to *be* flown; not to be packed into a metal tube like grease in a grease gun and extruded unchanged at your destination. But to inherit an empty sky, flirt with clouds; with canvas-covered wings and your own skill make a mock of gravity while an incense of burned Castrol and hot engine blows into your face: that is the essence of being young even if your earthbound self has to revert to middle age shortly after landing. It was a kind of miracle, really. The view ahead was through a V of struts, and sideways between the wings the sky was seen through an X of bracing wires. Yet the very airiness of this latticed cage seemed to emphasise the freedom. Free at last of the endless office work, the grim managerial grind, the bureaucratic demands of maintaining an operational bomber station in a cold war that seemed increasingly lunatic. He essayed a hectic sideslip and it was as if the draught on one cheek went right through his head, blowing clear the residues of daily life, the impurities of service politics and what felt like the leaden pellets of responsibility that were incrementally weighing him down. And so the thoughts came and went fleetingly amid the complex co-ordination of hand and foot that set the world beyond the cockpit twirling and pivoting in fabulous abandon.

Considerably rejuvenated and feeling slightly sick, Mewell at length glanced at the fuel gauge and compass and set a course for home. Wearsby's trapezium of runways soon appeared and he throttled back, steadily losing height. He picked out the taxiway by the control tower, keeping a sharp lookout for any other aircraft in the vicinity, but saw none. The airfield looked unaccustomedly deserted. It was evidently one of those mid-afternoon lulls. He lined up for the landing, waggling his wings to attract the caravan's attention but no lamp blinked an OK at him. On the other hand neither did it signal to him to stay clear. He touched down in a perfect three-pointer that simply added a dollop of cream to his pleasure, rolled out gently in about seventy yards, taxied aside and switched off. As he undid his straps with a sigh of satisfaction a blue Standard car came racing up. He unlatched both cockpit sides and suddenly experienced a brief flash of disorientation so powerful he wondered if he mightn't be having a stroke.

An officer in a wing commander's uniform had leaped from the car.

'And just who the fuck . . .' he began, but his voice tailed off as he saw the group captain's insignia. 'Oh. Sorry sir. I, er, thought you were someone else.'

Mewell didn't recognise the man and his puzzlement grew.

'Who are you? Where am I?' he asked.

'Mellaby, sir. RAF Blackstock,' came the equally puzzled response. There was a long pause.

'Oh bugger,' said Mewell mildly, standing up in the cockpit and looking around him, shaking his head.

*

'Bit of a balls-up, Pugs, I'm afraid,' he said some days later, raising his gun expectantly.

'These airfields *are* pretty close together round here,' his companion said sympathetically. 'They all look much the same from the air. It's a mistake anyone could make.' He then spoilt it by adding, 'Especially if his eyesight was going and he could no longer read a compass. And we'll overlook that he was once a navigator.'

'Yes, well, no need to rub it in,' said Mewell ruefully.

The two friends had met for an afternoon's rough shooting as they often did when they could get away from their respective duties. Group Captain Mewell was not much of a shot, as soon became apparent. There were two loud bangs and the pigeon he had fired at with both barrels went whirring off unmolested towards the airfield. He broke the weapon disgustedly and ejected two smoking cases on to the coarse grass.

'Bad luck, Spotty,' said Group Captain Tolbrooke equably.

'You've cheated, Pugs. You've obviously put all your birds into flak jackets. Plus this ammo of yours is all over the place. Look at this stuff –' Mewell took two fresh cartridges from the pocket of his shooting jacket. The red paper cylinders were stamped with black broad arrows. 'Christ, it's twenty-five years old.' He dropped them into his gun with hollow plops and closed it. 'What is this, Pugs – an austerity drive?'

'Mine seem to be working all right,' said Tolbrooke mildly. His game bag contained several corpses including a hare. 'I thought we'd use them up. We've just found a hundred cases of them in Stores. Apparently the government issued them at the start of the war so the chaps could cotton onto the idea of leading. If a rear-gunner practised how far ahead of a pigeon to shoot then he could supposedly bring down a Messerschmitt. I fear you would have made a very poor rear-gunner, Spotty.'

'That's probably why they chose to sit me up front –' The sentence was cut off by the bang of his companion's gun and a cock pheasant he had barely registered as getting off the ground thumped to earth. 'Golly, that was quick,' he said admiringly. 'I've got to hand it to you, Pugs old boy: you're pretty nifty with a gun.'

'I probably get more practice than you do,' said his friend. 'Oh dear, look at these spurs.' He had picked up the limp bird and was examining its legs. 'Hard as nails. Last year's model at least, maybe even the year before. An old survivor.'

'Until today.'

'Quite. He'll make stock. Or at least Belinda will.'

The two resumed their leisurely stroll. East Wittenham, some twelve miles to the south of Wearsby, was home to a couple of squadrons of Victor bombers. By some freak of surveying prior to 1939 its eastern boundary included several hundred acres of desolate fenland which, although surplus to military requirements, had never been returned to its previous owners. It now afforded rough shooting for the commanding officer and, come to that, anybody else on the station that fancied it. The two old friends valued these meetings as offering opportunity for some blameless privacy, unlike their respective houses full of adolescent children and wives. It was by sheer chance that they had ended up commanding adjacent stations in Lincolnshire. They had first met in 1944 at Stalag Luft I, up on the Baltic in Pomerania, both having been shot down a couple of months apart. After the camp was liberated by Russian troops they were repatriated and stayed in the RAF. Thereafter their careers had run roughly parallel although until recently they had not seen much of one another, largely because Tolbrooke had been stationed abroad a good deal in the Middle East and Singapore.

A couple of rabbits scuttled away but neither man made any effort to shoot.

'How's morale with you, Spotty?'

'Not very happy, to be honest. How about here?'

'Much the same,' Tolbrooke said. 'I suppose you heard we lost a nav radar the other day? Hanged himself in his garage.'

'Do we know why?'

'The MO wrote up the usual stuff about his balance of mind being disturbed. His wife said he'd gone very quiet recently. But I've had the rest of the crew in and they all suggested it was the QRAs. They're upset, obviously. A thing like that plays havoc with morale. He had a mongol son, you know, and wanted to spend as much time at home as he could, helping the wife. Of course at an admin level it also buggers up the crewing. I don't know about you, but in Victors we try never to split up the trio of captain, nav radar and nav plotter. That's the core of a V-bomber, isn't it? The AEO's got to be someone they get along with who can join the family, while co-pilots just come and go. So I've had to stand down the entire crew until we can get a replacement navrad they're all easy with.' Tolbrooke shook his head. 'And so it goes on, Spotty.'

'Doesn't it just. Since we can't be overheard, and I trust you're not wired for sound like one of those spy thriller johnnies, I don't mind telling you that I sometimes have my doubts about these iron men we've got at the top. Not about them as warriors, of course. Both LeMay and Grandy have brilliant war records, as did Bing

Cross. But that sort of inflexible *belligerence* of LeMay's sometimes fills me with alarm, I'll be honest. This "management control system" of his – it may be OK for SAC but it just isn't British. It's not the way we do things here. Yet Grandy evidently goes along with it. Maybe MCS *is* the right thing, with rules carved in stone for absolutely everything a bomber crew does every twenty-four hours. The right number of razor strokes when shaving, the correct way to lace up shoes, all laid out on endless bits of bumf and signed at every step. All right – I exaggerate, but not by much, Pugs, not by much. It's not a natural way to live and it's damned hard on the men.'

'I suppose if Armageddon's the alternative then hard is what we need.'

'H'm. Arguable. Sometimes the whole American approach feels to me more like brinkmanship than it does like deterrence. And if the past is anything to go by that's hardly ideal. Look at Korea. And if they're not careful it could be the same thing over in Vietnam.'

'It sounds to me as though you're having doubts about our entire mission, Spotty. Ought I to be having a word with the Pentagon, do you think?'

'Oh, feel free, old boy. That reminds me, there was a splendid USAF major at that bomb comp last year at Pinecastle who referred to the Pentagon as "Fort Fumble". I really liked that. You can't beat the military everywhere for taking the piss, can you?'

'Speaking of which, you might just hold my gun a second, would you?' Tolbrooke turned away and at a discreet distance spoke over his shoulder. 'You may be right about the brinkmanship. We did come awfully close over Cuba, didn't we? My Yankee friends tell me LeMay was pestering Kennedy day and night for a pre-emptive strike and damn nearly got his way, too. But Kennedy's nerves and political savvy prevailed.' The group captain turned, doing up his fly buttons. 'Still, Spotty, ours not to reason why. We're mere foot soldiers in all this. And I don't mind telling you this foot soldier's bothered by having one of his men commit hara-kiri. Frankly, it depresses the hell out of me.'

'I know, Pugs, it's bloody. I sometimes wonder if single men don't fare better. But they do say married men are more reliable, being more settled – supposedly.' An image of Amos McKenna passed briefly across Mewell's mental retina. Not rumours, exactly, but there had been intimations that his star pilot's current state was maybe not one of marital bliss. No-one wanted to pry into private matters but the squadron's readiness had to come first. He had pulled a few strings to get him and his wife better housed. A bit more space sometimes made all the difference. 'More settled,' he repeated. 'Did you get that psychologists' report thing from the MoD?'

'Yes, I remember hoping it wouldn't start a campaign badgering our chaps to get hitched. My married quarters are stuffed to bursting point as it is. I've got pilots as well as aircrew living in rented cottages up to eight miles away from the station.'

'Haven't we all. But we hardly need these brain-shrinkers to tell us what the matter is. It's not even the job, it's the damn silly way they want us to do it. The men are great: brilliantly trained, keen as mustard and totally dedicated. But they're not fools, Pugs, they're not fools. They read the papers, they watch the box in the mess.'

By tacit agreement both men had given up shooting and were carrying their guns broken over one shoulder.

'So it's dead obvious they must be discussing things,' Mewell went on. 'Why would their misgivings be any different from ours? It's damned wearing maintaining this state of constant alert even if we do understand the rationale. And I don't know if it's the same with you, but none of my lot like this aircraft pooling system, either. It puts everyone on edge, especially the crew chiefs.[†] And worst of all it hardly helps to know the bloody Navy's going to be taking over our deterrent role in five years' time. There's damn-all we can do about that.'

'No. Sometimes, Spotty, I feel the cold winds of fate blowing about all our shanks.' Nothing could have better indicated the long intimacy of these two men than the nicknames they used, particularly Group Captain Mewell's. It clearly antedated the television-era 'Muffin' by which his men informally knew him. 'To be honest, I'm doing my best to put my boy off any idea of a career in the service. I really think it's very doubtful he'd have a guaranteed future to take him through to a pension. Ever since that frightful ass Duncan Sandys wanted to replace our aircraft with missiles the skids have been under us.'

The two men had evidently elected to call it a day so far as shooting was concerned and were wandering companionably back in the general direction of Mewell's Allard, a distant blob of British racing green against the autumnal tussocks. From somewhere out of view in the distance there came a sudden thunderous roaring and a dark cloud could be seen billowing up above the horizon. In swift succession four Victors in a scramble take-off suddenly leaped out of hiding from beneath the bulge of intervening ground. Both men paused to watch with a professional eye as the rapidly nearing white bombers lifted steeply one by one into the bald grey sky then banked to port, showing their crescent wings. Towing sooty plumes, they dwindled into the high overcast on individual courses. Long after they had vanished that part of the runway in view remained smogged with slowly attenuating dark haze while the very soil of Lincolnshire seemed to go on yielding

---

† See Appendix 3, p. 295.

up the sonic punishment it had just absorbed, much as drawing-room curtains steadily exhale last night's cigarette smoke.

'Looking good, Pugs,' said Mewell judicially as the thunder melted away into the top of the sky. 'A shade more ragged than we're used to at Wearsby, of course, but still not at all bad.'

'Well, ours are faster than your tin triangles so we like a bit more airspace between them. And,' Tolbrooke added, 'at least they know where they're going. If you've managed to pass on your own nav skills to your lads they'll probably nuke York Minster under the impression that it's the Kremlin.'

Similar good-natured repartee brought the two men to Mewell's car where they shed their equipment. 'I'm sorry the boot's so small,' Mewell said without a trace of regret. 'We'll put your game in it and you'll have to carry the guns between your legs again.'

Tolbrooke opened the rectangular leather-covered case that had been propped in the passenger well. The rich antiseptic scent of Young's .303 oil rose from the green baize lining. The label inside the lid giving Cogswell and Harrison's London and Paris addresses was stained with it. He slotted his guns snugly back into their compartments. 'Funny: I look forward to cleaning them almost as much as I enjoy firing them,' he said happily.

'They're beauties, Pugs. I'm just sorry I never seem to do them justice. I'm not much of a shot. Never was.'

'We can probably forgive someone who got a gong for downing a couple of Dorniers in one night. Though I expect you only winged them. Wrong sort of ammo, no doubt.'

'Just get in the car, Tolbrooke. We at Wearsby have a way of taming East Witto Standard Vanguard drivers.'

'Oh Christ.' The huge V-8 engine chugged into life and Tolbrooke leaned back in his seat and braced one hand nervously against the vibrating aluminium dashboard while with the other he held the precious gun case upright between his legs. 'Spotty,' he said, just before Mewell could put the Allard into gear, 'what do you say we have a party?'

'What sort of a party?'

'You know, a thrash. Morale-boosting. All our crews together. Including any Canberra lads and other odds and sods we've got stationed.'

Mewell stared thoughtfully over the half-moon of glass that served as his windshield. 'Some joint whoopee, you mean? Not a bad idea. Ought we to get Coningsby along as well, do you think?'

'Ideally, yes. But the trouble is, once you ask them we'd be honour bound to ask Waddo. Your great rivals in the rugger.'

'True. Sounds like a recipe for mayhem. Still, even if discipline goes by the board for an evening it ought to cheer the lads up a bit. We'll need to get onto our lords and masters to see about redistributing QRAs for twenty-four hours and get their OK. Good idea, Pugs. And now as it's getting dark and it'll be coming on to rain at any moment and there's no roof to this car . . .' He blipped the engine, listening to it go from deep grumble to howl and back again with obvious pleasure, his head cocked. 'Reminds me – we had a Lightning pilot drop in the other day,' he said above the noise. 'Down to eighty pounds of fuel, can you believe? *Eighty*. Those boys like cutting it fine. So while they tanked him up one of our lads asked him what it was like to fly the thing. Apparently the real blast's the acceleration on take-off. "You know what?" he said. "It rolls your foreskin back." So, Pugsy, hang on to yours.' And with a whoop Group Captain Mewell let in the clutch.

10

At the opposite end of Wearsby's main runway from the fire dump, on the far side of rows of approach lights and an alarmed perimeter fence topped with strands of barbed wire, ran the main road. There, well to one side of the runway's central line, a spacious lay-by had been thoughtfully provided by highway planning. This was possibly to enable the British taxpayer to view the airfield and catch a glimpse of where his money was going. More plausibly, though, it was designed to allow the Soviet trade delegation's plane-spotters to take time off from promoting Sekonda watches. From beyond the fence the Russians had an excellent view through their binoculars of Wearsby's Vulcans on their operational readiness platforms in all weathers where, unless they were in the air or elsewhere on the flight line, the aircraft sat with their little entourages of vehicles in a plain state of readiness. The whole point of deterrence, after all, was for it to be no secret. The bombers were equally visible at night, each one drenched in the orange glare of sodium lighting. There was no missing them.

This morning, when he had driven down to the flight line, Chief Technician Baldy Hodge had glanced towards the end of the runway and noticed a familiar vehicle parked on the road beyond the fence. It was much too far away for him to be certain with the naked eye, but he thought it was bound to be the bloody Russkies as usual. Good; let 'em watch: they might learn something. He had a brief fantasy of one day rolling up in his new E-Type Jaguar and parking beside them in the lay-by just for the pleasure of seeing their grey, apparatchik faces register envy at the goodies that capitalism could so easily supply.

Lately, Baldy's colleagues had remarked that he had become fractionally less grumpy since the formation of the special 'P' Flight. According to the new dispensation XM580 was no longer subject to the centralised system for servicing and repairs. Instead, in a reversion to the old way of doing things, it once again became exclusively his aircraft. What was more, it now felt almost brand new. It and XJ791 had recently arrived back from Woodford having had various electronic goodies installed. Gone were the entirely ghost-white Vulcans of a fortnight earlier. The entire upper surfaces of both aircraft had been resprayed in a grey and green camouflage scheme for their new low-level role. Less obtrusively, there was a new aperture beneath the bomb-aimer's blister under the nose. Inside, filling the crawlway to this unused position, was a bulky box of tricks that now completely blocked the narrow sighting window. Some sort of experimental bombing sight, Hodge had gathered.

The pear-drops scent of fresh cellulose had penetrated even into the cockpit. Baldy was now sniffing this with pleasure as he stood on the access ladder between the pilot's seats watching the fuel control panel he had pulled out from beneath the main fuel gauges. He also kept a sharp eye on the centre of gravity indicator as the two bowsers below gradually filled the aircraft's fourteen tanks with some thirty-two tons of Avtur. He was not about to make the mistake that idiot young Cowans had made some weeks back when he had carelessly stood XJ810 on its tail while refuelling it. The lazy sod had done it from outside on the ladder beneath the wing, dialling up eighty per cent on the selector panel and just trusting the automatic system to distribute the fuel evenly. It hadn't. The rearmost tanks had filled first, the aircraft's centre of gravity had shifted aft beyond recall and the tail hit the ground and stayed there. Well, Cowans had learned his lesson and it served him right too. He'd been demoted to a mere erk pending being sent back to St Athan for retraining. Frankly, Saints was too good for him. If Hodge had had his way he'd have been out on his ear pronto, end of story. There was no room in the RAF for twats like that.

The fuel flow stopped at the ninety-eight per cent he had called for and, seeing from the display that it was correctly distributed, the chief technician closed the panel and backed down the steps from the flight deck before descending the main ladder to the ground. There he grimly surveyed the erks and tanker drivers as they rewound the hoses and earthing leads onto their respective reels in the two bowsers. Not that he was a mere overseer. Hodge was a big man, and those who had seen him taking a rare dip in a warm ocean in Aden or somewhere had realised that he could not possibly have acquired his upper-body musculature by standing around watching others work. Apprentices were depressed by the ease with which he could drag the thick fuel hoses to the aircraft with one continuous pull and, standing on the main wheels with his arms at full stretch, push the heavy couplings up onto the nozzles and seal them with a twist. 'That's all there is to it,' he would say, jumping back down and banging his work gloves together. 'Next time, you do it.' Then he would strike one of his peculiar attitudes. He had a repertoire of these odd postures which he would hold for a long moment like a shop window mannequin in overalls: both hands cockily on hips, or only one; one hand grasping the back of his reddish neck; occasionally both hands pressed to the sides of his face as though in an access of horror at the incompetence he could see around him.

Today Hodge was readying XM580 for a sortie up to the north of Scotland: the first since her return from Avro's and as far as he knew a routine test flight. No doubt it was designed to uncover any problems with whatever new gadgets had just been fitted. Even more than most at Wearsby he was curious to know why his and Flight Lieutenant Meeres's Vulcan had alone been earmarked for special treatment. Gossip abounded on the flight line as to the relevance of their new avionics fit, but maybe after all they weren't so special and any significance lay merely in their being the first of many. It was common knowledge that all Bomber Command's Vulcans and Victors were to be repainted in the new camouflage scheme, so it seemed likely these two aircraft were merely the first of the fleet to be dressed to meet their new low-level deterrent role. No doubt that had entailed some necessary adjustment to their navigation radars as well.

As the fuel bowsers pulled away Hodge signalled to a handler to start the diesel generator that supplied electric current for powering-up the aircraft. The coach arrived and the crew piled out, bulky and purposeful in their layers of specialised clothing and carrying their helmets and flight bags full of manuals and sandwiches. Their blue flying suits were topped off with vests with built-in life jackets whose yellow rolls around the collar shone as bright flashes of colour against the prevailing dull grey of the Lincolnshire day. Handing up their kit to each other they climbed into the aircraft.

'Wow,' said Amos, stopping for a moment to admire the Vulcan's new look. 'Don't you think she's rather handsome, Chief? Green and grey suits her. Smells nice, too. I trust all the tits and knobs are working?'

'All hot to trot,' Hodge confirmed, thinking as he handed him Form 700 to check that the Vulcan captain really did look like an RAF recruitment poster boy. Those dark good looks: very like Denis Compton in the Brylcreem adverts. He'd bet the ladies went wild over Squadron Leader McKenna, although truth be told there didn't seem to be many stories of Squadron Leader McKenna going wild over the ladies, even though he was known to enjoy a party like everyone else. No doubt he saved it all for that wife of his. Hodge rather approved of fidelity, which he habitually described as 'one owner-driver' in the manner of *Exchange & Mart*. Amos rapidly scanned the form, found nothing outstanding and climbed up the yellow ladder. Hodge followed. Standing behind the two pilots' seats the chief technician helped the men with their safety harnesses and then removed the safety pins from the ejector seats as well as from the canopy. The pilots stowed these in the appropriate pouches below the coaming.

Baldy gave a last look around the cockpit with a grunt of satisfaction before climbing back down the main ladder. He heard the hatch close above him as he pulled on his cloth helmet and took the long lead of its built-in headset and microphone from where it hung coiled on the nose-wheel steering jack, plugged it in and retreated some fifty yards behind the aircraft. From there he confirmed the movements of the Vulcan's control surfaces as up in the cockpit the pilots went through the check sequence while watching the telltale on the panel in front of them. Meanwhile the rest of the crew had settled in their seats and were reeling off the tedious litanies of their own system checks as Hodge signalled to a handler to fire up the Palouste air starter on its trolley. The Vulcan had its own onboard supply of compressed air for starting the engines but this was limited and better conserved for emergencies. Many an aircraft had had to put down unexpectedly on a strange airfield only to find that the single starter trolley they had there was unserviceable. Without their on-board starter they would have been stuck lifeless on the ground, and all for want of some compressed air.

In his headphones Hodge listened to the rapid patter of the crew over their intercom: 'Temperature selector – normal. Temperature control switch – neutral. Pitot head heaters – test and off. External lights – test and off. Tanks pressurisation – off. Nitrogen purge – off. Flight refuelling master – off . . .' So it went on. Baldy stood below on the concrete pan in the shadow of the giant wing with his head bowed, both lulled by it and attentive, like a bishop listening to a choir plough through the Te Deum and awaiting his cue. Unheard by him Gavin Rickards called up Air Traffic Control on the R/T: 'Five-eight-zero ready to start,' and received the expected response, 'Clear to start,' with the helpful addition: 'Wind is two-nine-zero at eight knots.' Now Amos's voice came over Baldy's headphones saying, 'OK, Chief, cleared to start. Ignition switch – on. Engine master switch – on. Clear four, Chief?'

'Clear,' said Baldy into his mike.

'Light on.' This was Amos confirming that no. 4 engine's air valve was open. The compressor bellowed and the hose from it went suddenly rigid.

Up in the cockpit Amos waited as he watched the engine's rev counter and oil pressure gauge climb, listening to the whine of the engine winding up before he moved the high-pressure fuel cock to slightly beyond the 'idle' position. He noted the jet pipe temperature was a satisfactory 350 degrees and throttled the engine back to idle. Everything was normal and he repeated the same sequence with the other three engines as his crew behind him continued with their own pre-flight checks, reading from the manuals. Nobody bothered to commit these lists to memory because nobody's memory was trustworthy enough. It all had to be done by the book.

As the three electronics crewmen sat shoulder-to-shoulder at their work stations Gavin Rickards fleetingly had an image of his treasured Austin-Healey Sprite and thought – by no means for the first time – how very different getting a V-bomber ready to fly was from simply leaping into a car and driving off. Or, come to that, from getting a Second World War aircraft into the air, a process that he'd once heard Muffin Mewell summarise as 'kick a tyre and light the fire'. As the air electronics officer, the young flight lieutenant had control over all his aircraft's myriad electrical circuits which had steadily been coming alive from the moment the Houchin generator had supplied external power. Now that the engines were burning and turning, the Vulcan's own generators made the aircraft self-sufficient. Somewhere on the ground below Baldy Hodge was even now shutting down the portable generator and disconnecting the cable. *Ground supply – off.* Like his two companions Rickards intently watched dials and clicked switches. He would now be doing little else until well after they had completed the sortie and landed again. If there was any romance left in flying it was largely confined to the minds of ordinary folk on the ground who might watch the delta bomber soar into the sky. From inside, and from the viewpoint of the crew facing backwards in the darkened compartment behind the cockpit, flying was almost entirely a matter of watching dials and displays and pressing switches until, after however many hours of bumping and lurching, the motion stopped and the main hatch popped with a hiss of nitrogen, daylight flooded in and they were in Cyprus or Norway or maybe back at Wearsby. Hopefully this discovery ought not to be a complete surprise to Vic Ferrit, the nav radar who had guided them there.

Out on the pan the compressor had also been shut down, disconnected, and everything cleared safely away behind the white line by the erks. Cocooned in the warm stench of burning kerosene beneath the roaring aircraft, Baldy Hodge still had a couple of checks to make. The first involved climbing up into the nose-wheel bay on an aluminium ladder to check the quivering hot-air trunking for leaks. There were none, which he confirmed to Amos in the cockpit overhead. Had this been an armed mission he would next have checked that the Vulcan's bomb doors could open and close in less than eight seconds, showing that all three hydraulic pumps were working. As it was he merely signalled to a handler to remove the ladder and walked out in front of the aircraft for the final check. This was to watch the air brakes move to all three of their positions. From there the resonance from the intakes with the engines at idle was just about bearable when wearing a headset.

'OK air brakes, Chief?' came Amos's voice faintly in his headphones. On each side of the aircraft there were two air brakes above the engine nacelles and one below. Amos and Hodge now checked them at 'mid', 'full' and 'in' and then repeated the procedure under emergency power. Finally, Baldy called up, 'You're good to go, Boss.' He waved to the handlers poised to drag clear the chocks from the wheels, walked back under the Vulcan, unplugged his headset and, gathering up its cable, retreated to the far side of the aircraft's nose where he could be seen from the cockpit in order to wave an all clear. Behind the cockpit's circular side window Keith Coswood in the right-hand seat could be seen raising a gloved hand in acknowledgement. Simultaneously the roar of all four Olympus engines rose to a howl and XM580 began to move forward, her nose turning to follow the taxiway and engulfing Hodge and the handlers in choking clouds of jet exhaust from which they vainly ducked, eyes streaming, behind the compressor and the generator. Judging from the fuel load Amos had requested, this sortie would last several hours. So instead of hanging around in the dispersal hut Baldy drove off in the battered Standard pickup to the sergeants' mess, reaching it just as his Vulcan went to full power at the end of the runway and began rolling.

Like a mother duck watching her chick take to water for the first time he eyed it as it gathered speed several hundred yards away, imagining he could hear the co-pilot calling out the knots: 'Ninety . . . hundred . . . hundred and ten . . .' With satisfaction he correctly predicted the exact rotation spot when at a hundred and thirty-five the nose lifted and she unstuck and went smoking into the sky amid almighty tumult, a racket that could set windows rattling for miles around. It was a sight and sound repeated a dozen times daily and he never tired of it. Yet this time it looked slightly different. Instead of a tilting white triangle diminishing into the cloud base, the new stripy paint job on the climbing aircraft made its outline less clear, maybe more stealthy, the disruptive patterning designed to make it harder for a fighter pilot to spot the bomber from above as it flew low over the ground. As XM580 tilted, her still-white underside gleamed for a moment like a gull against the grey before she vanished into the overcast. The crew chief turned away and went into the mess for a mug of tea and – if nobody had nicked it yet – a shufti at the *Daily Sketch*. It was more sensibly Conservative than the *Mirror*, and Baldy Hodge was a conservative man. Still, he did concede the Andy Capp strip made the *Mirror* worth the occasional glance despite it being a socialist rag.

*

Aboard XM580 the clipped transmissions between it and the control tower ('Understand transition three thousand feet') began to thin but the litany over the intercom continued until Gavin Rickards clicked the microphone switch on his oxygen mask, said 'Take-off checks completed' and removed his white bone-dome.

This revealed it as being nothing but a protective shell designed to fit over the cloth helmet which held the headphones. Bob Mutton, the nav plotter, did likewise before giving Amos a new course to steer over the intercom, adding 'Climb to thirty-eight thousand feet for our first turning-point.'

Now that the secret Oilcan radar system had been fitted to the two Vulcans their crews were mildly interested to see whether it worked. However, it was too important to risk being overheard by either the Russians or the Americans until the aircraft was definitely combat ready, so this sortie was more a way of testing everything else first. The same went for the new laser bombing system which had resulted in a mysterious box of tricks shoe-horned into Vic Ferrit's already crowded workstation. First things first: no aircraft ever returned from having new equipment in-stalled without immediately being taken up and tested. Even slight alterations made to its complex circuitry had a habit of causing seemingly unrelated problems. The briefing Wing Commander Ops. had given them earlier was to fly to the north of Scotland by a route that included Sunderland where, using the old system, they were to radar-bomb the museum from high altitude for old times' sake, and then on over Scotland to a stretch of the Atlantic west of the Orkneys where they could test the Vulcan's normal ECM radars and jammers with the help of an RAF Coastal Command Shackleton.

In due course the mobile ground radar in Sunderland 'fixed' the Vulcan far overhead in three dimensions. From this and the known trajectory of a WE.177 nuclear bomb it was immediately possible to calculate the accuracy of a theoretical drop. Almost at once Rickards received a radioed message that their radar pulse had scored a direct hit on the museum, theoretically obliterating County Durham. 'A good job jobbed there, Vic,' Amos congratulated his nav radar before leaning the Vulcan onto a new bearing supplied by Baa Mutton. Some twenty minutes later the northern coast of Scotland would have been visible between broken clouds had anyone aboard the aircraft been able to see it. But the view from the cockpit was, as usual, of nothing but sky until the aircraft banked slightly to starboard, which afforded the co-pilot, Keith Coswood, a brief glimpse of some dull green islands set in a steel-grey ocean.

The Shackleton with which Rickards had already made contact was one of several that over the last five years had helped keep up a twenty-four-hour surveillance of the Communist Bloc's intrusive 'fishing' fleets. These vessels tended to hang around the areas through which the Royal Navy's submarines most frequently passed on their way to and from their bases. Since they were in international waters there was little to be done about it. These so-called fishing vessels bristled with aerials and sizzled with coded messages and were also equipped with sophisticated gear to listen out for any submarine's distinctive sonar signature. The Shackletons periodically dropped passive sonobuoys to eavesdrop on the eavesdroppers and radio back what they heard. It was yet another small daily part of the great Cold War standoff in which both sides were on permanent twenty-four hour alert for the tiniest snippet of information that might fortuitously lead to a discovery or an advantage. It was this constant fluidity that eternally saved the game from the impasse of true stalemate.

Now the Shackleton, invisible some thirty nautical miles away to port, sent a series of code words to warn XM580 that the listeners were out in force. Rickards acknowledged and reminded Amos that their instructions in such circumstances had been not to try out Oilcan but to run a series of tests involving the usual Red Shrimp and Blue Diver jammers. They now took pleasure in swamping the Russian trawlers' various transmissions with noise before closing to within five miles of the Shackleton. This was where Rickards could test the radar in the Vulcan's tail that would warn of a Soviet fighter coming in stealthily from behind. The Shackleton obliged with a radar beam of the right wavelength and it plotted brilliantly on the tube in front of him.

After a further half-hour of flying patterns that included a swing northwards to the Shetlands, Rickards sent a message of thanks to the Shack and Baa Mutton gave Amos a heading for Wearsby where, forty-five minutes later, they picked up the control tower informing them that since their departure a late-afternoon mist had developed over much of the area. Mutton guided Amos down to the final approach when Wearsby's controller, with XM580 firmly on his radar, took over.

'Five-eight-zero, left three degrees. Resume your normal rate of descent and left three degrees, left three degrees and a mile to go. You're clear to line up for this approach. Final check. Short finals now, your heading is good. Look ahead for the runway slightly on your port side. You're on the glide path. You're on the centre line now. Heading is good. Spot-on the glide path. Look ahead and land visually. Talkdown out.' And through the murk ahead the runway's lights and the black and white piano keys at its end suddenly swam into clarity and Amos eased back on the control grip. The Vulcan's nose floated gracefully up and the forward view was lost as it flared, floating for an instant before the main wheels made contact with the runway with a slight jolt. He held it in this position while the speed bled off, with no view through the windscreen but of dark grey sky, keeping the line straight with an almost unconscious awareness of the speeding edge of the runway. He maintained the braking effect of this nose-up attitude for as long as possible. Not deploying the brake parachute would earn the gratitude of the team in their Land Rover who would otherwise have to retrieve it from the runway and repack it. Finally, the nose dropped and the nose wheels made contact and the brakes absorbed the kinetic energy of bringing this monster machine down to taxiing speed. The control tower cleared it to its stand where XM580 finally halted, the engines winding down. The crew were throwing off their harnesses as, at Amos's OK, Gavin Rickards popped the hatch and cold, damp air flooded in.

First up the ladder was Baldy Hodge, who went straight to the cockpit, took the stowed safety pins and swiftly made safe the pilots' ejector seats and the canopy. After a while the litany of shutdown checks was completed, the crew gathered up their bags and disembarked, Form 700 was duly signed and handed over, the crew bus roared off and Hodge was left with his aircraft on the pan beneath the high overhead lights. He and his lineys now went busily about, running checks and replenishing nitrogen bottles, climbing ladders and opening access panels, reading the two fatigue meters on the roof of the bomb bay (one for negative and one for positive 'g'). And in the chill, drizzle-laden Lincolnshire wind beneath the darkening sky the jet tubes overhead ticked as they cooled, and the landing gear made soft chinking noises as the disc assemblies shrank infinitesimally, giving up their heat.

11

Most mornings these days Jo McKenna would drive to the vet's clinic in Amos's ratty old Hillman Minx. At first she had dutifully caught the early local bus that stopped outside Wearsby's main gate, then had changed in Market Tewsbury to the slightly faster one to Mossop. The local bus dawdled and often broke down and even on a good day she would struggle to find a seat. There were notices painted inside its nicotine-tanned roof announcing fines for spitting, and she often stumbled over trussed hens lying on the floor, beaks agape. More and more she took to asking Amos for the loan of the car if he wasn't using it. It was not long before she was taking it as if by right, cutting her journey time down to less than twenty minutes. If the Minx's primitive radio was in a good mood she would find the Home Service and listen to Jack de Manio on *Today*, his voice coming and going amid the static and interference that Amos had told her was the result of all the military radio and radar beams criss-crossing the eastern counties. She often felt cheerful enough to sing along with the hymns that followed.

Her life, she felt, had been transformed. She could swing out of Brabazon Close and out past the guardhouse at the gate, turn right onto the Tewsbury road and become a civilian again. She left behind her the perpetual confused roaring of jet engines and a self-sufficient world dressed in light blue uniforms and obsessed with war; a world that could happily manage without her. It was a freedom she hadn't experienced for years. And as if that were not enough she had a job that gave her real pleasure and satisfaction. She had a new purpose in life. She had realised belatedly that she had a genuine affinity for animals. Even though she was nominally a vet's receptionist, sheer short-handedness often meant she was asked to help in the surgery. She had no formal qualifications for this but the vets assured her that, short of being able to give anaesthetics and wield a scalpel, she had the most valuable talent of all which was the ability to calm frightened creatures and make them relax. This, they assured her, materially increased their chances of recovery. Most mornings the practice's owners, Craig Maybus and Arthur Mealing, were out and about on their own, responding to calls from farmers that might be emergencies or merely routine visits. Her two very charming employers went about the country committing skilled acts of violence such as castrations and dehornings and earning widespread gratitude. Maybus & Mealing was the only decent veterinary practice for miles around Mossop and was clearly prospering.

Today was one of those Wednesdays Jo looked forward to because there was a walk-in surgery for pets in the morning. And better still, Avril O'Shea had promised to drive over for lunch. Five minutes before the surgery opened at 9 a.m. Jo parked on the gravelled area outside the substantial Victorian town house that had been Arthur Mealing's childhood home and still belonged to his family. These days much of the ground floor had been converted to a reception area, a waiting room, two consulting surgeries, a small operating theatre and – out at the back – what they called the 'recovery room'. This, the former scullery, held cages for animals in various stages of recuperation or expiry, many of the patients having bald patches shaved into their fur across which ran lines of purple stitches. The entire ground floor held a faint smell reminiscent of hot mice and TCP.

By ten o'clock both vets were busy and there were eight people in the waiting room holding a variety of cardboard boxes with holes punched in their lids and done up with twine from which now and then plaintive mewings and scrabblings could be heard. Occasionally one or other of their owners might whisper a few re-assuring words into a hole, but apart from that there was a dour British silence in the room. People sat staring straight ahead or kept their eyes on the Ministry of Ag and Fish's posters illustrating Colorado beetles on potato leaves. There was also a doleful twelve-year-old boy with scratched knees who sat sucking aniseed balls and dangling a dog leash with a choke chain between his legs so that its end traced the lino's pattern. Bored with that, he took a small mouth organ from his pocket and used a matchstick to un-clog grey fluff from its holes. Jo watched him through the open door from behind her desk. Little sod, she thought, doing that to his dog. At this point Craig Maybus opened his consulting-room door wearing a rubber apron over his clothes and a concave dent-ist's mirror on his forehead. He beckoned her in.

'Do you mind, Jo?' he said. 'I need a brief hand here. We'll hear if anybody rings or comes in. It's this dog.' He indicated a large an-imal of vaguely Airedale descent that was sprawled woozily amid puddles on the green American cloth that covered the table. 'I've got him sedated but I'm going to have to put him under and I need you to hold his head afterwards. The damned thing's wedged firmer than I thought.'

She cradled the dog's head as Maybus gave him another injec-tion, noticing how the animal had scratched the skin around one ear bare in its attempts to remove the marble. 'Pentothal,' said the vet. 'Good stuff but not very long-lasting.' The dog's eyes closed and she held his head and the ear flap up so Maybus could use his mirror to reflect the light from an Anglepoise lamp into the animal's ear.

'That's the trouble with something like a marble: there's damn-all to get a grip on.' He probed around with a pair of forceps. 'I've already tried washing it out but he took a dim view of that. I hoped we might get this out in a jiffy but I was wrong. If this doesn't work we'll have to keep him in for surgery later. No – I don't think I'm doing much good here.'

'How about . . .' said Jo diffidently. 'No – perhaps that's silly.'

'Go on. All ideas welcome.'

'I was just wondering if you took one of those rubber suckers off the sign in the window and held its knob with your forceps you might get a grip that way?'

Maybus looked up at her and gave a nod. 'Brilliant,' he said. 'Worth a try. This animal should be out for another five or ten minutes.'

Jo pulled the white notice saying 'Veterinary Surgeon' off the window with two brief quacks and handed one of the rubber suckers to Maybus who dabbled it in the water on the tabletop before grasping it in his forceps. 'Too big,' he said, straightening up after a moment. 'It wants cutting down.' He trimmed the sucker with a pair of surgical scissors and tried again. 'Ah,' he said under his breath. 'That's more like it. Let's see . . . Yes! Got you!' And he slowly withdrew a small blue marble with milky swirls.

'You're a genius, Jo. I always thought I wasn't bad myself at improvising ways out of trouble in a freezing barn at 3 a.m. But here you are in my own surgery with a peach of an idea. Ah – the poor beast's coming round. I'll take him into recovery and you can send the boy in to keep an eye on him for half an hour or so until he's fit to leave. I shouldn't waste your time trying to find out how the marble got there in the first place: it no longer matters. Lesson learned, I'd say. Or it bloody soon will be when his father gets our bill.'

For the next hour or two Jo sat in a small private glow of accomplishment. The boy and his dog left, both noticeably perkier than when they had come in. Various pets were handed over in their boxes and cages to Craig and Arthur, who retired to their separate consulting rooms for a while. Arthur was rather more acerbic than his partner and, Jo had discovered, instinctively took the animals' side rather than that of their owners. He now stopped off in Reception and said to Jo in an urgent undertone: 'What the hell does one do with a tortoise whose owner thinks it's "a bit under the weather"? It's all right for a GP: he only ever has one species to deal with. I have to make an excuse and go out and look at Merck's.' Of all the books on the shelves in the partners' office, the *Merck Veterinary Manual* was by far the most consulted.

Then at almost twelve o'clock and just when she was hoping the morning's work was tailing off towards the lunch hour, there came the crunching and popping of car tyres on the gravel outside and two uniformed airmen entered, one of them holding a large monkey. From the rings on their sleeves Jo could see at once they were pilot officers. She recognised neither of them, although it soon emerged they were from Wearsby and had been detailed off by Group Captain Mewell to bring the station's mascot, Ponsonby, for a check-up. It transpired that for the first time ever Ponsonby had been sick in Mewell's car a few days earlier and since then had not been 'back to his old form' despite the MO's best efforts.

Like everyone at Wearsby, Jo had heard of Ponsonby although she had never seen him since he hadn't been in residence more than a few months and was billeted mostly with the group captain and his family in their Queen Anne house a mile away from the airfield. She was surprised by the animal's size. He seemed well over two feet tall and might even be getting on for three. He wore a blue collar with Air Force roundels on it to which a long lead was attached. He looked about him apprehensively, his fingers gripping the pilot officer's lapel in a way that melted Jo's heart. At that moment Arthur Mealing came into Reception, glanced into the waiting room and said 'Christ almighty' under his breath. 'What the hell's *that*? Is there a circus in town or what?'

'He's a Barbary ape, the Wearsby station mascot. He's called Ponsonby.'

'Well I'll be jiggered. We've never had one of those in here before. What's the matter with him?'

'They say he's listless.'

'So would I be bloody listless if I'd been snatched away from my chums in sunny Gibraltar or wherever and held captive on an airfield in freezing Lincolnshire. Whose damn silly idea was that?'

'I don't know. I believe the group captain takes him for rides in his car.'

'Crikey. I've heard of regimental goats but this is ridiculous. I shall need ten minutes with Merck's. Barbary apes indeed.' He disappeared.

At that moment the front door opened and Avril walked in. 'Hi, Jo,' she said. 'How lovely to see you. Am I too early?'

'Rilly! No, not if you don't mind waiting a bit. Have you got the kids with you?'

'No, I've dumped them today. I'm footloose and fancy-free. H'm, I like your workplace.' She looked at her friend's desk and the filing cabinet and took in the colourful posters of wilting hens and lame horses on the wall warning of fowl pest and advertising tar-based remedies for laminitis.

'I'm afraid I'll have to wait until our last patient's out but he oughtn't to be long.' Jo nodded towards the waiting room. 'Come to think of it, you might be the expert we're looking for. You were reading a book about apes some months ago.'

'Golly,' said Avril, peering in at the solemn young officers and their nervous charge. 'Is that an ape? Or is it a monkey? I can't remember the difference now. It doesn't seem to have a tail. Is that how you tell? Ahh, look at its little pink face. Just like a scared child. What's the matter with it?'

'We don't know yet. But possibly nothing much worse than acute home-sickness.'

At that moment Arthur Mealing appeared and beckoned the two airmen and Ponsonby into his consulting room. The door closed.

'*Orang-utans Are not the Only Apes*, that's it,' said Avril. 'I remember the title now. Dr Prudence Summertown. She's just had another one out. Something like *The Passionate Body*.' She giggled. 'The newspaper said it told us a good deal more about lady apes than we ever wanted to know. She seems to be getting quite notorious. That Lord Boothby said he'd rather be caught in bed with the Kray twins than be seen having tea with Prudence Summertown.'

'Honestly, Rilly,' said Jo, half scandalised and half admiringly, 'the things you read.'

'Oh, I haven't read this new one and I'm not going to, either. But when you've got two small children you go mad if you don't read. Thank God for newspapers and *Listen with Mother* on the radio. And I've joined Boots' Booklovers Library. It all helps.'

At length the consulting-room door opened and the airmen emerged with Ponsonby, who seemed aware that his ordeal was over and now looked rather more relaxed. He had draped one long furry arm around the shoulders of the airman carrying him.

'Varied diet, that's what he needs,' the vet was saying as he followed. 'Just giving him leftover scraps from the kitchens isn't good enough, not by a long chalk. Despite his name he's a macaque monkey and not an ape, and in the wild he'd be eating leaves and fruit and roots and even the occasional insect. Go and catch some grasshoppers, the odd beetle, a moth or two. You know, give him a treat.'

The airman carrying Ponsonby looked wounded. 'We're trained to fly Canberras, sir. I don't think the group captain would approve of us wasting taxpayers' money on our hands and knees looking for grasshoppers. Especially not in November.'

'That's your problem. If you're going to keep an exotic pet it's your duty to make sure he's properly fed. Puffed wheat, indeed. Never heard such a thing. And no more pear drops, either, or else he'll be in for dental work. Tell that to his irresponsible keepers.' He put a brown bottle on Jo's desk. 'Also, he's lonely. Macaques are very social animals used to living in large troupes' (Good old Merck's, Jo thought) 'so he's bound not to be feeling too cheerful cut off from his mates, especially now that winter's coming. Mrs McKenna here will take the details of where we're to send the bill. Bomber Command? The Air Ministry? Kindly settle that with her.' And Arthur Mealing took his disapproval off into a distant reach of his boyhood home. A door closed somewhere with a bang.

'So, gentlemen,' Jo addressed the airmen briskly. 'Whom do I invoice? The OC Wearsby?'

'Excuse me, missus,' one of them said. 'Are you Squadron Leader McKenna's wife?'

'I am.'

'Oh, we were just wondering. I thought we'd seen you around the station. What do you think, Duggie?' he asked his companion. 'Have the bill sent to Muffin?'

'Why not? Perhaps mascots come under the mess? He'll pass it on to whoever.'

Jo made some notes and then stood up and took Ponsonby's spare hand in hers. 'You poor old thing,' she said. The animal stared back at her with liquid sad eyes. Then it swung its spare arm from around the airman's shoulders and onto hers. She took him into her arms, amazed at his weight. He nuzzled her neck like an infant but she quickly averted her face. His breath was astonishingly fouler than that of any infant she'd ever met.

'Heavens,' said Avril, getting a waft. 'Someone isn't using Amplex.'

'Yes, he's pretty niffy, isn't he?' said Duggie.

'Take him back to Wearsby,' Jo told them. 'But first stop off at the greengrocer by the wool shop and see if you can get him a banana. They don't always have them but there's nowhere else in town to try. Failing that, a nice sleepy pear. Give him a reward for having been so well behaved.'

'Huh, you haven't seen our car. There's a whacking great dollop of, er, monkey business on the back seat. Good thing it belongs to the RAF.' They left, Ponsonby giving the two girls a sorrowful parting look over the airman's shoulder. Shortly afterwards their blue Vanguard with service number plates scrunched away, a childlike face framed in its small rear window.

'Come on, Rilly, we're off,' said Jo. 'There's a place down the road where we can get a bite to eat.'

'Not too dear, I hope. The rent eats up so much and petrol's a terrible price. Imagine – five bob a gallon for us wretched civilians. Five *shillings*. No wonder the farmers round here get caught black-marketing their dyed stuff.'

'It's on me,' Jo said. 'You've come all this way and I'm in gainful employ these days. Is that your car?' she asked as they left and crossed the drive past a small Morris van with wire screens inside the windows in its rear doors.

'Heavens no – I can't afford to run a car. It's Jim's, my brother's. He got it in an auction. It used to belong to the GPO and it's got all these steel bins in the back for tools and spares for mending phone lines. I just borrow it sometimes. I only hope I can get back without a blowout. The tyres are completely bald.'

'The ones on Amos's aren't much better,' said Jo. They walked up Mossop High Street to the Pretty Polly Restaurant and Tea Room which had a green-edged Luncheon Voucher sticker in its steamy window. The room was quite full but they managed to find a table to themselves beneath a large framed oil painting of a multicoloured parrot perched amid riotous jungle leafage. It looked exactly like what it was: a picture commissioned from the restaurant owner's eighteen-year-old niece who was hoping to go to art school in Lincoln. The table was covered in oilcloth with a chintz pattern of bloodshot roses on which stood a cruet and a clot-necked bottle of HP sauce. A waitress brought them two handwritten menus.

'You see?' said Jo. 'That's not too bad, is it? Set lunch for one-and-eleven. That won't break the bank. Shepherd's pie and two veg followed by rhubarb tart and custard and, if we really push the boat out, we have the choice of Vimto, limeade or Kitty Cola. Or just a cuppa.'

'I think I'll settle for tea with mine.'

The two friends sat catching up with each other's news until the waitress reappeared with their lunch, which they attacked ravenously.

'Rather more mashed spuds than mince,' Jo admitted, plying the sauce bottle.

'It's not bad. Funny about the peas. I mean, here we are in an area that produces most of Britain's peas, so you'd expect them to be fresh, wouldn't you? But these things are dried. You can tell because they go all floury when they're cooked. Still, I suppose it is November. Even so, you'd have thought they'd have used tinned ones. You can get those in the Co-op for sevenpence.'

Aware that her friend was wittering, Jo said, 'Aha, something's happened, hasn't it, since we last saw each other.' She eyed her companion shrewdly. 'Don't tell me there's a bloke.'

Avril took a last mouthful blushingly. 'I don't know,' she admitted. 'Well yes, I have met someone. Clever you. But I've no idea if he's, you know, long term. He's got a mobile shop. I mean he owns it and drives it and everything.'

'He's forty-five and has three families scattered about the county.'

'Nothing of the kind,' retorted Avril indignantly. 'He's not yet thirty and he's unmarried and very nice-looking. He's sad, too, because he has to work so hard and drive long distances and work long hours so he hasn't had time to settle down and start a family. He knows all the farmers for miles around and buys stuff directly from them: parsnips, cabbages, carrots, potatoes, eggs, butter, even chickens, but of course those are pretty expensive. Obviously his prices have to take in his running costs in diesel and road tax and everything. But it's a real service because round us the buses aren't great and people live stuck out in the Fens and of course hardly anyone has a car. And if you're elderly or you've got small kids like mine it's quite a palaver going out shopping, it takes up so much time. If you're on your own you can nip in and out of the shops and do it all in half an hour, but not with kids. So Ted's a godsend as far as I'm concerned. He turns up at the door and he's got all sorts of stuff. He can even get bags of slack so I can make my own briquette things for the fire. Dad's been showing me how they did it in the war. You mix the coal dust with cement and water and pack it into those really small flowerpots and when it's hard you've got little flowerpot-shaped coal lumps. It's ever so much cheaper than buying proper coal eggs. As I say, old Ted's got pretty much everything I need.'

Jo dropped her voice still further. 'Including that?'

'Does a girl tell tales out of school?'

'She does if she wants her friend to pay for her lunch.'

'Well, I must admit he has occasionally parked his van outside the house overnight.'

'Ooh Rilly,' said Jo. 'You lucky thing. But . . .'

'No buts,' said her friend firmly. 'I know Marty would understand. It's nearly a year now since he went and, well, he's dead and I go on being alive and I don't know about you but I'm not cut out to be a nun. Also, I think children need a father, or at least a solid male presence in their lives even if he isn't their biological father. They're both still too young to remember much about Marty, anyway. It's a long time since I last heard Petey mention Daddy. It's awful, isn't it? The way things have of being heartless, even though it's nobody's fault? But please, Jo, don't mention Ted to a soul. Promise? I'm scared stiff that if the RAF hears about him they'll assume I've remarried and stop my piddling widow's pension. They would, too. They're quite mean enough to.'

After the first, any subsequent cups of tea came free so they both had refills while tackling the rhubarb tart, which had arrived tucked warmly beneath a quilt of brilliant yellow custard.

'It's like NAAFI custard,' said Avril reminiscently. They both laughed. 'But it's terrific you've got this job, Jo. It must suit you – you're looking heaps better than when I last saw you. And how's the new house? And, dare I ask, the old husband?'

'The house is OK. And Vulcan the rabbit's really good. Having a bunny hopping around the place makes it feel more like home even though I'm still finding leftovers from previous tenants, funny things. In the cupboard under the stairs, right at the back, there was a collection of dozens of empty brass cartridge cases, all different sizes. I mean, who would want those? I got Amos to give them to whoever collects up scrap metal on the station. And on top of the cupboard in the spare bedroom were boxes and boxes of those long wooden spill things men use for lighting pipes. Thousands of them, all dyed red. Who on earth would ever need so many? And given that they did, why would they leave them behind?'

'And Amos?'

Jo stirred her tea in a moment's silence before replying. 'He comes and goes, doesn't he? Mostly goes, these days. He comes home at night, pretty exhausted, and that's about all we see of each other. We're both out during the day. Ever since he got this special flight I told you about they're always off doing low-flying exercises. That's all he'll tell me but I don't suppose there is any more to know. It strikes me as pretty dreary, but there we are: he's only really happy in the air with his crew, all boys together doing their duty.'

Avril looked at her friend intently. 'You're sounding a bit different these days. You never used to say things like that. You're beginning not to sound like a service wife.'

'It must be this job,' said Jo. 'Thanks to Kay Hendry next door I've now got my own life and I'm doing something I like as much as Amos likes flying. I'm even thinking of studying to be a vet myself. Craig and Arthur say they'll help me and when I'm qualified they might even make me a partner.'

'That's wonderful, Jo. But suppose Amos gets posted? He's bound to, sooner or later. Either the squadron will move or he'll be promoted to wing commander and sent off elsewhere. If you're lucky it might be somewhere nice and tropical. But it's much more likely to be Germany or some godforsaken station in Scotland. Or if he's really unlucky the Staff College at Bracknell.'

'Exactly. And I shan't be going with him.'

Avril reached a hand across and laid it on the back of her friend's. 'Quite right,' she murmured. 'There comes a point. Good for you, Jo.'

12

It's *taking stock*, Amos thought as he jogged along: that's what the air force made so difficult. You were so seldom off duty or not surrounded by people or not working in the Vault mugging up targets. These days, come to that, you were spending a lot of time in the air doing low-level sorties over the Lake District or elsewhere in the British Isles. Hi-lo-hi was what everyone else was doing, plus endless rehearsals of the LABS manoeuvre: the low altitude bombing system whereby you flew in low, reared up to toss Blue Steel and carried on up with a half loop and roll-out at the top and away back the way you came but higher. Sooner or later both squadrons would be rotated out to Idris to practise LABS with inert bombs on the Tarhuna range in the Libyan desert.

Yet he and Meeres, supposedly having been earmarked for something special, were still waiting with the top-secret Oilcan radar system and the new laser bomb sight already fitted to both Vulcans and so far untested. Far from being sent off on spine-tingling missions, the two crews had spent most of their time either doing low-level sorties or else stuck on the ground expecting something to happen. The whole thing was actually very RAF. While they were waiting Amos and Terry had got a talented airman to dream up an appropriate device for their two aircraft. He had painted a perfect little Yogi Bear on the grey camouflage stripe just behind the roundel on the starboard side of the Vulcans' noses. Underneath each ran the motto: *Smarter than the average bear*. Besides being a near-universal catchphrase on the station at the time, this was felt by the two crews to express quite neatly their own distinction. Their colleagues were predictably disparaging and had already taken to referring to them as 'Boo-Boo 1' and 'Boo-Boo 2'.

Amos, wearing a tattered track suit and plimsolls, was now jogging along the Wearsby perimeter track on an early December afternoon, glad to be off on his own and heading towards his favourite haunt, the fire dump. It was only mid-afternoon but already the light was starting to go: a reminder that the winter solstice, the year's bottom dead centre, was only about three weeks away. The ambient light had begun to acquire a borderline quality: that moment when runway lights actually define a landing strip rather than being mere bright lamps dotted on either side of it. The red light atop the control tower also seemed to glow with a fraction more intensity as if someone had pushed a rheostat up a notch. The black gantry of the old water tower off to his right was stark against the sky and also carried a warning light. In the distance behind him came the sudden rising howl of a jet engine. It lasted a few seconds then died, almost immediately being repeated. Amos recognised it as a technician doing 'slam checks' on a Vulcan's engines on one of the dispersal pans, slamming the throttle fully open from idle to see how long it took the engine to spool up to full power: four seconds if everything was normal. Out of that sound a heavier drumming emerged and he turned to see a Transport Command Hastings on its run-out a hundred yards away behind him, landing lights glaring. As he watched, jogging backwards, the propellers of the two port engines blurred to grey before the bellow of the Hercules radials reached him, their gruff tone first acquiring a whine and then the whirring sound of the props themselves as the aircraft turned right off the second runway exit and trundled away from him. Amos turned back to his run.

Soon he reached the belt of trees. Behind it the fire dump's gates were open as usual and the great heaps of ruined airframes welcomed him with their desolate familiarity. He noticed that since his last visit the Coles crane had moved. This afternoon its jib hung, black and menacing against the grey overcast, above some evidently fresh remains. These were so battered it was hard to see what they might have been, but gradually Amos deduced they must be those of the Folland Gnat that had crashed a week previously a couple of miles away. The news had gone rapidly around the station, as such news always did, was laconically accepted and then forgotten. Some poor sod *but not me*. From uncorroborated word-of-mouth it was said that the Accidents Investigation Branch had determined the Gnat had been travelling at some 350 knots when its cockpit canopy had suddenly fractured and flown off, decapitating the pilot on its way. It would have happened in a split second without warning. Thereupon the aircraft had been seen to glide over Market Tewsbury in a mysterious near-silence, seemingly under control but rapidly losing altitude before stalling and flipping upside down into pasture near Burberton, missing a prize herd of Guernseys by thirty yards. The throttle lever was nearly closed, so maybe a final spasm had jerked the pilot's hand back. And here his silver coffin lay, scored and dented and with both intakes full of dried turf. He was an instructor aged thirty-three and they were still scouring the local countryside for his head.

Compulsively, Amos reached out and laid his hand on the Gnat's remains in a gesture he could not have characterised had he been asked. Sympathy? Solidarity? There but for the grace of God? He wondered why the late instructor had taken up flying in the first place. He must have joined the RAF after the war and would have qualified on Meteors and Vampires in the early days of the jet age. He'd done well to survive this long. There was no end to the things that could go wrong and kill you, especially in those days. You could faithfully run down every pre-flight checklist you wanted, you could get Pilot's Notes for the aircraft off by heart, you could do everything by the book, the Angel Gabriel himself could appear on the apron as you climbed into the cockpit to tell you the aircraft was in tip-top condition. And then twenty minutes later as you were breezing along with all gauges normal, wondering whether you'd be back in time to change and get to the garage to pick up the Riley after its decoke, the canopy shatters and in an instant the Riley and your whole universe vanish, dead circuitry tumbling in a helmet that somewhere falls to earth.

Mind you, Amos thought, there's an awful lot more to go wrong in a Vulcan than there is in a little Gnat. The electrical circuits alone are awesomely complex. On the other hand you've got so much more backup. The Gnat has a single engine. All you need is a flame-out or a bird strike on take-off and wham! you're probably dead. But a Vulcan has four engines and if one fails on take-off there's still more than enough power to get you round and safely back to earth. And you've always got that enormous wing on your side: lovely low wing-loading compared with the Gnat's.

Yet skinny swept-back wings undoubtedly held a magic. Like every boy who joined the RAF Amos had wanted to be a fast jet pilot. His adolescence had been filled with the post-war mystique of the sound barrier: that numinous, invisible frontier in the sky beyond which lay an unknown world in which it was said the very laws of physics broke down and no human could survive. Like any other science-minded adolescent he recognised this as journalistic piffle, if for no better reason than because it was perfectly well known that men had been flying faster than sound ever since 1947 and soon afterwards were doing it as a matter of routine. He remembered the first time he had gone supersonic when pulling a shallow dive in a Hunter. It had been over the sea off Selsey Bill and to be honest he'd kept his eyes glued as much to the altimeter as to the Machmeter because flying *into* the sea at low altitude was quite easily done in a moment's inattention at 660 knots. Of course it had been a thrill; of course there had been the sense of having joined an exclusive club; of course there was filmic romance in the knightly accoutrements of protective suit and helmet and dangling harness as one posed casually beside one's beautiful hi-tech steed.

Why then had he later opted for bombers? It seemed to have happened almost by chance: an opportunity to learn to fly a different kind of aircraft with multiple engines that involved sorties measured in hours instead of minutes. Amos turned his attention back to the Gnat on which his hand was still resting. He noticed that although what remained of the aircraft was battered almost beyond recognition, the landing light in the nose was freakishly intact behind the mud on its unbroken transparent dome. How did these things happen? He remembered doing a Blue Ranger to Edinburgh, South Australia and then flying up to Woomera in an RAAF Canberra. A lorry crew there had just retrieved the remains of one of Britain's Black Knight rockets being developed to launch satellites. It had fallen from the edge of space and had crashed a hundred miles down-range and here it was, a tangled heap of scrap metal and tubing. But when he looked at it more closely he could see that small sections here and there were completely intact: boxes of relays still with the assembler's crayon mark on the paintwork of their lids, looking like new; some perfect pipework neatly clamped to a bulkhead, the nuts still tight and sealed with a dab of paint. Amos had been unable to suppress the stupid thought: If I had been that relay box I could have fallen fifty miles from space to the desert floor and would still be in one piece. You just needed to know which piece to be in order to survive . . . It was a child's fantasy, like the one he could still remember having had when he was ten or so, imagining he was falling in a lift whose cable had broken. If he could gauge the instant before it crashed to the bottom of the shaft he could give a little jump off the floor and would survive while everybody else died.

And so one jogged to these secret elephants' graveyards at dawn or dusk and tried to take stock. Even so, Amos considered, I'm less bothered by the prospect of dying than I'm interested in what it is I really want. The awful truth is, I'm not very ambitious. I've made squadron leader by my mid-twenties and I'm the captain of a V-bomber. I'm not sure I want anything more. I don't want to end up like Muffin Mewell, a group captain with fearsome responsibilities. The high burn-out rate among senior ranks is no secret. In fact, I don't want responsibilities at all if they're all administration and no flying.

And suddenly as if from nowhere a strange thought came to him: Maybe after all the RAF wasn't my true ambition. Perhaps being a pilot is less my career than my way of being alone. Is that what came of reading Saint-Exupéry as a boy? Surely not the fascist-aviator so much as the seeker after majestic simplicity, the cockpit as monk's cell from which the view in every direction is implacable splendour behind which, like Lake District clouds stuffed with peaks, lurks one's own annihilation. Alone in that seat one could finally leave behind the wealthy and indifferent father, soar above the pompous and fatuous schools, transcend the timid former self. For wasn't the life of a pilot monkish in its way, with peculiar laws and disciplines to be learned by heart and practised until instinctive? He had heard there was a religious order who believed that so long as there remained a single person somewhere praying for the world, the Devil could not take it over and the final victory of Evil could be staved off. So what else was deterrence about, with devout aircrews on guard at all times? Like a monk one could be called from one's bed at 4 a.m. and be expected to go clear-headedly straight into the proper devotions. And eleven hundred miles east on the airfield outside Starobin, today's target, equivalent Russian monks would be getting up equally clearheadedly to man the MiGs and Sukhois protecting the Minsk-A sector.

In one respect, though, Amos felt anything but monkish. Having recently managed what the newspapers delicately called 'conjugal relations' with Jo, he was left with the guilty memory, impossible to suppress, of the image that had made it possible: Gavin Rickards in swimming trunks, standing in a blaze of sunlight on a rock in Cyprus three months ago, pensively watching the sea as it chirruped and glooped in the holes beneath his feet. Amos thought he had never seen anything quite as beautiful, even at school, and there seemed to be little further point in—

'Help you?' broke in a sudden gruff voice from behind. Amos jumped and hurriedly removed his hand from the Gnat's wreckage, turning in the same movement. He found a large, belligerent-looking corporal armed with a heavy torch.

'Er, no thanks, Corporal,' Amos said. 'I was just out for a bit of a run. Got to keep fit, really. I'm Squadron Leader McKenna.'

The corporal relaxed visibly, looking abashed. 'Oh, sorry, sir, I recognise you now. Excuse me, sir, we don't get many officers down here. Well, never, as a matter of fact. Watched you last Saturday, sir, putting Waddo in their place. Brilliant, that was. And Flight Lieutenant Pilcher. Best scrum-half we've ever had if you ask me. Seventeen–nine: a bloody walkover that was, and Pilcher going over two minutes before time just to rub it in. Sold their man a beautiful dummy, put it across him properly, that did. I bet Waddo are having a rethink now. Get rid of half their pack, I would. They just don't have our fitness, do they, sir?'

Still embarrassed at having been discovered deep in a reverie in the station's fire dump, Amos pulled himself together to meet this unexpected fan's enthusiasm. 'It wasn't a bad match but it certainly didn't feel like a walkover at the time. Once or twice they came damned close to seeing us off. That winger of theirs, Anderson, you've got to keep him marked every second of the game. That run of his in the first half from their twenty-five could have been fatal had Burdett not stopped him in time with only five yards to go. We were lucky. Anderson was the fastest man on the pitch, and you can't get away from that. You just have to recognise how dangerous he is. Do you play yourself, Corporal?'

'Used to, sir, up in Huddersfield. League, that was, not Union.'

'Ah, rough game, but good and fast. I sometimes think it makes a better spectator sport. But I mustn't stand gossiping. Do you have the time on you? I've come out without my watch.'

'Yes, sir, four-twenty sir.'

'I'd better be going then. When do you knock off – five?'

Amos took his leave with a genial wave his fan returned with an awkward gesture of his own that acknowledged the gap in rank between them but also the fact that since Amos was not in uniform he didn't have to salute him. Amos, who suddenly realised he was chilled after standing still for so long, began jogging back along the perimeter track. A good many lights had become more visible in the last half-hour, among them the red and green navigation lights of aircraft preparing to depart or being towed to a hangar. That made him think of the defective sidelight on his own Hillman Minx, and by extension to wonder what time Jo would be back in it. She had rather commandeered the thing these days. Still, if that was the price for keeping her happy and busy it was something he could live with.

Further speculation was blotted out by the crescendo of noise as a Vulcan passed him on the runway, nose just lifting, nav lights tilting as it eased into the air and bored upwards, Olympus engines blasting massive thunder over Lincolnshire. Just able to make out the serial number on the fin, Amos wondered where Spadge Eckersley was off to and his heart suddenly lifted with the vanishing aircraft. The job was going on and it simply outweighed everything else. It was not the solemn vow he had sworn that would keep him loyal to it, but an unvoiced allegiance he felt to the very ground his feet were pounding.

13

Even though the new equipment now fitted to Yogis 1 and 2 had yet to be tested, its top secret status meant that the aircraft had been physically sequestered from the rest of the station's Vulcans. Since they were no longer required to be on QRA readiness both aircraft were parked on the acre or so of hard standing beside 'C' hangar, out of the way of the two squadrons' day-to-day movements. An order had gone out that they were to be guarded at all times. Surveillance was made somewhat easier since they were never in total darkness at night: the lamps that lit the apron in front of the hangar were bright enough to spill some light around the side. A similar guard had now been doubled at one of the munitions dumps over on the far side of the airfield where a dozen inert practice bombs fitted with the prototype laser-guidance nose cones had recently been delivered.

To the station's contingent of RAF Police who did such guarding there was nothing new about any of this. Things requiring even more careful watchkeeping than usual came and went. The Thor missiles that had once ringed the base had now been returned to America, their place taken by home-grown Bloodhound SAMs. There were still American officers at Wearsby who were required for the dual-key system mandated by the use of US nuclear warheads in British weapons, but such atomic devices were kept in a bunker separate from that of conventional munitions. From the point of view of the Snowdrops detailed off for long spells of guard duty there was little difference between securing a bomb dump and standing by two Vulcans. The more conscientious ones spent the time patrolling from one aircraft to another, or maybe sheltering from the weather beneath one while keeping a desultory eye on its neighbour.

Corporal Brian 'Spikey' Caltrop was not one of the more conscientious ones. Personally, he couldn't see the point in mounting a separate guard on two aircraft on an already well-guarded and security-conscious airfield, but there you were. You stood around at all hours of day or night, basically waiting until a Land Rover turned up with your relief. Some other poor sod from 'B' shift would climb out with his dog and you would take his place for a trip back to warmth via the kennels. These days poor old Air Dog Bonzo was getting stiff with either age or cold and had recently begun scrabbling and whining a bit when getting into the Land Rover with the tailgate down. This worried Spikey because old Bonze was dear to his heart: they had been together for some time now and these early signs that the dog might have to be pensioned off sooner rather than later were disquieting. Lovely dogs, Alsatians, but sooner or later the back legs went. Like my own if this goes on, Spikey thought bitterly, stamping his boots to get the blood flowing.

He was now only ninety minutes into the shift he had pulled but already the damp cold of a December evening in Fenland had seeped into his feet and bones. He had heard that a Vulcan's wing had the aerodynamic effect of creating a slight breeze beneath it when the aircraft was parked, and he could well believe it. A series of head colds was to him irrefutable evidence that his regulation white-topped cap was quite inadequate protection against the weather. As a special dispensation he was allowed to wear a greatcoat over his blue uniform so long as he wore the 'Mars bar' armband on his left sleeve. Underneath he wore the white webbing belt with the holstered thirty-eight revolver which, in his humble opinion, was bloody stupid. Having to unbutton your greatcoat first hardly made for a quick draw. Not that he'd ever once had to draw his gun on duty other than at the range, unfortunately. Frankly, the prospect of having to shoot someone was by no means unwelcome. In any case he thought it was time they issued the new 9mm Browning Hi-Power automatics. Now *that* was a weapon that could knock the stuffing out of your average CND protester or Communist intruder.

Such thoughts, familiar as they were, lulled Corporal Caltrop's vigil. Against all regulations he was sitting on Yogi 2's starboard landing gear with one leg between the tyre and Bonzo. He could feel the leaning dog's warmth through the wool of his trousers. Truth be told, they had both fallen into a doze that was closer to suspended animation. Even the scream of a power tool and clatter of dropped equipment coming from the nearby hangar failed to keep them alert, while the occasional din of aircraft coming and going was so commonplace as to make no impression. In Spikey's case a booze-up the previous evening had resulted in one of those nights when he found it almost impossible to sleep properly. The hangover had passed but left him feeling underslept and internally delicate. Hunched against the cold and with his back against the leg of the landing gear, he had been staring off towards the lights of the ops block, the officers' mess and Wearsby's various admin buildings, all of which, he knew, were warm and well supplied with hot beverages. In this mesmeric trance he might even have nodded off for a moment because a particularly loud noise in the hangar fifty yards away brought him back to life. He yawned and glanced at his watch. Jesus Christ, he thought: over another frigging hour to go.

He eased himself to the ground and gave a gentle tug on the thick leather leash. Bonzo gave a sigh and got stiffly to his feet. Man and dog stretched and began ambling across to Yogi 1, their breath grey in the night air. The two Vulcans were parked with thirty-odd feet of space between their wing tips. Spikey Caltrop was halfway over before he took in that the aircraft's hatch was open and the access ladder down. That was wrong. Odder still, there seemed to be no light on inside, although it was hard to be certain because the slight spillage of light from the front of the hangars reflected off the cockpit glass. Yet no sooner had he registered this than there came a series of flashes from inside that were visible in the canopy's porthole window and the open hatchway. His first thought was of an electrical circuit shorting. Now very much awake, the corporal unbuttoned his greatcoat and also the flap of his canvas holster. Something about his level of alertness must have communicated itself to Bonzo because the dog gave a low growl that Spikey silenced with a quiet 'Zt!' Drawing his revolver – at last! – he took up a position to one side of the ladder and called up with his best sentry's rasp: 'Who goes there? Identify yourself!'

From inside a voice said crossly, 'It's all right. It's only me.'

'Who's "me"?'

'Ernie Hodge, you arsehole. Who did you think it was – fucking Santa Claus?'

A bulky shape intermittently lit by the torch it carried appeared at the head of the ladder and began descending. On reaching the ground Baldy flashed the light briefly across the corporal's face. 'Oh, it's you, Spikey,' he said. 'Nearly gave me a bleeding heart attack.' He pushed the ladder up until it clicked, then swung himself agilely up onto a nosewheel and pushed the yellow button in the underside of the fuselage. Irrelevantly, Caltrop noticed a small loop

149

of slender brown cable sticking up from the side pocket of the pad-
ded jacket the crew chief was wearing. Overhead the access hatch
closed with a sigh. One-handedly, Baldy felt for a key, found the
lock and turned it before hopping back down. Close up, the corporal could feel the man's intimidating animal strength. 'Now that's
security,' said Hodge. 'You see this horribly expensive example of
state-of-the-art Cold War weaponry?' He flashed his torch at the
expanse of the Vulcan's underside before shining the light on the
key he was holding. 'And do you realise what sort of lock they put
on it to stop people stealing it? A bleeding Morris Minor car lock,
that's what. Any average burglar could open it with a bent wire in
five seconds. So it's a good job we've got blokes like you standing
guard, Spikey. Not that I saw you when I arrived. Intuition tells
me you were dozing off under the other one over there, or am I
wrong?'

'I was over there but I certainly wasn't dozing,' said Caltrop
hotly, aware that this was turning out to be an episode he would
probably not include in his duty report later. 'But who would have
guessed you or anyone else would come creeping around here at all
hours? You want to watch it, Hodge: it looks suspicious, not even
turning the lights on. Might have got yourself shot.'

'Hardly "creeping" to drive up and park in front of the hangar in
plain view. I walked over, opened the aircraft and went in without
so much as a challenge from you and Lassie there. I didn't turn the
lights on because I didn't need to: I only nipped in to collect the
fuelling forms I'd forgotten.' Hodge half withdrew some folded papers from a pocket. 'Right? In and out in two minutes. As it is I
shall probably be on the mat for being late with the bumf so I'd
be obliged to you, young Spikey, if you'd do me the favour of forgetting I was ever here. In return I shall do the same about your
serious dereliction of duty, which I fear under Queen's Regulations

150

would carry the death penalty for both you and Rin Tin Tin if I reported it.'

'Yes, very funny.' The corporal holstered his gun and rebuttoned his greatcoat. 'Come on, Bonzo,' he said to his dog. 'We've probably caught a saboteur red-handed but we've got to pretend it doesn't matter.'

'Hardly in my own best interests to sabotage an aircraft I shall be flying in,' retorted Baldy, walking away toward the front of the hangar where Caltrop now saw a car was parked, its paintwork misted with dew and without colour beneath the glare of the overhead lighting.

For the next forty minutes until at last the RAF Police Land Rover came to relieve him, Spikey Caltrop pondered the episode. He thought again of the odd flashes he'd seen. Had they simply been the random gleams of a torch? He supposed so. All the same, how did a man like Baldy Hodge – renowned all over the station as a stickler for doing things by the book – not only forget some refuelling documents but come back for them at a time when he ought to have his feet up by the fire at home or be feeding his face with toad-in-the-hole in the sergeants' mess? Another twelve hours weren't going to make any difference. Nobody would be checking the paperwork of fuel loads in the crew chiefs' office tonight. Oh well, he thought: just one of those minor mysteries. At this point the headlights of the Land Rover speeding towards him put everything out of his mind other than the thought of a bite to eat and getting warm again. He removed one of his white gloves, reached down and fondled the dog's ear. 'We're in luck, Bonzo,' he said. 'It's the relief of Mafeking.' The reliever was Pogo Willis, who jumped out looking to Spikey's jaundiced eye like someone with a hot meal and several tots of the right stuff inside him.

'All quiet on the Western front?' asked Willis as his own dog, a fierce animal named Mixer, bounced from the back of the vehicle.

'Dead quiet. And dead cold. You're welcome to it.' He bent to boost Bonzo up into the back. The animal's coat was soaked with dew. 'Come on, old sport. Let's get you in and dried off.'

14

Suddenly the two converted Vulcans were scheduled for some bombing practice using the new guidance system. The nav radars, Vic Ferrit and Julian Caddy, had been well briefed and had already spent considerable time using a simulator that introduced them to this very different method of bombing. Meanwhile, more of the bombs had been delivered to Wearsby. Their steel casings were painted white. Aerodynamically, they were identical with normal 750lb bombs except that their fins had been enlarged into vanes big enough to guide the bombs once they had picked up their target. For practice purposes they were, of course, inert, being filled with nothing more dangerous than concrete. However, their snout-like nose cones were discreetly shrouded from prying eyes with sheaths made from orange canvas which the armourers were already calling 'bomb johnnies'.

The sortie called for each aircraft to drop six bombs from varying heights at low speed. Their objective was a squat concrete tower out on the Donna Nook bombing ranges. This was an area of gloomy tidal flats at the mouth of the Humber where V-force aircraft quite often practised. This tower, known to all as The Bosun, was no bigger than the base of a lighthouse and just as massively constructed. As much an aiming mark as an actual target, it had been built in the early 1950s when its flat top had been painted with a chequerboard of black and white squares. It would be nice to record that this design had long since been obliterated by the impacts of practice bombs, but the truth was that The Bosun had very seldom been hit. The sands around to a radius of half a mile concealed thousands of tons of ordnance while the erosion of The Bosun's paintwork was more down to salt and seagulls' excrement than it was to any accuracy on Bomber Command's part.

Even while the two Vulcans were being bombed-up one of the limitations of this newfangled laser-guidance system became obvious. Met reports were indicating a layer of cloud at three thousand feet drifting in towards the target area from the Pennines. It would probably reach Donna Nook in about three hours' time. The general consensus was that since it was impossible to use any visual bombing system through cloud, if ever this new gadget was to impress anyone it was going to have to do so by being amazingly more accurate than the existing technique.

As the armourers' tractors pulled away the bomb trolleys, now empty except for a heap of canvas nose-covers, the final decision to go was hurriedly taken. Amos and Meeres taxied their aircraft out, turned into the light prevailing wind and took off with a rolling start one after the other. Since Donna Nook was only about forty miles distant neither Vulcan climbed higher than a couple of thousand feet, turning eastwards out over the sea and following the coast up. Within minutes their objective was in sight. The sky was still clear at their level: scattered cloud began at about five thousand feet. Gavin Rickards had already contacted the ranges and had confirmed that the observers were in place and ready.

'You on the ball, Vic?' Amos asked over the intercom. 'We'll do one dry pass to get your eye in.'

'Ready, Boss.' Vic was intent on the newly installed circular screen that showed a remarkably detailed view of the terrain over which they were passing.

'Two thousand,' said Baa Mutton next to him.

'Roger.' Vic saw The Bosun's image drift down from the top of the screen, sinking across its graticule. His right hand was on a new little joystick with a thumb switch. He moved this until the target was centred in the grid and pressed the button. The laser marker under the aircraft's nose sent a stream of coded millisecond laser pulses that struck The Bosun and were reflected, being instantly picked up again and appearing in the centre of Vic's screen as the target. There it stayed, the picture electronically frozen even as the bomber passed overhead, until the increased deflection became too much and the view reverted abruptly to that of normal terrain.

'OK, Boss, it's just like in the sim,' said Vic. 'Let's do a live one.'

Amos banked Yogi 1. The bomb doors opened, half retracting into the sides of the bomb bay: a neat piece of design to lessen their drag. XM580 straightened up and once more made a run across The Bosun. This time the aircraft gave a slight lurch as Vic released one of the bombs.

'Bomb gone, Skip.' Below them and behind, the electronics in the nose of the bomb picked up the sparkle of the laser impulses Vic was sending being returned by the target. Little electric motors moved the vanes, guiding the falling ordnance. There was a small pause. Then –

'It's a hit!' Rickards relayed. 'Bloke says we've knocked a corner off.'

'Blimey, that's a first for any new piece of equipment I've ever known,' Amos observed to Keith Coswood beside him.

'Bet we can't do it again.'

'Cat in hell's chance. We'll probably hit Grimsby.'

'Don't. Just *think* of the paperwork.'

Yogi 1 came around over the sea as Terry Meeres made his run in the second Vulcan. His bomb was ten yards shy. This was very accurate by usual standards but thirty feet could make all the difference if one were trying to take out a really difficult target such as a railway bridge. Those were practically immune to anything other than a direct hit. Amos's next run was a thousand feet higher and slower at 240 knots. 'Those clouds are going to scupper us,' he said, pointing as he lined up. 'We're not going to get any higher today.' Once again the Vulcan gave its little lurch as Vic toggled another bomb. This, too, was called as having shattered against The Bosun. There were cheers from the compartment behind.

'Well, dang me: the bloody thing seems to work,' said Keith. 'I can't wait for the next bomb comp. It should give the Yanks something to chew on.'

'Oh, they've probably got something just like it, except it can brew them a hot drink at the same time.'

'We'll still give 'em a run for their money. *And* do it on NATO standard coffee.'

After dropping all their bombs the two Vulcans headed for home. The first squall had hit and tiny meniscuses of water pooled, quivering, at the corners of their windscreens. Once the crews had been debriefed it was clear this first trial had been a great success. After receiving seven direct hits and one low ricochet The Bosun was reportedly looking scarred, mottled with the fresh marks of today's damage. Had the bombs contained high explosive much of it would have been demolished.

'But we keep quiet about it,' said Group Captain Mewell at the end. 'No need to go telling your mates in the squadron.'

His caution was scarcely necessary. By the time the crews had changed and filled out all the necessary paperwork the episode was already beginning to blend into the mounting tally of all the sorties they'd ever flown. The bread-and-butter routine of Cold War flying was as always followed by hours of filling out forms and reports and writing up log books, and with the certainty of doing it all over again tomorrow.

15

At Lindsey Air Station in Wiesbaden, which hosted the headquarters of the USAF in Europe, Lieutenant General Gus Moon closed his office door before unlocking the pouch that had arrived on the overnight flight from Washington DC. Standing, he riffled idly through the contents while trying to dislodge a stubborn fragment of breakfast bacon from between two molars with his tongue. Boring ... boring ... semi-boring ... aha! A document with the Defense Intelligence Agency's blue seal caught his eye. He picked it up and sat down at his desk. Its Top Secret heading was followed by the code word CORAM, meaning information that must on no account be seen by a NATO ally. That was fine by him. Had it been left to Gus Moon he would have shared as little as possible with most of them.

He noted that the original document had been forwarded from Headquarters Command, USAF, where it had been copied to just two other names besides his own. Both were high-ranking colleagues and one, General Hubert T. Buchinger, was a personal friend. Moon read on:

DIA agents in the United Kingdom report RAF Bomber Command may be in possession of (i) a new radar system, and (ii) a new bomb guidance system. Both are subject to UK level 3 security and probably of near-deployment status. If true, this suggests development has taken place unilaterally, care having been taken expressly to shield these projects from US eyes. The Director suggests discreet, repeat discreet, enquiries be made of Strategic Air Command base commanders at both RAF Mildenhall in England and Offutt, Nebraska to ascertain whether any information about the existence of these alleged new systems has yet been divulged by their British counterparts. An affirmative answer would also confirm the reliability of DIA sources.

The Agency notes there were rumors within SAC after Exercise Skyshield II in 1961 that the success of the RAF's Vulcan contingent was due to their employing a radar technique or ECM advantage to which SAC was not made privy. This has since been discounted as a face-saving device on the part of NORAD. In our opinion these latest intelligence reports may simply be a 'Chinese whispers' resurgence of this old rumor. It may now have been embellished to include an alleged new British bomb guidance system that could rival or even exceed our own Paveways that are nearly ready for deployment.

All the same, in view of these reports and the great urgency of deploying the best available battlefield technology in South East Asia, the Agency respectfully suggests the Air Force take steps to ascertain the reports' validity. This might conceivably be achieved by means of joint USAF/RAF exercises.

'Well, well,' said Gus Moon as he laid the document down. The DIA quite often got its facts right. The idea that the British might be pulling a shitty surprised him, but not very much. In his career he had made good friends with several RAF types, some of whom were now high-ranking officers. There might well be matters of

159

national pride at stake here. Britain's V-bomber force was a perfect example of the store the Limeys set by doing things their own way with their own equipment. Moon didn't doubt that if they really were working on something new they would share it with the USAF as soon as it was ready.

At this moment his aide, Captain Polick, came in to give him the good news that his meeting at 11:00 with the French general had been cancelled on account of the general's ill-health.

'Great,' said Moon. 'With any luck he won't recover and I shall never again have to listen to him passing on complaints from that pain-in-the-ass de Gaulle. The Frogs are going to pull out of NATO anyway, and the sooner the better.'

The last time they met, the French general had had the nerve to wag a warning finger about Dien Bien Phu and what he called 'Indochine' generally. 'You watch out,' he'd said. 'That General Giap's a military genius.' Moon had been hard put not to retort that the yellow fellow might well be a genius, but he'd been facing the fucking French Foreign Legion, or whatever it was, and not the combined military might of the United States. A very different ball game, monsieur.

It was no secret that his assignment to USAFE was getting Moon down. Despite not having flown an aircraft in eleven years he still thought of himself as basically a stick-and-rudder man. Yet this command required him to be more of a diplomat than anything else, and it severely tested him almost daily. There were times when NATO seemed less a partnership of allies and more a rabble of warring tribes. Despite the imminent threat of mutually assured destruction in the northern hemisphere and an increasingly bloody communist insurgency in Southeast Asia, some of America's so-called allies seemed to be more focused on endless squabbling, especially about their equipment. Tomorrow, for instance, he would be having yet another meeting with the Germans about their F-104 Starfighters. The aircraft had already earned itself the newspaper nickname of 'Widowmaker'; but whose fault was that, given how much extra avionics gear the Krauts had insisted on stuffing into them? No surprise the damn things were overweight and fell out of the sky. In that case the Dutch would soon come calling to complain that their own F-104s were inferior because their avionics weren't as advanced as the Germans'. And finally the Italians would bellyache that they'd heard the Dutch aircraft were getting an upgrade that would leave the Italians' own Starfighters as the weak link in the southern chain. The widespread rumors that Lockheed had only been able to sell the aircraft by means of widespread bribery didn't help, either.

Still worrying at his shred of bacon, Gus Moon sighed and reached for a cable slip.

TO: GEN BUCHINGER/USAF HQ CMD JBAB 12/3/64. YOUR DIA COMM OF 12/2/64 NOTED. REMEMBER RAF HAS VULCAN SERVICING FACILITY AT OFFUTT SO EASY TO CHECK IF SYSTEMS ALREADY DEPLOYED. SURELY IF ALREADY IN GENERAL USE WE WD KNOW? SUGGEST I GET JOHNNY PIERCE TO INVITE RAF TO RADAR/BOMB COMP ASAP STRESSING NEED FOR BEST AVAILABLE FIT. CONFIRM AUTHORIZED SOONEST. VAE VICTIS MOON.

He had Captain Polick take this down to signals and find him some toothpicks. Wiesbaden was five hours ahead of Washington DC so he wouldn't be hearing from Hubie until after lunch at the earliest. Meanwhile the rest of his mail was waiting. He worked his way through the usual dispiriting news in the form of yesterday's cables and reports from South Vietnam. It was clear to Gus the war would have to escalate massively. The air force was already building up its forces in Tan Son Nhut and Bien Hoa, and sooner or later McNamara would surely authorise fighters and bombers to strike north of the 17th parallel. At which point they'd come into the sights of the SAM batteries the Viet Cong had got from the Russians. Gus knew what that would mean. Back home public attitudes about the war might be overwhelmingly supportive, but he had a premonition he knew was shared by some of his colleagues that things might not be so easy. He vividly remembered his own days as an air force base commander in Korea and the hell that was unleashed on his pilots who crossed the Yalu River. Technology had improved a lot in the last fifteen years, and not just on the American side. All the more reason to ensure that if the British ECM and bomb guidance really was superior, their secrets should be shared without delay.

At 14:30 his aide brought him a flimsy envelope. Inside was a message from Hubie Buchinger:

TO: LT. GEN. A. MOON/USAFE HQ LDY 12/3/64.
AUTHORIZATION CONFIRMED FOR PIERCE
INVITATION RAF BOMBER CMD RADAR/BOMB
COMP SOONEST. VAE VICTIS HUBIE

Colonel Pierce and Gus Moon went back a long way – to World War II, in fact, when Johnny Pierce had been Gus's wingman flying P-51 Mustangs with the 8th Air Force out of southern England. Now, many years on, Pierce was commander at Wheelus Field in Libya. This was rapidly turning into the biggest American air base outside the United States, its importance increasing daily as pilots posted to Vietnam stopped on the way for intensive practice of low-level strikes on the Al Watia and Al Usara bombing ranges. When they had last met Johnny told him they had just built the most accurate possible replica of a Soviet Guideline radar installation out in the desert and this, too, would be used for pilots staging out to Vietnam. It would be the perfect place to find out whether the intelligence reports about the British had been correct.

Lieutenant General Moon unwrapped a toothpick and dealt decisively with an infuriating remnant of lunch. Europe did at least have that to recommend it: it was a toothpick culture. Then he lifted the receiver of his red telephone and placed a call to Colonel Pierce at Wheelus.

16

After a late-night sortie that saw both 'P' Flight Vulcans back at
5 a.m. Baldy Hodge spent a couple of hours superintending Yogi
1's refuelling and dealing with a minor hydraulic leak on the nose-
wheel steering jack. Then he made a prodigious breakfast in the
sergeants' mess before commandeering the technicians' runabout.
He and several of his colleagues had clubbed together and bought a
ten-year-old Jowett Javelin from a wing commander who had been
posted to Singapore. With full access to the RAF's workshops they
had rebuilt the car's odd, flat-four engine into something considerably hotter and it was generally admitted that it went 'like the
clappers'. Its availability on any given day was decided on a first
come, first served basis.

Now Baldy was speeding to Lincoln through wintry lanes. On
the seat beside him was a small packet addressed to a Catherine
Smithers in Liverpool. It contained a film cassette from the tiny
Minox B camera they had given him the previous year. He assumed 'Catherine Smithers' had the same relationship to a living
person as 'John Parsons' had to himself. A conscientious man,
Baldy Hodge was aggrieved at having to send the film off unex-
posed in all but a handful of its fifty frames. Had that stupid twat
Caltrop and his dozy dog stayed asleep for only a couple of minutes
longer he could have used the lot. As it was he'd only managed to
take a few pictures of the new radar set-up – whatever it was – at
the AEO's station. He had hastily hidden the flashgun and battery

pack in a corner under the work desk, reasonably safe in the knowledge that he would be the next person to enter XM580 and could spirit them away in a tool bag. They were too bulky for him to have carried out under Caltrop's nose. The MP wasn't *that* stupid.

But he wasn't that bright, either. The keys to all the aircraft were hung on a board in the dispersal hut, and if the poodle-pusher had been on the ball he would have checked back to see if XM580's key was there. It shouldn't have been if Hodge had taken it to get the documents. But in fact it would have been there anyway because Baldy had long ago had a duplicate made. Nobody knew about that, least of all the Squadron Engineering Officer. Still, regardless of whether the MP's suspicions had been aroused, it was not going to be easy to arrange another opportunity. The policeman's blundering intervention had left Baldy with an unfinished job. He had yet to photograph the other new equipment that had been installed on the navrad's side of the desk. He wondered how much anyone could deduce about how an instrument functioned from its photograph.

Not much, he hoped as he wrestled blasphemously with the car's peculiar column-mounted gear lever, briefly slowing for some cretinous yokel on a bicycle. It was a major preoccupation of Baldy's to convince himself that the information he collected from time to time for 'Catherine Smithers' and her friends hardly amounted to spying as such, and much less to genuine treason. Baldy and his conscience very often consulted one another in great detail and always concluded unanimously that the information he was supplying was of little material use to an enemy. In this ever-competitive Cold War Vulcans themselves were rapidly approaching obsolescence in terms of their technology and in any case, as Baldy would gratuitously remind the sergeants' mess, the days of the entire V-force as constituting Britain's deterrence were numbered. Anyone who could read a newspaper knew it had little more than four years' life left in it before the navy took over. At which point he, Baldy, was O-U-T *out*. He had given the best years of his life to the RAF, had been rewarded with a pittance, and had what he considered a miserable pension to look forward to if he retired at thirty-nine. However, a trained and experienced ex-RAF chief technician had real value on the open market. Some of these Middle Easterners who were modernising their air forces simply threw money at you for a short-term commission. True, the idea of three or five years spent getting his knees brown somewhere up the Gulf held little charm for Baldy Hodge but still, Arabs weren't really nig-nogs in the proper sense and in fact some of them were all right. The point was, their *filoos* was good.

Because of course it was all about money. Unknown to everybody but himself and his wife, Baldy Hodge had one single-minded mission in life. This was to buy a decent house for his parents, and particularly for his father. Each snatched visit to see them in their rural slum near Thame renewed both his indignation and his determination that they must have better in the years they had left to them. Their present hovel was a disgrace. On the edge of flood-prone water meadows, it was the end cottage of a row of five meanly flung up in the mid-nineteenth century to house estate workers. It was damp and draughty with the unmistakable smell of galloping dry rot. His dad had been forced by illness to re-tire from the railway in 1961, aged only fifty-nine. He had worked from the age of fourteen when he had been taken on as an apprentice at Didcot by the Great Western Railway. From there he had risen to drive the Cheltenham Spa Express in the mid-1930s: one of their crack trains with gleaming cream-and-chocolate coaches. That was when Baldy had been born in the modest but solid railwayman's house in Didcot that GWR had built for its engine drivers. After the war GWR was swallowed up into British Rail by government decree – a socialist government, needless to say – and there wasn't an ounce of proper paternalist decency in that lot. After years of breathing coal dust Dad's lungs had gone and he and Mum had been obliged to quit their home after nearly thirty years and plough all their meagre savings of eight hundred quid into that mouldering pigsty. It would have been a point of honour for any son to see them properly rehoused.

Such thoughts came habitually to Hodge when he was by himself: evidence of a narrow but steely determination of purpose. Family came first, end of story. He knew perfectly well that his fantasies about splurging on an E-Type were just that. He would dearly have loved one but there was no way he would spend a penny on self-indulgence before he'd rescued Dad from the mildewed dump which was plainly making his chest worse by the month. It was gall to him that his father was so proud of the clock that BR Western Region had presented to him when he left. Baldy had instantly recognised that, though quite good, it was still very much an other ranks' clock and would have cost British Rail hardly anything. Yet his father could see only a great honour in recognition of great service. It had pride of place on the cream-painted mantelpiece in their tiny parlour which had a clinking brick floor laid straight onto bare earth across which slugs left silvery trails overnight. Upstairs the bed linen was always limp with damp and there were sponge-like growths near the ceiling in the spare room. That was what came of heating with paraffin, Baldy had told them. He'd heard those Valor stoves chucked out a gallon of water for every gallon of Esso Blue they burned. He never visited his parents without loading the car's boot with bags of coal for their minuscule grate. He had already paid to have the cottage's outside privy brought inside: the first house in the row to enjoy this luxury.

All in all, Baldy reckoned (usually loudly and publicly) that his native land had got its priorities arse-about-face. Instead of spending untold millions each year on joining America's panicky nuclear crusade, Britain's first duty – like that of any self-respecting country – should be to ensure decent basic living conditions for its own people. Quite why certain of his colleagues thought this the raving of a dangerous radical was beyond him. It certainly didn't in any way hinder his equally vigorous contempt for CND activists and long-haired peace protesters. A dose of National Service would soon have sorted out those layabouts, so what had the prats in Westminster done? They'd only abolished it to save money, that was all. Hodge had heard of false economies but this was ridiculous.

Having reached Lincoln in a blaze of interior rhetoric he parked the car outside the Cornhill Market and made his way to the Post Office where he dispatched the packet to Liverpool. Then he went to the National Provincial Bank where he deposited £90 in fivers. With rudimentary cunning, Hodge had realised that it might attract the attention of tax snoops if he kept on putting large sums of money into his Post Office savings account, so he had opened accounts in several different banks at branches within reasonable driving distance of Wearsby. Next time it would be the turn of Martins Bank in Grantham. A similar primitive caution made him ring the changes on the post offices he used for sending the occasional packet to Catherine Smithers in Liverpool, to Brian Sumption in Doncaster and to Ivy Trousdale at the Dippy Doughnut in Ipswich. He received his instructions by phone from a public box by ringing a Barnsley number, which you could now do by STD. This number seemed to belong to a betting shop. He would ask if Cardew's Reward was running in the two-thirty at Gatwick, whereupon he was abruptly asked to wait and a man's voice speaking an absurd plummy English would tell him in a very few words what was required.

Baldy had often thought this a pretty laboured form of identification since he was sure Gatwick racecourse hadn't outlived the war and these days most of its hallowed turf lay beneath the new airport. Still, the whole system by which he passed on information and received instructions and payment seemed to him reasonably foolproof. By means of ordinary letters and public phones he avoided all that over-intricate tradecraft so beloved of spy story writers: all those 'cut-outs' and 'dead drops' and 'brush passes', not to mention invisible inks. It was all simple and straightforward and obviously planned so that he need never step out of his role as a chief technician. Until now he had not been asked to supply information that he couldn't gather without arousing suspicion in the normal course of his work. Indeed, this was the basis of his firm opinion that he was doing nothing that could remotely endanger either his colleagues or his country. He had never kidded himself about the cash 'John Parsons' periodically received from France. It was, he knew, ultimately Moscow's money. But he was surely fooling rather than helping these idiot Commies. He didn't see how such mundane information as the names of people who came to lecture or the layout of the station's kitchens could conceivably be of the remotest value to an enemy.

That being said, Hodge recognised that this taking pictures of the Vulcans' new equipment had definitely pushed the stakes up a notch. It was by far the riskiest assignment he'd yet been given. Yet such was his self-confidence after nearly two years of easy money that he felt no nervousness. The important thing was that at last he was closing in on the £5,000 goal he had set himself as the sum needed to buy his parents a really decent home. Somewhere in

Devon would suit them, he thought. He had heard it was a warmer climate down there.

Feeling that the cold, grey weather and a successful trip had entitled him to a small luxury, Baldy, whose sweet tooth was as notorious as his bitter pronouncements, went into a confectioner's and lashed out 1/6d on three bars of Fry's Five Boys chocolate: a favourite of his since childhood. Then, placidly munching, he steered the Jowett one-handedly back down the Lincolnshire byroads to Wearsby.

In the city he had just left a man wearing a rat-coloured trench coat and a trilby went into the National Provincial Bank, showed a small wallet to a cashier and asked to speak to the manager.

17

The great morale-boosting Christmas Dining-In Party was now imminent. As initiators of the plan, Group Captains Mewell and Tolbrooke had tossed to see which station would host it and Mewell, to his perfectly concealed dismay, had won. It would take place at Wearsby on 12 December. He and Tolbrooke had decided after all not to invite Waddington and Coningsby stations: Waddington because of Wearsby's recent trouncing of them in the rugger, which would have guaranteed mayhem; and Coningsby because their Vulcans had just been transferred to Cottesmore, leaving them temporarily bereft of bombers and wide open to the sort of mockery that would equally provoke unrest. Instead they had judiciously invited their nearest neighbours to the north: RAF Blackstock and RAF Tapsley, who flew Vulcans and Victors respectively. Both stations' commanding officers had enthusiastically accepted, agreeing that a bit of seasonal cheer was just what their QRA-weary crews needed.

At Wearsby preparations had long been in hand. Two immense marquees had been erected on the lawn behind the officers' mess, each joined to the other and connected to the main building by a canvas tunnel. The enclosed space was floored with varnished deal panels. Heavy-duty fan heaters, normally used in the hangars, had been wheeled over and installed in the marquees while electricians improvised lighting gantries. On a raised dais at the end nearest the mess was the top table for the stations' commanders and their guest of honour, Air Vice-Marshal Vernon Catterpox. The AVM was the highest-ranking officer in Bomber Command whom Mewell and Tolbrooke had been able to get at short notice and, truth be told, neither was overjoyed that he had accepted. Their invitation was motivated more by tact and courtesy than by any real desire for the man's company. They had been hoping to get another brass hat entirely, a man who was still very much one of the lads despite his age and rank: a man who in 1945, under the influence of a punch made up of equal parts of brandy, sherry and Mackeson's stout, had ridden his AJS motorcycle up the main staircase of an officers' mess in a bomber squadron being visited by Winston Churchill and, unable to stop, had smashed through a door on the landing, revealing the great man himself dressing for dinner. The motorbike, embedded in the wardrobe, had stalled in a dense blue cloud of fumes. Churchill, joined by his aide, went into a dignified 'To-what-are-we-indebted' speech while the airman picked himself up, looked blearily about him and became aware that he was being addressed by a fat man in his underwear. 'Oh do fuck off, there's a good fellow,' he said and collapsed unconscious to the Ministry of Supply's carpeting. 'If you insist,' was Churchill's mild rejoinder. As a result the airman had achieved undying fame as the man who'd told Winston Churchill to eff off and whose subsequent career had obviously been undamaged since he now wore an Air Marshal's rings. At the time it had probably done him no harm that he was a pilot with two DFCs and a DSO and a national reputation as a fearless bomber captain.

'*Catterpox*,' said Tolbrooke with a sigh. 'You know, Spotty, I've never rated the man. He wants to be popular, that's his trouble. Did you ever in your life know anyone who badly wanted to be liked and who actually was?'

'Can't say I did, Pugs, no. But we're stuck with him now. They say he's an amateur conjuror.'

'Oh God, I hadn't heard that. I only hope . . . well, just think how it might backfire.'

Both men lapsed into brief introspection, imagining the awful spectacle of an Air Vice-Marshal trying to do conjuring tricks for a hundred and eighty-eight unsober bomber crews.

'No, he'll have more sense,' said Mewell. 'Surely?' he added.

Mewell had given orders that Wearsby's chefs should push the boat out when it came to the dinner menu. Thirty-five stout turkeys had been ordered from a local farmer and, dispatched and dressed, now waited on racks in a walk-in freezer behind the kitchens. Forty Christmas puddings from Joe Lyons in Lincoln were similarly in readiness. The question of drink arose.

'Plentiful,' Mewell said decisively.

'Naturally, sir,' said the mess steward. 'I really meant what kind of drink?'

'Beer, just so long as it's not Watney's Red Barrel, which is frankly gnat's piss.'

'We don't stock that in the bar, sir. I suggest Tolly light. That's the most popular we have and it's local. I'll lay in some extra barrels from Cobbolds.'

'Good man. Also wine, we'll need. Nothing too extravagant. They may not be stone-cold sober to start with and the Accounts department won't wear shameless expenditure. Most of the men aren't really wine-drinkers anyway, are they?'

In the mess steward's experience most of the men would drink anything and cheerfully finish an evening on methylated spirits if offered it, but he didn't say so. 'It's true we don't serve that much wine in the mess, sir, except on dining-in nights. I would suggest white rather than red. It tends to be cheaper.'

'Well, see what the NAAFI can get us. I've heard the Algerians have started exporting the stuff in cardboard boxes.' Group captain and steward looked at each other and shuddered. 'All right for you,' said Mewell. 'Just remember, whatever the men get I shall have to drink, too. It would hardly do to give them North African battery acid while we at the top table indulge ourselves with a choice Burgundy. Not on, I'm afraid. There'd be a riot. If the NAAFI can't do it you'll have to get it locally. There'll be a bonded warehouse somewhere. And isn't there a Lovibonds in Mossop? They could probably do us a couple of dozen cases of Blue Nun. Think on your feet.'

The hardest part of the arrangements had been getting High Wycombe to agree to losing four V-bomber stations for forty-eight hours. This naturally involved loading other stations with extra duty. Mewell had had a terse phone conversation with a voice of authority in a command bunker somewhere under Buckinghamshire who had tried to cut down the crews' absence from duty to twenty-four hours. The group captain patiently explained that it was against all regulations to drink on the day before flying, and these men were definitely not going to be in a fit state to man the nation's nuclear deterrent a mere twelve hours after a binge as majestic as this was intended to be. Eventually the point had been conceded and the party was officially on.

Mewell's order to push the boat out was not confined merely to food and drink. In his view Wearsby's honour was at stake as the host station, and the Christmas-themed decorations were lavish. The walls of both marquees were hung with purple nylon drapery stuck with yellow stars which the station's wives and WRAFs had spent hours cutting out of heavy art paper. The drapery was also liberally hung with silver balls. At the end of the marquees furthest from the top table was a large Christmas tree whose tip reached the canvas roof. A team hand-picked from the rugger XV had liberated it by night from a plantation near Market Tewsbury. Its branches were hung with tinsel, coloured lights and more silver balls. A line of tables pushed end-to-end stretched along each side of the tented space, facing each other across a clear area in the middle that formed a corridor between the dais at one end and the tree at the other. Gaily coloured streamers criss-crossed overhead. A sound system had been rigged with tannoys attached to the lighting gantries. This was partly for the benefit of after-dinner speeches but mostly for the music. A group had been hired from London by a pilot officer alleged to have connections with what he called the 'pop' world. The Beatles, the Searchers and the Dave Clark Five having pleaded prior engagements, a quartet calling itself Heavy Sausage had agreed to come and play for after-dinner dancing. They claimed to be exponents of 'the Tottenham sound'. This, the airman assured them, translated as 'loud'.

Even afterwards it was conceded that the event's logistics had been well planned. A fleet of coaches was laid on for the guests, impeccably timed so that irrespective of the distance they had to travel they would all arrive together at Wearsby on the dot at 19:00. Mess Dress 5B was specified on the invitation so that everyone would in theory be neatly dressed with a black bow tie and a white waistcoat. In the event not every airman who disembarked at Wearsby that evening could any longer be described as neat. It was obvious that many of the guests had come prepared for an alcohol famine and had brought their own supplies. In many cases ties were already awry and waistcoats not as pristine as they had been at the start of the journey. At least the occasion had been blessed with fine weather: a chilly night with the odd patch of fine mist. The fleet of Bedford coaches drew up and parked in a neat row. Before their drivers went off to the warmth and hospitality of the sergeants' mess they each placed a large painted sign in front of their coach with the name of the station to which they would be returning.

Even so, early portents suggested that not every contingency had been planned for. Amos began to get an inkling of this when he discovered that for no reason he could fathom the guests had been seated according to function rather than squadron. Thus all captains were together, all co-pilots, all navrads, and so on. The result was that virtually everyone at table was a stranger to everybody else. Worse still, they had been grouped in what looked suspiciously like a descending order of status, with the pilots nearest the top table and the rest filling the remainder of the marquees with the AEOs down at the end next to the Christmas tree. Possibly this arrangement contributed to a helpful stiffness at first, a degree of formality that allowed everyone to find his place and be standing vaguely to attention as the four station commanders and their guest of honour filed in and took their seats. But shortly after everyone had sat down and the waitresses began circulating it became evident to Amos that this decorum was not set to last. From down by the tree there came a muffled detonation and a bread roll shot the length of the tents and smacked against the linen cloth draping the top table and concealing the superior officers' eminent legs. A cheer went up. A second explosion sent another roll humming through the air to ricochet off a corner of the lighting tower and smack into the back of a co-pilot's head. He flung down his napkin and lurched unsteadily to his feet. From the back of the marquee came a chorus of 'Ahh, diddums!' and a third explosion. The roll-gunner had found his range by now and the missile took the co-pilot squarely in the fly buttons. Having identified his assailant by the tin tennis ball tube and the can of lighter fuel he was holding, the incensed victim ran the length of the tent towards

176

him, scattering alarmed waitresses, and launched himself across the table. With a crash of glass and silver the two men disappeared amid fresh cheers, the silver balls tacked to the nylon drapery jiggling violently as they grappled.

With some presence of mind Group Captain Mewell pulled the microphone stand towards him and his voice filled the marquee.

'Gentlemen,' he said, admirably managing not to sound reproving. 'I should hate to think that all these turkeys had died in vain. At least let us do them justice before open warfare breaks out.'

This provoked another cheer, this time one of assent rather than ribaldry. The silver balls stopped jiggling and the two combatants separated. The co-pilot returned somewhat unsteadily to his seat, smoothing his hair and brushing pine needles off his mess jacket.

'I mean,' he addressed his fellows as he sat down, '*someone* had to sort him out, don't you think? A godforsaken runt of an AEO from East Witto?'

'Oy,' came a voice of protest. 'I'm from East Wittenham. Not got anything against us, have you?'

'Not unless you fire bread rolls at my balls. Come on – we both fly Victors. That means – ' he belched glassily – 'that means we must have balls in common.'

'You certainly talk it,' his neighbour said soothingly. 'Have a drink.'

Now the Blue Nun began circulating in quantity, and any remaining reserve in people's behaviour disappeared. Amos was sitting opposite someone he thought he recognised who identified himself as a Vulcan captain from RAF Blackstock named Simon. They soon discovered they had both taken part in a bomb comp in Nevada the year previously.

'Skittish,' Amos observed, gesturing with a laden fork at the assembled company.

'It was always going to be,' Simon said. 'It's probably not a bad idea to give everybody a chance to let their hair down once in a while. Gets the moans out of them.'

'And God knows there's plenty to moan about,' another neighbour chipped in. 'What's that arsehole Chatterbox doing here? Who invited *him*?' He pointed with a turkey drumstick at the top table.

'I can't place him,' Amos said. 'I must be too pissed. Is he an arsehole?'

'Copper-plated. He's the one who . . . you remember that Vulcan crash at Heathrow back in fifty-six? Returning from that world tour thing, showing our fabulous new bomber off to the natives around the world?'

'Yes, but Catterpox wasn't involved in that. I'm pretty sure it was Podge Howard in the left-hand seat with Harry Broadhurst as his co-pilot. C-in-C Bomber Command, no less.'

'Ah, but Chatterbox's role came later. You remember they were coming in to land and Howard undershot and they hit a field at a rate of knots and bounced into the air again. On the way up Howard discovered he had no more elevator control. They were terminally fucked and they knew it, so he and Broady punched out. They were still hanging under their chutes when the other poor sods touched bottom – four of them because the real co-pilot was sitting behind. He'd been bumped to sixth seat so Broady could be in the office for the final leg. They all went up in the fireball as Podge and Broady drifted to earth.'

'There can't be anyone on Vulcans who doesn't know the story,' said Amos through a mouthful of stuffing.

'You'd think so wouldn't you, but I've met those who don't. It's almost ten years ago now. Also, in our line of business we don't much like talking about fireballs, do we? Incidentally, is that your private bottle you're hogging there?'

178

'Oh, sorry.' Amos pushed the Blue Nun across the table. 'So where did Catterpox come in? Bloody silly name.'

'Well, after the crash there was this terrific outcry in the press. How come pilots have bang seats while the workers in the coal-hole behind don't? Is this the old British class system at work again? Chatterbox was the one they fielded to explain it to Fleet Street and he made a balls-up of it.'

'I think I do remember it vaguely,' said Amos. 'I was more worried about O levels at the time.'

'Too right he ballsed it up,' interjected his other neighbour, who had been listening while gorging on roast potatoes and bread sauce. 'He made out it had nothing to do with class and was just a matter of economics. Retrofitting bang seats in the aft compartment of all the V-bombers would mean massive structural re-engineering, de-dah, de-dah . . . Huge expense, aircraft being taken out of service, all that.'

'To be fair there wasn't much else he *could* say, really.'

'True. But once the newspapers had made jokes about his name they asked how come the bombers had been designed like that in the first place. Not quite so easy to answer.'

'Hangover from the war, perhaps?' hazarded Simon. 'They were designed in the forties, after all. Pilots cost more to train?'

'Yes, and I expect they also thought the pilots were officers and gentlemen while the blokes in the back were most likely noncoms. But that wasn't what got Chatterbox into trouble in the service. Crews didn't like him telling the public that no-one in the back ever gives baling out a second thought because they're far too busy with the job to worry about that chance in a million of things going blooey, and anyway they have total confidence in their mates up front.'

'That was him?' said Amos, glancing blearily at the top table.

'I guess he was probably right. Frankly, if we thought about everything that might happen we'd never take off at all. But no-one who isn't us should be allowed to say so, and especially not to save official face. So you're right: the man's an arsehole. I wonder what he last flew? Other than a mahogany bomber.'

'He's got gongs,' said Simon, squinting at the object of their discussion on the top table. 'I'd guess Ansons on nav training in 1944.'

During this attempt at a proper conversation there had been plentiful signs that things elsewhere in the tent were hotting up. The level of din had increased so that most exchanges were now shouted. The bread-roll gunner was back in action, this time trying to pick off the coloured balls on the Christmas tree. A cheer greeted each one that burst into shards of glass. Dense missiles of moulded pudding were also sailing across the room accompanied by drunken cries of triumph and rage. By now several of the waitresses seemed the worse for wear and, evidently scorning to run from the scene, decided instead to take shelter beneath the tables where they disappeared behind the fall of white linen. Presumably they found succour since they gave no sign of re-emerging.[†]

*

Meanwhile, over in the sergeants' mess Baldy Hodge stifled a belch and said, 'Now this is what I call a proper Christmas dinner.' Liberal portions of turkey, stuffing and chipolatas had just been served and a case of Blue Nun that had found its way over had been well broached. 'You wouldn't believe the crap we've had to put up with recently.'

'The food's usually bad, then?' asked one of the bus drivers who, like his fellows, was employed by Eastern Counties and was getting

---

† See Appendix 4, p. 297.

double overtime for this special Saturday night job.

'It bloody has been,' said a scrawny corporal. He was recently back from Bristol where he had been doing a course on the Olympus 301 series of Vulcan engines. 'And we all know why, don't we?'

'*We* don't,' said the driver.

A sergeant caught Baldy's look and said warningly, 'Now, Mr Hodge, there's no need for tales out of school. Let's just say there have been problems here in the catering department recently, and leave it at that.'

Baldy paid him no heed. 'It's hardly a state secret, though I bet they'd like it to be one. Anyway, this gentleman's got a right to know how his taxes get spent. They've just uncovered a racket here,' he told the driver. 'Quartermaster and accomplices have been black-marketing our good quality supplies, buying cheap crap and pocketing the difference. Three-day-old bread and condemned meat.'

'That's not very kosher,' the bus driver said. 'I'd be a bit narked.'

'Welcome to the RAF.'

But after this contentious sally the Blue Nuns did their rounds and worked their magic, spreading an unbuttoned conviviality through the slightly staid atmosphere that normally prevailed when outsiders were present. On the other hand it might have been the quality and quantity of the food that gradually lulled the company into an amiable repletion. For the moment the men concentrated on doing the meal justice and even Baldy Hodge seemed content to forgo further bolshy comments as he intently squashed his roast potatoes so as to soak up the maximum amount of gravy.

18

Three hundred yards away in the tents behind the officers' mess unabashed rowdiness continued to prevail. Then suddenly a spontaneous lull spread as the diners' attention became focused on an unusual spectacle. Appearing from nowhere, a Barbary ape had loped to the centre of the marquee. The animal was wearing a neatly tailored uniform jacket whose sleeve rings identified it as an air commodore. In one hand it clutched a small bottle half full of ruby red liquid. It peered woozily about, clearly puzzled. A collective shout of laughter went up, some of it a little strained, as though certain diners were wondering whether they had finally begun seeing things and at any moment a troupe of pink elephants might enter this circus tent. The sudden noise obviously startled the animal. He made an impressive leap and lithely swung himself one-handedly up the lighting gantry to the top. There he perched beneath the marquee roof and took a long pull at the bottle which he then flung into the void below.

'Christ almighty,' said Simon. 'What the hell's *that*?'

'That's Ponsonby,' Amos explained. 'He's our station mascot. Strange: he always used to be a pilot officer. He seems to have been promoted.'

'Blimey. An air commode monkey. I like it.'

At that moment Group Captain Mewell reached again for the microphone and chose to address his errant pet.

'I say, Ponsonby, can you hear me?'

Predictably, a great shout of 'Yes!' went up from the diners.

'No, shut up you lot,' said Mewell. 'That's our station mascot and he outranks you all. He's an air commodore and very ring-conscious. So please show some respect for his rank and for his state, which he can't help because some bastard's been feeding him Cherry Heering.'

By rights this amiable address ought to have had a soothing effect; but drink and a general impatience with rank of any sort now seized the assembled company. It was evident from the violent billowings and rain of silver balls that revellers had penetrated behind the nylon bunting and were rampaging between it and the tent wall. A hand emerged to a cheer and draped some female underwear on one of the branches of the tree. The external canvas wall must have become unpegged from the ground because two old-fashioned, sit-up-and-beg service-issue bicycles were slid in and sounds of drunken bets being taken could be heard above the general din. A bike was hoisted onto each of the end tables and mounted by dishevelled airmen, their bow ties dangling and their hair tousled. A voice shouted: 'Gennelmen! I give you tonight's great contest! On my left here, for the honour of his station, Barney Haggerty, the Pride of Tapsley. And on my right, for the honour of East Wittenham, Godfrey Stebbing. Gennelmen, lay your bets ... Thank you, thank you. A clean ride, please, gennelmen, and no gouging. First off the table the other end the winnah! On yer marks ... Get set ... *Wait for it* ... Go!'

The competitors were soon aware that track conditions made the going hazardous. Halfway along, and making speedy progress through glasses, plates and lumps of pudding, the Pride of Tapsley's front wheel encountered a Blue Nun bottle on its side and he made an impressive exit from the race, taking with him quantities of food, crockery, and still-seated diners. On the other side Flying

Officer Stebbing was going canny, avoiding the worst obstacles and apparently unaware that his rival was already out of the race. But in the last stretch he abandoned caution and, accelerating, plunged off the end of the tables to a shout of acclaim from his backers. For the moment he was unable to relish his victory since he had laid his head open on a corner of the dais and lay unconscious beneath his trusty steed. A cry went up for a nurse, and eventually a girl emerged from beneath a table dabbing at her lips with a napkin which she then folded and applied to F/O Stebbing's forehead.

'Give him the kiss of life, darling!' shouted someone.

By now the ranking officers on the top table had realised that all hope of maintaining some sort of order was lost. Nevertheless Air Vice-Marshal Catterpox got to his feet and reached for the microphone.

'Now look, chaps,' he began, 'this is pretty disgraceful, you know. A joke's a joke and all that, but . . .'

In the hail of missiles and chorus of boos that greeted his remarks his lips could be seen still moving, but the booming tones had stopped. Someone had sabotaged the sound system. As if he recognised this as a definitive moment Group Captain Mewell also got to his feet and with a curious drunken dignity gave the rioters a salute so snappy he almost fell. The boos quickly changed to cheers. A ragged chorus of 'For he's a jolly good fellow' broke out as he ushered the rest of his guests down off the dais and back along the tunnel into the mess. Groupie had abandoned the field.

A second bicycle race had meanwhile been organised and F/O Stebbing was dragged clear just as a flight lieutenant from RAF Blackstock soared off the table's end, miraculously landed upright and, adroitly avoiding the dais that had undone his predecessor, plunged into the marquee wall which cushioned his fall.

Like many others Amos was now on his feet. He needed air.

Tipsy as he was, he felt no urge to continue. Also, he was wondering how the rest of his crew were faring and decided to see if he could find any of them. He now thought it was probably just as well the seating arrangements had split them up because it made 'P' Flight's crews less open to resentful attack from their peers than if they had all been sitting together. His progress through the milling revellers was slow because he found somebody had been spreading liberal amounts of brandy butter over the floor. On all sides people were slipping and falling, clutching at others and pulling them down too. It was at this moment that the terrified Ponsonby, whose presence overhead had momentarily been forgotten, burned his hand on the back of one of the lamps and lost control of his bladder.

Eventually Amos managed to win through, exiting beneath the marquee wall on hands and knees just as the Christmas tree inside was toppled with a great crash of decorations. The cool night air outside was remarkably reviving. There were others outside wandering about in dazed fashion. In their bedraggled mess kit they looked like survivors from a disaster at a state occasion. Off to one side was parked a London double-decker Routemaster bus in disguise. It was sprayed pink; its windows were curtained and there was an immense blue sausage painted on its side. From within came the sound of laughter and guitars being plucked. On the step at the back were several seated figures.

'Are you lot the group?' he asked as he approached.

'Right, man,' said a youth.

'I don't think you're going to be needed, you know,' said Amos. 'Things have got a bit out of hand.'

'A bit?' said another. 'It makes Tottenham Town Hall after one of our gigs look like Westminster bleeding Abbey. Anyway, your sound system's buggered, isn't it, and we're not setting up our own

185

just to have you lot bugger that too. You must be joking.'

From far down the perimeter track towards the fire dump there came the sound of engines and a crashing noise. Some of the lads doing a demolition derby? Amos began making his way homewards, surprised in a muddled sort of way that he was both drunker than he'd thought and also depressed or something. Maudlin? Was that the word? Or was that his father's college at Oxford? Ahead of him there were two figures in an odd posture. No – as he came closer he could see it was one figure kneeling by a fire hydrant, being sick. 'Oh Gawd,' he heard the figure say weakly. 'Oh shit.'

'I blame the nuns,' Amos said as he came up. The figure made an effort to stand and he recognised his AEO, Gavin Rickards. 'Oh, it's you, Gavin. Ill met by moonlight. Need a hand?'

'Boss?' said Rickards uncertainly, blinking in the sodium glare of a street light.

'That's me. Where are you going?'

There was a pause. 'I can't remember.'

'Where's your car?'

'Dunno. Why?'

'Because they may be organising a demolition derby and you don't want them to take your Sprite.'

'Shit, no.' The thought seemed to sober the boy up a little. 'No, it's in the garage over there –' he waved a hand. 'Miles away. Where I live. Oh God.' He leaned across the hydrant and put his head in his hands. 'I wish . . . I think I drank too much. Just a bit. I wish I was in bed. Or dead.'

'Come on,' Amos said, putting an arm around him with great protectiveness. 'Come back to my place. It's quite close and you can sleep it off there. It's Sunday tomorrow, isn't it?'

Together they set off a little totteringly, their arms about each other. Presently they came to the little net of roads where the married officers lived in suburban exclusivity.

'This where you live?' asked Rickards. Then, like a ten-year-old, 'Are we nearly there?'

'What does that sign say?'

'Brabazon Close, it looks like.'

'Good, that sounds right.'

With Rickards propped in the flimsy porch Amos searched his mess jacket for the key and, to his surprise, found it. 'OK, sshhh. My wife'll be asleep.' He let Rickards in and guided him into the lounge without turning on the light. The street lamp a few doors up shed a feeble bilious glow into the room. 'You sleep on the sofa. I'll get some water. We'd both better tank up. It'll help tomorrow.'

Amos felt his way to the kitchen, rebounding a little off unexpected doorframes, and returned with a jug of cold water. He found his AEO sprawled on the sofa, sound asleep. With a vague feeling of disappointment Amos drank deeply from the jug, kicked off his shoes and lay on the floor with a cushion under his head and the rancid candlewick hearthrug over him. He gave himself up to the room's steady circular motion. After a while it lulled him into unconsciousness.

Sometime during the night he was awakened by something soft and warm pressed against his face. 'That you, Gavin?' he murmured, suddenly almost sober and filled with a piercing tenderness. He reached an arm across and with a shock found Vulcan the rabbit. Half paralysed with cold, Amos went for a piss, came back with an armful of coats and lit the gas fire, leaving it on low. It did little to warm the room but the increasing glow of the perforated fireclay mantles and occasional soft popping sounds were comforting. The rabbit moved close to it, its bulging eyes reflecting orange dots. With almost maternal care Amos threw a couple of coats over the faintly snoring Rickards. Then, as though he had reached an irrevocable decision, he too crawled beneath them, putting an arm around his sleeping crewman. To his surprise and pleasure Rickards did the same to him, although it might have been no more than a dopey recognition that the sofa was barely big enough for both of them.

Sometimes in drunkenness a few things can become clearer. Feelings swim up from where they have long been pressed down and stand there, suddenly blatant, making it impossible to deny their familiarity. (Of *course* it's that. It has always been that, and you know it . . .) Amos experienced just such a recognition as he listened to Gavin's heart through the vomit-stained mess jacket. It filled him with profound relief as well as tenderness. This was something that went back to childhood and had been thrust into the shadows, there to remain inchoate and unfinished. Now, belatedly, it was able to put on adult shape and clothing. He ran a hand through the boy's springy hair and was amazed to feel the arm around him tighten. Instantly and from nowhere came an inner view, as clear as a photograph, of the row of plane trees outside his study window at school, the blond patches on their trunks marking where they had shed their scabs of bark. Just one of those baffling but pin-sharp images that have no meaning, he thought. Even so, much as he had disliked his school, he could well recall the depression that had marked his final days there. He had been haunted by the sense of dispersion: of old friendships and alliances about to be broken up and scattered even as people swore they would see each other again at university, at reunions, at Old Boys' dinners. They would keep in touch; of course they would. *Atque in perpetuum, frater, ave atque vale.* Catullus's words by his brother's grave. They sounded like any school's – or squadron's – true motto.

Almost ten years later, on a sofa in his married quarters, Amos

188

fell prey to a melancholy that hovered on the faux-tragic edge of self-pity (yet another side to drunkenness). This desired and breathing body to which he clung in order not to fall represented an impossibility, above all in the service. The permanence that love pretends to claim for itself is victim to many things more banal than mortality. Sooner or later, if he didn't blot his copybook, Amos would be bumped up to wing commander and sent off to God knows where. In the meantime Gavin could equally well be sent anywhere. It might be years before they ever met again. A hopeless tear ran down Amos's cheek before he sidled into sleep.

When he woke again grey daylight had crept into the room. He was alone on the sofa. His head ached. The gas fire was extinct, he noticed. Presumably the meter had run out. Getting stiffly to his feet he went along the corridor into the kitchen and was surprised to find quite a domestic scene. Jo and Gavin were sitting at the table with mugs of coffee and the rabbit was crouched in one corner with a lettuce leaf sticking out of its mouth. There was a tube of Alka-Seltzer and a yellow tin of Bisodol powder together with a white-rimed glass in front of his AEO, who was wearing a borrowed coat over his flimsy mess kit.

'Oh dear, oh dear,' said Jo. 'Look what the cat brought up.'

'You see before you,' Amos said, dragging up another chair, 'two survivors of multiple assaults by blue nuns. They're vicious creatures.'

'You look ghastly.' His wife got up and put the kettle back on the stove. 'I prescribe black coffee and Alka-Seltzer.'

'And how are you, this fine morning?' Amos asked Gavin.

'Not as bad as I deserve to be. Thanks for bringing me back last night. Otherwise I'd have been found stiff and stark under that hydrant like one of the babes in the wood.'

'Pity the babe who's as pissed as you were. How's the head?'

'I'll live.'

'I heard you come in,' said Jo.

'Sorry. We tried to be quiet. I thought it better to sleep downstairs rather than wake you.'

'So I saw. You looked very sweet together when I peeped in on you this morning.'

Suddenly Amos knew without doubt that Jo understood everything. He also knew it was the formal end of their marriage. In his hungover state it seemed less important than whether his wife would gossip about it and create a scandal to appease her outraged womanhood or something. Yet he couldn't really find it in himself to care. Infinitely more important was to discover what footing he and Gavin were now on. He dreaded hearing the boy claim not being able to remember a thing, followed by a return to the joshing but respectful mateyness of any close-knit crew member with his captain. He yearned, yet dared not presume.

'Sound asleep as you both no doubt were,' Jo was saying with one eyebrow sceptically raised, 'you presumably missed the excitement.'

'Excitement?' said Amos. 'What was that?'

'They had to call out the fire tender. Apparently some idiot went and set fire to the marquee. Burned to the ground.'

'Crikey. Anyone hurt?'

'Not according to Kay and Ronald. It must have been one hell of a party.'

'It was,' said Rickards. 'I've never seen anything like it.'

'Gavin's been telling me about it,' Jo said. 'To be honest it sounds perfectly disgusting. What kind of behaviour is that for grown men entrusted with nuclear weapons?'

'Pretty much what you'd expect, actually. Somehow, atom bombs don't leave you much choice.'

'You're just being silly, Amos. Anyway, heads will have to roll, surely? People booing an Air Vice-Marshal off the stage. It sounds like a mutiny.' She mixed a couple of spoonfuls of Nescafé powder into a mug of boiling water and gave it to Amos, who ladled in a good deal of sugar before he began sipping.

'Ahh, that's a life-saver, Jo. Thanks. Yes, well, I expect there will be repercussions, there usually are. Disciplinary hearings. Even fines. If they've destroyed the marquee, quite a lot of fines. Any injuries will be deemed as self-inflicted and if they're enough to stop someone flying he'll probably get handed a fizzer.'

But Jo seemed not to be listening. Having made his coffee she had gone over to stand by the back door, looking out of its glazed upper half. 'Amos,' she said. 'Come here. What's going on at the chapel?'

Amos and Gavin got to their feet and went over. Jo opened the back door and they went out and stood in the cold where they could see the station chapel off to the right over the low fence. It was an ugly building that had evidently been thrown up to minimal Air Ministry specifications, presumably just after the war: a stylistic hodgepodge that might be vaguely described as Congregationalist Gothic, with broad steps up to an arched entrance, plain brick elevations broken by pointed windows and a flat roof. This Sunday morning it was a scene of activity that had nothing to do with religious observance. A crowd stood in front gazing upwards. Sitting on the roof was a dilapidated little Morris 8 that Amos at once recognised as belonging to the chaplain. Although it made his head ache he couldn't help laughing.

'That's Wheezing Jesus's car,' he said. 'Jim's done it after all. Good for him.'

'Who's done what?' asked Gavin.

'Jim Ledbetter. Jo, you remember that house-warming thing that

191

Dominic Purdue and Joy threw for us when we moved in here? Before his wife dragged him home old Jim was suggesting putting the padre's car on the chapel roof for a prank. It looks like he's done it. Brilliant. I wonder how he managed it.'

At that moment the sound of an engine announced the arrival of the Coles crane from the fire dump, its heavy sheave block swinging from the top of the jib. As the driver positioned the crane beside the building it was obvious this same jib was just long enough to have swung the car onto the roof by means of the four wire ropes and hooks dangling from the block. However, it was equally obvious that somebody was going to have to go up in order to fix them to the car. Almost as soon as Amos had the thought the fire tender arrived with its extendable ladder. The crane halted, block swinging wildly, and at that moment a small, squat figure appeared on the roof. It was wearing a little tattered RAF uniform jacket and looked quite distraught.

'Oh my God!' Jo exclaimed. 'There's that poor ape, the mascot, whatshisname.'

'Ponsonby.'

'For God's sake, what callous bastard put the poor animal up there?' Jo was suddenly red in the face with rage. 'Is there no limit to the *cruelty* of the shits on this station?'

'Maybe it was a mistake,' hazarded Amos lamely. 'Perhaps he was asleep in the car when they put it up there.'

'Oh yes, a likely tale. And he never noticed, I suppose.'

'Well, he was pretty sozzled, you know.'

'*Drunk?*'

'Cherry Heering, apparently.'

'Whoever did that ought to be shot. Just taken out and shot.'

'Mm. It wasn't me, Jo, and it wasn't Gavin here. We were whacked out in the lounge.'

They watched the wretched Ponsonby lope around the edges of his confinement, stopping here and there to peer down and evidently concluding there was no way that even a monkey from Gibraltar could climb down sheer brick walls, let alone a monkey with a hangover. Just then he seemed to notice the crane jib swinging beside the car and shambled across. Obviously wondering whether if he climbed onto the Morris's roof he would be able to reach the jib and shin down it, Ponsonby paused for a moment beside it, looking down. At that moment the heavy sheave block, swinging in, caught the side of his head and smashed him against the car, the impact bouncing the pitiful body outward over the edge where he fell in a tangle of outflung limbs, his air commodore's jacket fluttering, out of sight to the ground below. There was an awful silence.

'You fuckers,' said Jo almost conversationally; and Amos had never before heard her say such a thing. It was extraordinarily shocking and he felt a quick embarrassment that Gavin should have heard her. 'You *fuckers.*'

19

Early in the New Year Wing Commander Ops was briefing the two 'P' Flight crews while Group Captain Mewell sat to one side, his chair half-turned towards the blackboard. The time had come for both Oilcan and Vector (the code name assigned to the laser-guidance system) to be tested against some realistic opposition.

'With the Admiralty's co-operation,' Wingco was saying, 'we have arranged to run Oilcan against a set-up on one of our nuclear submarines of a pretty good version of the three Soviet acquisition radars used for their Guideline missiles.

'At this moment she's en route from Faslane to an area a couple of hundred miles off south-west Ireland called the Porcupine Sea-bight. We're hoping the trials can be made the day after tomorrow. This will depend to some extent on the weather. January off the Celtic Shelf is not exactly the ideal time for a submarine to dally on the surface, but for reasons the group captain will shortly explain we're having to get a move on. The other constraint is if there's the wrong sort of shipping in the area. I'm told we can rely on Shack-letons patrolling for twenty-four hours prior to the sortie. We don't want those famous Russian trawlers listening in, or anyone else, come to that. Sir?' he glanced over at the group captain.

Mewell got to his feet. These days he was looking a little care-worn, Amos thought, and had been so ever since the Dining-In Party. Naturally, no-one at mere squadron level was privy to the things that must have been said at command level, but Amos and the others thought it safe to assume that poor old Muffin had got a bollocking. In addition, he was known to be sad about Ponsonby's demise. The animal had spent much of its time in the group captain's house with his family, not to mention the intimate moments it had shared with him while roaring up and down the airfield in his Allard. Mewell was visibly making an effort to tighten things up at Wearsby, and disciplinary action had recently been taken against several people for offences that before 12 December nobody would have bothered about. These days, even the hairier members of the sergeants' mess would think twice before demanding their bar stay open after 23:00. The Snowdrops with their dogs had doubled their patrols of all Wearsby's dispersals.

'Gentlemen,' he said, 'as Wing Commander Imber says, this radar exercise will take place the day after tomorrow unless either Coastal Command or the Admiralty reports snoopers or weather conditions that make it dangerous for the sub to remain on the surface. So far the Met boys are giving encouraging signs. You will be on six-hour call in case we decide to bring it forward. The exercise has been code-named "Canteen". You navigators will find the rendezvous co-ordinates in the Vault so after this you will go and plan your routes out and back. Both aircraft will go with ninety-eight per cent fuel in case there are last-minute changes or for some reason you need to stooge around in the area. We're not expecting to need it but short-notice tanker backup will be arranged.

'Now, we have recently received an invitation from the Americans to participate in an exercise of their own. This will take place on the Libyan ranges near Wheelus Field. They, too, have set up a mock Guideline missile radar complex and we have had a specific request from USAF's European headquarters in Wiesbaden that we compete against it. We are ninety-nine per cent certain it's pure coincidence that the invitation should have been issued at this particular moment, and that it has nothing to do with our new anti-radar system. We're still confident that nobody apart from ourselves knows it even exists. In any case we've brought Canteen forward so as to give you AEOs some final practice.

'We have accepted their invitation to participate, but in the usual spirit we're treating it as more of a challenge, so we've issued them with one of our own as a sort of quid pro quo, if you like. This will be a bomb comp using Vector. We have simply said it will be for guided bombs but we've not specified a laser system. They'll be free to choose whatever kind they like. You'll be based at Luqa for the duration of the exercise and a supply of the new munitions is already on its way there. So far, the practice runs you've been having show consistently impressive results. We're hoping you'll be able to score points by showing our cousins that they don't have the field to themselves and that Britain can still invent and innovate, and so forth. With luck we'll surprise them by slipping this kit in under their radar, so to speak. I've been told that a real success with Oilcan, in particular, would be a very useful bargaining chip, but to what use this might be put only the top brass knows. At our humble level, though, it would definitely go some way towards knocking out a few dents this station's honour has suffered recently. I need not elaborate, gentlemen.'

*

Canteen day duly dawned and found Yogis 1 and 2 in the air and heading for the Atlantic. The two Vulcans flew together, getting regular fixes from stations they passed until Bob Mutton called up Amos on the intercom saying, 'Just passing Swansea on the left, Boss. Come a couple of degrees right and we'll be on the money.' Amos acknowledged and made the course alteration. Soon they were over the Celtic Sea with some three hundred nautical miles to fly to the rendezvous point. Despite this being January it was one of those rare, cold days with perfect visibility. Even the sea below showed little movement. This was perhaps unsurprising from fifty thousand feet; but here and there the odd oil tanker heading towards the Bristol Channel left a wake spreading in a fan still visible even when it was ten miles wide, and where two wakes intersected they made moiré-effect interference patterns that could be clearly seen from the cockpit side windows. This argued an almost flat calm, which was exactly what the Met men had said, based on reports radioed in by ships in coastal areas and further out in the Atlantic. Just for a change, the weather gods were smiling. Amos thumbed the mike switch.

'You still awake, Keith?' he asked his co-pilot.

'No.'

'Good. Fancy a spell?'

'I could do with the hours.'

'You have control.'

'I have control.'

Amos leaned back and stretched. Then he got back on the intercom.

'Captain to AEO: how are you doing there, Gavin?'

'OK, Boss. I'd guess another five minutes to radar contact with the sub.'

'Remember each aircraft does three passes: one at high level and one at low level with Oilcan alone, then another one at low level with Oilcan plus chaff and the rest of the ECM while jinking.'

'Roger. Also confirm that Yogi 2 will reverse our first two passes. They'll go high when we go low and vice versa, but always slightly behind us. That way we also check on possible interference to see if we get running rabbits on our screens.'

Ten minutes later Vic Ferrit called up Amos.

'Skip, Yogi 2's started descent.'

'Roger, Vic. Thanks.' There had been agreement beforehand that radio silence between the two Vulcans was to be maintained except in emergency so that no unnecessary hint of the exercise should be given to the unseen ears that were ever-pricked over every horizon, no matter how empty it looked. It was astonishing how much might be deduced from so little information. Both aircraft had been given a short list of previously agreed code words for brief communication with the submarine, even though it hardly seemed that it would have been a security risk to have wished the boat's skipper a good morning. Sometimes up here in the cockpit, gazing out over the curved world, Amos felt the absurdity that an ideological confrontation among earth-dwellers nine and a half miles below should also reach up to embrace this thin, sub-zero region and, ever since Sputnik in 1957, even space itself. Thereafter this squabble for temporary world dominance had effectively tainted the planet's every molecule, and in gloomy mood Amos could see no reason why it shouldn't eventually spread to the moon and the nearer planets as well. Yet it seemed daft to squabble over territory that no human could inhabit for long. If you baled out merely at this height you'd be dead in seconds without a pressurised suit, your blood within nine degrees of boiling point, and it wouldn't matter a row of beans whether you were capitalist or communist or pacifist. For the umpteenth time it struck him as a damn silly way for human beings to organise the terms of their brief lives in their one and only home.

Amos had always liked to indulge his private thoughts while flying, but on this occasion something was nagging at him. It had to do with the last thing he'd heard, whatever it was . . . yes, about *rabbits*. With a little adrenal stab he realised the connection: that Jo had taken Vulcan the rabbit with her when she went. She had said nothing and left no note. When he had returned home to Brabazon Close one evening a few days before Christmas he had known at once from the echoes that it was an emptier house than the one he had left that morning. Eventually Kay from next door had come round and told him with some embarrassment what he had already deduced – indeed, must already have predicted, so unsurprised did he find himself to be. A young woman had turned up with a car and she and Jo had loaded it up with various boxes and bags and they'd simply driven away. The vast expanse of sea and sky through which he was now speeding at Mach 0.86 suddenly felt like a world that was dismayingly void instead of supportive. With another pang Amos thought of Gavin sitting only half a dozen feet away. His crew and its bonds of trust and friendship seemed a small thing and flimsy to set against the implacable physics of things far beyond the Vulcan's windscreens. Not for the first time he wondered if he would still be in the RAF in ten years' time.

Suddenly Gavin himself broke into his thoughts. 'AEO to captain, I'm getting the boat now. We've swapped IDs. In three minutes I'll deploy Oilcan. We're to carry on straight to target without any evasive measures.'

'Roger. Keith, did you get that?'

'Roger, Captain,' said Coswood. His right hand was light on the control handle's pistol grip as he disengaged the autopilot. 'Basically, we carry on as we are while Gavin back there works his electronic miracles.'

'A hundred nautical miles to target . . . now,' said Bob Mutton. 'Flying time to target ten minutes, thirty seconds.'

'Got you, Baa,' said Keith, his eyes on the Machmeter beneath the coaming directly in front of him.

Five minutes later Rickards came back. 'Hey, Boss, this gizmo works. They got us twice and they've lost us twice. They're still hunting. And that's when we're going straight and level with no countermeasures . . . Hang on; they may have got us again.'

There was some more silence broken by Vic Ferrit. 'We're nearly over them, Boss.'

'Five seconds,' said Bob. 'Course and altitude corrections coming up.'

In response to these Keith Coswood began a slow right-hand bank as his left hand eased back the power to seventy-five per cent. The Vulcan could be felt slowing as it lost speed and height.

Amos said: 'AEO, keep an eye out for Yogi 2.'

'Got him, Boss. About ten miles behind and climbing. Our heights will intersect in a few minutes but with this separation maintained.'

The exercise proceeded uneventfully. The two aircraft swapped altitudes and repeated the run. Coswood took Yogi 1 down to five hundred feet and for the first time the two pilots caught a brief glimpse of the submarine as they approached: a black whaleback with a tall sail outlined by flecks of white foam lost in the middle of a sunlit ocean empty to the horizon. Amos took over control for the final run which he made at a thousand feet while Rickards used the entire range of the aircraft's jamming devices and deployed various types of chaff. On this run, after the submarine's radar had briefly picked up both Vulcans at forty-eight nautical miles' distance, no lock-on had been achieved and it was left baffled and trying to reacquire the big deltas even as they overflew and, banking steeply, climbed away for the last time towards the north-east.

As they were nearing the Bristol Channel Amos suddenly remembered something and clicked his switch. 'Captain to AEO.'

'Yes, Boss.'

'What about those running rabbits of yours. Did you see any?'

'Nothing to speak of. A bit on that last run when Yogi 2 was so close, but that's normal. I don't think Oilcan makes the interference any worse. It's too focused.'

'I got the odd bunny on mine,' came Vic's voice. 'But like Gavin says, no big deal.'

While Keith Coswood flew them back to Wearsby Amos thought again of the rabbit that had just hopped out of his own life. Since Jo had left him he was aware that his crew, normally so relaxed and informal, were now fractionally less so when he was present. He would intercept anxious glances as though he were being examined for signs of emotional fragility after a tragic bereavement. The truth was that he missed the rabbit more than he did Jo. He had grown fond of old Vulcan who, to be honest, had never done much other than hop and chew and crap. But Amos had liked the unfathomable look in his dark and bulgy eyes. Sometimes he had caught the animal gazing at him, unwinking, in an oddly companionable and intimate fashion, which was more than his recent wife had done.

The real conundrum was, did any of those anxious gazes conceal a suspicion of the true state of affairs? In that respect the service was quite as bad as school had been. It was in the nature of hermetic institutions that everybody's private radar was sensitively attuned to detecting special friendships as well as hidden enmities. One never knew when they might cause a subtle shift in the balance of power. In any hierarchy the whole hidden drama of who–whom was never far from people's calculations . . . Might Amos induce Gavin to leave the service if he were to do so? Absurd. The boy had his own career to think of. It was hopeless to think anything could ever come of it, whatever 'it' was.

But Wearsby's Air Traffic Control was talking to Keith Coswood, and Amos broke off his sad musing to busy himself with the usual disciplines of approach and landing. In a separate part of his brain, though, he briefly revisited one of his earliest reactions to Jo's departure, which was the glum realisation that any moment now he would be booted out of Brabazon Close and back into a caravan.

20

Jo and Avril were sitting in the kitchen of Avril's rented house. Outside it was a frosty Fenland Sunday with an enormous blue sky in which the sun, like a great cold bell, hung low. The children were at their grandparents'. Earlier, Avril and Jo had done the washing in the scullery, a quarry-tiled room a step down from the kitchen containing a gas stove, a large earthenware sink and a mangle. At the back of the scullery was also a recently added door leading into the outside lavatory so that one no longer had to go out of the house in all weathers.

The kitchen, with its lino floor beneath which the ends of floorboards showed here and there as rectangular prominences, was an altogether warmer place. The stove in its alcove beneath the mantelpiece gave an occasional sigh as its coals shifted behind the double doors with their little mica windows. It was a companionable sound, as was that of the women sipping mugs of Ovaltine at the table. The mantelpiece itself was decorated with a row of little paper golliwogs from pots of Robertson's jam. The washing was drying on the airer hauled up to the ceiling: the children's clothes, chiefly, which had simply frozen stiff on the line in the garden earlier. A ginger cat was dozing on the ironing board, its wrists tucked in. Anyone coming through the side passage from the street and glancing through the kitchen window would have thought it a tranquil domestic scene; and so it was, outwardly at least.

'I don't get it,' Avril said for perhaps the twentieth time. She was referring to a visit they'd had earlier that day from two plainclothes policemen wearing Homburg hats and raincoats and looking just as they did in the cinema. They were asking questions about Avril's friend Ted who had the mobile shop: questions she had been quite unable to answer, such as 'Did you ever have any reason at all to suspect that some of the items Mr Timperley had for sale might have been stolen?'

'Of course not,' Avril had answered. 'How could you tell? I mean, if you went into Griffiths the petrol station to buy paraffin, how would you know if it was genuine Aladdin Pink or something they'd got on the black market? Come to that, how would you know if the brandy on sale in the wine shop hasn't been smuggled in from France by night in little black kegs?'

Detective Inspector Hammersley and Detective Sergeant Dibley had smiled those tight, bleak smiles by which policemen convey that they don't mind those they question scoring the odd debating point because they are privy to a larger picture which will shortly become horribly clear. On this occasion, however, they left the picture opaque.

'So what's Ted done? Or supposed to have done?' Avril demanded.

'Oh, no charges have been laid yet, Mrs O'Shea. We're just making some preliminary inquiries, asking people in this area who are known to have been among his customers. For instance, can you tell us if you ever saw any meat aboard his vehicle?'

'Meat? Well, he's got a fridge in the back and often has chops and sausages and sometimes chickens. I'm just another customer. Why don't you ask him?'

'Oh, we will when we find him.'

'What do you mean, *find*?'

'He's not been home for days, madam. I suppose you don't know where he is, do you?'

'Why should she know?' Jo, having been listening in the kitchen, had been unable to stop herself coming into the hall and breaking in. 'You heard her: she's just a customer of his.'

'And you are?' The inspector's pale eyes had switched to her beneath lifted eyebrows. Jo noticed the skin on his forehead was slightly rough and peeling as though he'd caught a touch of the sun, although it was probably chapping from the winter wind. She mentally prescribed Nivea cream or Snowfire.

'I'm Mrs McKenna and I'm an old friend of Mrs O'Shea's.'

'Do you live here?'

'It's none of your business where I live.' One thing about being – or having been – a service wife, you did feel confident and even slightly immune when dealing with civilian police. They were nothing like as serious a prospect as the RAF police. 'As a matter of fact I've been staying here a few days. I was living at Wearsby until then.'

Both women caught the glances which Hammersley and Dibley exchanged. 'You were living at RAF Wearsby, were you?' the senior man asked.

'I was. I'm . . . I'm married to Squadron Leader McKenna.'

'I see. And I suppose you don't know where Mr Timperley is, either.'

'Not only do I not know where he is, I've never even met the man.' The DS burrowed in his raincoat and came out with a photograph which he handed her. 'No,' she said, 'I've never seen him. I don't recognise him at all.'

After a few more exchanges the two detectives had left, saying it was likely they would return in due course. Since then Avril had been repeating 'I don't get it' and compulsively making Ovaltine.

Suddenly Jo said, 'I wonder if I'm being stupid, Rilly. I've only just remembered something. At about the time of that incredible

Christmas Party I told you about there was a rumour going around Wearsby that people had been arrested for being involved in a plot to do with food in the sergeants' mess. Amos might have mentioned it and my neighbour Kay Hendry did – you know, she was the one who helped me get the vet job in Mossop? I remember she did say there was a scandal about black-market food supplies or something but I'm afraid I didn't pay it much attention since I had rather more urgent things to worry about. Now I come to think about it, could there be a connection with your Ted? Those two coppers did seem to perk up when I mentioned I'd been living at Wearsby. You don't think he's involved in anything fishy, do you?'

Avril gave a little sigh and lifted a crinkled scab off the top of her Ovaltine with a teaspoon. 'I know, I know. You did warn me.'

'I warned you he might have other women, not that he might be a crook.' The two friends looked at each other and both simultaneously shook their heads slightly. 'You and me – we're not doing too well, are we?'

'You've still got a husband,' Avril reminded her. 'And no children.'

'Technically true: Amos and I are still married. But not in any other sense we aren't. I don't see how we could be after that.'

'That' referred to the night of the Christmas party, which had been a constant topic of conversation between the two friends.

'I just *knew*, Rilly. Seeing them together on the sofa, even if they were asleep and couldn't avoid embracing if they didn't want to fall off . . . I mean, one of them could have slept on the floor, couldn't he? In fact it looked as though one of them had started out there. There were cushions and stuff. They looked *intimate*, somehow, as if they'd been doing it for ages even though I'm fairly sure they hadn't. No, the moment I saw them everything fell into place. Amos's iffiness about, you know, lovemaking, and suddenly remembering how often he would talk about Gavin – much more than he did about the others. You were right all along.'

'Poor Jo.'

'I suppose . . . Not really. It would be hypocritical of me to make a great song and dance about it. I already knew I couldn't stick life with the RAF for ever. No, all this does is give me a solid reason that anybody would recognise. Not that I can use it. I've had enough of Amos and his world but I wouldn't want him sent to jail. Or ruin young Gavin's life, either. He's actually rather a sweet boy, innocent in a way. I've no idea if he knows what he's got himself into but that's his funeral. If he's old enough to die for his country, and all that.'

Now Avril got up and made some more Ovaltine. It seemed very comforting in the circumstances. The afternoon outside the windows was turning to dusk. 'Frost tonight,' she said as she stirred in the hot milk. Placing a mug in front of her friend, Avril said, 'I'm afraid I have a confession to make,' and she told Jo about a night long ago when she thought she might have seen Amos kissing someone in an alley near the Serpent's Tooth. 'I feel bad about it,' she ended. 'I really ought to have told you at the time. But I wasn't sure and I couldn't risk telling you something like that if it wasn't true, could I?'

'I don't know, Rilly. I'm not sure I'd have believed it anyway, not then. Anyway, it's water under the bridge now. I know it sounds funny but that's not really what bothers me about Amos. It's that whole way of life he's involved with. Maybe with Marty you saw something different because he flew helicopters and spent a lot of his time doing rescue work. Airlifting badly burned stokers off ships or winching up birdsnesting boys stuck on cliffs – that's decent, worthwhile work. But what those Wearsby crews are doing is different, somehow, or else it makes them different. That

Christmas party . . . You know, in a way it was actually *mad*. Even that might have been overlooked, I suppose. But deliberately getting that poor animal drunk and terrified out of his mind before driving him to his death – I'm sorry, that's just not forgivable, Rilly. I know Amos didn't do it personally because he was asleep on the settee with his boyfriend, but he was part of it; some of his friends were involved.'

'Mm. It was a shitty thing to do, all right, but maybe you're being a bit harsh about the other stuff, Jo? Plenty of people round here would say the job Amos and others like him are doing is very worthwhile. They'd probably say that helping prevent nuclear war is rather more important than rescuing people who get stuck on cliffs. Marty used to say he was thankful he wasn't doing Amos's job. He said the strain did something to you, day after day spent studying targets, towns in the Ukraine whose inhabitants had done nothing to you but who you might at any minute have to drop a bomb on. The whole spirit of it has to be cold and scientific but also aggressive, and all at the same time. I think that sort of life must take its toll.'

'Oh, you can see it doing that,' agreed Jo. 'It's one thing to get these guys highly motivated for something but it's another if you're going to keep them at that sort of pitch indefinitely. It changes them. I could see it in Amos. It made him *cruder*, something like that. Rougher. If you're a hundred per cent professional bomber there isn't any per cent left over for you to be an ordinary husband about the house, is there?'

Avril glanced at the clock on the mantelpiece. 'I think we've probably had enough Ovaltine. We could have some tea before I go and fetch the kids,' she said, 'though we needn't worry about them. Nan and Grampa love having them. When we come home I'll put them pretty much straight to bed.' She took the kettle from the top of the stove and into the scullery where she lit a gas ring to bring the water all the way up to boiling.

'Do you think those policemen know about you and Ted?'

'That's just it: you can never tell how much coppers know. Perhaps they went to his house and found a list of his customers including my name and they were just working through the list? I know he kept a notebook because sometimes he gave credit if you were too skint one day. It was very neat and businesslike with names and addresses and dates. That's one of the things I like about him – he's punctual and professional. There again people round here are that nosy, one of them might have seen him parked outside one night and they'd have probably told those detectives. That's people round here: all smiles and good neighbours if you meet them out shopping; but they'd shop you too behind your back, given half the chance.'

That morning Jo had made a sponge cake in Avril's Wonder Oven: a metal affair with a thermometer set in its circular lid in which one could bake things by standing it on an ordinary gas ring. It was supposed to be more economical than having to heat an entire oven. This particular cake had raspberry jam in the middle and Jo now cut them both a slice each.

'You weren't really banking on him, though, were you?' she asked Avril.

'I suppose not. It was just nice to feel, you know, wanted again after a whole year of being a widow and a mother. Someone warm next to you. I really miss that part of it. Also, I do believe children need two parents. Petey definitely needs a man in his life. So at the back of my mind I admit there was always the thought: by a miracle someone decent might come your way. But the decent ones don't always want to take on someone else's children, do they? Ted's very nice in the bedroom department but if it turns out he's not all

I hoped he might be in the other departments I don't know that I've lost anything very much. I'm not pinning too many hopes on him. Fewer still after this morning.'

'Bloody *men*.' Jo gazed at her tea and smiled wanly. 'I'm beginning to think a nice reliable nine-to-five orang-utan might be a safer bet after all. Perhaps I should get on to that lady scientist and get a few names and addresses . . . I'm so grateful to you, Rilly, taking me in like this. But short of going back to my parents I couldn't think who to go to.'

'You did exactly right. It's lovely to have company. Also, it's nice to have someone who can help out. The kids adore you, so you've made my life a lot easier in the last however long it is. Three weeks? But I know it's much harder for you to get into work these days without Amos's car. That's an awful bus ride first thing in the morning.'

'True. But I still love the job, Rilly, and it'll get better once winter's over. It's the getting up in the dark I hate. Thank God you were able to borrow your brother's car to move me from Wearsby, otherwise I don't know what I'd have done. Called Pickfords, probably. I just had to be gone by the time Amos came home.'

'I wonder what he's been doing since you left?'

'Oh, the same as always. Flying, or talking about flying. Drinking in the mess or in town with the boys. For all I care he may have got young Gavin to move into Brabazon Close with him. That would give the true-blue neighbours something to talk about, let alone the barrack warden.'

21

The two Vulcans were being prepared for their ranger to Libya. Based at Luqa in Malta, they would fly their desert sorties to the ranges south-east of Wheelus AFB, a distance of only a little over two hundred nautical miles. The base commander at Wheelus had extended a warm invitation to the two crews and was offering refuelling and overnight facilities as needed, but Bomber Command evidently felt it would be better if the Vulcans were based on an RAF station, where any spare parts for the aircraft would be more easily available. That was them being heavily tactful, Amos thought; it was more likely their chief concern was to keep Oilcan and Vector away from snoopers, even if they were our allies. But regardless of where they were to be based, the crews were looking forward to Exercise Praying Mantis, as the Americans were calling it. Predictably, the Wearsby wags had already renamed it. Even the lineys out on the pan now referred to it as Fraying Panties.

The two crews' chief technicians, Baldy Hodge and Barry Venn, would be coming along as well in the sixth seats, although they would not fly on the actual sorties to Libya. This was for reasons of safety rather than security. Several of the runs would be at low level and a fourth crewman might fatally slow the evacuation of the crew compartment in the event of a low-level emergency. But the two men would be invaluable if there were some mechanical problem. Baldy Hodge spent the day before the trip inspecting his aircraft with great thoroughness. He even remembered to look out his passport, although over the years he had flown to stations all over the world without once having to produce it. Having your F.1250 was all the ID you needed, and any scruff-arsed country that thought otherwise was one he didn't fancy going to.

As soon as he had known he would be going to Luqa Baldy had called the betting shop in Barnsley, quoted Cardew's Reward and had passed on the information to the plummy voice. The voice had told him that someone in Malta would contact him for the rest of the photographs. Baldy had made it clear to the voice that he would expect decent money in return for them since the job was very much riskier than anything else he had undertaken. 'Noted,' was all the voice had said and the connection was broken after only fifteen seconds. Baldy had been obliged to make the call from the public box outside Wearsby's main gate: a breach of his normal cautious practice made unavoidable by his being unable to get away for more than a few minutes. At least he couldn't be overheard there, unlike in the sergeants' mess. The kiosk smelt of fresh paint and as yet no-one had hastily scratched phone numbers onto any of its surfaces. In fact the entire box was new, the GPO having finally replaced the old booth that had been partly demolished by carousing airmen some months earlier.

As he worked, Baldy was irritated that he hadn't yet had an opportunity to complete photographing the new equipment. But security in general on the station had recently been tightened. Instead of regular patrols there was now an MP and police dog on continuous guard beneath each of the two 'P' Flight Vulcans. No-one knew the reason for this new regime. As always, rumour talked of spies; some hazarded it was connected with the black-market food scandal in which three arrests had already been made on the station. More cynical gossips claimed that poor old Groupie had put up such a black over the Christmas party affair it was as much as his career was worth to risk anything else that might suggest he wasn't running a tight ship. But Baldy packed the Minox and the flash-gun, confident that things were bound to be more relaxed in Malta and that sooner or later a suitable opportunity would present itself. He wasn't fussed about it. Things were always dozier abroad, especially in Mediterranean countries.

His more immediate concern was trying to imagine everything that might go wrong with the aircraft. He began to assemble suitable spares and equipment to take with them in a two-ton pannier that would be carried in the Vulcan's bomb bay. First to go in was a spare tail parachute – a bulky pack weighing all of two hundred pounds which he nonetheless picked up and heaved in by himself. Some spare radio sets went in, a dozen gallons of red hydraulic oil and, given the Olympus engines' notorious thirst for oil, twenty gallons of the stuff. Better safe than sorry. Sundry other parts were added and Hodge topped off his selection with his own Elswick Hopper, incongruous though a bicycle looked in the bomb bay of a nuclear bomber. He had years of experience of his aircraft being parked on a pan at the far end of a runway in the tropics, a mile's blazing walk from the nearest building. He had frequently made it clear in his distinctive manner that he was buggered if he was going to be stranded out there on the edge of Bongo-Bongo Land replacing a fuse while everybody else roared off in the only available transport to a nice cool mess with the rhythmic swish of overhead fans and beer so cold it numbed your mouth.

Now that his bicycle was stowed Baldy could see there was room enough left in the pannier for the crews' kit, which was much neater than having to stow it inside the aircraft in the bomb-aimer's niche, anchored beneath a cargo net. But in any case the new bombing kit was now taking up all available space. Baldy liked his aircraft pin-neat, which is why it pained him after sorties and

QRAs to find the floor of the crew compartment littered with wrappers from Spangles and Blackjack chews as well as empty sherbet fountain tubes that had rolled away underfoot. On one occasion he had even found an immense gob-stopper welded to the floor next to the nav plotter's seat. He assumed the man had spat it out when called on suddenly to use the intercom. A bloody childish sweet anyway, Baldy thought sourly. The thing was almost the size of a golf ball. It only needed a serious bump from a turb to lodge it in your windpipe and that would be it for a vital component of Britain's nuclear deterrent: incapacitated by a gob-stopper. When flying, the chief technician favoured jelly babies himself.

Meanwhile his counterpart, Barry Venn, was engaged in the same job on Yogi 2, parked alongside. Periodically the two men trotted over to shelter from the winter weather beneath each other's aircraft and compare notes. Naturally, both of them knew the purpose of Exercise Fraying Panties, just as they knew that the code words Oilcan and Vector referred to the new systems that were to be tested in Libya. Group Captain Mewell might have ordered this knowledge be restricted to the two aircrews, but even he would have known such things couldn't be kept secret for long from the engineers who in many respects knew the aircraft more intimately even than the men who flew them.

'Ever been to Luqa?' asked Baldy. 'Well, I have, and it's got something all these stations have that share runways with a civil airport. *Civilians.*' He managed to get a fair amount of disgust into the word and Venn nodded sympathetically. The only civilian aviators that military aircrew rated seriously were ex-RAF or, at a pinch, ex-USAF: the rest were frankly more or less of a liability. 'Though to be fair, the local tassafs at Luqa are a step up from your usual native grease-monkey, probably because we've trained them a bit over the years.'

'Tassafs?' queried Venn.

'That's what they call them there. TASF – Transit Aircraft Servicing Flight. We'll probably be parked on tassaf dispersal. They're local Maltese boys but they can do most things in the way of regular service and repairs. They're not really used to having crew chiefs like us coming along so I suppose they've had to learn how to do some of our work themselves. One or two of 'em are not too dozy.'

Venn recognised this as a positive accolade from Baldy, whose generosity with praise was usually illustrated behind his back by jokes involving Scotsmen and Jews. 'Well, I must say it'll be nice to get away. Fenland in January – I mean, it's just not designed for human beings, is it? Look at it.' Venn swept a gloved hand at the hissing sleet that temporarily obscured the control tower three hundred yards away. 'I always feel we're under water here. We might as well be stationed on Dogger Bank or somewhere. Still, I'll say this for Vulcans – they do keep you dry on the pan. Not like bloody Beverleys, where the wing's too high to give you much shelter, specially if it's blowing.'

'Even so, my lad, don't expect to get much of a tan in Malta.' This was Old Hand Baldy speaking. 'It can get pretty cold in the Med at this time of the year. It ought to be better than this, though. Tell you the truth, I don't really like these trips as much as I used to. Must be getting old.'

'You're not alone, Ernie. It's so effing uncomfortable. You squat there in the dark on that survival pack trussed up like a ruddy turkey and feeling airsick while your feet freeze, hour after hour of it. Don't get me wrong: I love the job. I wouldn't do anything else. It's just the flying I don't like.'

'I'm taking hydraulic oil, are you? They're ninety-nine per cent certain to have drums of the stuff at Luqa but it's that one per cent

215

that flips the shit into the fan. It doesn't take more than some faulty swaging.'

'It's already in. True – all we need is what happened Tuesday and we're sunk. That was XJ810 again.'

'Bloody jinxed, that aircraft. First Cowans stands it on its tail while refuelling, stupid prat, I hope he's freezing his balls off at St Athan in Welsh Wales right now. And then that caper the other night. Nobody's fault here, just crappy manufacturing. Either a pipe's end is properly swaged or it isn't. Don't talk to me about quality control in British industry. We've become a nation of shoddy workers. If you ask me, it's high time we learned from the Yanks. They build their aircraft like Swiss fucking watches compared to ours.'

This was a familiar Baldy theme and could be heard aired at any lunchtime in the sergeants' mess. It was always forceful and usually baffling because one could never quite work out what his own position was, other than dissenting. Some said he sounded like a Communist, others like a reforming patriot. He would very often quote his favourite film, *I'm All Right Jack*, in defence of the British worker who was forced into sloppiness and unionised militancy by inept, self-interested management. Ever since that toffee-nosed arsehole Duncan Sandys had screwed it up, said Baldy, the aircraft industry was a shambles. You raise his salary and boost his morale with some decent management and your British workman will give you quality second to none . . . Although nobody in the mess quite believed this, the large and truculent Baldy was someone to whom you instinctively murmured assent from behind your copy of *Reveille*, especially when his ears glowed like red flags.

The present pretext for his outburst was an incident three nights ago when one of the flexible hydraulic hoses to the brakes on XJ810 had torn loose on landing and sprayed oil over the port main bogie's disc packs. It was sheer luck it happened where there were erks with the right kind of fire extinguishers to put out what could have become a major fire. It was just the sort of incident neither chief technician wanted to happen to one of their planes when they were away. Eventually Baldy Hodge trotted back to Yogi 1 and completed his own checklist of things he might need before supervising the ground crew as they ran a painstaking external inspection of the aircraft. For the moment the weather had lifted somewhat. The wind stocking near the threshold of the runway was stiff in the cutting breeze that was coming from the north-east and bringing over sudden flurries of snow and sleet. In the intervals between them visibility improved so that in the distance the occasional car or lorry could be seen on the main road or parked in the lay-by beyond the perimeter fence. In the other direction the pale grey tower of Market Tewsbury church stood clear for a while against the more leaden grey of the sky. In these intervals Hodge as usual strode about in the open making a variety of his trademark spastic gestures, apparently in involuntary response to what he thought of as the lineys' blundering incompetence as they went about their tasks.

*

On the morning of their departure the two crews went out to their aircraft at dawn to make them 'combat ready' so the more laborious of the crew-in checks could be dispensed with later. They then went off to breakfast, Baldy Hodge treating himself to a mammoth feast with Barry Venn at the aircrew diner. As he observed with an air of weary experience, one never knew on these trips where the next meal was coming from. When at last the coach drew up outside he got Amos to sign Yogi 1's Form 700 while bringing with him the form's travelling version for the trip.

The Met report favoured a take-off by mid-morning, after which they said more snow was on the way. Baldy followed the crew up the ladder into the cramped and dark compartment, which almost immediately became still darker as the hatch closed with a hiss and a thump. The two small porthole-like windows, one on either side of the AEO's and navrad's positions, were always kept covered. The chief technician understood the reason but still cursed the gloom as he took his place. His ad hoc seat was the lid of a toolbox on the floor. He began strapping himself tightly into his bulky parachute, from which further webbing went to the survival pack that dangled under his ample bottom and which would form an unyielding and lumpy cushion for the duration of the flight. Finally, he clipped himself into the even more restricting safety harness attached to the bare metal frame on the bulkhead with the leather pad for his head. Warplanes were definitely built with functionality rather than comfort in mind.

Once seated, panting slightly and trussed with sundry straps and buckles into a semi-crouch, Baldy plugged in his own intercom connection and listened to the crew carrying out the irreducible minimum of pre-start checks before he heard the turbine outside feed compressed air to the first engine for start-up. Soon all four engines were running and he heard McKenna given the clear-to-go. Almost at once the pilot blipped the throttles to unstick the aircraft from the slight icing around the tyres and Baldy could feel her begin to move. Everything outside had been handled well, he conceded grudgingly. No difficulties with the chocks, and nor should there have been. A problem sometimes occurred on the pan if a QRA ended in a scramble and an over-eager pilot had the power up to eighty per cent or more and held only by the brakes. There was a point at which the tremendous thrust simply overcame the brakes and the aircraft would start to move regardless. It wasn't that the brakes failed, simply that the Vulcan would move even with the wheels locked solid. If the lineys weren't quick enough to remove the chocks the tyres could half override them, making it impossible to pull them free, which always led to an abort and a serious black mark against whoever was in charge – usually the chief technician. Baldy was an old enough hand to ensure that when his aircraft was scrambled the chocks were pulled almost completely away before the pilot gunned the engines. In this way only the last inch or two of the long Toblerone-shaped blocks remained in front of the main bogies and could be wrenched free or even scrunched aside by the massive tyres.

Now Yogi 1 was lined up at the threshold of runway two-four and Hodge was listening to the familiar pre-take-off checks: brakes on, throttles to eighty per cent, check all gauges normal, airframe anti-icing on, parking brake off, main brakes off, engines to full take-off thrust. Since he was facing rearwards the increasing acceleration threw him forward against the harness. He listened to the co-pilot calling out the speeds up in the cockpit barely six feet away, announcing when the rudder became effective, 100 knots – 120 – 140 – 160 – V1, rotate – lift off – 170 knots – climbing out – undercarriage up. He cocked a professional ear for the clunking sounds beneath him of the doors closing and the latches engaging. The ambient noise suddenly became quieter as the airflow outside smoothed and the reflection of the engines' blast from the ground no longer reached them.

The AEO's voice could be heard calling the checks.

'Undercarriage up – all lights out.'

'Up and lights out,' came the co-pilot's response.

'Flaps up.'

'Flaps up.'

'Cabin air supply on.'

219

'Cabin air supply on.'

'Heat on.'

'Heat on.'

And eventually Rickards said 'Take-off checks completed.'

Soon they had reached the top of their climb, had levelled off at cruise power of ninety-three per cent and were settled into what was scheduled to be a flight of three hours and eighteen minutes. Baldy's seat on the survival pack soon became so uncomfortable he released his harness and stood up as much as he could with his heavy parachute on. He slackened its straps and then took the pack off altogether before standing on one of the vertical steps to the cockpit. That put him between the tall backs of the pilots' eject-or seats, a position he often took on flights he accompanied. From here he could keep an eye on various dials and gauges while also enjoying what he could of the limited view afforded from the Vul-can's windows. He was thankful neither of these pilots smoked. In the past he had flown with a captain who, in defiance of reg-ulations, lit up a pipe in the cockpit and, once the auto-pilot was engaged, sat back and read a book, puffing contentedly. On a flight to Khormaksar in Aden, one co-pilot had managed to get through the whole of Mickey Spillane's *The Deep*, and that leg had included some tricky in-flight refuelling. Baldy didn't mind the reading but he did object to the smoking, even though the captain concerned had tapped all his ash and dottle into an old St Bruno tin rather than on the cockpit floor.

They flew south-east, high above a tossing ocean of cloud that was dumping sleet onto unfortunate mortals below. Baldy re-membered the first time he had stood between the pilots in a Vul-can cockpit, astonished at how little they could see from their sup-posedly majestic vantage point. Not only was the cockpit cramped, with the pilots sitting shoulder to shoulder in their bulky gear.

They seemed to be sunk up to their noses in a trough entirely lined with gauges and switches and black trunking. Forward vision through the steeply-raked fan of five small shatterproof panes was squeezed between the high coaming of the instrument panel bulking up in front of them and the low canopy – itself lined with knobs and controls – frowning down almost to meet it. It was only when you stood hunched in this space capsule of a cockpit that you appreciated how vital were the two periscopes the AEO could use to view most of the aircraft's underside as well as much of its upper surfaces. They were the only way to get any direct sight of what was happening outside.

At about the trip's halfway mark, when they had just entered Italian airspace, the rations were broached and various sandwiches, pork pies and chicken legs divvied up, passed around and swapped. There were Thermos flasks of fruit juice, tea, and the infamous 'NATO standard' coffee: very hot, very sweet and very strong. Not much more than two hours had passed since Baldy had eaten his monumental breakfast but he found himself quite able to pack down a heroic lunch on top of it. 'Eating Command' was living up to its reputation. Crews might be yearning for a crap, and supernumeraries might be accommodated in discomfort approaching that of the extreme confinement used by professional torturers, but no-one was going to starve to death on one of Bomber Command's aircraft. In point of fact aircrew mostly ate in-flight meals for the same reason that civilian passengers did: to alleviate boredom rather than hunger.

When everyone had finished Baldy made sure everything was packed away and the Thermos flasks stowed before once more buckling on the survival pack that doubled as his cushion and strapping himself back into his crouch on the wooden box top. Within twenty minutes the AEO was in touch with Luqa and just after they had passed over Agrigento on the south-western coast of Sicily Yogi 1 began its let-down. From the Tyrrhenian Sea onwards the clouds had apparently cleared completely. Now Baldy could imagine a fisherman glancing up to see their contrail fray and stop, the Vulcan's white triangle still too small to see against the blue of the sky, its jet resonance probably lost in the slap of waves against the boat. A bare half an hour later they came into Malta from the south-east, low over Birzebbuga, and touched down on runway three-two before taxiing to the dispersal area. With a sigh of ni-trogen the door opened and foreign-smelling air spilled into the Vulcan: a scent of sun-baked bricks and sea and dusty cement that told Baldy he was definitely abroad.

*

The crews were warmly received and happy to leave their chief technicians behind with the aircraft, supervising refuelling and other post-flight checks. Baldy Hodge and Barry Venn were given strict orders to allow nobody aboard unsupervised and never to leave the aircraft unlocked and without an armed guard, which would be supplied. They left Baldy retrieving his bicycle from the bomb-bay pannier, the sight of which caused some amusement among the tassaf erks. Vulcans were still a comparatively exotic sight in Malta and attracted the usual awed attention. It was diffi-cult to associate them with ferrying battered old bicycles about the world.

Once the men's own kit had been retrieved and loaded aboard the crew bus it drove them off to change out of their flying gear. This was Gavin's first time in RAF Luqa and he was surprised by the activity and sheer variety of military aircraft there. Behind the coming and going of RAF Land Rovers, Bedford trucks and fuel bowsers he noted like a boy plane-spotter the parked aircraft they passed. He recognised four photo-reconnaissance Canberras belonging to 39 Squadron with their camouflaged upper surfaces and sky-blue underwings and bellies. His colleagues simultaneously pointed at half a dozen Canberras from Wearsby that would be flying to and from RAF Idris and the Tarhuna range to practise toss-bombing. In addition he counted two Shackletons, three Hunters, a Javelin, a Meteor, two Hastings transports, a Britannia of Transport Command from RAF Lyneham and a de Havilland Devon from the Idris Flight. There was also a USAF C-54 Skymaster he thought might well have flown across from Wheelus. There were a couple of NATO and French aircraft as well as an Italian air force Fiat jet. As the bus drew up a large Argosy transport was lumbering into the air, probably heading for the Middle East somewhere or maybe Changi, Singapore. It was all bustling evidence of the extent of Britain's military presence around the world. The thought was inseparable from a feeling of pride and confidence. He suddenly felt his future secure.

*

At six o'clock that evening Baldy Hodge decided that now was as good a time as any to try for the pictures he needed. Get the thing over and done with. With any luck the reward could bring his savings up to the magic £5,000 mark. With that he would buy the house and see his father and mother properly installed. Then he would serve out his remaining four years while immediately quitting this hole-and-corner stuff which fell so dismally short of any James Bondian romance. There were never going to be Aston Martins and bikini'd temptresses in his life. Not that Baldy had ever expected them. He was content to take the money and keep his head down.

With the key to XM580 around his neck he transferred the

flashgun and battery pack from his duffel bag to a canvas toolkit. The little Minox camera went into a breast pocket. Before closing the toolkit he armed himself with a heavy double-ended spanner that he tucked down the leg pocket of his overalls. You never knew abroad. Then, taking the torch he had thoughtfully brought, Baldy left his quarters, mounted his trusty bike and pedalled off past the brightly lit flight lines. The two Vulcans were parked nose-out in comparative seclusion on the far side, lit by the mournful bluish light cast by two widely separated and very tall mercury va-pour standards that made the camouflage stripes on the aircraft's tail fins stand out starkly. The evening was chilly but dry – a big advance on bloody Lincolnshire, he thought. As he neared the aircraft he could see a white-topped Military Police Land Rover parked to one side. The figures of two policemen with their dogs emerged from each of the shadows cast by the great wings. The one guarding XM580 came up to him as Baldy dismounted and leaned his bicycle against the main landing gear. The MP shone his torch directly into Baldy's eyes.

'Yes?' said the policeman curtly.

'I'm the crew chief of this aircraft and I need to look at something. And get that bloody torch out of my eyes, you great moron. I can't see a thing.'

'You could try to keep a civil tongue in your head,' the man ob-served, lowering the light to examine the name stitched to Baldy's overalls and the toolkit slung from one shoulder. Hodge returned the compliment, learning from the MP's stripes and ID tag that his interlocutor was one Corporal Wooderson. 'Anyway, Chief Tech-nician Hodge, nobody's going into this aircraft tonight, not on my watch. So you may as well get back on your bike. Sorry about that but I've got my orders.'

'So have I,' said Baldy belligerently. 'I've got a lot to do. We've got a critical exercise the day after tomorrow.'

'Yes, and I've got a critical boss and I'm a lot more scared of him than I am of you. I don't suppose you're a Russian spy but my orders are to treat everyone as if they were. So how about you push off and come back tomorrow.'

And then Baldy Hodge did a very rash thing. He raised his hand and jabbed a forefinger the size of a carrot at the MP, saying 'Now you listen to me . . .' but before the words were out the dog went for him, sinking its teeth into his left forearm with a gruff snarl. With a yell of pain and surprise, Baldy did something even more stupid. With his free hand he fumbled the spanner from its long pocket and brought it down on the animal's back with a savage blow. The dog gave an oddly human cry and fell away.

'Reg!' the policeman shouted, retreating a few steps as he reached for the flap of his holster. But his companion was already there, gun in hand, attracted by the raised voices. Seeing the spanner with which Baldy was now prodding at his mate to keep him away and, in the gloom beneath the Vulcan mistaking it for a pistol, Reg shot Baldy in the thigh. Baldy collapsed to the concrete, the spanner clanging away.

'You OK, Timber?' On a long leash Reg's dog, hackles raised, was standing guard over Baldy, who seemed to be writhing in a pool of hydraulic fluid.

'I'm all right but the bastard's hurt Beefy. Shine your torch?' He slid the loop of his dog's lead from his wrist and knelt by the animal, stroking its head. Beefy was trying to get to his feet but his back legs wouldn't work and he only moaned, looking up at his master as though he knew it was the end for him. 'Smashed,' concluded the policeman, having gently felt the dog's back. 'Completely smashed.' He unbuttoned his holster. 'You go and call it in.'

'What about this guy?' Reg flashed his light over the groaning

Baldy and revealed the hydraulic fluid to be a spreading lake of blood.

'Fuck him. First things first.'

Reg and his dog jogged across to the Land Rover. Before they reached it the policeman knelt behind Beefy, gave him an affectionate pat and shot him in the back of the head. Apart from a twitching forepaw the animal lay still.

'And how I wish I could do the same to you, fuckface,' said Wooderson chokingly, getting up and going to stoop over Baldy, his boots twin black islands in a crimson sea. But he saw at a glance it would be a wasted bullet. There was far more blood on the concrete than could possibly remain inside the big man, who suddenly began to look shrunken. As Timber Wooderson bent over him Baldy opened his eyes very wide and said weakly, 'Dad? Is that you, Dad?' and with a sigh died. Wooderson straightened up and holstered his weapon. In his shock all he could think of was the endless questioning and paperwork this was going to bring. 'Why me?' he murmured towards the sky. In the distance flashing lights appeared, converging on the scene.

22

Unaware of what had happened in their aircraft's shadow, the two crews had already left the station for a night on the town. Some locally stationed officers who claimed to know the right places drove them to the Phoenicia Hotel at Floriana on the outskirts of Valletta. Apparently its Pegasus Bar was a favourite watering-place of BEA aircrews – most of whom were ex-RAF – as well as of air hostesses. At any rate it was deemed a good place to start. The Luqa station commander had already been in touch with Wheelus to announce the safe arrival of their guest participants in Praying Mantis and was told they would be expected the day after next. Tomorrow would be a day for nursing hangovers and running yet more checks on the Vulcans to make sure they would not only be fit to fly but capable of giving a good account of themselves.

'Bring on the hosties,' a flight-lieutenant on Canberras said happily as he parked his battered Singer Gazelle outside the grandiose, triple-arched portico with 'Hotel Phoenicia' incised in the stone-work along the top. 'They joined the airline for travel, duty-free and *pleasure*. Which just happen to be the exact same reasons why we joined the RAF. Right, chaps? Time to get our ends away.'

In the Pegasus Bar Gavin and Ken Pilcher, his opposite number from Yogi 2, felt themselves gravitate together less because they were both AEOs than out of some kind of resistance to the general atmosphere of extroverted booziness. Ken had recently married a nurse and was maybe still under the restraining influence of his marriage vows. He was also something of a car freak and Gavin was happy to talk about vehicles they had driven or longed to drive. Yet as they nursed beers together at a small table Gavin was conscious of how often he glanced across the room to where Amos was standing at the bar. He was aware also of something like envy for the others in that group: all of them pilots of similar rank. He recognised one of them as a wing commander from Wearsby's Canberra squadron and couldn't entirely suppress the idea that together they really did look like an élite. He thought Amos in particular looked absurdly like an Ealing Studios version of a quietly heroic bomber captain.

Ever since the night of the Christmas party Gavin had tried not to think too much about his increased intimacy with Amos. It had undeniably disturbed the otherwise meshing clockwork of his life. Life in an active squadron was made orderly by ritual and routine, most of it too demanding ever to qualify as boring in any normal sense. Anything that upset this by falling outside the normal round of daily duties and occasional benders was hard to deal with, especially if – as now – it also reminded him of a younger self he hoped had disappeared for good.

At that moment Ken abruptly broke off a disquisition about Jim Clark's brilliance as a racing driver, raised an arm and exclaimed, 'Good Lord, there's Brian Tatchell. I had no idea he was in Malta. Would you excuse me, Gavin? I've not seen him since Swanton Morley.' He got up with his beer and went off to greet a foxy-looking fellow with a gingery moustache. Gavin thoughtfully finished his own beer and was just considering getting a taxi back to the airfield to make an early night of it when a girl sat down at his table. Her sultry dark looks reminded him instantly of a film actress he couldn't place. One of the 'Carry On' films – that was it: Fenella Fielding in *Carry On Regardless*.

'Hello, I'm Veronica,' she said. 'What's a nice boy like you doing all on his lonesome? Oh, don't worry, darling, I'm not on the game. Just bored, basically, as you're looking.' Her breath smelt of alcohol as she chattered on about the awful *tedium* of Malta while Gavin tried to work out an appropriate response. He wasn't used to girls making the first move. He found himself mildly attracted by the dark hairs on her forearms. 'Quite a dull place, this bar,' Veronica was saying. 'I vote we sneak off and I show you something of the island. You've never been here before? Well then, come on.' Seeing Gavin hesitate, she asked a little satirically, 'Do you need permission? Get your senior officer's OK?'

'I was just . . .' He cast a glance at the rest of his colleagues at the bar, severally engaged in drinking and chatting up various floozies. 'No.'

His new friend put on a mohair cardigan and led the way out of the Phoenicia, down the steps and into the night. Parked among the ornamental palms was a maroon Daimler Dart that, in the scattered lights filtering through fronds, appeared almost black. It was an enviable car although Gavin had always found its prognathous grille worrying, like someone whose mouth bulged with too many teeth. Still, as the proud owner of a Bug-Eye Sprite, he reflected that he was probably in no position to be picky or competitive about the aesthetics of British motor designs.

'We'll keep the hood up, I think,' she said. 'It's too chilly otherwise.'

Soon they were out in what passed for open country in this small island. He had the impression of stony fields with tumbledown walls topped with prickly pear, an endless succession of small shuttered villages and immense churches. In the distance frequent flashes and showers of coloured balls in the sky were evidence of more than one firework display. It was a clear night with a large moon and there were occasional glimpses of the sea. Veronica drove with what people called 'flair' when they didn't want others to think they were scared.

'I told you what I do but you haven't told me what you do,' he said at length, his legs braced stiffly in the dark.

'Nothing yet, darling.' She flashed him an ambiguous, dashboard-lit smile. 'Well, Daddy works for Mitchell Cotts. He's always on the move. He goes to Tripoli to look at their dreary supermarket there, or down to Mombasa or Rhodesia or Tanganyika – whatever they're calling Tanganyika these days. Or South Africa. He's hardly ever here. Mum's bored out of her tiny skull. Freddie's away at Oxford. I shall be going to the Slade shortly.'

'The Slade?'

'The School of Fine Art. London, you know? The capital of England? I want to design jewellery . . . Sorry – this is a bloody silly car for a place like this. You really need a Land Rover here, something with a bit of clearance.' She was bouncing the Dart down a stony track towards what looked like a cliff edge where the world stopped abruptly. They halted with a flurry of pebbles beside a small stone house. 'Mum bought this place for Freddie to study in. That's a laugh. Boys like Freddie don't study. So I sometimes use it. There's a great view of the sea if you happen to like sea.' She switched off. 'So what does your father do? Is he also in the RAF?'

'No, he's a GP. In Devon.'

'Truly rural.'

'It is, rather. But I always wanted to fly and had a knack for electrical things so I didn't follow my father. Amos says I'm no great loss to the medical profession and I expect he's right.'

'Amos?'

'Squadron Leader McKenna. He's the captain of our Vulcan. A terrific sort.'

'A terrific sort? Oh, was he the tall one at the bar? The film-star-good-looks one?'

'I suppose so, yes. It's true, he is very good-looking.'

'He looks queer to me. My brother's queer and so are all his friends at Oxford. I can always tell.'

After the initial shock Gavin debated whether to invent a firm defence of Amos as a happily married man but decided it was too late in every sense. Anyway it wouldn't be worth it. This languid, sophisticated girl beside him clearly inhabited a world so different from his own there could be few discernible points of contact.

'And I've yet to make up my mind about you,' Veronica added.

'If you were in any doubt,' said Gavin bravely, 'why did you invite me out?'

'Oh, I like challenges. A girl can get mortal bored on this ghastly Catholic island. *You're* not a Catholic, are you? Let's go in. There should be some bottles and things.'

The rough little cottage faced east, and when in the morning Gavin opened the shutters he winced at the blast of sunlight before being struck by the magnificence of the panoramic view, which was of the molten heave and glitter of sea to the horizon. Sections of nearby cliff were of desert-coloured rock. A dry breeze smelling of marine things with an underlay of something aniseedy from the tough vegetation filled his lungs and slightly cleared his aching head. From somewhere came the distant whanging and jangling of church bells.

'Milk and sugar in your coffee, I suppose?' Veronica called up from the kitchen.

'Please.'

'Hard cheese. There isn't any. You get it black or not at all.'

On an ancient wireless set she found the BBC World Service. The news seemed to be mostly about the escalating war in

Vietnam. They drank their coffee in silence until Gavin said with a self-deprecating laugh, 'I'm sorry, Veronica. I really had much too much to drink last night. You know how it is.'

'I do indeed,' she said with a weary trace of bitterness. She patted his hand condescendingly. 'That's your alibi, darling, you stick to it. Handled with care it could serve you for life.' After a little: 'You'll be wanting to get back now?'

'I'm afraid so. We're off to Libya tomorrow on an exercise,' he added indiscreetly.

'How very dreary for you. Darling, I've *been* to Libya with Dad and it's utterly frightful. There's bugger-all there, you know. Roman ruins, yawn yawn. A few nice olive groves and vineyards that Mussolini's Italians planted along the coast around Tripoli. Good for Il Duce, frankly: they're about the only green things in the country. A few of the old Sicilians who farmed them are still there. In Tripoli itself it's just ex-Bedouins and Texan oilmen in frightful check shirts. Thirty miles inland it's desert and wadis and escarpments and sand dunes and that sort of thing for X thousand miles all the way down to Chad or Niger or one of those other non-countries. Forget Libya.'

'Oh, it's just an exercise for a day or two and anyway we'll be based in Luqa and flying down. We won't set foot in Libya.'

'Bully for you.' But Veronica had already wearied of this topic and they left the house and got into the car whose dew-wet soft top was already tautening in the sun. On the drive back to Luqa Gavin thought Malta looked much how he'd imagined Libya might: a sandy-coloured landscape with blocky, whitewashed buildings seen against a gentian-blue sky and garnished with vicious succulents. It was also dotted with skeletal iron windmills, presumably for pumping scarce water from artesian wells. In addition to ancient British cars, the narrow roads were full of blowsy, shambling buses with bright paintwork displaying unpronounceable destinations full of x's. In due course Veronica dropped him back at Luqa and his erotic adventure, such as it was, was over. She sped off with a non-committal wave and he found he was relieved to be back in the RAF's ample and reassuring bosom. He could see in the distance the two Vulcans' camouflaged fins sticking up above the other parked aircraft. This, at least, was a familiar world in which he felt properly at home. His first act was to have a thorough shower. Then he went to the mess for breakfast, which was humming with the news of Baldy's shooting.

'You mean, shot *dead*?' said Gavin incredulously, forkful of bacon arrested in mid-air.

'Doornail. It probably wasn't on purpose but the Snowdrop hit his femoral artery and he bled out on the spot,' said Vic Ferrit, not (it struck Gavin) entirely without relish. 'It's true I never really took to the guy. He was an odd sod but you had to admit he was a top-notch chiefie. But that's still not the real punchline. Guess what they found on him? Only a spy camera complete with flashgun.'

'You're joking.'

'I'm not,' said Vic. 'I got it from Amos, who's just been with the CO here. It's all heavily under wraps but it looks like old Baldy was working for *them* on the side.'

'You mean the *Russians*? *Baldy*? I don't believe it.'

'Join the club, dearie,' said Vic amiably. 'No-one here wants to believe it, you can bet on that. But why else was he trying to get into the aircraft at night with a camera? More importantly, why aren't these Vegenins I've been taking doing a damn thing for my headache?'

'All hell's breaking loose,' confirmed Ken Pilcher, at that moment joining them with his coffee. 'They don't know whether to shit or go blind. How much has been compromised? They haven't the foggiest.'

233

'Sabotage?'

'No, they think that's unlikely,' Ken said. 'After all, he was flying in it.'

'True,' agreed Vic. 'My reading of our late lamented chiefie is that he was too devoted to his aircraft to do it deliberate damage. I don't think he cared much about us, but he did about his precious charge. He struck me as pretty much wedded to the thing.'

'So what about Frayed Panties?' Gavin asked. 'Do you think it'll go ahead?'

'God knows. You can bet all sorts of scrambled phone calls and coded telexes are whizzing between here and High Wycombe at this very moment. Personally, I can't see any reason for cancelling if old Baldy was just freelancing on his own behalf. I say we get some more toast,' Ken said. 'All this drama has given me a real appetite.'

By lunchtime both Vulcan crews had been informed that the exercises would go ahead as planned. Yogi 1 would just have to get along without its crew chief for a few days but that shouldn't be a problem. By mid-afternoon much of the shock had worn off in the absence of any more information. The local technicians had meanwhile connected both Vulcans to the ground power supply and Gavin had spent an hour in his aircraft's crew compartment running his own check of the extensive electrical systems. He then went outside to sit on one of the main wheels, watching the air traffic coming and going on the runway. He noted that the inevitable Snowdrops and their dogs were never far away. After a while a dusty RAF Land Rover drew up and Amos came and joined him.

'Jesus, what a to-do,' he greeted Gavin. He hitched himself with a groan onto an adjacent tyre. 'Talk about a right royal kerfuffle.'

'What's the latest?'

'Well, old Baldy's still dead. That's about the only certainty. I had to go to the morgue and identify him for the groupie here. Bit of a shock, seeing him lying there the colour of chalk. They say he's completely exsanguinated. Not a drop left in him. His only bit of colour was that tattoo on his arm, "Dishonour Before Death". At least his motto came true in the end,' said Amos grimly. 'I suppose they'll be flying him home.'

'You don't think we might have to take him?' asked Gavin. 'In one of our panniers with his bike?'

'It's a thought, but I expect he'll go in a Transport Command hold, packed in dry ice. The thing is – and no gossiping, OK? – groupie here has gathered from London that security were already suspicious of him and would probably have arrested him the moment we got back. But the brass were too keen to see these exercises go well to risk acting just on suspicion. The whole thing's an absolute shock. Who would have thought old *Baldy* of all people . . . ?' his voice tailed off as he shook his head disbelievingly.

'He was always going on about money, wasn't he? He certainly didn't earn as much as some of his juniors. If you ask me, that's asking for trouble.'

'Mm. Well.' There was a moment's silence. 'Anyway,' said Amos in a subject-changing tone of voice, 'onward we go. We've now got to concentrate on putting up a good show against the Yanks. Incidentally,' he glanced at Gavin, 'I'd be interested to know what happened to you last night. I last saw you at the Phoenicia, enmeshed in the toils of a femme fatale. So – how did it go, if I may ask?'

'I don't really know,' Gavin said, feeling himself blush. 'She seemed sort of eager and bored at the same time. I've never met anybody quite like her.'

'Oh, she's the same with everyone. Some of the lads at the hotel know all about Veronica. Apparently she's an old hand. She lies in wait like a vampire for innocent-looking boys like you, then takes them off and sucks them dry. She's famous for it.'

'*Now* he tells me. Thanks a lot for letting me know. And there was I, thinking she wanted me to take a look at her Daimler's wiring. Either that or she was a Soviet spy hoping to seduce me into giving up secrets.' Gavin didn't like to think about the indiscretion of having mentioned the Libyan exercise to her.

'But she didn't.'

'It might have been more interesting if she had. I don't really think I'm cut out for these casual capers.'

'You mean as a spy victim or vampire victim?'

'Either. Both, really. I – I'm afraid I'm not much of a sexual athlete, Amos. Or I haven't been so far. Maybe I need more training sessions.'

Amos gave him a sideways smile. 'Maybe we both do, although you obviously made out better than I did last night. I just sat around with some empty-headed air hostesses who were drenched in that Blue Grass perfume my wife liked. I didn't fancy either of them although it would have been a pushover. Instead, I watched our Vic getting wasted. A couple of hours ago he made a light lunch of Alka-Seltzer and he and Baa are now working out our course for tomorrow.'

There was a thoughtful pause while the two airmen stared out across the airfield watching a pair of photo-reconnaissance Canberras take off, turn to starboard and head away eastwards as they gained height. 'Akrotiri, for a bet,' said Amos. 'It's the right direction for Cyprus, anyway. Off to do some snooping in the Middle East somewhere.'

There was another pause. 'I . . .' Gavin began.

'Mm?' Amos turned to look at him with an encouraging lift

of the dark eyebrows that reminded Gavin so much of Gregory Peck's.

'I just wanted to say I'm sorry about Jo, Amos. It's almost like death: nobody dares say anything. But I liked her.'

'Yes,' said Amos after a bit. 'I did, too. There's no real mystery. We got married too young. People do. And then sometimes I suppose they just grow out of each other. I don't think she should ever have married into the service. She came to hate what I'm doing. What we're all doing, really.'

'That's hardly your fault. If anything, it's the fault of politicians.'

'Yes, but she didn't just mean that. She used to say I was married to this –' he pointed a finger upwards at the immense wing overhead. 'She said I was far more interested in it than I ever was in her. And you know, she was absolutely right. When all's said and done.' He looked up and then patted the landing gear's massive leg at their backs. 'It's still *beautiful* to me, this aircraft. Did you know they planned a civil airliner version of the Vulcan back in the mid-fifties? It was going to be the Avro Atlantic. It was dropped because they never got enough orders from BOAC to justify it. So many missed opportunities.'

A brief silence fell. Then, as if Amos thought Gavin was owed further explanation, he added, 'When I was posted to Wearsby as a captain – well, you'll remember it since it's not so long ago – my long-suffering wife probably thought I would settle down into the model husband who's on top of his profession and I suppose comes home in the evenings and stands in front of the fire with both hands in his pockets, jingling his small change, puffing on his pipe and probably calling her "Kitten".'

'That doesn't sound like you.'

'Nor is it.' Amos glanced sideways at Gavin. 'I can't see you being like that, either.'

'No. I don't have the interest. I suppose I'm not very good at domesticity, or those sorts of relationship. The only time . . . look at the *size* of that thing,' he pointed to where an Argosy transport was starting its take-off run five hundred yards away. 'If it's the one that was here yesterday it's one of 70 Squadron's. I think they're based in Cyprus.'

They both watched as the immense twin-boom aircraft gathered speed. As with most large aircraft seen at any distance, it still seemed to be moving at a walking pace halfway down the runway. The combined note of the four Rolls-Royce Dart turboprops reached them more as a frantic groan as finally the bulbous nose tilted and it lifted off.

'You never think they're going to make it,' Amos said, watching with a pilot's eye. 'Sometimes, of course, they don't . . . You were saying?' he prompted. 'About a relationship?'

'Oh, nothing, it's silly. I was a kid. It was at school. And it certainly wasn't a relationship.'

'Ah, school. And?'

Gavin shifted on the Vulcan's tyre. 'It really was nothing, Amos. I was in the CCF and getting mocked for being what they called "Corps-keen", which at my place was a black mark against you. I used to spend a lot of time in the signals hut. I really loved that place. It was freezing cold most of the time although you could work up a decent fug with the stove going. It was somewhere I could retreat to because very few others went near it. I was perfectly happy alone there doing repairs on the Corps's radio equipment. Whenever I think about it I can still smell the smoking flux coming from a hot soldering iron. I was a serious radio ham in those days, collecting QSL cards from contacts I made all over the world. The only fly in the ointment was this older guy who began pestering me and in the end always seemed to be in the hut when

I was. For a long time I thought he was like me and just interested in working new contacts. But that wasn't all he was interested in.'

'So you fought to protect your honour?'

'No – far more pathetic than that.' Gavin laughed. 'Poor bugger. I just went on fiddling around with valves and frequencies and squelch buttons as if nothing was happening and eventually he just gave up. Maybe I was like you in a junior sort of way. I mean, too absorbed in what I was doing to be interested in much else.'

'Oh, I was interested, all right,' said Amos after a glance towards the policeman who was safely out of earshot. 'There was always *someone*, you know. At school, at Cranwell.' He paused and took a breath. 'Just as there is now. You. But I expect you knew that.'

There was a brief, frozen silence before Gavin said, 'I wasn't quite sure.'

'You can be now,' Amos said bleakly. 'Knowing what I've always known about myself, it was wrong of me to have married poor old Jo. I did love her in a sort of way, just not in the *right* sort of way. But I really thought it might cure me. That night of the party proved the opposite. Though actually I knew it was hopeless the moment you joined the crew.' Absently, he picked at the longitud-inal grooves in the tyre next to him. 'I'm fated, you know. I shall always be on the wrong side of everything. The law. Normality. Marriage. Even love. I do try hard to make up for it by . . .' he ges-tured silently upwards at the great wing. 'Otherwise it all seems too empty.' He paused. 'And you? Since I'm being so frank?'

'I've never been really sure,' Gavin said. 'But, well, you're defin-itely the most important person in my life at the moment.'

'Ah. At the moment.'

'You know what our problem is? I've been thinking about this a lot recently. You and I have spent all our lives in bloody *institutions*, right from when we were children. Prep school, public school, and

239

now the RAF. All along we've been pretty much insulated from the outside civilian world by our own laws and discipline: our own codes and traditions and ethos. Even vocabulary. When you think about it, the RAF's got so much in common with our boarding schools it's really just a semi-adult extension of them.'

'Jo used to say that. Poor girl, she never got used to it.'

'Exactly. But you and I can recognise what goes on because it's so similar to boarding school. Quite apart from the peculiar customs and slang there's all that rumour, jealousy, rivalry, arse-licking, sneaking, toadying, bullying – or at least victimisation of one sort or another. It all goes on. *And* love, of course. But I don't think people who haven't lived in an institution ever completely understand it. It might help if they'd been to prison, I suppose. I do know that grammar-school types like Vic and Baa are often baffled by the sheer pettiness of much that happens, even now. The one thing they don't reckon with is how *emotional* things can become. But to you and me all that became familiar when we were eight – or whenever we were first sent away to school.'

'Those hothouse relationships.'

'Precisely.'

Amos glanced at him and nodded briefly, then away at a Hastings that was just bringing its engines up to take-off revs at the end of the runway. With a heavy drone it began to trundle along until after a few hundred yards something abruptly changed in the engines' note. They saw the whirling discs of the propellers alter as the pitch changed and the pilot throttled back. The aircraft lost speed.

'He's aborted,' said Amos. 'I wonder why.'

He got up to walk out from beneath the Vulcan's wing when there was a peculiar whistling swish and something like a tall, twisted black plank embedded itself with a startling thud in the ground right at the edge of the concrete apron, a bare five yards away.

'Bloody hell,' Amos exclaimed, jumping. Gavin joined him and together they inspected the object. 'Have you any idea how lucky we are?'

'It looks like a propeller blade.'

'That's exactly what it is. If we'd happened to be standing out there it could have sliced us in two. A few yards more and it could have done mortal damage to poor old Yogi 1. Imagine what that might do to thin aluminium skinning. It would go right through a fuel tank.'

'Had it gone the other way it could have sliced through the Hastings.'

'They were dead lucky. Except now they'll be grounded for a bit and there'll be an inquiry.' He nodded toward the big transport, which had turned and was taxiing towards a runway exit on three engines. They could now see the stilled starboard inner propeller was gap-toothed. Between them they tried to pull the blade from the ground but it was too deeply embedded to budge. 'I suppose we'd better notify them where it landed.'

Amos went over and spoke to the MP. Then he and Gavin got into the Land Rover. Before they moved off Gavin impulsively put his hand over his captain's where it lay on the squab seat between them. 'It's hopeless, isn't it?' he said quietly, his eyes suddenly full of tears.

'Of course it is,' said Amos shortly as he started the engine. 'It always was and it always bloody will be. You're everything to me, but what's the good of it?' He let in the clutch with a bang.

23

Some time after ten o'clock the next morning the two Vulcans lifted off Luqa's runway and flew a graceful curve until they reached a modest altitude on their heading across the Mediterranean. Almost immediately they picked up Wheelus Air Traffic Control and a new course. Exercise Praying Mantis would be deemed to have started once they crossed the Libyan coast, which they were requested to do at two thousand feet. Thereafter they would lose height so as to reach the radar installation at the Al Usara desert ranges as low as they liked. At their present speed, flight time from the coast would be approximately seventeen minutes. The first day's radar exercise effectively consisted of mock bombing runs. These could simulate both a European Theatre retaliatory attack using a nuclear weapon and an attack on a SAM base such as American aircraft were currently engaged in over North Vietnam. It was not long before Vic Ferrit, Yogi 1's nav radar, had confirmed his aiming point some one hundred and forty miles distant and had it firmly locked into his system's computer.

Uncharacteristically for the time of year, the day was again cloudless. In the cockpit Amos was flying and Keith Coswood was glancing regularly through the circular side window by his head. In due course he got the first visual of the coastline where the wrinkled sea met the camel-coloured African continent in a thin line of white. Almost dead ahead and partly obscured by the Vulcan's nose was a patch of regular shapes that might have been a small city. 'Tripoli coming up, Skip,' he told Amos. 'Twenty miles or so.'

Both Vulcans lost height without decreasing speed and, having obtained clearance, crossed the coast directly over Wheelus on a desert heading. Vic reported having established the American air base as his 'initial point', some eighty miles from what in a live bombing run would be weapon release. At that moment Gavin detected a radar contact from the distant ranges and flicked the switches that brought Oilcan into operation. He had instructions to use normal ECM and now brought his jammers into action. The Blue Diver antennas buried in each of the Vulcan's wing tips began blasting electronic noise which would immediately have forced the target radar to employ its range gates in order to exclude as much of it as possible. The two Vulcans were now down to three hundred feet or so and five miles apart, and had begun jinking manoeuvres to increase the acquisition radars' problems. Gavin in Yogi 1 and Ken Pilcher in Yogi 2 then added their Red Shrimp jammers for good measure. These were mainly designed to confuse anti-aircraft artillery, but it was precisely the AAA emplacements around targets in North Vietnam that were currently the problem.

In this way the two Vulcans went twisting across the desert floor to Al Usara. At forty miles' distance the two nav radars, Vic Ferrit and Julian Caddy, changed to a larger scale and used the stubby little joysticks in front of them to put their aiming markers on the target. This course information went straight into the navigation computers and thence to their aircraft's autopilots. Had this been a live bombing instead of a radar comp the pilots could have let automation take over completely. Their aircraft would have flown themselves to the target and released the bomb at precisely the right moment. But down low today, both captains were going to do this manually. This was real flying. Their co-pilots called out the altitude as the camouflaged Vulcans tilted like mottled sails above a rushing landscape of scrub and stones that came into momentary view with each banking manoeuvre. In the distance a huddle of huts, vehicles and radar arrays appeared. There was even a marked circle with a large helicopter sitting in its centre. No-one aboard either Vulcan had more than a glimpse of it. They were concentrating on dials and screens. Calm voices on the intercom simply told the pilots that they had passed the weapon release point. Amos eased back on his control handle, slightly turning it, and with gentle pressure from his foot gaining a little height in a broad turn so as to put some distance between Yogi 1 and the radars before coming in for another run from a different direction.

'What luck, Gavin?' he asked.

'They've lost us, Boss. They couldn't have got a missile after us unless they'd done it visually and sent up all three. But we'd have chaffed and jammed them out of the sky. This kit really works.'

'Good stuff, you guys,' Amos relayed to his crew. 'We'll give them another three or four runs and then head for home. Maybe they've got Yogi Bear on the mess TV back at Luqa.'

'Nah, Malta's bound to be behind the times. It'll be something crappy like *Whirlybirds*, bet you. Rescuing brainless dogs and kids from canyons. Just a twenty-five-minute advert for Bell helicopters.'

In this way short bursts of banter intercut some high precision low-level flying. On one of the climb-outs Amos asked Keith if he remembered ever being warned about shitehawks here.

'Someone said something about it at breakfast this morning. They don't tell tales about them here as they do in Aden. Apparently a Shack hit one at twenty-one thousand feet over Khormaksar recently. You wouldn't believe a poxy great bird like that could get up that high, would you?'

'That's thermals for you. You'd think they'd need oxygen.'

'We'd be on it, for sure. But they're scavengers, aren't they? They only hang around places where there's garbage to peck at. This Libyan wasteland looks a bit short on edibles, even for shitehawks. Let's hope the guys stuck out here at Al Usara have been told to take their rubbish home with them when they fly back at night.'

All in all, it was a triumphant sortie. Neither Vulcan was ever subjected to a radar lock-on long enough for a SAM to have got anywhere near them. Game, set and match to Oilcan, as Baa Mutton remarked after setting a course for Luqa. By the time they recrossed Wheelus at eight thousand feet the radar operators out in the desert had no doubt reported their own failure. The radio message that came up was laconic. 'Thanks, guys. We thought we'd make it easy for you on the first day.'

'Don't worry, we'll try harder tomorrow,' Amos sent back. 'We've got 'em rattled,' he added to the crew over the intercom. 'Well done, you chaps. That was fun.'

Day two of Exercise Praying Mantis being the bomb comp, the crews were out early while the Vulcans were being bombed up with the inert rounds. They looked much the same as ordinary iron bombs except for the enlarged vanes and their snorkel noses tipped with transparent domes that were revealed when the orange hoods were removed. Each aircraft carried six. The pilots had already memorised the instructions on the conduct of the competition. Six runs were to be made from any angle, at various heights from five hundred feet to twenty thousand. Strict altitude separation would be vital: two USAF aircraft were also competing: an F-105 Thunderchief and a B-52. The F-105 was the type currently being deployed daily over North Vietnam in 'Wild Weasel' bombing raids against strategic targets, and the target at Al Watia the competitors would be trying to hit apparently reflected this.

Some hours later as he banked Yogi 1 at a thousand feet over the desert range Amos said 'Holy shit!' as a long, narrow iron structure came into view below. It was a full-scale railway bridge on girder legs, perhaps a hundred and fifty yards long, standing in the wilderness all by itself. Presumably modelled on a real bridge somewhere in Hanoi's territory, it was complete in its detail of cross-bracing and concrete pilings at the base of the legs. The structure stood perhaps eighty feet high – it was hard to judge from the air.

'Talk about no expense spared,' said Keith as they banked around it. 'And a bastard to hit: the thing's full of holes. Not like the old Bosun out at Donna Nook.'

'I guess that's the idea. Near misses just don't count. We'll just have to see what Vector can do.'

But it turned out that from five hundred feet Vector couldn't do much. Both Vulcans' bombs fell in the bridge's thin shadow and were scored as near misses.

'We're too low, Skip,' Vic said from the back. 'There's no time for the vanes to guide them. It'll be better higher up.'

They turned in a large climbing sweep over the desert while behind them the two American aircraft made their passes. They, too, scored near misses. It was a different story from two thousand feet, however: both Vulcans scored direct hits on the bridge. Cheers broke out over the intercoms. Down on the ground, a safe three miles from the target in a reinforced and air-conditioned bunker, the Range Officer radioed up the results with an added 'Good shooting, guys. See what you can do from five.' The F-105 also scored a hit, launching its bomb from an underwing pylon. Score: two–one to the RAF but with another four runs to go. The Vulcans climbed to five thousand feet and, even to their own nav radars' surprise, scored two more hits.

'You couldn't have done that yesterday, Vic,' observed Amos acidly.

'Too right, Skip. I was seeing double till lunchtime.'

Once more they came around in a broad climb and more of the horizon came into view, now including a faint sight of the Mediterranean on the edge of vision to the north. Visibility was not as good as on the previous day: there was more sand in the air and Amos wondered whether as they bombed from greater heights this would defeat the laser system. But what could be seen of the ground was intimidating enough: an endless hinterland unbroken by road or feature.

'Blimey,' said Keith as the pale mud-coloured panorama tilted up one side of the windscreen. 'It's bloody identical in every direction. Imagine being stuck down there.'

'Don't even joke about it,' said Amos, and at that moment there was a loud bang that shook the aircraft. 'What the hell was that?' They both leaned forward against their harness, rapidly scanning the panels in front of them for emergency lights and aberrant readings.

'Bird strike?' queried Keith.

'Number four jet pipe temperature rising,' said Amos. The aircraft was vibrating and the starboard wing wanted to drop. At that moment the number four engine fire warning light came on. 'Damn. Fire drill, Keith.' The co-pilot immediately pulled back the right-hand throttle lever and shut off that engine's high- and low-pressure fuel cocks. As the revs began dropping he pressed the extinguisher button.

Amos found he was having difficulty holding Yogi 1 in anything like a normal attitude. The right wing still wanted to drop and the entire aircraft was yawing violently. He was having to use both hands on the control grip but took one away long enough to click the intercom switch. 'Captain to AEO,' he called Gavin. 'We have a fire in number four engine. Get off a Mayday, then call Yogi 2 to get a visual on our starboard wing.'

'Roger.'

The fire warning light for number four engine had gone out when Keith had pressed the extinguisher button but now it came back on. The vibration had increased to an unpleasant shuddering that no amount of tinkering with trim seemed to alleviate. Suddenly Terry Meeres in Yogi 2 came on the radio.

'Yogi one, I've got you. The underside of your starboard wing is well ablaze. You've got flames coming out of the engine doors.'

'Fire in number three,' broke in Keith, seeing the light on the panel, automatically pushing the extinguisher button and pulling the throttle lever back. 'Jet pipe temperature rising.' He closed off the fuel supply to that engine, including the cross-feed cocks to both it and its neighbour. The Vulcan immediately crabbed to the right under the asymmetric power. With full rudder Amos pushed the remaining two port engines to maximum thrust and put the aircraft into a shallow climb. He knew they were almost certainly going to have to abandon and the higher they could get, the better for the crew in the rear compartment.

'Nav radar, nav radar,' he called Vic. 'Jettison all bombs. Repeat, jettison all bombs.'

'Roger, Skip.' There was a lurch as the three remaining bombs fell away. 'Bombs gone.'

'AEO to Captain: I've just had a gander through the periscope. Confirm major fire in the starboard wing.'

At that moment both starboard warning lights went out.

'Captain to AEO,' Amos called back. 'Lights are out. The wiring's probably burned through. Hang on while I get us another visual from Yogi 2.'

Terry Meeres was a safe half-mile away to starboard, keeping pace with his stricken companion and also in a shallow climb.

'Yogi 1, your fire's worse,' he called. 'You won't put it out, Amos. Get out now. I'll watch and mark you.'

'Roger, Terry.' Amos cut him off and clicked the intercom switch. 'Captain to AEO: prepare to abandon. Prepare to abandon.'

'Roger, Boss,' came Gavin's matter-of-fact voice. From his tone he might have been agreeing that now was a good time to break for coffee instead of acknowledging that he would shortly have to entrust his life to a large piece of nylon. Even in this crisis Amos felt a pang of pride for the boy's courage and professionalism.

What neither he nor anyone else aboard the Vulcans could have observed, however, was one of those fatal mischances that can haunt airmen for the rest of their lives. At the normally safe distance of a mile away and three thousand feet lower, the B-52 was also banking to bring itself around after its latest pass at the target. Its camouflaged swept-back wings were hardly visible against the desert floor. Unnoticed by anyone above, the trajectory of Yogi 1's three jettisoned bombs met that of the huge aircraft at a closing speed of over five hundred knots, the combined ton of steel and concrete smashing into it behind the cockpit at the wing roots. In an instant the aircraft's back broke, the main spars crumpling and the wings folding, its fuselage turning turtle. As it broke up the intact nose section with the five crewmen fell separately into a wadi, the rest of the bomber raining down piecemeal within a half-mile radius. An immense cloud of dust and sand billowed up to mark the spot.

Six thousand feet overhead, all unaware of this, Amos was still trying to keep Yogi 1 under some sort of control. The vibration was increasing, its frequency becoming higher. The juddering was now severe enough to blur vision and it was becoming hard to read the instruments. Further delay would clearly be suicidal.

'Captain to crew: Abandon. Abandon. Abandon.'

*

In the rear compartment the 'abandon aircraft' panels were now glowing brightly on the console in front of the crew. As nav radar it was Vic Ferrit's task to go first and open the hatch. By now the vibration in the aircraft was so heavy it was causing g-forces and Vic had to operate the inflatable cushion on his seat to boost him to his feet. Staggering from handhold to handhold like a seaman on a storm-bound trawler, he reached the door lever and rammed it past the emergency detent. To his relief the hatch opened with a bang and daylight exploded into the darkened compartment. He had an impression of a fawn carpet somewhere beyond the brilliant rectangle in the floor and sent the yellow ladder off into space. Thank Christ the landing gear's not down, he thought; at least we won't be smashed against the nose leg when we jump. The lowered hatch would now act as a slide and as his eyes adjusted he could see the glow of the fire reflected on the metal, bounced back from the white underside of the Vulcan's wing. He checked to see that Bob and Gavin were on their feet and ready to follow, gave them a quick thumbs-up and launched himself down and out, tumbling into a confused slamming of light and roaring air until his canopy cracked open and he was wrenched upright and dangling.

*

From a safe distance Terry in Yogi 2 watched and relayed his observations to Amos. 'OK, one's out . . . two . . . three. They're all out and they've all got good chutes. Go. Good luck.'

In Yogi 1's cockpit Amos and Keith hastily pulled out all their connectors. In the instant that Amos released his grip on the control handle the Vulcan became uncontrollable and reared up into the beginning of a stall from which both pilots knew there would be no recovery. Amos indicated to Keith that he was jettisoning the canopy, which promptly flew up and disappeared in a clap of sound. The noise of the airstream and the two port engines at maximum power suddenly became deafening, yet there was surprisingly little wind buffet inside the cockpit. He signalled 'Go!' and with a bang Keith pulled the face-blind handle and vanished in a cloud of cordite smoke. Amos sat as upright as he could to minimise spine damage then punched out himself, the mad blur of explosive acceleration and tearing wind succeeded by a rush of relief as his canopy deployed and he could see his seat tumbling off below. As things stabilised and his brain caught up with him he noted another parachute off to one side and below: Keith, presumably. He strained to see Gavin's chute but the ground was still revolving and he lost all sense of direction until he spotted the nearly vertical slash of dark smoke standing in the air nearby at whose end a vast wounded arrowhead was plunging earthwards towing a scarlet banner of flame. A second later Yogi 1 dissolved into the desert almost directly below him. He actually heard the sound of the impact through his helmet. A deep crimson fireball instantly erupted through dust clouds. It reminded Amos irrelevantly of a peony in his aunt's garden. The way the dust and smoke came boiling up towards him and then frayed to one side indicated a stiffish breeze at ground level. This was evidently going to carry him a little way beyond the crash site. He was thankful the aircraft had managed to gain what little extra height it had.

As he floated down he was aware of the continuing roar of jet engines as Terry Meeres stooged around the crash site in large circles, keeping well above the descending parachutes. But there was no time left for watching the Vulcan. The ground was rapidly coming up to meet him and he concentrated on making a good landing and not breaking a leg on a boulder or coming down in a thorn bush. In the event he made a copybook touchdown, rolling over and smacking the release to prevent himself from being dragged. The canopy billowed, dented and collapsed and he got to his feet and stood there unfastening his helmet and rubbing an elbow. The remains of Yogi 1 were blazing a bare quarter of a mile away, pouring smoke into the bald blue sky with occasional dull explosive thumps. He thought the entire emergency had lasted no more than four minutes: the activity compressed so he could still hardly believe that in so short a time his aircraft had gone from being a triumphant participant in an exercise to an incandescent pyre in the desert. His mind was still trying to catch up with events when he heard the whapping of helicopter blades. Following the sound he saw a twin-rotor H-21 Shawnee approaching, presumably dispatched from the Al Usara radar site. That's quick off the mark, he thought, assuming it had been alerted by his Mayday call. No doubt it had come to pick up his crew, guided from above by Yogi 2, which was still flying low-level circles over the area. But he was surprised to see the Shawnee settle near another dust cloud a couple of miles away. Still, knowing that his parachute would have been visible, Amos began gathering up the shrouds and canopy. He heard a shout and, looking around, saw Keith approaching with his own chute hastily bunched in his arms. The RAF didn't approve of pilots returning without their parachutes.

'What a way to spend the day,' was his co-pilot's greeting. 'What the fuck was it? Did we hit a shitehawk?'

'Who knows? Whatever caused it, I'd guess number four shed some turbine blades and then probably the whole disc. It wouldn't be the first time that's happened to a Vulcan. But they'll have a job getting much information out of that –' Amos waved a gloved hand towards the fire. It was burning smaller now and cleaner, the smoke a lighter shade. 'I watched her go in. There won't be a lot left. Good – here come the others. Two of them, anyway.'

Bob and Gavin came up, also trailing roughly bundled parachute silk. Amos's eyes met Gavin's and spoke silent volumes, but what he said was, 'Has anyone seen Vic?'

'No, he was first out, though, so he's probably on the far side of that,' Bob indicated the bonfire. 'He'll be along. So what about Oilcan and Vector and the NBS film?' The aircraft's highly secret navigation and bombing system was a top security concern in the event of a crash. 'I know the Yanks are our allies but our instructions were pretty clear.'

'We'll just have to hope nothing identifiable's left of either. But I'm also hoping Terry thought to get in touch with Idris and they can send some chaps over. They won't be experts but they can at least stand guard until the Air Ministry sends a team down. Meanwhile, no mention of any special equipment.'

'Right. I believe our taxi's here. Can't think why they took so long.'

'What did I say yesterday? It's bloody *Whirlybirds* after all. The irony of it.'

The 'Flying Banana' had landed fifty metres away and the four walked to it through the ochre dust its sagging, still-twirling rotors were stirring up. Two American airmen greeted them and helped them into the machine's capacious interior.

'You OK, you guys?' one asked.

'Fine, thanks.' Amos looked around anxiously. 'Have you seen my nav radar anywhere?'

A major who must have been in the cockpit came round to the door. 'You the captain?' he asked Amos. 'Glad you four got out OK, but I'm afraid you need to brace yourselves for some real shitty news. Your buddy didn't make it. Your other guys were watching from above and saw what happened. Maybe he'd broken an arm and couldn't steer his chute. He drifted straight into the fireball.'

'Oh Jesus,' muttered Gavin.

'Yeah, it happens. We lost a Thud driver the other day. Same thing. Whammo, out safely and then straight into the fire. But there's worse to come. You won't know this, and nobody's blaming you, but you lot downed our Buff.'

'*What?* We were nowhere near it,' said Amos.

'I know, but your bombs were when you jettisoned. They fell right on top. Broke it up like a pretzel. That's what that dust cloud was out yonder –' the officer stretched an arm towards the desert beyond the smouldering remains of Yogi 1. 'No survivors.' He shook his head sadly. 'Score: five of our guys, one of yours, plus two large aircraft. It's been a goddamned expensive exercise, this, and nobody's fault. We'll get you back to base now.'

For the short flight to Wheelus the remaining members of Yogi 1's crew were silent, each busy with his own thoughts and not meeting the others' eyes. Not that conversation would ever have been easy, given the deafening clatter inside the machine. But the expression on the face of the major sitting against the bulkhead in a webbing seat told Amos he knew exactly how they would be feeling. Enjoyment converted to tragedy in the twinkling of an eye. The horror of the unintended consequences of what they had done in order to survive, the guilt of having survived, the shock of a friend's death mixed with fervent private prayers that Vic was already unconscious or, better, dead before he drifted helplessly into the holocaust on the desert floor. Familiar enough emotions to airmen on active service anywhere.

*

Later, none of the Britons could fault the courtesy and kindness extended to them on behalf of the USAF by the base commander, Colonel John Pierce. Tall for a man who had squeezed himself into F-86 cockpits to fly combat missions over the Yalu River in Korea, with a sandy crew cut and freckled forearms, he was there in immaculate sun-tans to greet Yogi 1's crew when they landed at Wheelus. They stepped out into the familiar scenery of an active airbase, to the whine of jet engines, the shimmering thermals and smell of burning kerosene. The colonel introduced himself, shook them all gravely by the hand and hustled them into a van which drove off in the direction of the obviously residential side of the base. Soon Amos and the others found themselves sitting somewhat incongruously in their dust-stained flying kit in a bungalow with palm trees in its front garden, the house being set in a concrete-paved street looking for all the world like an averagely prosperous Californian suburb. Gavin noted the blue Ford Fairlane parked in the next-door drive. A basketball hoop set over the garage door clearly marked the houses out as married quarters.

When a white-jacketed Filipino had served them cans of freezing beer, Colonel Pierce said: 'Gentlemen, 'I'm sorry to have to welcome you to Wheelus in such circumstances. My sincere condolences to you all on the loss of your crewman – Flight Lieutenant Ferrit, I think? – in the dreadful accident this afternoon. My apologies for spiriting you away to this house with what looks like unseemly haste, but I considered it better for everyone if you're away from curious stares. It goes without saying that absolutely no blame attaches to you for what happened at Al Watia. You had an emergency and were not to know our bomber was below you. We're all aviators. We all know what the deal is. As you'll guess, on a base as active as Wheelus we're none of us strangers to these things. I can guarantee no-one here will be anything but sympathetic.'

The colonel went on to inform them that he had already spoken to RAF Luqa and arrangements had been made for Squadron Leader McKenna to do the same just as soon as he wished. The bodies of the five USAF men would arrive shortly. A search would be made for that of Flight Lieutenant Ferrit once the wreckage had cooled sufficiently, although this might not be until first light tomorrow. He understood a small team from RAF Idris would also be flying in to help with the search. Since tomorrow was Sunday, Colonel Pierce said, 'it would be deemed a graceful act' if all four Britons attended a short service in the base's chapel. 'Not a funeral, of course, just a public acknowledgement that we airmen know our lives often hang by a thread, the other end of which is held by Almighty God.'

Fall out Roman Catholics and Jews! Amos heard an irrepressible inner voice add in memory of his Cranwell days.

'On a lighter note, you gentlemen have sure given us much to think about. Yesterday's exercise definitely revealed an imbalance in our respective radar capabilities' (one way of putting it, Gavin thought to himself, exchanging a swift covert glance with Amos) 'and today's bomb comp, cut short as it tragically was, already looks as though it will yield highly valuable data. You gave a first-rate account of yourselves. Strictly from the military point of view, then, Praying Mantis has been a success. I believe it will be seen as having been of crucial value in our joint fight against godless communism, and we can be consoled that our comrades we mourn today gave their lives in the most urgent challenge our free world faces.'

It was good, appropriate stuff, and Pierce did it well. Once in private, though, each of Yogi 1's crew was surprised at how quickly he felt like shedding the subdued mode. *He had survived.* Once again it had been some other poor sod's number up. That it had been old Vic's turn merely strengthened his own claim to be genuinely invulnerable. Before long, something lighter began stealthily to break through the sombre mood, although the generous supply of Pabst and Schlitz may have helped.

In the event they spent another thirty-six hours at Wheelus while the inevitable formalities were completed. Each crewman gave a statement that later would be used for the board of inquiry. At midday on Monday an RAF Transport Command Devon arrived to ferry them back to Luqa, where they each gave further statements, including ones relating to Baldy Hodge's death. It was two more days before they could hitch a lift back to the UK. During that time an RAF team combed through the wreckage of Yogi 1 in the desert, but no trace of Vic Ferrit remained beyond some distorted buckles from a parachute harness. Investigators examining the engines gave as their preliminary opinion that a bird strike was the most likely cause of the disaster. 'One mangy fucking bird causing all that death and destruction' was a thought common to everyone on board the Hastings as it droned them slowly and vibratingly back to Wearsby. It felt an ignominious way for a Vulcan crew to come home.

2012

24

Amos had spent most of the previous day driving up from the West Country. He had long ago ruefully acknowledged that his former taste for speed was much diminished; he supposed this was yet another thing he could put down to age. But a night in the B&B somewhere near Lincoln restored his spirits even before he spotted Ken and Annie Pilcher in the breakfast room that morning.

'Hullo, Pins,' Annie greeted him as he went over to their table. Though smiling, she was giving him what he recognised as one of her professional medical looks. 'Are you OK? We were betting you might chicken out at the last moment.'

'Couldn't afford to. I went ahead and booked this place the moment you sent me the bumf about the reunion. It was a way of ensuring I wouldn't back down. I refuse to be stung for a cancellation fee. What about you?'

'I wish we'd done that,' Ken said. 'For a while yesterday I thought we'd have to pitch a tent to rest our old bones in. Everything's booked solid for twenty miles around. Everett tells me there are just over two hundred coming.' Unlike Amos he was wearing the old 319 Squadron tie as well as a dark blue blazer with silver buttons and a gold-worked RAF badge on its breast pocket. 'A miracle there are that many of us left above ground, if you ask me.'

'We're tough buggers to kill, Fishy, that's why. God knows the RAF tried hard enough back in the old days. I put it down to that

261

Eating Command diet of ours. Plenty of health-giving cholesterol in those wonderful flight-bag rations.'

'I might point out that Ken's having these sausages under a special dispensation,' his wife said firmly, 'so he'd better make the most of them.' She had been a Princess Mary nurse when they were married. 'After this weekend it's back to yoghurt-and-like-it.' She had retired as a principal matron, which Amos thought ranked her equivalent to a group captain or something.

'You see how she bullies me?' Ken edged a piece of fried egg unsteadily on to the corner of a piece of toast and ate it with obvious pleasure. He had left the service a mere squadron leader before setting up the business in which he had so spectacularly prospered.

'Are you going up to Wearsby straight after this?' Amos asked them.

'Straightish. We need to find a garage first: we've blown a fuse somewhere and none of the bloody windows will open. Don't you just hate modern cars? What was wrong with winding-handles, I should like to know?'

'You mean you haven't come in one of your flamboyant museum pieces? I thought it paid to advertise.' Ken's company restored classic cars for what his brochure odiously described as 'a bespoke clientele'. 'What was wrong with that monster you were swanning about in before Christmas?'

'The Hispano-Suiza? Sold it, unfortunately, and you don't want to hear for how much. A beauty. But the engine was over ten litres, and at current petrol prices this journey would have bankrupted us well before we'd reached Reigate. Anyway, because of my shy and retiring nature I thought Annie and I would blend in a bit better with a cooking car. We leave the showing-off to others. I now wish we hadn't. That J-12 had silk-smooth window winders, as well as headlamps a foot across. So where are we going to buy a fuse for our wretched Japanese heap?'

'On a Saturday?'

'Come on, even in the wilds of Lincolnshire somebody must sell fuses. We'll look around. At this rate I'd say up at the airfield round about twelve. I assume nothing much will happen until well after lunch. We'll be largely a gathering of old buffers, don't forget. I'd bet on most saving themselves for the dinner tonight. We'll take it easy this morning. Give Annie time to powder her nose.'

'And you time to get the egg off your tie,' said his wife tartly.

'Oh blast, I haven't, have I?'

An hour later as Amos neared the airfield he began to recognise familiar landmarks. Good God, he thought as a skeletal structure loomed behind some trees: a huge rectangular iron reservoir atop a tower of girders, the whole thing painted black. It's still there. He remembered it as a useful landmark to glimpse out of a Vulcan cockpit's side window when on finals. He could see the tank was now considerably rusted and had become partially hidden behind trees that had grown up around it. The rest of the landscape, though, looked flatter and bleaker than he remembered. No elms now, of course. Everything seemed to have been strangely denuded in the last, well, how long? Had he really not been back to his old station for *over forty years*? It didn't seem possible. All the intervening time spent plodding up BOAC's and then BA's seniority ladder had distanced him from that earlier and arguably happiest part of his life. Still, he had kept in touch with a few of his old mates, some of whom had stayed on and risen to the dizzy rank of air vice-marshal and the like. Amos had retired just before the turn of the new century as the airline's most senior Boeing 747 captain, with his silver hair looking disconcertingly like Captain Oveur in *Airplane!* played by Peter Graves.

Suddenly the otherwise familiar road sprang a junction off to the right that he didn't recognise. He passed it and slowed. The new road headed off towards what should surely have been runway two-four – yes, it would have to go slap across it to those new buildings . . . The car moved forward and Amos could now see what looked like a factory with a sign proclaiming the name and logo of a brand of flat-pack furniture. Beyond that the road evidently continued towards a group of new office buildings visible in the distance. So would that be where the old fire dump had been? Disoriented and faintly dismayed, he let the car amble on towards the main gate. This looked unchanged but for the absence of armed military police and their dogs. On the grassy island in front of it stood a down-at-heel twin-engined transport aircraft as the gate guardian. A Viking? A Valetta? He couldn't remember, but thought that in his day they'd had a Whitley, a real bomber, appropriately enough for a Bomber Command station. He wondered what had happened to it. He turned in at the gate, feeling an atavistic urge to fumble for his F.1250, and carried on to the old admin block, which from a distance didn't look too different from what he remembered. He presumed the other end of the runway two miles off was unchanged and that it still stopped as it had forty years ago at the main road.

He became aware of the tall shapes of tail fins above the hedge. They've at least got a Victor, he thought to himself, plus that dirty white rounded slab poking up over there probably belongs to a Hastings or similar old transport. Once through the gates he could see a substantial collection of aircraft off to his right, parked on a big stretch of grass he didn't remember. After all, the place was now billing itself as Wearsby Air Museum. Signs pointed to a car park behind the admin block which was now labelled 'Ticket Office and Shop'. Amos left the car and went in. An enormously fat woman sat behind a counter on which was a spread of brochures and guides, a plate of rock cakes and a till. Suspended on steel cables from the ceiling of the large room behind her was what looked like the dusty port wing of a Chipmunk.

'I'm here for the reunion,' Amos said. 'Do I need to pay an entrance fee?'

'Bless you, no. For this weekend you're a Cold War hero, and heroes get in free here. Anybody else we squeeze dry.' She laughed with such good humour Amos found himself smiling. It was a warm day and a fan on the table behind her turned its face mechanically from side to side like a celebrity bestowing smiles, regularly stirring a Union Jack on a stand. 'Just wear your reunion badge, though.'

Amos took it from his jacket pocket and dutifully pinned it to a lapel.

'You need to go out –' she raised a bolster-like arm dimpled with cellulite and indicated a direction off to the left – 'and look for the big white marquee next to Hangar 2. Have you been to Wearsby before?'

Wanly he smiled. 'I was based here in the sixties.'

'Really? Was that the time of the spy scandal?' She studied his faux-Hollywood looks. 'Maybe we met in the old days? I used to work in the NAAFI here in sixty-eight.'

'I'm afraid I'd gone by then. So you're a local?'

'Stayed on, got used to the Fens, met a bloke, had a family, got fat. My life story, by me. You'll find a few changes here if you've not been back since then.'

'I've seen some of them already. They've chopped off half of runway two-four and replaced it with an industrial estate.'

'Yes, they did that ooh, three years ago now. You couldn't get a V-bomber in or out now even if you wanted to. We were offered a Nimrod 2 last year but nobody fancied landing it and taking a chance on stopping in time. I bet in the old days you lads would have done it like a shot, but this is an elf-'n'-safety generation we've got now, isn't it? So what we're left with is just stuff that can get in and out easily: light aircraft, executive jets, gliders, the odd helicopter. It's really sad but I suppose we all have to move with the times. Have a rock cake. I made them this morning.'

At that moment a family party with three children came in so Amos thanked her and took his leave, munching the rock cake and heading towards the large marquee he could see bellying slightly in the light breeze. Outside stood a blackboard proclaiming 'Cold War Reunion – Reception'. He was disgusted to feel a crawl of apprehension in his stomach. He paused at the entrance, breathing in the nostalgic military smell of sun-warmed canvas. Inside, the walls were lined with trestle tables bearing various items for display or possibly for sale: bits of old machinery, models, books and manuals, photographs. A short man wearing an RAF blazer and a badge identifying him as Chris Everett came forward to greet him.

'I'm the fellow you sent your cheque to. If you'll just sign in I'll find you your ID.'

'Amos McKenna.'

'McKenna, McKenna.' On the table inside the door were rows of ID badges, presumably in alphabetical order since Everett immediately found the right one. 'You must excuse me,' he said as he handed it to Amos. 'I don't know you, do I?' Amos was suddenly aware that his own clothes might be a little too studiedly civilian: brownish slacks topped by an American light sports jacket with a discreet check pattern, a plain white shirt open at the collar. 'That's the worst of these things. We all come to feel we're the last of the many, but there are still quite a lot of us around who were on V-bombers even though we certainly didn't know everybody else at the time. And of course it *was* rather a long time ago and we all change, well, physically. Unfortunately. Which squadron were you?'

'I was in 319.' He drifted away, leaving Everett with his brow furrowed as if in an attempt to remember something until his attention was distracted by a fresh batch of newcomers to the tent. Amos wandered around looking at the models and memorabilia. He recognised several pieces of V-bomber hardware that had presumably been salvaged when the aircraft had been broken up: one of the long bladder-like pee bottles they had known as 'rubber kippers'; a nav radar's little joystick with its white bobble; some cardboard packets of chaff billed as 'Window for I-Band radar'; a copy of Pilot's Notes for a Victor Mk. 2. The people behind these stalls looked far too young ever to have used the things they were selling. Some were women, although he had a feeling they weren't ex-WRAFS. Overhearing one of them extolling a radar altimeter to a grey-haired man, Amos realised that these were enthusiasts dedicated to the point of obsession who no doubt travelled around from one aviation event to another. They probably knew as much or even more about a navigator's instruments of nearly half a century ago than he on the flight deck ever had. He had long since learned not to underestimate the true devotee.

Years ago, back in the days when he was at last firmly in the left-hand seat of a BA airliner and interested passengers were still allowed to visit the cockpit in flight, a lad of about fifteen had been shown forward who appeared to be almost as familiar with a Boeing's fuel transfer system as Amos. The boy had explained about shifting the fuel between tanks as it was gradually used up so as to maintain the aircraft's trim, casually referring to the plane's centre of gravity as its 'cg'. Impressed and inwardly amused, Amos had been mischievously tempted to live up to the character wished upon him by *Airplane!* and ask the boy if he ever hung around gymnasiums or had been in a Turkish prison. Instead, he congratulated him on his detailed knowledge. The reply had been matter-of-fact. 'I'm a Rafbrat,' the boy said. 'My dad's a wing commander. I'm pretty much qualified on Chipmunks.' Amos had often wondered whether he and the other precocious visitors to his cockpit had eventually taken up flying as their profession. As warmly as he had felt at the time about their obvious enthusiasm, he thought bleakly that they might have done well not to join the RAF in the last decade or two, especially after 1991 when the Soviet Union finally imploded and the world changed.

The marquee was steadily filling up with new arrivals. It was also becoming noticeably hotter. Amos felt increasingly distinctive in his mufti. The men – old codgers, as he thought of them, even though they were largely his own age – nearly all wore the unofficial uniform of ex-service types: badged blue blazers, grey flannels, crested ties. They had the benign yet stubborn expressions of people glimpsed filing out of Sunday matins in country churches where the Book of Common Prayer and the King James Bible are still used and 'The Church's One Foundation' still sung. These gentlemen peered myopically at each other's lapel badges like visitors to a gallery who first check the legend beneath each painting as though unable to see it until they know who the artist is. Then they read the other's clothes in confirmation. It was all done in an instant, quite casually, before conversation was struck up. Now and then came exclamations of surprise and pleasure. Hands were wrung, elbows grasped, long-time-no-sees exchanged. For the most part the women in their decent dresses beamed impartially.

A burgeoning gloomy rage began to overtake Amos that he had ever allowed Ken to talk him into coming. Social events were not to his taste at the best of times and this one promised to be as grim as any. He had certainly never been to a reunion of his old school, though God knew the old school kept pestering him even now for handouts to finance their new squash courts or chemistry labs: shameless begging letters that assumed his deep sentimental attachment to a place he'd been forced to attend for five years nearly sixty years previously only because his father had paid heavily in a straightforward business transaction. It was too easy to imagine how much – or how sadly little – former friends and classmates would have changed over that great gap of time. It looked like being much the same deal here at Wearsby. Gazing across the tent, Amos was certain he recognised a former officer whom he disliked on sight before remembering why. The man had surely headed some sort of inspection – TACEVAL? Weapons Standardisation Team? – and had given him and his crew an exceptionally hard time, causing them briefly to lose their combat-ready status. Amos could no longer recall their exact offence but the sense of injustice had clearly outlived it by decades, ready on the instant to spring back to life at the mere sight of a man who now looked like a jovial bishop.

Amos's gloom settled like precipitate in a test tube. This whole business of trying to turn the clock back was doomed and silly. What were these bits of ancient aircraft for sale but religious relics? Fragments of machines long since defunct but still for true believers imbued with the charisma of a British aviation that no longer existed. That dull-looking round metal gadget, for instance, bristling with stubs of snipped-off wiring and labelled as a transponder from a Lightning fighter's fuel tank. Presumably the magic these things held was reserved for people who had never flown such aircraft on a daily basis, just as fragments of a saint's tibia would acquire value the further away they were from local folk who could actually remember the cantankerous old hermit in his smelly cave.

Amos wandered to the marquee's entrance for a breath of air without the nudging stink of hot canvas. Fifty yards away was an open-fronted tent he hadn't noticed on the way in, despite its being festooned with banners and posters. Loudspeakers rigged on either side were extolling the triumphant and hugely costly resurrection of Vulcan XH558 while appealing for yet more funds to keep it flying from its new home at former RAF Finningley. In any but the shortest term it was, he thought, a doomed enterprise. Had it been in support of one of the faintly ludicrous old crocks that Fishy liked so much puttering their way from London to Brighton each year in the veterans' rally, it might have made sense as an exercise in harmless nostalgia. It was surely well within an averagely rich man's pocket to keep an ancient Daimler or De Dion Bouton on the road. Even keeping wood-and-canvas biplanes in the air, as the Shuttleworth Collection heroically managed, seemed to him entirely reasonable. But to maintain a half-century-old V-bomber in airworthy condition struck Amos as an exercise in futility. He knew better than most the Vulcan's extreme mechanical and electrical complexity. Any slight defect or malfunction in an obscure component would risk its permit to fly being withdrawn. Its fatigue life must anyway be nearly up. In any case, what was it all for? What could a flying Vulcan accomplish beyond a temporary moistening of the eye and further weight added to the burden of useless regret for an era lost and gone? It had something of the melancholy of Professor Challenger's pterodactyl escaping from London and hopelessly winging its way back towards its prehistoric lost world in South America. Anything needing resurrection was by definition dead, and hence beyond any true revival . . . At this moment, and with relief, Amos spotted Fishy and Annie approaching the reunion tent.

'Ha! Off already?' Ken inquired.

'Debating.'

'Really, Pins. Imagine thinking you can come to a do like this without being rat-arsed first.'

'You, I presume, are?'

'Coasting, old thing. Coasting quite pleasantly. Feeling no pain.'

'He insisted,' explained Annie, 'in celebration of having found a fuse for the car. Medicinal purposes only, of course. And I'm doing the driving.'

'You'd better get your ID, Fishy.'

'Right. Quick look-round and then I suggest we bugger off and get some lunch. The fat woman in Reception told us there's a buffet at the local golf club. Why don't we wander up there and get stuck in. Then when we're suitably primed, we can start meeting and greeting. Trouble is, I suspect most of the chaps we wouldn't mind seeing again are either dead or in a sunset home for the terminally confused.'

'If you remember, that was precisely my point when I tried to resist coming here. It was you who talked me into this whole thing.'

'Did I? Oh well, it'll do you good. Sharpen up your people skills. You've spent too much of your life sitting in cockpits, cut off from the rest of us ordinary punters, taking refuge behind locked doors and gold braid. This –' Ken paused at the entrance to the tent and cheerfully surveyed the chatting men in blazers as though they might be potential customers for one of his monstrously expensive cars – 'this is the real world.'

'I feared as much,' said Amos.

Now that he was with Ken and Annie he felt a little less vulnerable. This was as well, since on the stroll back to their Lexus in the car park it proved impossible not to pause now and then, looking at the wartime brick buildings and the 'C' type hangars and being slightly dazed by the memories they insistently brought back:

lapel-graspers each determined to tell its tale. Yet for some reason it was the sight of Market Tewsbury church tower a few miles off across the airfield's expanse that most vividly brought the past back. Amos was aghast at a sudden conviction that maybe he had never really left Wearsby; that it was the rest of his life which had, after all, been purely vaporous. The intervening forty years he had spent flying the aerial corridors that latticed the planet now felt to have left not a trace behind them: mere contrails that high-altitude jet streams had dissolved to the thinnest of thin air.

25

After lunch Amos and Ken returned to Wearsby Air Museum. They had left Annie with some old nursing cronies she had bumped into with the promise that they would all meet up again at the buffet supper that evening. By now Amos was feeling less apprehensive, partly mellower for a few drinks and partly because neither he nor Ken had yet found any of their contemporaries from 319 Squadron. He was beginning to hope they were the only ones present at this reunion.

They had been told that the Vulcan and Victor on display were closed to the general public this afternoon but would be available to any of the reunion guests to visit at will. Amos and Ken strolled towards them through a graveyard of monuments to the post-war British aviation industry. Many of the aircraft on permanent display were beginning to show their age. In some of the older ones black or green spots of algae had begun to invade the cellulose paintwork, especially on the underside of fuselages and wings. Here and there acrylic windows and cockpit canopies had acquired a yellowish crazing of microscopic cracks or else a milky opacity. Tyres were flattening, the rubber cracking along the folds. However, it was apparent that the two V-bombers on display spent much of their time inside the nearby hangar. They had a far more cosseted and spruced-up look even if, as Amos had learned over lunch, neither aircraft had any engines and had to be towed in and out of its shelter. They reached the Vulcan and Amos stood for a moment looking at it like someone meeting an ex-lover and discovering, with a mixture of awe and chagrin, that they hadn't aged at all.

'By God, it was a beautiful aeroplane,' Amos said at length. 'I wonder what this old girl's history was.'

'XM592,' said Ken. 'Ring any bells?'

'None. On the other hand, without digging my old log books out of the loft I doubt I would recognise the serial number of a single aircraft I flew in the RAF. Would you?'

'I doubt it. But can't you even remember the one you had to jump out of in Libya? It was called Yogi 1.'

'Yes, and yours was Yogi 2. I can recall *that* incident all right, no problem. The only time in my entire career I ever had to eject. A bad day, that.'

'You're telling me. I still remember us going round in circles as Terry Meeres told us he could see five chutes and then one of them going into the fire but of course none of us knew who it was. All we could do was bugger off back to Malta and wait for news. That was no fun, either.'

'No.' Amos was appraising the Vulcan. 'You know, Fishy, they really were magnificent beasts.' He noted the red covers blanking off the intakes, the shining sleeves of the landing gear, the fully inflated tyres and the gleaming paintwork that suggested someone had gone to the expense of giving it a re-spray.

'That they were. Works of art in their way.' Ken's was a professional car restorer's eye. 'It's hard to believe we could design and build these things over half a century ago when these days we can barely put a bloody glider together. Shall we go inside? You first, Captain.'

It was more than strange taking that first high step up to the bottom rung of the yellow ladder. It required a slight effort that

Amos couldn't recall having to make in the old days. Going up into the aircraft was like revisiting a childhood home and finding it at the same time intimately familiar yet curiously miniaturised. It seemed incredible that this, his long-ago workplace, should have shrunk to such tiny dimensions. Had the pilots been able to revolve their seats like the crews', all five men would have been little further apart than if facing each other around a small table in a hotel lounge, albeit on different levels. *And the smell* . . . Despite its years of public exhibition the aircraft had retained more than a ghost of that military smell he remembered at once: Avro's black paint, perishing rubber, webbing, kerosene, oxidising grease, wiring harness.

'Christ almighty, Fishy,' he exclaimed. 'I can't believe it was ever this small.' Decades of flying big Boeings had accustomed Amos to flight decks that were like ballrooms by comparison, where one didn't have to be a contortionist merely to sit down. An atavistic prompting made him choose the left-hand seat, into which he sank after manoeuvres that made his ageing joints creak. With much groaning and cursing Ken squeezed beside him into the co-pilot's seat which gave out a huff of expelled air.

'You know the awful truth?'

'What's that, Fishy?'

'It's definitely a young man's aircraft. I remember on long flights we sometimes used to swap around if one of the drivers wanted to stretch his legs. He'd take my seat and nick my Spangles and I would sit here and pretend to fly the thing for twenty minutes. It was on autopilot, of course. But I don't remember it being this difficult to get in and out of the seat. You realise our shoulders are actually touching? Anyone would think I'd got fat.'

'You have.'

'Don't *you* start, Pins. It's quite bad enough hearing Annie on the subject . . . Crikey, you really couldn't see much out of these things, could you? You're sort of sunk down.'

'I know. The side window was more useful most of the time.' Amos's left hand was on the control stick, his right on the throttle levers, feet on the pedals. Without thinking, he found the knurled knob to the right of the control column that adjusted the pedals and turned it to accommodate his long legs.

'Do you reckon you could still fly this thing, Pins?'

Amos gave a wistful smile. 'Like a shot. No problem. It would all come back as soon as we started doing the checks, I know it would. All that training, all that practice: it's indelible. The only thing is, I might not be able to lay my hands on everything quickly enough. This layout's a pretty clutter compared with what I was used to in 747s. Different instruments, too. Out of the Ark, some of these. You certainly couldn't call this a glass cockpit. Even so, it's still a bloody miracle when you think this was designed well over sixty years ago. But yes. I could fly it *and* land it. No question. You know those smartphones that have inductive charging? That's what it feels like sitting here. This seat's a sort of wireless power source, and the longer I sit in it the more I shall get recharged.'

'So do you still regret Annie and I talked you into coming?'

'Well . . . not so far, I suppose. But then, I've yet to run into someone who knows me as the station's black sheep.'

'Oh come on, Pins. We've been over this a dozen times. Nobody will remember all that. It was a hell of a long time ago. Water under several bridges.'

'So you say. But only this morning that fat woman in Reception asked me if I'd been here at the time of the spy scandal. *She* knew about it. It's OK for you, Ken, even though you were on the same exercise. But I was the captain. Just so many things stacked up I felt jinxed. I mean, why did it have to be *my* chiefie selling stuff to the Russians? And then getting shot dead in Luqa? And why did some bloody vulture have to pick on *my* aircraft in the middle of that wilderness? And why did that wretched Buff have to fly slap into my three bombs? And why did poor old Vic get out safely only to drift into our bonfire? Plus, of course, there was all that gossip about my marriage break-up and, well, you know.'

'It was just happenstance, the whole lot of it, Pins. Everybody recognised that.'

'Of course it was, but I was still tainted. I've often thought if we'd all been a bit more on the ball we might have noticed in time what our chiefie was up to – what was his name? Hodge, Baldy Hodge. But we had a mass of our own stuff to concentrate on, didn't we? There simply wasn't time to wonder whether every erk who laid a hand on the aircraft might have been in the pay of Moscow. That's why we had security and MPs everywhere. But no. Shit sticks, Fishy. And in the military that's fatal.'

'Mm. Do you remember the rumour that Hodge might actually have been spying for the Yanks? It was probably a lot murkier than we imagined. Anyway, the important thing is your crew stuck up for you, don't forget that.'

'You all did, for which I'm eternally grateful. Old Mewell turned up trumps, too, although he could just as easily have thrown me to the wolves. Poor old Muffin. Coming on top of that incredible Christmas party and those black-marketeer commissaries, a spy scandal affecting his station must have been the kiss of death to his career. But good on him, he supported us all to the hilt. I often wonder what became of him. As you know, I lost touch with just about everyone when I left the RAF, even with you and Annie. There was a huge gap.'

'Of course I stayed on quite a bit longer than you did,' Ken said. 'But we all got a bit out of touch once they stood down that special flight of ours and we were split up and posted. It was just the

Air Ministry's knee-jerk way of dealing with practically any scandal, from chaps going to bed with each other to high treason . . . Doesn't it all seem *silly* now?'

Amos was clicking switches and twirling trim wheels reminiscently. 'I hardly ever see you and Annie these days, Fishy. Do you know what happened to any of our lot?'

'The odd rumour, mainly. Oh no, wait – do you remember Jim Ledbetter? He was in 319 with us.'

'Ledbetter. Ledbetter. Sort of familiar but I can't put a face to him.'

'He was a co-pilot who was eventually sent off to 230 OCU.'

'Christ, Fishy, your memory's amazing.'

'Not really. He turned up about eighteen months ago as a potential customer for a classic car. I thought I'd told you but I suppose I can't have done. So we had a few drinks and refreshed a lot of memories. I liked him a lot. Wasn't he a neighbour of yours during your short stay in married quarters here? He told me he was the one who originally thought up the plan to put the padre's car on the chapel roof. You remember that, of course.'

'Do I ever. Indirectly, it was the immediate cause of my marriage's collapse. Old . . . what was his name? Wheezing Jesus, that's it.' Amos and Ken laughed, staring through the Vulcan's windscreen and seeing nothing that was outside in the afternoon light.

'Jim said he'd heard that Terry Meeres is still flying in Canada somewhere as a veteran private pilot. He was a good egg, was Terry. Best captain I ever flew with. But Jim wasn't in touch with anyone on a regular basis . . . Do you suppose Jo's still around here?'

'Jo my ex? Who knows? Last I heard she was going to marry a local vet after our divorce had come through. She'd be over seventy now,' Amos heard himself say in some astonishment. 'Probably a grandmother several times over. I hope she's been happy. She can't have failed to be happier than she would have been if she'd stuck with me. I was the world's worst husband . . . Fishy,' he suddenly broke off, 'do you reckon we did any good?'

'What? Oh, you mean with this – ?' Ken waved a hand at the cockpit.

'Yes. The Great White Detergent. The whole nuclear standoff bit.'

'Well, there never was a nuclear war so I guess you could say it worked. Hundred per cent success. That's if you believe the Soviets ever really intended to attack us.'

'But we did believe that, Fishy. Just about everybody did at the time. It was deadly serious, wasn't it? That's what people forget. Or else they're too young to know what it was like. We all of us lived for – what, about thirty years? – with the constant possibility of being annihilated in the next fifteen minutes. Politics have never been so serious since.'

'Al-Qaida?'

'Dangerous arseholes but not *nuclear* arseholes. At least, not yet. No, that Cold War period was scarier for longer than anything in the history of this planet simply because we could all of us have been wiped out. But we've got such short memories that the whole era has faded for everyone except old farts like us who remember what it was like and maybe – just maybe – helped to keep the balance. Amazing to think you and I knew more about dozens of towns in Russia, and in far greater detail, than we ever did about places like Market Tewsbury and Mossop and Lincoln. Remember those hundreds of hours of target study day after day, month after month, year after year? And nowadays, Fishy, I often ask myself: was it worth it? By the time you and I were flying, both the Soviets and the Americans had their ICBMs hunkered down in silos in Ukraine and Kansas, and thanks to NORAD and our early warning at Fylingdales total retaliation was guaranteed anyway. End of planet. So what were guys like us doing pottering about the sky at a few hundred knots in our ageing Vulcans and B-52s and Tupolev-95s, telling each other we were keeping the peace?'

'Earning a living,' said Ken firmly. 'Having fun. And by golly it *was* fun a lot of the time.'

'Can't deny that,' Amos admitted. 'Lots of great flying, lots of great people. Only young once, and all that. But when I look back it sometimes seems like just one more shining, multi-trillion-dollar cause that somehow turns out to have been utterly pointless. Like Vietnam, come to that. Millions dead all over Indo-China, and to what end? None whatever. Good old godless communism was going to implode anyway. We're fools to go on getting caught up in these things. We just repeat the same mistakes endlessly, and always will. It's in our genes.'

'I . . .' Ken began, but at that moment there were loud voices from below and behind them and the sounds of elderly men heaving themselves aboard.

'Do you think they'll have kept the rubber kippers?' someone asked, nearing, then 'Ah, the office is occupied.'

'No, no,' said Amos, trying stiffly to clamber out of his seat. 'We've been here quite long enough. Risk of becoming maudlin and philosophical, you know. I'm afraid you'll have to back up a bit. We're not as flexible as we were . . . Were you in 319?'

'No, 552. Victors. Mostly at East Wittenham; 1967.' The stranger on the steps was a portly cove in a blazer.

'After my time, I'm afraid. Ken and I will leave you to it but you'll have to squeeze into the coal-hole to let us out. I'd forgotten how bloody small these things were even though I flew one for years.'

'Could it be that we've all got bigger?' said the man as he and his companion perched in the crew's seats to allow Amos and Ken past and back down the ladder to the ground.

More elderly men in blazers were gathering around the two V-bombers, passing lunchtime gas and rehearsing old times.

'You remember when they invented snatch plugs for still faster scrambles?' one was saying. 'As you moved forward things like the cable from the ground power unit automatically pulled out so no time was wasted with lineys having to disconnect manually. And do you remember the Vulcan that towed a ground power unit when the snatch plug failed to disconnect? Poor bloody captain had no idea he was starting his take-off run with a damn great generator on wheels still plugged in behind him. Luckily someone in the control tower wasn't asleep and radioed him to abort. Problem was, the Vulcan had brakes but the GPU didn't, and it was obvious the thing was simply going to catch up and smash into the under-carriage and do God knows how much damage. But the ground crew piled into a van and rushed along to stop the unit rolling and damage was averted . . .'

Tales from back when. Suddenly, neither Amos nor Ken felt like mixing and mingling, so they set off behind the old officers' mess (now reincarnated as 'Wearsby Resources Centre', whatever that meant) on the road that led eventually to the network of streets where the old married quarters had been. It was strangely unsettling how much of the airfield was unchanged, and how much different. Certain buildings seemed passably maintained and looked as they always had; others were on the edge of dereliction. It was like wandering among the ruins of some great monastery destroyed under Henry VIII, and they the bewildered shades of monks recognising exactly where their cells had been but appalled by littered turf and obliterated holy places; seeing with pangs the still-standing arched door they had built to the chapter house but which now gave onto a gravelled car park with disabled toilet facilities. What now of all the precision, the devotion, the constant ritual? The whitewashed kerbs and shaved grass? What now of the tannoys once bolted everywhere whose whooping klaxons had preceded the clipped and urgent tones of somebody at High Wycombe, the Voice of God summoning them day or night to a no-notice mass generation of aircraft, a Micky or a Micky Finn or just another QRA?

Amos found the houses in Brabazon Close nearly unchanged except cosmetically. The windows and front door of his old quarters had been painted a pale mauve and it now had a satellite dish screwed to the chimney. He guessed all these houses had been sold off by the MoD in the early 1980s, offered at knockdown prices to serving personnel who later sold them on at a pretty profit to civilians when the RAF left Wearsby for good. There were plenty of cars parked in the street which in his day had been practically empty. Well, it was a Saturday after all. He supposed that on weekdays the people who lived here now commuted to nearby towns like Mossop and probably as far afield as Grantham or Lincoln. The whole estate had a very civilian feel and held nothing of interest, not even many memories.

The nearby building to which he did feel drawn was shuttered and had a derelict air to it. He and Ken stood in front of the chapel and took in the boarded-up windows, the groundsel growing between the stones of the shallow steps in front, the padlocked chain threaded through holes bored in the main doors.

'Hideous, wasn't it?' said Ken admiringly. 'That flat roof, the pseudo-Gothic arch, the whole air of religion catered for on the cheap. "Fall out Roman Catholics and Jews!" – remember those parades from training days?'

'I certainly do. I just want to walk around the outside if you don't mind, Fishy. You remember my AEO, Gavin Rickards? He wrote to me after I'd left to tell me they'd put in a special stone or something.'

They made their way along the wall. Somebody with savage machinery had recently cut back what looked like thickets of hydrangeas and buddleias and other shrubs that had sprouted in the abandoned flower beds. Here and there were stones embedded in the ground still bearing a few traces of paint as though they had once demarcated a parking area. When they reached the rear of the chapel Amos was pleased to see that the station's sports field his former garden had overlooked was still unchanged. Some children were shooting footballs at a goal down at the far end. Their shrill voices came sadly on the breeze.

'Is this it?' called Ken.

Amos joined him and found a pale memorial stone let into the base of the chapel wall. It was criss-crossed with snails' mucus, but the engraved legend was perfectly legible:

IN FOND MEMORY OF
AIR CDRE B. A. PONSONBY
THIS TABLET WAS PLACED
BY HIS FRIEND GP CAPT N. MEWELL
'FAITHFUL TO THE END'

'Good Lord,' said Amos after a silence, more touched than he could have imagined. 'What do you think the "B. A." stood for?'

'Barbary Ape?' Ken hazarded. 'Old Muffin must have been awfully fond of the animal, anyhow.'

'I'm afraid "Faithful to the end" is a bit wishful. I actually witnessed the wretched Ponsonby's demise, and I think you'd say he was *terrified* to the end. Possibly still pissed as well.' But even as he spoke the thought came to him that Mewell might have been referring not to his pet's faithfulness but to his own. 'Poor Jo. She completely lost her rag over it. In fact I owe these last forty-odd years of regained bachelorhood largely to the wretched, exiled Ponsonby.' Amos paused and for an instant his face fell into lines of extraordinary sadness. 'That fellow who came to buy a car off you, Jim Ledbetter, the one who engineered this whole episode – I . . . I don't suppose he mentioned Gavin, did he?'

His friend glanced at him sympathetically. 'As a matter of fact he did, Pins, but only to say he thought he'd heard on the grapevine that he'd got married, had some children and had split up. I didn't want to tell you because Jim was a bit vague, and who knows what drivel the grapevine distils?'

And that was the only mention of the matter either of the two old friends made that day. In due course they drove in their separate cars to the nearby golf club for the buffet dinner. At first Amos was daunted almost to the point of fleeing by the great throng of scrawny or portly ex-nuclear warriors wearing crested ties, but Annie deftly headed him off and distracted him to the point where both were impressed and amused by the spectacle of septuagenarians heaping and re-heaping their plates. The phrase 'Eating Command' followed by guffaws was frequently heard, just as jokes about prostates and piss tubes were made in the Gents. Amos, finally, was reassured to be recognised and greeted warmly by one or two other members of 319 Squadron who plainly held nothing whatever against him and were quite simply happy that he had given oblivion the slip and had returned after so long.

Yet among the ghosts haunting the long tables was one as much of valediction as of nostalgia. A half-forgotten array of names and faces was inevitably fading, linked with touched-up anecdote and reminiscence. But what had definitively passed was an era, taking

284

with it the skills and machines that had been underwritten by an entirely different world and way of looking at it.

'I suppose,' mused a bald gentleman who had once looped a Victor bomber in a moment of exuberant irresponsibility, 'I suppose in terms of sheer professionalism, striking power and global presence, the RAF we knew was at its zenith.'

'But the writing was on the wall.'

'But the writing was on the wall. Polaris and all that.'

'I meant more for Britain. No more empire, general pulling-in of horns, downward spiral.'

'Ah, that. Yes, well, by God we were lucky chappies, weren't we? Blasting around the sky all over the world? I could never believe they were *paying* me to do it. It's odd. Mention the sixties to people today and they think of drugs and hippies and rock-and-roll. *Our* sixties were rather different, weren't they, but quite as wild if not more so, and all paid for by the taxpayer. Just unbelievable. Fantastic fun. Nail-biting fun. The best kind.'

At last Amos, Ken and Annie made their separate ways back to their B&B with farewells and mutual hopes for future meetings ringing in their ears. Amos insisted to Annie that he was perfectly able to drive and promised to see them both at breakfast. The night was moonless and sparklingly clear. On impulse he stopped in a lay-by about five miles from Wearsby and turned out all his lights, the better to see the sky. It was a pilot's sky as he had so often seen it from a cockpit on his lonely journeys: the wraparound black sheet of the firmament and its printed stars. Suddenly he was ambushed by an immense grief. At that moment he would have given his life just to be able to thumb a switch and hear Gavin's voice from behind: 'That you, Boss? What kept you? I've been waiting so long.' Resting his head on the steering wheel, Amos had to delay the resumption of his journey because for a long moment he couldn't see for the exasperating tears which at length he blamed on alcohol.

*

Some three weeks after the reunion, the local newspaper carried a front-page headline that read GRUESOME FIND IN TREE. The story was of an old poplar in a field near Market Tewsbury that had been felled because it was a danger. It was only when the farmer returned next day to cut it up that he discovered, wedged in a fork between two branches that had grown to encase it, a hard white helmet full of ancient bird's nests. When these were removed the farmer found the helmet also contained most of a human skull. Someone suggested that it might have a connection with the old airfield at Wearsby; but as of going to press, the paper said, police were baffled.

Appendix 1

Skyshield II

To this day, several mysteries still surround Skyshield II (pages 24). Perhaps the most notable is why, after over half a century, the USAF's final report on the exercise should still be officially classified as secret. British conspiracy theorists, in particular, might be interested to learn that eight years after the exercise the Ministry of Defence in London, in a response labelled 'top secret' to a query from their man in the British Defence Secretariat in Washington, made it clear that British documentation was missing: 'We have been unable to trace official records of Exercise Skyshield II.' In a further cable on 8 April 1969 they were more specific. 'Unfortunately all records have been destroyed. We have however established that the Bomber Command Research Branch did not report on the Exercise, which suggests that the USAF kept the overall results very much to themselves.'

This is strange indeed. The British military, like their civilian counterparts in Whitehall, are not in the habit of destroying records. Besides, there is no need. Documents that might prove embarrassing are simply filed away, Sir Humphrey Appleby-style, in some obscure annex where they might possibly be stumbled upon a century later. It seems equally unlikely that Bomber Command's Research Branch never reported on the exercise. We know from an MoD cable that the Research Branch had British observers on the ground at several US radar installations during Exercise Big Photo, if not for Skyshield II itself. It would have been of the utmost concern to them to learn how the Vulcans' ECM fit performed against the mock-ups of Soviet SAM radars since this was crucial to the entire deterrence strategy. We can only conjecture that the USAF and/or NORAD refused to allow them access to the relevant data afterwards.

The reason for the flurry of transatlantic cables between Whitehall and the British Defence Secretariat in Washington early in 1969 was itself peculiar. The BDS had suddenly been asked by the Pentagon to supply information about Skyshield II so that it could be used as evidence in a forthcoming hearing of the US House of Representatives' Committee on Appropriations. Congress's belated interest in an exercise that had taken place eight years earlier was triggered by a sensational article in the 1 February 1969 'Newsletter' of issue no. 73 of an obscure and slightly mad journal, the *Washington Observer*. Headed 'TREASON STORM', this repeated an allegation it had made in its issue no. 25 back in 1966 that the RAF's Vulcan bombers in Skyshield II,

> equipped with a new type of gear producing electro-magnetic waves that simulate magnetic storms, flew over New York, Chicago, Washington DC, Detroit etc., photographing their 'targets' with clocked film, without being detected by the ground defenses. The latter reported 'no overflight,' but when confronted with the clocked film taken by the ground radar, found that 'atmospherics, due to magnetic storms' had occurred at the very moment when the Vulcans' film showed the passage of those nuclear bombers over the cities in question. The operation was a great success from the viewpoint of the RAF commanders, who had been urging their American colleagues to install the same gear on the B-52 bombers.

It showed conclusively that the Soviet nuclear bases could be knocked out with the greatest ease in one single raid, before the Soviet authorities even learned that the magnetic storms over the USSR had been artificially induced.

What made Congress in 1969 take an interest in a sensational (and more than a little dotty) story they had ignored in 1966 can be explained in one word: Vietnam. In the intervening three years the war in Vietnam had become hopelessly bogged down. In particular the 1968 Tet Offensive had furnished vivid television images of North Vietnamese troops and Viet Cong cadres, long presumed wiped out, suddenly appearing as if by resurrection and pinning down US marines behind their half-tracked vehicles. This had had a decisively depressing effect on the American public's support for the war. The *Washington Observer* was evidently pandering to a growing desire to look for scapegoats and had repeated the allegation of its earlier issue that the British had a hush-hush electronic device that could 'produce artificial magnetic storms enabling large bombers to pierce any air defense in the world'. So why was this miraculous gadget not fitted to SAC's B-52s, thus saving the lives of countless American airmen? The paper alleged this was because 'successive US Administrations have honored a secret Executive compact with the Soviets prohibiting the installation of this electronic device on US aircraft'. Why so? Because, the *Washington Observer* claimed, President Kennedy had done a deal with the Soviet Union that there should be only two nuclear superpowers, the USA and the USSR. 'All efforts were to be directed towards the elimination of England as a nuclear power. But this [British] invention, which put Soviet Russia at the mercy of RAF Bomber Command, risked undermining the whole set of premises on which a Soviet–American partnership and eventual alliance could be sold to the American public.'

Ludicrous as this flight of fancy might seem, it was clearly enough to provoke questions in the House of Representatives, calls for a Committee on Appropriations hearing, and in turn a request from the Pentagon for information from London about this alleged British super-weapon. The initial cable from the British Defence Secretariat in Washington is classified 'Top Secret. UK Eyes Only' and reads (with the punctuation restored):

HAVE BEEN REQUESTED BY DDR AND E [Department of Defense, Research & Engineering] AT PENTAGON TO OBTAIN INFORMATION TO BE GIVEN AS EVIDENCE TO HOUSE APPROPRIATIONS COMMITTEE ABOUT EXERCISE SKYSHIELD II IN 1961. DDR AND E WANT CONFIRMATION THAT SPECIAL TACTICS AND ECM DEVICES WERE USED WHICH SUCCESSFULLY DEFEATED NORAD. ALSO IF THERE WAS HIGH LEVEL AGREEMENT (KENNEDY/MACMILLAN SUGGESTED) THAT DETAILS OF EXERCISE WOULD NOT BE RELEASED. APPARENTLY USAF UNABLE OR UNWILLING TO RESPOND TO DDR AND E. APPRECIATE UK MAY BE IN SIMILAR PREDICAMENT. REGRET LACK OF WARNING OF THIS SUBJECT UNAVOIDABLE. EVIDENCE REQUIRED BY 2100Z HOURS WEDNESDAY 19TH. GRATEFUL FOR ANY RELEASABLE STATEMENT OR BACKGROUND INFORMATION SOONEST.[†]

As we know, this resulted in the claim that London were unable to

---

[†] National Archives: MoD: DEFE 24/654.

trace any official records of Skyshield II. In a later cable drafted to BDS Washington the MoD said, in part:

IN ANY EVENT WE SHOULD NOT BE PREPARED TO RELEASE ANY INFORMATION WITHOUT CONCURRENCE OF USAF WHO MAY BE ACTING LOYALLY TOWARDS RAF.

[. . .]

IT IS NOT REPEAT NOT CLEAR IF 27 SQN'S SUCCESSES WERE AGAINST NORAD OR MOCK UPS. RESULTS AGAINST LATTER PROBABLY STILL HIGHLY CLASSIFIED. SIGNIFICANT THAT NO DE-BRIEFING OF CREWS WHO TOOK PART IN USA ALTHOUGH MEMBERS OF BOMBER CD. DEVELOPMENT UNIT WERE PRESENT AT GROUND STATIONS.

[. . .]

FCO UNABLE TO TRACE ANY HIGH-LEVEL AGREEMENT ON DISCLOSURE OF INFORMATION. THE THEN HEAD OF S6 DOES NOT REPEAT NOT RECALL ANY SUCH AGREEMENT.

[. . .]

SUGGEST YOU REPLY TO PENTAGON THAT IN TIME AVAILABLE WE ARE UNABLE TO PROVIDE ANY FACTUAL INFORMATION. IF USAF ARE PREPARED TO GIVE EVIDENCE WE SHOULD WISH TO BE CONSULTED AND TO BE GIVEN SUFFICIENT TIME TO EXAMINE EVIDENCE.

As for the reason why, over fifty years after the event, the USAF's final report on Skyshield II remains classified, it is inconceivable that it could still have security implications and equally impossible that there could still be technological secrets to give away. The answer – as nearly always in such cases – is most probably to spare someone's blushes. Sir Humphrey would have understood.

Appendix 2

Stealth

A myth has recently grown up about the Vulcan bomber having a low enough RCS (radar cross-section) to qualify it as an early 'stealth' aircraft. This is ridiculous. When it was designed in the late 1940s questions of stealth were simply not considered: much of Avro's design skill was concentrated on the barely understood aerodynamics of the delta planform (p. 77). It was sheer chance that burying the engines in the wing roots was to become one of the measures adopted for stealth design over thirty years later. In fact, this was a common feature of early British jet design and was shared by many aircraft of the period including the other two V-bombers, the Valiant and the Victor, as well as by the de Havilland Comet airliner. The idea of the Vulcan with its massive delta wing as having been 'stealthy' – a whimsy nowadays often repeated by journalists as fact – has been nailed by the authors of the *Avro Vulcan Owners' Workshop Manual* (Haynes, 2010) who included one of the Vulcan's most distinguished test pilots, Tony Blackman. They wrote: 'In truth the Vulcan, like other large aircraft of its time, possessed a large radar signature.' That being said the Vulcan, like any other aircraft, could become marginally less visible at certain radar wavelengths and at certain angles.

Ever since the late 1980s, when the bizarre design of Lockheed's F-117 Nighthawk ground-attack aircraft became widely known, public misconception has grown as to the ability of 'stealth' technology to render an aircraft invisible to radar. No doubt Hollywoodian special effects of people donning 'invisibility cloaks' (the all-time child's fantasy) have fed into the idea that stealth technology is already doing this job for large machines such as aircraft and ships.

It isn't. In this context 'stealth' just means limiting as much as possible the degree to which the machines of war can be detected by radar and other means. To date, and for the foreseeable future, nothing is completely proof against some form of detection – whether using radar, infrared equipment or ordinary eyesight. This was brought home painfully to the Americans during the Kosovo war when in early 1999 a precious F-117 was shot down over Serbia (and another severely damaged) by Soviet SAM missiles using a long-wavelength radar-guidance system that dated back to the 1960s. Worse, the downed Nighthawk was in good enough condition for its 'stealth' design secrets to be thoroughly investigated by Russian and (probably) Chinese technicians. Even more embarrassing was the incident in December 2011 when an unmanned top-secret American 'stealth' drone, a Lockheed Martin RQ-170 Sentinel, was not merely detected when it overflew Iran but induced by the Iranians to make a perfect landing when they fooled its default homing programme into thinking it was back at Kandahar in Afghanistan. Presumably its secrets, too, have now been fatally compromised.

Appendix 3

The aircraft pooling system

For some years before this story opens Bomber Command had gone back to operating a 'pool' system for its aircraft (page 107), whereby a particular crew was not assigned a particular aircraft with whose idiosyncrasies they and their crew chief became familiar. In fact this idea dated back to the Second World War. During the Battle of Britain each pilot had had his own aircraft which was serviced by its own ground crew. This not only made for loyalty between him and the men responsible for keeping his machine airworthy, but it meant that the pilot grew to know his own aircraft intimately. But under the pressure of war this was soon perceived as an extravagant use of ground crew and it was decided that savings could be made by changing to a pool system. Under this, aircraft were all serviced centrally and pilots simply drew whichever machine was ready. This can be seen as an early version of the 'rationalisation' that is the frequent bane of twenty-first-century life, as when few NHS patients ever see the same hospital doctor twice running, presumably on the assumption that all doctors, having supposedly been trained to the same standard, are equally good and therefore interchangeable.

However, this was emphatically not true of aircraft built much before 1975 and the slow dawn of the CADCAM era (Computer-Aided Design/Manufacture), when they were all effectively hand-built. This resulted in tiny disparities one from another which could produce considerable differences in handling, especially at high subsonic speeds. Not surprisingly, crews much preferred to stick with an aircraft they knew. The pool system of servicing, as it affected V-bomber crews, was therefore a source of disquiet and was unpopular with everyone but Whitehall's time-and-motion men.

The blithe bureaucrat's assumption that all aircraft of a particular type must be identical was to lead to one of the MoD's most notorious and expensive mistakes. This concerned the Nimrod MRA4 maritime patrol aircraft, intended to be the upgraded version of the existing Nimrod MR2. MR2s were based on the old Comet airframe dating back to the late 1940s and when in the late 1990s the contracting company, Flight Refuelling Ltd, tried to mate these older sections to the newly designed wings, it was found to be impossible. Nothing matched up. The original fuselages had all been hand-built in the days before CADCAM whereas the new wings had been constructed to computerised tolerances. This was a major reason why the project's costs soared uncontrollably, leading to its cancellation in 2010 when it was £789 million over budget and more than nine years late. Any old V-bomber crew chief in retirement could have told them what would happen; but it is a peculiarity of the modern system that nobody ever consults the people who actually know things, especially if they are over sixty and 'out of the loop'.

Appendix 4

High jinks

Readers may find the goings-on at Wearsby's Christmas party (p. 180) implausibly exaggerated. If so, they should consult ex-members of the RAF of that generation who are temporarily prepared to sacrifice loyalty for honesty. These now staid and often respectable members of society will probably be able to give accounts of similar occasions, perhaps including the Dining-In Night on an RAF station in the Middle East during which the officers' mess was set on fire and gutted. They will almost certainly have heard of the most notorious of them all, the legendary 1 Group Dining-In Night.

This took place at Waddington in 1965 and was vastly bigger than the event at Wearsby. Virtually the entire V-force's crews were present, some 750 guests in all. It is still not clear what the idea behind this grand occasion was but it is presumed that the Air Officer Commanding 1 Group at the time, Air Vice-Marshal Stapleton, thought it would be a way of congratulating and even thanking the V-force for its dedication and success. What officialdom completely underestimated was the depth of feeling among the men: the smouldering grievances caused by the rigid and often petty regulations that governed practically every aspect of their lives; the endless QRAs and target study; and the feeling that things might drag on indefinitely thus – or as long as the nuclear stalemate lasted.

A great many of the diners at Waddington had arrived already drunk and armed with bangers and other fireworks, some eager to settle old scores with members of rival squadrons. Sir Harry Broadhurst, a former Air Officer Commander-in-Chief of Bomber Command, was a guest of honour even though he had retired from the RAF four years previously and was therefore technically a civilian. As he walked in to take his seat at the top table he was loudly hissed, a breach of manners that must have been shocking to many of those present, and savagely so to Sir Harry. 'Broady' had once been a popular senior officer; but this popularity was irrevocably – if unfairly – damaged as the result of the Vulcan crash at Heathrow in 1956 when he quite rightly ejected to safety. It was not his fault that the four men in the compartment behind the cockpit did not have ejector seats. However, for this final leg of the celebratory flight – which was due to be met at Heathrow with a good deal of pomp and ceremony – he had insisted on swapping places with the aircraft's usual co-pilot, who had to go and sit behind. Visibility was poor, with rain and heavy overcast, and on a final approach in such conditions it was customary for the man in the right-hand seat to call out the altitude while the pilot flying concentrated on his other instruments and on picking up the beacons at the end of the runway visually. In the aftermath of the accident many airmen argued that had the usual co-pilot been in the cockpit the disaster might never have happened. 'Broady' was not only inexperienced on type; he wasn't calling out the heights. The result was that the pilot, Squadron Leader Donald Howard, must have been made additionally tense by the weather conditions, the restricted vision from the cockpit that all Vulcans shared, and from having the chief of Bomber Command sitting next to him. Instead of aborting and diverting to a backup airfield where conditions were better, he evidently decided to go ahead and risk a landing. Fatally misjudging his approach, he touched down in a field of Brussels sprouts 600 yards short of the runway.

All the crew who died in XA897 at Heathrow that day had been Waddington men, which probably contributed to 'Broady''s reception at the 1 Group Dining-In Night there nine years later. Thereafter the dinner swiftly and famously descended into total anarchy, so much damage being done that reparations eventually had to be levied from all 750 guests via their mess bills.